ADVAI
THE ⌐⌐⌐⌐ ⌐⌐⌐⌐⌐

"A thrilling ride that kept me up late reading. As a fan of all things related to railroads, this book met my need for trains, adventure, and the strength of human character all in one place."

—**Michelle Kempema, executive director**
Colorado Model Railroad Museum

"What a story! *The Last Zephyr* is full of richly detailed descriptions of passenger trains, volcanic eruptions, disasters, and leadership in a crisis, all in an emotional adventure tale full of vivid characters and dramatic situations. I couldn't put it down and was very sorry when the book came to an end."

—**Walter Alvarez, best-selling author of**
T. Rex and the Crater of Doom

"Embark on a wondrous journey within – the only bittersweet element is that every turn of the page brings you closer to bidding farewell to this splendid tale. You'll never look at Moffat Tunnel the same way again."

—**B. Travis & Kate Wright,**
Rollins Pass and Moffat Tunnel Historians

"This book has it all: a dynamic storyline, relatable characters, and of course, trains! It's a perfect read for anyone who loves riding the rails and adventuring. I just couldn't put it down. Along with CB's insightful quotes, everyone is sure to gain something out of this book."

—**Bryson Sleppy, Trains.com/Model,** *Railroader Magazine*

THE LAST ZEPHYR

THE LAST ZEPHYR

C.B. BLACKFOREST

ALDER PRESS

Golden, Colorado USA

ISBN 978-0-9725955-1-3
Library of Congress Control Number: 2023911155

Cover photograph by Mel Patrick
Back cover photograph by Derek Brown
Book cover and interior design by Mike Corrao, Mayfly Design (mayflydesign.com)
Map Illustration: Matt Kania
Editor: Marly Cornell

Alder Press
alder-press.com
P.O. Box 7401
Golden, Colorado
80403

Alder Press donates a portion of the proceeds from this book to the Colorado Railroad Museum for the preservation, restoration, and presentation of Zephyr related artifacts.

Dedicated to cousin Matthew, his parents, and all the rest of the clan. Family makes all the difference!

CONTENTS

PREFACE

This story has its origins millions of years ago, when the complex geologic structure far below Yellowstone National Park and the Rocky Mountains was created. But I will forgo all the prelude and get right to the train ride that, in many ways, came to symbolize humanity's eternal will to survive. What happened is part of the history of the most pivotal moment in the entire twenty-first century.

As often happens in monumental times, seeds of love are sown when life itself seems to hang in the balance. Such was the case for many who rode the Zephyr, including my parents.

The best place for me to start our story is thirty years ago, as the world neared the end of the turbulent 2020s. A disturbing late-night conference call came from the man who later became my geology professor and mentor during my college years.

CHAPTER 1

YELLOWSTONE

"Civilization exists by geologic consent, subject to change without notice."

—Will Durant

SUNDAY, 10:00 P.M.

"People are going to die! We have to get the word out and evacuate everyone—NOW!" Dr. Michael Sayers couldn't have been more forceful.

Sara Blackburn, the head of Homeland Security, was annoyed. "What do you want us to do, tell everyone west of the Mississippi that they have to go live somewhere else for who knows how long? Come on, Dr. Sayers, be realistic!" she said.

It had taken weeks for Sayers to get the attention of the highest level of the US government. Now the video conference with Blackburn was only happening because of the shocking news that many parts of Yellowstone National Park had risen ten inches in just twenty-four hours. Not only that, surprising signs of renewed volcanic activity were reported at Dotsero near Glenwood Springs and in Hot Sulphur Springs. Worst of all, a super volcano complex even larger than Yellowstone and thought to be long extinct, appeared to be roaring back to life. The La Garita Caldera located in Southwest Colorado was suddenly causing well water to boil and spewing powerful sulfur smells. Swarms of small earthquakes were recorded from Montana to New Mexico. Sayers put forth his most compelling arguments and evidence. It wasn't enough.

The scientist was defeated. Blackburn, realizing the conviction of the man she just dressed down, and the implications of doing nothing, asked about the probability of the eruption happening within the next week. Sayers couldn't know for certain, but he guessed 70 percent.

That wasn't high enough to convince Blackburn to take the draconian measures Sayers advocated. Instead she agreed to temporarily close the National Park and send out an advisory for people living within a hundred miles of the predicted epicenter.

After the call, Sayers's boss was livid. "Mike, are you trying to get this office defunded? You just asked a member of the President's cabinet to tell half the country to run hundreds of miles away from home. Damn, man, did you think she would say, 'Yes, let's do that right away!'?!"

Sayers sat quietly, head down, as his boss continued the angry rant laced with sarcastic bite. "Listen close, Mike, I should fire you right now. I would, if you weren't the most-talented geologist on the team. So here is what's going to happen. You'll be in Grand Junction on Tuesday for the Bureau of Land Management meeting. You deliver your presentation in person, and don't say a word about Yellowstone. Let me make this very real. If you are not there, or if you try to use that event to stir up panic, your job, your pension, and your reputation will be gone. Is that clear?"

"Yep, it's clear," Sayers said humbly.

His wife heard the whole thing from the other room. After the call, she came into the study. "What do we do now, Mike?" she asked.

He looked at her in a way that broke her heart. After taking a moment to gather his thoughts, his countenance changed from that of a crushed man, to someone who was determined to save at least his own family. He told his wife to immediately pack up the kids in the car and race south as fast as she could. He would still attend his Tuesday meeting, then fly to Brownsville, Texas, to meet them. "With luck," he said, "the calderas will give us enough time."

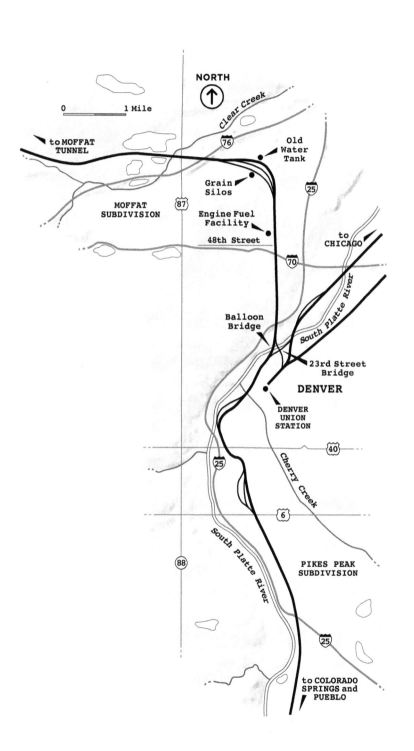

CHAPTER 2

TRAIN DAYS

"Everyone secretly loves trains. Rail fans have the courage to publicly admit they do."

—CB

Denver had the most beautiful passenger train station and platforms in America. Sweeping white arches of steel were draped with overlapping gleaming white canopies covering the platform area. At first glance, the station was inspiring, simultaneously modern and dramatic while still being in tune with its historic architecture. The famous neon "Travel by Train" sign, which advertised rail journeys for more than seventy years, was still perfectly perched atop the massive stone building.

Denver Union Station (DUS) was always busy after the half-billion-dollar renovation was completed in 2014. Train Days, the most important event on the rail fan calendar, made it even more crowded. The big draw to Train Days was the UPR BIG BOY.

Heat emanated from the massive steam engine's boiler. The crowd of train fans could feel the energy. Steam wafted from underneath the black maze of pipes, rods, and tanks. The smell of burning oil in the firebox hung in the air. That greatest vestige of the steam era sat on DUS Track 5 with a string of bright-yellow streamliner passenger cars with gleaming silver bogies stretching clear to the bumper behind it.

Just one track away, and only seven years younger than the much larger Train Days attraction, sat another relic of railroading lore. Patiently waiting near the end of Track 4 was a 1949 Budd built stainless steel round-ended dome/observation/sleeper train car. In the eyes of many rail fans, that shining beauty was perhaps the best example of the finest, most elegant form of mass human conveyance ever invented. Freshly delivered from a year of painstaking restoration at shops in Strasburg, Colorado, the car was finally qualified by regulators. It was ready to carry passengers on the high iron of Class 1 rail. The car was none other than the "Silver Sky."

Ben Batton, of the Colorado Railroad Museum, had coordinated the team of people and organizations that got the car to that point. The tall and neatly groomed man stood on the platform, looking at the fruit of his efforts with great satisfaction. He had spent years of his life, mostly volunteer time, working on the project. It all came to a pinnacle today.

The project began a decade prior at conductor Nicholas Jay's house. Nick had called Ben to talk about what he had found in a derelict state in a tiny train yard in the upper Midwest. As they sat on his patio overlooking the Big Ten Curves of the Moffat subdivision, enjoying chips and fruit smoothies Nick's daughter Juliette made, Nick told Ben the great news: He found the most famous train car ever to serve the public in America–the Silver Sky.

CHAPTER 3

CREW BRIEFING

"Railroaders are masters of monotonous adventure."

—CB

Four familiar faces sat around the Denver crew room table on the first Monday morning in September, Labor Day. They were one level below the main floor of the Great Hall at Denver's historic Union Station. Between them, they had over 120 years of seniority and railroad experience. They were the crew of the number-one job in Denver—the regular assignment that the highest seniority members of each craft usually bid for. They were the operating crew of the Zephyr through the Rockies.

Conductor Nick was at the head of the table. He looked dignified with his "salt and pepper" hair and crisp uniform. With only months left before retirement at the age of sixty, he was determined to finish his career with the same energy and enthusiasm he had started with as a brakeman thirty years prior. For Nick, a lifelong train fan, conducting the Zephyr wasn't just a job; it was "livin' the dream!" He showed up early, as he always did, to get train orders from the dispatcher printed and placed at each seat for the crew. The crew log was open to the correct page so each worker could sign in.

The oldest of the group was a crotchety but lovable engineer named Larry Cohen. In spite of his rough exterior, Larry had a heart of gold. He was sitting where he always sat for the morning crew briefing—at the opposite end of the table from his conductor. Larry had over thirty-eight years "in the seat," a term for a locomotive engineer operating a railroad engine. He looked young for his age and kept himself in top physical condition. He was one of those guys who could retire at any time with full benefits, but kept working because it was better for his family situation. Even so, everyone knew he would retire soon. Knowing he was a "short timer" gave him a bit more freedom than the others on the crew to speak his mind. Over the last few years, Larry's rants about sports, politics, religion, or anything else under the sun had become legendary. He was best known for spilling his guts while riding in the van to the train station from the hotel in Grand Junction. Among the Denver-based crews, Larry's diatribes had become known as "The Morning Grind with Larry Cohen."

The second engineer was Christina Emmerson. She was quiet, self-confident, and one of the growing number of female locomotive engineers in the system. She didn't speak out much, but that did not mean she was disengaged. She was just more contemplative before speaking than most. Christina was a great colleague. Everyone trusted her professionalism and skills without question.

Nick's assistant conductor had been with him for several years. Her name tag read "Renate Sebastian," but everyone just called her René. She excelled at organization and neatness. Usually, she beat Nick to the station and had the paperwork all laid out. But that day the crowds on her commuter RTD train were so big, she had to wait for the next departure. Still she was twenty minutes early for her sign-up time. But she was annoyed. She was out of her routine because of the Train Days crowds.

René joined the railroad after a successful career in the hotel industry. Even though she and her husband were on solid financial footing, she wasn't ready to leave the workforce. She chose passenger railroading as her second career for the same reason lots of people are drawn to the trains—the unexplainable mystique of the rails. Although René was nearly as old as Nick, she was twenty years behind him in seniority. That made Nick the conductor in charge. The two worked well together as a team, as seasoned railroaders usually do.

All four were more than just colleagues, they were best friends. They spent more time with each other than with their own families.

Nick and Larry were almost like brothers after decades of safely running trains together.

It was 7:05 a.m. Still fifteen minutes until going on duty. Everyone thought Nick would be glowing and raving about the Silver Sky. They had heard him talk with great passion about the project that had finally come to fruition.

To their surprise, the first topic Nick brought up had nothing to do with trains at all. Instead he expressed concern about the news he heard on the radio while driving to work. He asked if the other members of the crew had heard it. They all had some idea of what was happening.

Larry spoke up. "Yeah, so the Parks Service is evacuating Yellowstone because of heaving ground?"

"That is what I heard," Nick said. "It's unusual that the ground all over the park would have places that swell up like that; I think they said almost a foot. It has happened before, but not more than just an isolated pocket and a few inches here or there."

René chimed in, "I suppose there will be something happening soon. It will be interesting to see how many people in Cody or Jackson Hole try to quickly sell their houses this week," she said, as they all grimaced mildly.

Nick got the joke and chuckled, but he was alarmed. "This really could end up being serious, guys. We could be in for something cataclysmic," he said. "Who knows? It could end up being anything from a small puff of steam blowing off, to an absolutely devastating eruption that wipes out all of Yellowstone Park and most of the western part of the US, or anything in between."

"All that may be true, but they would tell us if they really thought it was that bad. They can predict things like that nowadays," Larry said.

Nick disagreed. "I don't think we are that good at predicting geological events yet."

Nick looked at Christina and could tell she was worried. He tried to back off his scary doomsday talk. He suggested that the rise in ground level probably wasn't that big a deal. He said the evacuation of people was just a precaution. "In all probability, a bunch of water seeped in under the earth's crust, got hot, and steamed up. Real soon that steam will find a way to the surface and the ground will resettle. Kind of like a blister, once it pops, everything will be fine. It could end up being a really awesome show—way bigger than Old Faithful, but not deadly, if people keep their distance. That is why they are ordering the evacuation."

"That's right," Larry said. "Speaking of steam, did you guys see the BIG BOY out there? What an amazing piece of machinery. Did you feel the heat coming off that boiler? I don't know how those guys ran them things day after day for twelve hours at a time in the summer. I'd melt and die."

René wanted to turn the subject to what she thought was the big issue of the day. "Hey, what about Nick's big day, guys? How does it feel to have the Silver Sky ready to roll after you put so much effort into that project?"

They all clapped, smiled, and looked at the conductor.

"I can tell you this," Nick said, "anyone can start something. The trick is to finish. Today, although it sounds arrogant, and maybe it is, but I don't care—I feel like a winner!"

René reacted to his admission with typical affirmation, "You *should* feel like a winner. You did a great thing getting that train car back on the rails, and now you get to be the conductor on its first trip behind the Zephyr."

Nick knew that most of the work had been done by the team Ben Batton mustered together. "Actually, René, my main contribution was just to initiate the project. Other people did the heavy lifting. You will get to meet a lot of them out on the platform. The whole team is out there. Those are the folks that really made the Silver Sky happen."

The phone rang. The caller was Joyce Smyth, manager of the entire Zephyr operation. Joyce was no stranger to the crew. Her hands-on approach meant she knew everyone and everything that was a part of *her train*. A church-going woman from the south side of Chicago, she added charisma and faith to everything she did. She always said what she thought, and was not afraid to dole out criticism when needed. Yet everyone felt loved by her, because they were. She was sort of like everybody's mother. Joyce loved people—especially those who worked for her.

What now? Nick thought.

Joyce started talking fast. "Nick, listen, I know you're busy getting the Zephyr ready and Train Days and all that. But you need to know you have a United States senator on board today. He and his wife are also my friends. Just make sure we treat them like everyone else—with exceptional hospitality."

Nick answered as he usually did, "We got this!"

Joyce replied with a touch of critical encouragement, "Oh I know you do. Just go easy on your PA announcements. They are great, but you do tend to get a bit long-winded. Now go have a wonderful trip, and God bless."

"Hey, wait a minute . . . ," Nick said into the phone, but his boss had already hung up. Nick was annoyed; he was very proud of his famous scenic announcements.

Nick looked at the standard railroad time clock on the wall: 7:20 a.m.; they were officially on duty. "Okay, we've got a job to do, let's get 'er done."

Nick called the dispatcher in Omaha to activate their train orders and let him know the Zephyr would be on time westbound. After the routine conversation was finished, the dispatcher added that trains in the Yellowstone vicinity were being advised to be alert for any seismic activity. Nick said he had heard a bit about it, and hoped all the railroaders up there would be safe.

Back on train number 5, which had just arrived from Chicago, inbound conductor Mindy was on point, watching the shove into the dead-end tracks of Denver Union Station. She passed commands to the locomotive engineer via the radio. "Number 5, good to shove ten cars. Let's go a bit easier than normal—lots of people in the area. OVER."

"Roger, ten cars for #5—go easy. Out," the engineer said over the radio.

At least fifty people had scanners on the platform, listening to Mindy and her crew of professionals do their job. It was almost too much for a die-hard rail fan: The BIG BOY, the Silver Sky, the inbound Zephyr, and all the other display booths that were set up—Train Days indeed!

As a joke, several mops and buckets were placed around Union Station. The idea was to be ready to clean up any excessive foaming messes. Mary and Margaret, two sisters who worked as station agents in Denver, and their husbands were on their way to Hawaii. Their plan was to ride the RTD A line to Denver International Airport to catch their 9:40 a.m. flight through San Francisco. They came early to set out the mops. For decades, train fans were referred to as "foamers" by railroad employees because some fans got so excited when they saw a train that they were said to foam at the mouth. The two couples knew Nick and the other serious train fans at work would get the joke.

After Mindy finished coupling the Zephyr to the Silver Sky, she turned and saw Margaret and Mary. They were smiling broadly as they used their mops in mock sarcasm to soak up imaginary foam at Mindy's feet. The conductor was mildly humored. With a mocking grin, she pointed out a spot they had missed.

CHAPTER 4

SCANNING

"The beauty of train travel is, in large part, the people that travel by train"

—CB

René was using her electronic mobile device (EMD) to scan quick reference (QR) codes of passengers lined up on platform #4. The coach attendants, Tim, and Dan, were by her side. Right at the front of the coach class line were Leonard Gonzales and his family. Leonard had gotten tickets on the Zephyr for himself, his wife, and two young kids. They were on their way to Glenwood Springs for a long weekend of fun at the Hot Springs pool, rafting on the Colorado River, and rides at the amusement park. Gonzales was a Marine who had served in Iraq. He wore a ball cap emblazoned with the Marines logo. The eagle, globe, and anchor were tattooed on his forearm.

"Thank you for your service to our country, and for taking your family on the train," René said respectfully as she scanned Leonard's phone.

"Thanks, we are excited," Mr. Gonzales said with a smile.

Right behind the Gonzales family was a sturdy-looking man in his mid-twenties with a ballcap on backward. For luggage, he had a backpack, roller suitcase, and good-sized tool bucket. Doug Klaus was a contractor on his way to help a friend with a kitchen project in Grand Junction. René saw the tools and asked if Doug had weighed his stuff. He had. He assured her that it was right at fifty pounds. She took his word for it and moved down the line.

About forty feet back in the coach class line were four large men in their fifties and sixties. They were all wearing CU Buffs gear: shirts, hats, even socks. They had been football players for the University of Colorado in the 1980s. They were on their way to Glenwood on the train. Their plan was to take a limousine to Aspen for a reunion. They were looking for their fellow teammate, Paul Brown, who was supposed to be onboard already.

Just as René finished scanning the tickets of the four former athletes, she heard a single voice start a chant. "*Who dey think dey beat dem Buffaloes? Who dey! Who dey!*"

All four men plus the guy who started the chant repeated the obnoxious cheer, only much louder.

René squinted her eyes and pulled her head into her shoulders in a helpless effort to block her ears, since her hands were full of seat checks and her EMD.

All five men laughed and gave each other high-fives, and hugs.

Tim had their seats assigned in the premier coach section. He said they could go right to the train. The friends thanked the crew members, and walked together down the platform.

Car attendant Dan looked at his colleagues, Tim and René, as the five men walked away. "Well, we know who to draft if we need a good defensive line on this train," he said in jest. Dan was known as a passionate football fan who loved all things Packers. Most of his analogies were related to the gridiron.

They all grinned and continued to the next passenger in line.

René was scanning tickets for a family of five booked in regular coach class. She noticed they were only going to the first stop on the line, Fraser at Winter Park. "What's going on in Fraser?" she asked the mom in a sort of rhetorical manner as the EMD computed the QR code.

The mother, Jessica Knight, said that they were going to the Zoppe' Circus that evening, and staying three nights at a bed-and-breakfast.

René looked up with surprise. "Oh, I have been to that circus several times in Wheat Ridge. Have you seen them before?"

"Nope, first time. We're really excited," Marshall Knight said, as he gathered their kids and baggage for the short walk down the platform.

"Well, you are going to love it, and the kids will never forget it. Make sure you meet Nino the clown. He is the best!" René said.

Dan handed them their seat checks; their car was right next to where they were standing.

Meanwhile, Nick was getting sleeping car passengers scanned in and sent to their respective cars. For him, seeing the large number of people getting on in Denver was a great thing. He loved trains and railroading, but it was the train staff and passengers, the people who made each trip on the Zephyr interesting and fun.

"Hello, Pamela. Hi, Mr. Abraham," Nick said to a couple going to Salt Lake City in room 18 of the 540 car. "Just go toward the front of the train and look for the CAR 540 sign. Rashid, your car attendant, should be at the door waiting."

"Got it, thanks," said Mr. Abraham.

"Can we ride in that car?" his wife asked with a humorous grin as she pointed at the shiny Silver Sky.

Nick looked in the direction she was pointing and saw James and Brewster, two of the VIPs on the Silver Sky, standing not far away. "You don't want to ride with those bums," he said with a chuckle.

"Hey now, be nice," James said so everyone could hear.

The friends all had a good laugh. Dr. Pamela Abraham laughed with them. "Clearly you train people are a close-knit group," she said.

"Don't tell anyone, please," Nick said, continuing the banter.

But it wasn't just banter. Those guys were some of Nick's best friends. They had worked together on their mutual passion for years.

Close-knit for sure, Nick thought as he continued through the line of sleeping car passengers.

People who passed through Denver on the train could step off during the fifty-minute break while the train was being serviced.

Knut, an athletic European sports reporter, and Olivia, his girlfriend of many years, had literally run through the crowds of Train Days to get to Whole Foods Market. They were back with only moments to spare and two bags of moderately overpriced vegan sustenance.

Another passenger, Yao Ping from China, was more interested in infrastructure and trains than stocking up on fringe supplies. As an engineering student, he was dumbfounded that a busy city like Denver, that was long north to south, would have a north to south train station, but no through tracks. *Surely I am missing something here*, Yao Ping thought as he surveyed the track layout. *No way the people of Denver would spend so much effort to build such an impressive train station that was so impractical*. But they had.

The last passenger in line looked rushed and rather haggard. He was traveling in the premier coach section of the train to Grand Junction. His ticket was for four people, but only he was there.

"Where is the rest of your group?" René asked, after scanning the man's phone.

"I sent them south by car," he replied impatiently, as his phone rang. "Excuse me," he said as he put the phone to his ear.

"Here is your seat check, just go forward two cars and look for seat 26," Tim said.

The man walked past, only half-listening.

"Who is that guy, and what is his problem?" Tim asked René.

She looked at her device. "His name is Michael Sayers. I have no idea what his issue is, but he said he sent his family south."

"South? That's rather odd," Tim replied.

René and Tim had been working in public transportation long enough to sniff out a person with troubles. Sayers fit the profile. He was clearly not a poor man, but he was in a distracted hurry, stressed, and had an odd story about his missing family. People with those kinds of peculiarities were usually running from the law, in a bout of domestic violence, coming down from an addiction, or they had just lost a loved one. Regardless of what the problem was, it wasn't good.

"I will keep an eye on him," Tim told his assistant conductor.

On platform #4, near the sleeping car vestibules, a group of family members had gathered to meet Jay and Diana, who were passing through town as they traveled from Chicago to San Francisco. Their three daughters were there, along with most of their thirteen grandchildren and five great-grand kids—a real treat for all of them.

Jen, the car attendant, took a family photo for them in front of her car. The group was planning to browse the Train Days displays and have coffee at Pig Train Coffee inside the station after the train left, taking away the patriarchs.

All passengers getting on in Denver had been processed and were onboard the train. Nick was headed to the dorm car near the front of the train—car 540.

René checked out the rear of the train to make sure mechanical contractors had installed the necessary safety gear properly. She saw the back of the Silver Sky with its amazing, rounded end and sculpted dome. Two red marker lights were brightly illuminated inside protruding shrouds of protective stainless steel—one on either side of the car. Above the concave roof at the end of the car was a darkened mars light embedded in a large housing that resembled an upside-down keel. An artistic drumhead was attached to the back door of the car. It was a perfect replica of the original 1949 Zephyr logo, with a neon depiction of the Golden Gate Bridge and art deco block letters.

What a perfect-looking rear of a train, René thought.

The Silver Sky had been the rear car on the first ever run of the Zephyr to California on March 20, 1949. Now, more than eight decades later, at 8:04 a.m. and 30 seconds, conductor Nick gave the order to engineers Larry and Christina, "Train number 5, pull on signal indication DUS track 4. OVER."

Just as it had done years before, the Zephyr, with the Silver Sky bringing up the marker lights, glided out of Denver Union Station. Onboard were 245 souls from all over the world, every lifestyle, every socioeconomic level, and a multitude of faiths. No one aboard had any clue that this odd amalgamation of humanity would soon be bonded together like few groups have ever been.

Hundreds of people were photographing the Zephyr as it pulled away from Denver Union Station. The end of the Silver Sky glided by the front of the BIG BOY. The band stopped playing, even the musicians wanted to watch the historic moment.

"Could there ever be a more glorious railroad scene?" Ed, the leader of the steam engine project, asked rhetorically.

The crowd watched silently. Then when the marker lights were gone, a cheer from all in attendance rose up spontaneously as the band leaned into "Happy Days Are Here Again."

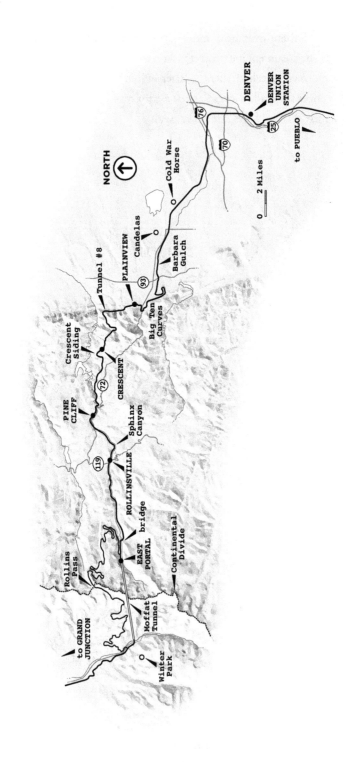

CHAPTER 5

RAILS THAT CLIMB

"Going to the mountains is like going home."

—John Muir

René made the usual safety announcements on the public address system (PA). Nick was busy on the radio, talking to yard masters, dispatchers, and engineers about permissions and authorizations for the track the Zephyr would run on. He donned his reflective vest in preparation for lining the manual switch on the Platte River bridge. René told the passengers that Nick would be giving scenic announcements throughout the day. She was all business.

The train stopped on the old wooden deck bridge with steel and concrete supports. Only a few such bridges were still in service on the Zephyr route. As Nick lifted the lever of the switch just west of the 23rd Street diamond track, a place where railroads intersected at right angles, he glanced upstream to the recently rebuilt Balloon Track bridge. That span over the Platte connected North Yard on the Moffat route with the southbound Joint Line that goes to Colorado Springs, Pueblo, and beyond. It looked strong and robust.

Nick wondered how long it would be until the bridge he was on would be replaced. He called to his engineers, "Number 5, pull over."

Reagan was delighted! His radio scanner caught all the action. He heard Nick and Larry. He knew the lingo. The speaker was loud enough for his mom to hear it all.

"DUS, Mom, that means Denver Union Station! All of us train fans know that."

She smiled sweetly at her son.

"Number 5, that's us! We are really going to California!"

Claire loved Reagan, he was her precious boy, but he was a handful. Reagan had been born with autism. He was high-functioning and high-energy, and insatiable when it came to trains. Claire and her husband Terry figured out how to support each other as they raised their son. Adapting to the care demands of a special needs child pushes parents to make difficult decisions. Such was the case with Terry and Claire. He focused on earning the money to support the family; she stayed home and sacrificed her career for the needs of their son. The arrangement was working so far, but Claire found herself mostly alone with Reagan.

The boy loved trains, and he loved his extended family. Claire's saving grace was her family. Her parents, brother and sisters, cousins— all loved Reagan. The whole family still lived in neighborhoods near the La Grange, Illinois, train station. They were a constant source of support and distraction.

Reagan's life was blessed because of those people who were related to him. Claire's dad had stepped up the most. He was with Reagan every week. Together they went to places like the Chicago Museum of Science and Industry just to see the model trains run. Reagan could do that for hours. Sometimes they just sat along the tracks near their home counting cars and locomotives. It was his grandpa who bought the train trip from Chicago to California for Claire and Reagan. He planned to come along too, but his health was declining rapidly. Just the thought of going on a long train trip made his hips ache. Reagan didn't seem to realize it, but his grandpa was an old man.

On the morning Claire and Reagan went to Chicago to board the Zephyr, Grandpa handed Reagan his railroad scanner and charger. He looked squarely at his grandson and said, "You have seen me use this thing a hundred times. You're ready. It's yours now." He gave Reagan a laminated card with the radio frequencies of the entire Zephyr route.

Reagan was speechless. He held that scanner like a mother holds a newborn baby. This was the greatest moment of his life! (Reagan actually had a lot of "greatest moments.") The trip was Reagan's fifteenth birthday present. He and Claire were riding the best train in America all the way, from start to finish.

Terry was happy for his son and wife. He wished he had the time and money to join them on that trip. To him, eating in the diner, having sleeping car accommodations, and all the rest sounded like great fun. But he was a working class guy. He and Claire had met while they were both working in the motor pool at Fort Hood. He always worried about how much money he spent. His life never included luxurious vacations or fancy cars.

Claire knew all about the conflict Terry faced as he toiled away for her and Reagan. She could feel the compassion and love her husband felt for his son, and for her. She wished desperately that Terry could join them on this trip. The familiar emotions welled up inside her: grief versus gratitude, anger tempered by anxiety, love overshadowed by loneliness. A familiar pattern. She could either start to cry, or get that nonsense out of her head right then.

Never mind all that, Claire thought, *we are doing this!* She had never seen Reagan so excited and thrilled.

"We are really going into the Rockies on the Zephyr!" Reagan repeated again and again.

Claire bit her lip to help hold back tears and nodded affirmatively. *Damn right we are*, she thought.

The train sped up as it went by Prospect Junction. They passed busy North Yard with its engine fueling station, marshaling yard, grain elevator, intermodal facility, and commuter rail maintenance shops.

Later that day, an "important train" was supposed to roll through North Yard. The BIG BOY was going to pull up to the massive steel water tower, or "water crane," as such structures were called in the old railroad lexicon. The tank was located just north of the Pecos Junction control point switches. It was to be used to fill the boiler and water tender of the massive steam engine. That tower had rarely been used in the last seventy years, but was restored with a spout and filter system specifically for Train Days.

Speed on the Zephyr increased. The two 4,200 horsepower locomotives whisked west over road crossings equipped with "Quiet Zone" technology, where engineers didn't need to sound the horn.

Passengers got their first good view of the mountains as they passed Old Town Arvada, the hub of a western suburb of Denver. The Rockies beckoned in the brilliant sunlight. The sky above the peaks was cobalt blue. Pine forests separated the city from mountain tops like a picture frame. Radiant white clouds accented the whole scene. Although it was a typically dry, late-summer day in Colorado, life seemed to emanate in every direction.

Dr. Michael Sayers was not enjoying the scenery. He had just gotten a disturbing call from his boss in Golden, Colorado. "Mike, you may have been right. The big one might be starting soon. Ground all over northwest Wyoming is sinking and bulging back up again . . . five feet in some places, and in just two hours! Not only that, the Dotsero volcano is venting heavy," the man said. "I may have signed your death warrant, making you go to Grand Junction. Please forgive me."

Mike decided right then to get off the train at the Granby stop and pay whatever it took to charter a plane and pilot to fly him south, where his wife and kids were headed, to outrun the calamity to come.

Oblivious to the terror brewing hundreds of miles to the north, a huge crowd filled the ball fields of Ralston Valley High School for the Labor Day soccer tournament. That evening, the All State Youth Orchestra was to perform as a "drone works" light show filled the sky for all the participants and surrounding community.

Nick used the PA to draw everyone's attention to the event, and brag that his daughter was in the cello section of the orchestra. As the Zephyr passengers looked at the soccer fields, people at the games looked right back, beckoning the engineer to blow the whistle. Christina obliged them and let 'er rip, loud and strong.

Crossing over Indiana street, passengers could see Pikes Peak to the south and Longs Peak to the north. Those two 14,000-foot mountains are more than 160 miles apart, but so tall that they could both be seen at the same time from that vantage point. James Peak is right between them, but only 13,294 ft high. Seasoned rail fans knew they would travel underneath James Peak through the Moffat Tunnel in just about an hour.

At that very moment, emergency text alerts went out to every phone within 200 miles of Yellowstone National Park with an order to immediately evacuate the area by any available means. The message was signed by Sara Blackburn, director of Homeland Security. She was finally convinced that the United States was about to be hit within hours by a natural disaster worse than a nuclear bomb explosion.

Some people sitting on the right side of the train noticed a statue of a red horse next to the tracks. Nick was in the parlor car talking about it. "That is a monument placed as a memorial to the men and women who worked at the Rocky Flats nuclear weapons trigger factory during the Cold War. Many of those workers died relatively young of cancer and other health issues, possibly related to the work they did at Rocky Flats."

One mile further west, the train went by numerous metal water diversion troughs. At that point, the tracks cling to the side of a steep slope on the north side of Barbara Gulch. Nick continued his narration, "The ground underneath the tracks here has a thick layer of bentonite clay just below the surface. That clay is weathered volcanic ash that settled in salt water millions of years ago. Bentonite is very expansive when wet, making it difficult to keep railroad tracks level. These drainage aqueducts redirect water and snow melt away from the tracks to mitigate the effects of the clay under the roadbed."

Velocity slowed as the Zephyr went under the Highway 93 bridge. The Big Ten curves, one of the most famous spots for railfans along the route, lay just ahead. Winding around a series of 10-degree turns and climbing the 2.2 percent grade forced the Zephyr's engines to work a little harder than usual. Christina fluctuated between notch 5 and 6. They rounded the famous string of hopper cars welded to a defunct track. The retired equipment was placed there to act as a windbreak after a freight train was blown over in 1969. Since then, no train had

had an accident, in spite of the notoriously stiff breezes that regularly whipped through the area.

Nick commented on the PA, regarding the view of the skyscrapers in Downtown Denver. "Folks, rarely is the air so clear, the sky so blue, the city so dazzling as it is today. Soak it all in. You never know when you will get a chance to see Denver in all its glory again."

Above the Big Ten is a siding called Eisele at Fire Clay. The roadbed cuts into the side of Eastridge at Blue Mountain. Nick pointed out the brilliantly colored layers of sediments exposed by the gash in the hillside that David Moffat and his men chiseled out to build the railroad more than 120 years before. Nick said one layer in particular was very different from the others: pearly white and about two feet below the top of the cut.

"We are 400 miles from Yellowstone. That layer is derived from ash that emanated, most likely, from a Yellowstone eruption 660,000 years ago. Imagine the power it took to thrust that much material this far!"

Dr. Sayers heard Nick's words over the loudspeaker in his coach car. His first thought was that Nick was close, but still wrong. He was describing the Lava Creek B ash found at Leyden, not Fire Clay.

After he got over his typical scientific need for accurate minutiae, Sayers thought to himself, *Does that guy have any idea how ominous his narration is?*

René knew Nick had a good idea of what was going on at Yellowstone from their crew briefing. She tracked him down, found him in the crew dorm car, and gave him a good scolding. "You know a lot of people on this train have heard the news about Yellowstone this morning just like you did. Stop trying to scare them, please."

After winding around Blue Mountain, the train crossed over a small bridge that went over Highway 72, Coal Creek Canyon Road. Christina, in the 313 cab, commented to Larry on how the number of people living in that area had grown over the years.

"I know," Larry said. "They just keep adding houses and cars and people, but they never add enough roads or schools or stores. And what if there is a huge flood like in 2013, or a big wild fire like Superior in 2021? You think all those people up there can get through this tiny little road to safety?"

"Finally!" Jay said to Diana, as they sat on the preferred right side of the parlor car. "We're in the mountains. Now we get to the good stuff."

Moments later, the Zephyr entered tunnel #1. Nick's voice came on the PA again. "This is the first of forty-three tunnels between Denver and Grand Junction, Colorado. We will go through the first twenty-seven tunnels in the next twenty-eight miles, culminating with the world-famous Moffat Tunnel that will take us over, and under, the Continental Divide."

Climbing at a steady 2 percent grade, the Zephyr was well above the prairie below. Views out over the Great Plains were almost surreal; endless flatness collided with impossible undulations. Scattered among the steep hills, massive spires of stone, called the Flatirons, poked skyward.

David Halliday Moffat came to these hills in 1903 with an army of 20,000 railroad builders. His goal was to construct a standard gauge railway from Denver to Salt Lake City, and on to the Pacific. He never made it all the way, but he did drive his rail line *through* the Rockies, not around them. His chief engineer, H. A. Sumner, chose to weave through the Flatirons above Eldorado Springs. It took moxie to decide to build a railway among the rockslides and cliffs of that route, but it paid off. That choice created one of the most scenic passenger rail routes in the world. On the Zephyr that Labor Day, nearly everyone aboard agreed.

In the parlor car, Nick commented that passengers could look straight up through the sightseeing windows at all the rocks that had still never fallen on the tracks. It was a sobering thought, looking at thousands of tons of fractured stone high above them on nearly vertical cliffs.

After a few moments, Nick got back on the PA. "I would like everyone to know that you are on one of the safest railroads ever built. Between 1904, when the first trains crested the Rockies on the Moffat line, until today, not one passenger has ever lost their life due to a railroad accident of any kind. We have not been perfect, but every effort has been made by our host railroad, and our own company to keep that record from ever changing."

Rounding Crescent siding, high above the deep chasm between the tracks and Gross Reservoir, the Zephyr passed a parked train full of rail. Nick commented to René how nice it was that the UPR had installed concrete ties all the way from Denver to Moffat Tunnel over the last two years. "I know it's because of increased freight traffic, which can cause us delays, but I really do appreciate the enormous investment. Now they are even preparing to put in brand new rail! I will get to end my career on the best tracks money can buy!"

CHAPTER 6

BAD BEHAVIOR

"The only thing necessary for the triumph of evil is for good men to do nothing."

—Edmond Burke

Not everyone was enthralled by the scenery and quality of the railway. Andy "Rad" Richardson had been drinking heavily. By the time Nick was talking about Gross Reservoir on the PA, Rad was too drunk to care about anything. He was not used to so much booze, having been in prison the past few years, and most recently having stayed at a shelter in Naperville, Illinois. When his bottle was empty, he went to Sammy, the lead service attendant (LSA) working the coach class snack bar, to try conning her out of another shot or two. Instead she cut him off and suggested he try to sleep until he was more sober. Back at his seat, he began getting fidgety. He was feeling like he had waited long enough— he remembered a pretty young woman he had seen a few rows away.

Ingrid was alone next to an empty seat. Susan, Ingrid's seatmate, had gone to Sammy's snack bar, one car ahead and downstairs.

Rad saw his chance to get close to the young foreigner who he perceived to be insecure. He went up and asked her how she was doing and if he could sit with her. He sat down, not really giving her a chance to say no. He asked her where she was from.

She looked at him skeptically and said, "Austria."

"Cool, kangaroos and an opera house, right?" the ignorant ex-con asked.

"No, mountains and Mozart," she replied without an ambivalent smile.

"Are you traveling alone, or with that older lady?"

She didn't answer, thinking, *Susan is a beautiful woman who is perhaps in her late forties, but certainly not old.*

Rad kept talking. "Because I am traveling alone, just sort of exploring the West. If you want a travel partner, you know, we could travel together."

Ingrid was dumbfounded. She wondered, *Is this creep really thinking I would want to spend any time with him at all?*

She replied, "I am meeting friends. I am fine alone," in a tone that said, *GO AWAY!*

Rad persisted. "Really, I think you should hang out with me—I can take you to my beach house in Cali. It's amazing!"

His lie was so obvious that a woman two rows forward, who was eavesdropping, let out a sharp scoff as if to say, "Liar!"

Ingrid tried to politely say no and ask him to leave, but Rad kept accosting her. He slid a bit in her direction, sitting too close for comfort. His hand reached for her knee. His bad breath blew on her.

She was just about to call for help when help appeared.

"It's time for you to go back to your seat, Mister." Zachary Miller's voice left no doubt that he was prepared to do whatever it took to stop Rad's unwelcome advances on the beautiful woman from Europe.

The entire train car was silent. People looked for Dan the car attendant, or one of the conductors. But no staff members were in the car at that moment.

"The girl and I are talking. You go mind your own Amish business," Rad said to Zach condescendingly, only half glancing toward the powerful, chiseled farmer.

"Get up and go back to your seat now," Zach said in a low, quiet tone that left Rad with only two choices: comply or fight.

"Please go, I do not want to talk to you," Ingrid pleaded with Rad, afraid she would be the cause of a physical altercation, something completely unacceptable in her worldview.

Rad looked at Ingrid, feeling betrayed, then at Zach, who had the physical power to easily pummel the skinny ex-con if he chose to do so.

L.T. Miller watched his grandson's courageous action to protect a stranger. He was proud of the moxie Zach was showing, but saddened by the truth the incident was revealing about who the boy really was in his heart. He and the rest of the Amish clan sat silently. Their strictly pacifist culture commanded them to not get involved.

Zach didn't want to be a hero. He had asked his younger cousin to go find a conductor—fast, while he kept an eye on "that guy."

But Dan, the car attendant, was in the diner, having his late breakfast break, and the conductors were in other parts of the train. Zach decided he couldn't let Rad continue to escalate his unwanted advances. Several people in the train car were feeling the same urge.

Zach took a quick glance, hoping the conductor would open the end door of the car. No one was coming. He saw Rad physically move in on Ingrid, and saw the girl clearly try to back away. In Zach's mind, it was time to either stand up and act, or be a coward.

L.T. Miller turned away from the scene and looked forward stone-faced. The others in the Amish group followed his lead. Zach had made his choice, a bigger choice than most people in the train car realized. He had decided he was not going to sit passively while another person needed help. He chose to be a man of action. Zach knew what his behavior meant. His Amish way of life was probably ending right then and there.

Rad turned to meet the challenge. Zach neither attacked nor retreated. He just stood there without flinching. Rad, in his booze-fueled anger, was getting ready to punch the powerful Amish man.

"That's enough!" came the shout from Susan. She was shocked at the sight as she entered the upper level of the 512 car. The muscular, good-looking young Amish man was staring down the creepy guy, and that jerk was sitting in her seat!

"You!" she said, pointing at Rad's eyes, "get the hell away from her, and get out of my seat. NOW!"

Rad took a quick look around. All eyes were on him. No one

looked like they were on his side. After a brief silence, the angry ex-con relented. "This is crap!" he said out loud, as he got up and stormed toward the stairs. He stumbled, slamming into the water fountain cabinet on the way, and disappeared into the lower level of the next car.

Zach had not struck the man in anger, and the young woman was safe. The prayers of the Miller clan had been answered.

Susan looked at Zach. Zach looked at Ingrid. Ingrid looked back at Zach. Then Zach looked at Susan, not knowing what to do next. It was a magic moment.

Susan, who knew a thing or two about love at first sight, saw a hopeful gleam in Zach's eye as he looked back at the young woman he had just defended. *This could be interesting*, she thought.

Ingrid's thoughts were racing. Relief, embarrassment, confusion, and fear were in her mind. That was to be expected. What surprised her was her desire to keep looking at this clean-shaven man wearing odd clothes who had come to her rescue.

The hurried footsteps of a man bounding down to the snack bar on the lower level of car 511 were ominous. Sammy peered down the hall. *Oh boy*, she thought, as Rad tripped forward in her direction. There was no good will in his demeanor at all.

"I want two shooters of Jack!" he demanded brusquely.

"Listen, I told you just a few moments ago, I am not serving you any alcohol. Now please leave, or I am going to call the conductor." Sammy was calm but stern.

Rad continued in a drunken voice, "Call him, I want to talk to him about what a . . . " He stopped himself from uttering the swear words he would usually use. He was still sober enough to hope he could stay out of trouble.

"You know what? Never mind!" he said, and started to go up the stairs. But with each step, his anger grew. He turned around. "On second thought, forget that! Call your stupid little conductor. Cause I'm gonna complain about you!" he said, pointing right at Sammy.

Rad dove into a diatribe of swearing that would cause a military drill sergeant to blush.

Sammy felt threatened. She grabbed her PA mic. "Immediate assistance needed in the lower level snack car 511!"

Now she was mad, and a little scared. Seconds tick by slowly once the call for help is made, and the person who made the call is alone with the troublemaker.

"You really think I'm scared of you, or him? Lemme tell you, I messed up more punks that thought they was somethin' in the joint than you ever saw. I ain't scared of your conductor."

Tim, the premiere coach attendant, was first down the stairs. He had heard the end of Rad's "tough-guy talk." The oldest man on the crew, Tim was undaunted. "Sir, back up and say no more!"

Conductor Nick had had enough. He guessed immediately what the issue was. On his way to the 511 car, he was stopped by Susan. She was looking for some help after the incident between Rad and Ingrid.

At the same time, a ten-year-old Amish boy started talking fast at the conductor. Susan interrupted the boy and started to say how Rad was being suggestive and inappropriate with a female passenger.

Nick was short and to the point as he kept hurrying to Sammy's aid. "Don't you worry, we got this."

As he spoke, Jim, the bartender from the parlor car, passed by in a near dead sprint.

Nick knew Rad had to be removed from the train as soon as possible to ensure the safety of passengers and crew. Without waiting for confirmation, he got on the railroad radio. "Number 5 conductor to head end. We need police to remove a possibly violent male, approximately forty years old. OVER." Nick was rapidly walking through the train as he made the call to end Rad's journey 1,000 miles short of California.

"Roger, police at Pinecliffe. OUT." Larry toned up the dispatcher with the local tower three-number code.

BEEP came the pleasant sound indicating that the message to the operations center had been received. "UPR Omaha Dispatcher 80. OVER."

Larry told the dispatcher about the need for police. Arrangements were made for the exchange. Milepost 36.93—Pinecliffe, Highway 72 crossing.

Even a drunk scoundrel knows when the deck is stacked against him. Rad felt the weight of consequences for his actions catching up to him. In one last hope of avoiding repercussions, he slithered back to his coach seat in the 512 car.

René, Tim, and Dan were already watching him. Conductor Nick saw the staff members in the 512 car through the window in the door. Being satisfied that Rad was under surveillance, he went down to the 511 car snack bar. Sammy told him the story about how she had cut Rad off from alcohol, and about his second attempt at more booze.

Jim was with her, still holding his wine glass polishing cloth from the parlor car.

Nick assured her that the guy was being removed ASAP, and that she would not have to deal with him anymore.

Nick went upstairs and back to the 512 car where Rad was sitting.

The seedy guy started talking before Nick could get a word in. "Hey, man, I'm sorry 'bout that, bro, you know, with the chick in the little store thing. We're cool, right?" Rad put out his arm for a handshake with the conductor.

"Understood," was Nick's response while standing straight and strong, and demonstrably NOT shaking Rad's hand.

After a quick crew briefing with René, Nick went downstairs without making any more eye contact with Rad. He opened the window on the lower level of the train car. A Boulder County sheriff was already waiting at the grade crossing in his SUV. The train slowed to a crawl.

"Two cars number 5. OVER. That will do. Out," came Nick's commands to the engineers.

Christina stopped the train with the vestibule of car 512 right in the middle of the railroad grade crossing on Colorado Highway 72.

Rad was still in his seat upstairs. Assistant Conductor René and other crew members were all keeping an eye on him. The mood was tense. Once the train stopped, everyone jumped into action.

"Let's go, your trip is over," René said to Rad as she came up behind him.

"Oh no, I am so sorry. I didn't mean to upset anyone. Please don't do this."

"Too late, cops are waiting outside. You can walk off and just go away, or they can come up here and arrest you. Your choice." René had given that speech quite a few times in her ten years on the rails. She was an expert at it.

Rad thought through his options. He was mad. Mad at René, mad at Nick, mad at the train, mad at the other passengers, and mad at God. He wanted to lash out and "bust up all of them jerks!" But most of all, he wanted to stay out of jail. He gathered his composure, and the few belongings given to him by the shelter back in Naperville. He slowly got up and headed for the stairs.

Nick only took a moment to explain the situation to the sheriff's deputy. Four automobiles were already backed up at the crossing being blocked by the motionless train. One was a military grade Humvee and a driver that reminded Nick of his G.I. Joe toy from when he was a kid.

Nick had to speak loudly to be heard over the clanging of the crossing gate bells. René followed Rad off the train. The angry man was not being accused of a crime, but he was not welcome on the train any longer. The only thing needed from the sheriff's deputy was the assurance that Andy Richardson safely left the property.

Rad was humble. He was hoping to avoid any more escalation. An arrest would violate his prison release terms. "Yes, Sir" was all he said when the officer asked him to step away from the train.

"Number 5, proceed west, delayed in the block. OVER," Nick called out on the radio.

"Roger, number 5 departing west at Cliff, delayed in the block. OUT." Larry responded.

Christina pulled the throttle, and the train eased away from the road crossing, and from Andy "Rad" Richardson. The incident had cost the Zephyr ten minutes.

Nick was not happy. It had started out to be such a perfect day. Now he would have to hustle through his station stops to get back on schedule by the time the train reached Glenwood Springs. Then there was the annoying paperwork that had to be filled out and sent to a multitude of railroad officials.

Nick did not take the time to feel sadness for Rad's plight in life. His only concern was that the drunk man might cause problems for some of the people living in the canyon. Nick lived near Pinecliffe. His home community was made up of some of the most decent people he had ever met. He wished he had asked the sheriff to get Rad back to Denver.

René had other thoughts. She was a compassionate person. She wondered who Andy's mother had been, where she might be, and imagined how she would ask forgiveness for her son.

René's exterior image was strong and determined, but on the inside, she was full of empathy. She had always felt the pain of others, and tried to understand why people behaved badly. She liked to assume people were basically good. If they were not kind, she wanted to believe that it was only because rough circumstances caused them to act badly. That worldview had been shaken to the core by years of seeing random people at their worst on public trains. But her benevolent opinions about human nature were not completely gone yet. She secretly grieved for Andy Richardson.

Neither Nick nor René thought for a second that the ten minutes Andy Richardson just cost them would be of any major importance.

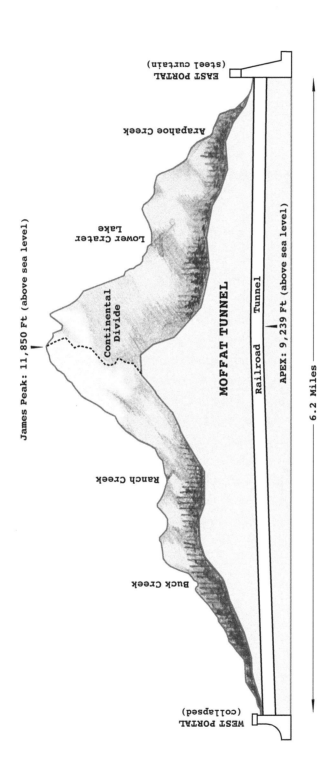

James Peak: 11,850 Ft (above sea level)

EAST PORTAL
(steel curtain)

Arapahoe Creek

Lower Crater
Lake

Continental
Divide

MOFFAT TUNNEL

Railroad Tunnel

APEX: 9,239 Ft (above sea level)

Ranch Creek

Buck Creek

WEST PORTAL
(collapsed)

6.2 Miles

CHAPTER 7

THE MOFFAT TUNNEL

"The most important part of a tunnel is that it isn't a cave."

—CB

The Rad distraction caused people to forget about scenery or geology for the time being. One thing Nick had always felt strongly about was keeping passengers informed regarding things happening with their train. He thought through what to say on the PA at that sensitive moment. Once he was ready, he pressed the button on the mic. "Folks, Conductor Nick speaking. I am sorry about the delay we have just incurred. As some of you already know, we had an incident. You see, a person on this train chose not to respect our rules, your train crew, or fellow passengers. As a result, we were forced to have law enforcement escort that individual off railroad property. Again I apologize for the disturbance, and thank you for your understanding. Now let's have some fun railroading! We are coming up on Lincoln Hills, Rollinsville, Tolland, and the world-famous Moffat Tunnel."

The Zephyr rumbled over the west switch of the Rollins siding, as the PA came to life throughout the train once again.

"Ladies and gentlemen, may I have your attention please, this is Nick, your conductor. In just nine minutes we will be entering the Moffat Tunnel. We will need nine minutes and twenty-four seconds to go through that longest tunnel on our entire route. Even though we have a powerful venting system in the tunnel, we ask that you not go from one train car to another inside the tunnel. That will help us keep our environment inside the train clean by keeping any exhaust from our locomotives on the outside. So if you are not where you want to be when we get to the tunnel, go there now, so we can keep the doors closed while we are in the tunnel."

René was still in the coach cars. "René to Nick, PA works great, but maybe use it less. OUT"

Nick was humored to hear that. *How ironic*, he thought. He had fought for years to get better reliability of the PA and several other systems onboard. Finally the mechanical department had the money, workers, motivation, and parts to keep all those important little details working. Now he was being asked not to use it as much as he wanted.

The train climbed even higher. Two young cowboys came out to wave at the train in Tolland. "Number 5, clear at West East Portal, let's go to the tunnel channel. OVER." Larry's voice was calm and confident as always.

"Tunnel channel. OUT," Nick answered.

An empty track curved away to the north. It was all that was left of the Rollins Pass track. That twenty-four-mile line was a standard gauge bypass that went over the top of the Great Divide. It operated from 1904, when rails first penetrated that area, until 1927, when the Moffat Tunnel became operational. Two large maintenance buildings for the tunnel were north of the tracks. Adjacent to the main line track, the East Portal siding sat unused.

As the train entered the tunnel, Christina barely noticed a big UPR maintenance truck and two men with hard hats and safety vests outside the tunnel entrance. Without fanfare, the Zephyr slipped into darkness.

East Portal at Moffat Tunnel is a huge concrete building that houses ventilation fans, back-up electrical generators, a maintenance office, and a powerful steel gate to seal off the entrance. It sports an inscription on a tall tower above the entrance: MOFFAT TUNNEL, 1923–1928. North of the tracks on the outside wall is a large brass plaque that is the door to a time capsule containing artifacts from the construction of the facility. It is an imposing structure to say the least—more like a fortress than a train tunnel. Trains had to travel almost ten yards before they were really in the mountain, not just in the portal building.

Several moments of tunnel darkness passed before Nick's now-familiar voice came on the PA again. He had this idea that people, especially travelers, wanted to know where they were. He loved giving his Moffat Tunnel speech.

"Ladies and gentlemen, as you can tell, we have entered the Moffat Tunnel. This 6.2 mile long, 15 feet wide, 26 feet high bore through the main range of the Rockies is the highest point reached on the connected American railway system at 9,239 feet above sea level. Tracks crest near the middle of the tunnel, directly over, or some would say under, the Continental Divide. That Great Divide separates waters flowing to the Atlantic from those flowing in the direction of the Pacific, the two greatest oceans of our planet. The tunnel was blasted out between 1923 and 1928. We will travel for nine minutes and twenty-four seconds in the tunnel before emerging at Winter Park Resort. There is one last thing I should tell you: as we cross the Great Divide and are at the highest place any regular train can go in North America, we will also be as deep into the crust of the earth as most of us will ever go in our lifetime, with more than 2,500 feet of solid granite directly above our heads. Now sit back and enjoy the scenic wonders inside the Moffat Tunnel. Thank you."

A few chuckles sounded in the parlor car. People lucky enough to ride the Silver Sky saw the light of day disappear behind them as the steel gate closed downward from top to bottom.

"Train number 5, running air. OVER," Larry reported. Each passenger train that goes through the Moffat Tunnel had to test the brakes before passing over the apex. Nick felt the retarding of speed. "Good runner number 5. Out," he called on the radio.

Another minute passed. Everything was proceeding as uneventfully as ever. Until it wasn't.

CHAPTER 8

EARTHQUAKE!

"Wisdom in an emergency is aided by abundant experience
in normality."

—CB

"What's going on up there? OVER!" Panic was emanating from Nick's voice as he barked into his radio. No response.

The 540 car was rocking side to side with rhythmic violence. Concern elevated to terror. *SCRAPE!* The top left side of the train car bounced against the wall of the tunnel and shot back to the other side. The axel springs in the bogies, those massive steel encasements that hold the wheels to the train car, made groaning creaks as they were fully compressed, perhaps for the first time ever. Without the solid walls of granite forcing the car to re-right itself, the high double-decker train might have tumbled over. Fear was quickly replaced by the realization that the worst possible scenario, a derailment, was happening in the worst possible place, 2,500 ft. below the shoulder of James Peak.

Nick caught his breath as he tried to gather his composure.

"We don't know what's happening! Are you okay?" Larry's voice was no less panicked, but there was also an inquisitive tone as if to say, *This makes no sense.*

Christina was in the seat at the controls. As the train started to sway, she instinctively set air to apply the brakes. Then the rocking movement intensified.

"Full service!" Larry yelled, begging Christina to stop the train.

"I'm already there!" she responded. They could both see light at the west portal of the tunnel. It was still about half a mile away, a distance that suddenly seemed enormous. The two locomotive engineers wanted nothing more than to get to that light. They were sure the train had derailed.

Christina looked at the air pressure gauges: BRAKE PIPE 85 PSI. Had the train derailed, the brake pipe hose would have most likely come apart at the gladhands between derailed cars, and sent air pressure plummeting to zero. *Oh good, maybe we are still on the rail*, she thought.

The train was rapidly slowing down, 30 mph, 20 mph, 10 mph. Christina felt a glimmer of hope. *Maybe we can still drag ourselves out of here.* She was just about to release the brakes and make a dash for the west portal of the tunnel, and the radiant sunshine of Winter Park.

Larry imagined all kinds of chaos behind him. Twisted train cars piled up in an unmovable jam, wedged into the fifteen-foot-wide concrete walls of the tunnel. His thoughts were halted by the piercing scream from Christina. *Oh no!* Larry thought, as he stood up to look closer. He opened his mouth, but no words came out. His eyes were as wide as they could get, but he could not see forward.

"The light at the end of the tunnel is gone!" Christina yelled. "Holy Crap!"

The darkness ahead of the still-moving train didn't compute for either of them at first. Then with rapid expansion, a cloud of dust billowed into the beam of the 313's powerful headlight. Within seconds, the Zephyr was engulfed. Five mph. *WHAM!* Full stop.

Christina hollered, "Cave in!"

The impact was intense, but not deadly. Christina's quick action on the automatic brake handle at the first indication of trouble had slowed down the train enough to avoid disaster when the plow of the lead locomotive crashed into the boulders of the collapsed tunnel at about four mph. It was a hard enough stop to knock anyone still standing off their feet.

Nick made a second call, "Are you guys alright?"

No response. Nick's sensory inputs were all confused. The train was still rocking back and forth as if it was running fast on a bad track, but he knew what he had felt a second earlier—a familiar feeling he hadn't experienced in years, but he recognized it instantly. Impact! Like that of a hard joint, when two train cars come together too fast in a yard while coupling, or when an engineer shoves too far and cars smack the bumper at the end of a stub track. Years of yard work on switch engines had given him enough experience to know what he had just felt. But it didn't add up. His mind was trying to understand how the train could have such an abrupt stop and still be moving. Then it dawned on him.

He thought and yelled at the same time, *"It's an earthquake!"*

Christina twisted the reverser switch from forward to back up like a race car driver shifting gears. Her other hand simultaneously grabbed the red automatic brake valve lever and pulled it all the way toward her. She didn't even realize she had instinctively grabbed the black handle throttle and yanked it all the way—notch 8!

"Back up!" Larry yelled. He assumed rocks were still coming down and that their only hope was to go east, to get as far away from the cave-in as fast as possible.

"I'm on it!" Christina yelled right back. She didn't know what the status of the train or track behind her was, but she knew she didn't want to stay where they were. The engine slowly began to roar louder as the RPMs of the diesel engines increased. Amps rose on the meter. The locomotive had never stopped rocking even after it hit the wall of rocks. Nothing could be seen outside the windows of the cab through the dust. The feel of the engine didn't jive with the indications on the gauges.

"Come on, go!" Christina thought in a panic. Then panic turned to a terrified feeling, like sinking deeper underwater with no way to reach the surface. The feeling was caused by a little light that had come on. The implications of that light were devastating. WHEEL SLIP.

Her heart sank. Larry felt like he would throw up. Amps kept building up—over 1,000. Another light: SAND. Helplessly, the two looked at the gauges. When steel wheels slip and begin to spin on steel rails, adhesion drops to near zero. If the wheel slip didn't stop real soon, the train was hopelessly stuck. If they couldn't find a way to move the train back, they and the more than 200 people on board were most likely going to be crushed by more cave-ins or suffocate in the cloud of dust.

On the lead unit, the one Larry and Christina were sitting in, the front axle was barely touching the rail. Rocks from the cave-in had wedged under the traction motor housing of the front bogie. The rear truck didn't have enough adhesion to the rail to pull the front wheels of the locomotive off the rocks and shove the entire Zephyr backward up a 0.8 percent grade at the same time.

All eight wheels of the lead unit began to spin in place. Radar told the onboard computer that the train was not moving. The speedometer told it that the wheels were turning. The incongruity triggered the programmed response: Light up the warning to engineers and apply sand to the wheels.

"Bite!" Larry yelled. Bite is what railroaders call it when the powered wheels grab the rail and move, rather than spin in place. The speedometer read 10 mph.

"We aren't moving—the wheels are just slipping," Larry said with a hint of reservation.

Christina slammed the console with her fist. "Back up, damn it!"

She feathered the independent brake lever, the control that applies brakes to the wheels of the locomotives only. Suddenly . . . *scrape, pop, drop!* The train lurched backward!

Nick was running through the baggage car on his way to find out what had happened to his engineers when he was thrown face first to the linoleum floor by the sudden rocketing backward of the entire car. He got back on his feet. The train was moving—but it was going east!

Who's watching the shove? he thought.

Without taking the time to think about it, he began instinctively falling back on twenty-nine years of rules, classes, and experience on the rails as a response to the confusing menagerie of sensory inputs that didn't make sense. He started running in the opposite direction to protect the end of his train that was moving blindly backward.

As wheel slip was detected, both locomotives automatically gritted the rail below the struggling wheels with sand. Finally, enough bite was achieved on the second unit to pull the lead engine's front truck off the rocks and shove the Zephyr to relative safety in the eastern end of the tunnel.

The clouds of dust visible in the headlight started to blow backward, like it was being sucked into a vacuum. "We're moving!" Larry was gripping the arms of his chair so tightly, his fingers dug into the black vinyl.

"The whole train must be on the rail," Christina said with a relieved voice, choking back tears.

"Don't worry about speed, just get us out of here!" Larry commanded.

"I'm giving it all we've got," Christina said, as if to tell Larry that she didn't need orders from him. She knew what she was doing. She didn't know what was happening to the tunnel, but she did know how to handle the engines.

None of the crew understood why the tracks and tunnel, the very foundation of their world, were convulsing. They were all in a fog, trying to react and catch up with circumstances they had never encountered before. A light passed by the cab window. It was a tunnel emergency refuge point.

Oxygen—we might need those bottles if this dust gets much worse, Larry thought. *Never mind that,* he decided in his head. *It's more dangerous to stop—we've got to keep moving.* He kept his thoughts to himself.

Speed increased. "We're doing 30 mph!" Christina yelled over the roar of the engines. She smiled, seeing that the air was clearing. They were escaping certain death by cave-in. Her emotions were pulling at her like she had never felt before. She wanted to hyperventilate in fear, but her mind was determined to stay focused on the primary objective: get her train, her crew, and her passengers out of that hellhole as fast as she could.

There will be time for losing it later, she told herself.

She pushed the throttle forward. Notch 7,6,5,4, IDLE. They were going backward blind at 45 miles per hour through a tunnel that might have collapsed into a solid wall of deadly rock.

"God help us!" Christina said in what was for her more of a real prayer than a catch phrase.

"So far so good!" Larry replied.

"Just hang on," she told Larry.

Finally the odd rocking of the earthquake subsided. The movement of the train started to feel "normal" to the crew. Relief was creeping into the thoughts of the engineers as they made sure they kept control of the train.

"We might have dodged a bullet," Larry said.

James, Brewster, and the rest of the VIPs in the Silver Sky found themselves suddenly leading a move eastward. They were monitoring the radio transmissions (as all well-versed rail fans do). They knew the peril they were in.

James called to Alex, "Man the e-brake! They are shoving away from a cave in and can't see."

Alex was the only trained railroader in the private car. He threw open the small coffee table top over the brake valve and stared intensely out the back window. Ben had already turned on the big mars light, lighting up the whole tunnel for a hundred yards.

Nick's race through the train was frightening to everyone on board. Regardless of their questions and panic, they got out of his way, knowing instinctively that his task was of utmost importance at that moment. He was trying to reach the back of the 512 car—the last public coach on the train. Dan was already there. He had the door unlocked and open. The car attendant had been around long enough to know Nick or René would be on point once the train started going backward.

René had been in the diner when the earthquake started. She began to run for the rear of the train just like Nick, once she felt it going backward. She got to Dan first.

"I'm on the rear, we're good for at least ten cars. OVER!" came a female voice on the radio.

Finally the bold, yet frightened engineers had some visual direction. Larry grabbed the mic from the middle of the dashboard. "Ten cars! Good to have you back there. Can you see through the dust? OVER."

"YEAH! It's cleared up," René transmitted. "I can see ten cars at a time—shove ten! The trouble is the private car. I've got to drop down to get on point. OUT."

René dropped the mic and grabbed the lower rung of the safety bars at the end of the 512 car. She swung herself down.

Brewster heard what she said and ran to open the end door of the vestibule on the Silver Sky. He got it open right as René finished lowering herself through the narrow space between the bottom of the bi-level walkway and the top of the private car diaphragm.

"Ten cars again number 5. OVER!" It was Nick. He had made it to where Dan was guarding the now opened end of the train. He gave a car count while René tried to get through the Sky.

René rapidly weaved her way by the private bedrooms, past the bar below the dome, and up into the lounge area in the rounded end of the fancy train car. Everyone in the car was staring at her with scared expressions as she ran to the windows.

"René is on the point number 5. Shove ten. OVER!"

Before the engineers could answer, a different voice cut in on the transmission. "Omaha to train number 5, can you hear this radio? OVER."

Inside Moffat Tunnel, the railroad has a series of radio repeaters that allow transmissions from the dispatcher on a specific tunnel frequency. The dispatcher's voice was trembling.

Larry answered, "Number 5 here. We are alive and moving east as fast as we can—the freaking tunnel is caving in. OVER!"

The dispatcher's response sounded dismissive to their message, considering the monumental implications of what Larry just said.

Instead of addressing the cave-in, the voice coming from the UPR dispatching center in Omaha said what was required by an urgent memo: "Listen closely. We have a national emergency. Apparently, Yellowstone National Park has just completely blown up. Authorities are telling us that all trains must immediately depart main tracks *if at all possible* and stop. Everyone west of the Mississippi River is to take whatever cover they can find. Be prepared for the possibility of very hot and toxic fallout of volcanic ash. OVER."

Forty-eight mph. Christina moved the throttle to dynamic braking

SET UP by instinct. The Zephyr had crossed back over the apex of the Moffat Tunnel. They were going backward downhill toward Denver. She tried to swallow, but her throat was paralyzed.

"Ten cars again, shove. OVER," René said in a shocked tone.

"Train number 5, the dispatch center is being evacuated. I've got to go. Just . . . OVER. Oh my God . . . "

The crew in the tunnel could tell that the dispatcher, their only link to the outside world, was suddenly completely distracted, mixing words and absent from their conversation.

"Dispatcher, you want us to stop right here in the tunnel?"

The radio made no reply.

"Dispatcher, you do realize the tunnel is caving in on us?"

Larry's tone of voice was clearer than his words. *We ain't stopping!*

Finally the dispatcher's voice could be heard again. "Guys, this is bad—the pictures on the live cam monitors . . . my family . . . I've got to go. I am so sorry. Good luck. I'm so sorry."

"Good for ten more cars number 5. OVER." René tried to stay focused on the immediate job at hand, which was getting the train out of the tunnel safely.

"Ten. Roger," Christina was trying to process what she had just heard. Larry and Nick were doing the same thing.

"Where is the emergency brake valve?" René asked Alex, who looked like the one to ask.

"Right there," he said, pointing to the lever connected to pipes inside a fancy curved encasement next to the rear door.

"Come in, dispatcher," Larry called.

No one answered. He repeated it three times to no avail.

"Clear for another ten cars. OVER."

"Ten," Christina replied.

Several seconds passed. Christina held the train speed steady at 45 mph.

"Ten cars again," René called out, a little less sure of herself than before. The signal far ahead was red.

"What in blazes is going on?" a loud voice yelled in Nick's direction as he tried to see through the dark tunnel from the coach car. He was rapidly trying to think through the situation.

More voices and questions started coming at Nick like a slow building riot. "Are we in trouble?"

"Is this as bad as it feels?" The cadence and volume of passenger voices grew.

Nick did not turn to acknowledge them but stayed focused like a laser on the job at hand. He knew René had the point. So he pushed his way to the middle of the car and downstairs to the PA. He would try to calm the passengers.

Nick's voice was heard throughout the train. "Folks, this is Conductor Nick. Obviously, we are experiencing an emergency. The crew is working feverishly to get us to safety. Please, everyone MUST stay calm and seated, and allow us to do our jobs. We have some of the most-experienced train crew members and engineers in the system. We will work the problem. Just please give us space and keep calm. We will give you all the information we have as soon as we can."

The ability to multitask is something Nick could do well—speak and think about something different at the same time without missing a beat. While he was calming people with his PA announcement, he made up his mind on what to do.

"Stop the train number 5. OVER," Nick called out on the radio.

Christina slammed the automatic brake handle to full service, being careful not to go too far and place the train brakes in an emergency stop, which would have required three minutes to recover from before they could get moving again. She was afraid Nick was seeing more rocks falling.

The thought that she was going to die finally got to her. She started tearing up. She realized her emotions had her gasping for breath. She looked at Larry in fear, hoping for some kind of reassurance. She saw the older man with thirty-eight years of railroading experience smile as if to say, "I know." She saw the tears on his face too. There was comfort in that moment of shared terror.

Nick's radio transmission was different. His tone was decisive, but not alarming. He was choosing to take charge and pick between hopeless choices. The track was clear, no rocks or damage from the earthquake at all. There wasn't even any dust from the cave-in, which was now several miles west of where they were. He had never been great in high-pressure situations. Suddenly he faced more pressure than he ever dreamed of. But it was no dream; it was a nightmare, and it was real.

The train slowed rapidly.

"Crew brief," Nick said into the radio. He had not made the decision that the train would stay in the tunnel, only that they would talk about it and decide together.

"Is the track clear?" Larry was clearly impatient and scared, on the edge of panic.

"Track is clear; the air is clear. I just think that we have time to decide if we should go outside, or shelter in the tunnel with a whole mountain protecting us. OVER."

"Are you kidding me? What if there are more rocks falling?" Larry was almost yelling into the radio.

Christina turned to Larry, tears still on her face. "Maybe Nick's right. He knows a lot about geology. He knows more about Yellowstone and eruptions than we do."

Christina wanted out of the tunnel as much as anyone, but if Omaha was evacuating the dispatching center, the place they call "The Bunker" that could withstand an F5 tornado, it must be *really bad* out there.

Larry, like everyone else, was scared. But he had always been able to handle the heat and keep his cool. He thought he'd seen it all, but this was way beyond anything he ever experienced before. His mind was racing through the options. Nothing was a sure bet. In fact, no choice seemed any good at all. He had to assume the world outside that they had left just a few minutes ago—a world of incredible beauty and life, was gone, or soon would be. Larry figured they should get the train out of the tunnel and then come back in if it got bad out there. He radioed Nick with his thoughts.

"Larry, if the ash cloud gets here, we won't have time to get back in the tunnel and shut the gate. Volcanic clouds travel at up to 600 miles per hour!" Nick said it with certainty.

In fact, he wasn't too sure about the speed of the ash plume, but he knew it could really move. He also feared blast debris—balls of molten rock falling from above at supersonic speeds.

Larry could tell by the tone of Nick's voice that he was confident in his assessment. Larry worried that if he and Christina tried to keep shoving the train out of the tunnel, Nick could use the emergency brake handle in the train cars to force a stop. No need to have a further discussion. He knew what Nick was suggesting, and he knew what had to be done. They would stop, inspect the situation, and then shove out of the tunnel when all was clear.

The train stopped. "Shut the engines down; do it fast. We have to preserve the air in here. OVER."

Nick's transmission was too late for Larry. He was already pushing the red button that shut off both locomotives.

"Tie off the hand brakes," Christina said into the radio.

"Roger," Nick said.

The engine RPM meter read zero. The main engine of the 313 had rumbled to silence. Within seconds, the 309 went quiet as well.

Larry had shut down the oxygen-guzzling locomotives in record time. The Moffat tunnel was eerily still.

Christina centered the reverser switch and placed the parking brake lever to the APPLY position.

Oh God, let this be the right decision, she prayed.

CHAPTER 9

CHAOS

"Calamity and calm tend to chase each other."

—CB

The brief moment of quiet was shattered by the ratcheting of hand brake chains as Nick started securing the train. René did the same on the Silver Sky. Nick decided that only three brakes were needed by rules with the 0.8 percent grade on the tracks inside Moffat Tunnel. After he tied the brakes on cars 512, 511, and 510, the magnitude of his passenger problem came into focus.

René had gotten off the Sky at the vestibule steps and was starting toward the 512 car when she heard the starting of a diesel engine behind her. When the Museum had the Silver Sky renovated, they added a self-contained HEP diesel generator that automatically came on thirty seconds after power from the locomotives was shut off.

"Kill that engine!" she yelled back up into the car.

Brewster, James, and Harry scrambled to the control locker. Sean was already there. He hit the red HEP Emergency Shut Off button. The engine in the undercarriage of the Silver Sky sputtered to a stop. Only floor lights remained on inside the tail car of the train.

The calm garnered by Nick's previous PA announcement was fading fast. Panic and fear were welling up again. For the first time since the odd rocking began, the mighty Zephyr sat motionless and silent in the dark.

It's over, Nick thought, as he dared to believe the worst of the emergency had come to an end.

A few seconds after the end of motion, most lights went out because Larry shut off the locomotives. Without power from the engines, HEP died. Only emergency illumination was left on the train. Mechanical silence became almost audible when the constant drone of the air-conditioning blowers ceased.

Passengers were letting their fear and confusion slip out audibly.

Nick knew he and the engineers were not completely on the same page about sheltering inside the protection of James Peak. Once done tying the third hand brake, Nick ran to the stairs in the middle of the 510 car from the brake end (B-End) door. He leaped two steps at a time to the bottom. He had his coach key in his left hand and rapidly shoved it into the lock of the PA closet. He grabbed the mic. He stopped and took two deep breaths. He got ready to give the most important announcement of his career.

Reagan was in his economy sleeping car room with his mom, listening to the radio scanner his grandfather gave him for the trip. They had heard it all. Claire said to Reagan, "Nick's got this. It's scary, but we will be fine."

She could tell Reagan started to melt down in fear. For the teenager with autism, there were just too many sensory inputs all at once for him to process.

She said it again, "Trust me, Conductor Nick will get us out of this. Just breathe deep, and let's listen and see how he does it." She smiled at her son. He took lots of deep breaths and did his best to calm down. "One, two, three, four . . . " Reagan was trying to refocus by counting fingers—a trick that usually worked for him.

All these years of therapy and special ed need to pay off today, Claire thought as the intercom came to life.

Marshall and Jessica Knight had three terrified children to keep calm. Kids don't usually do well in dark places, especially when everyone around them is scared. All five gathered together in one double seat of the 511 car.

Marshall told the kids that he didn't know what was happening, he didn't know why the train had jumped around so much. He didn't know why the lights went out. "But," he said, "we do know that we are together. So we are just going to pray for the train guys and girls to fix everything, and wait for them to get us out safely."

Marshall's daughter asked when they'd see Nino the clown.

Jessica hugged her little girl. "We don't know, darling."

In the H room of the 531 sleeping car, a man named Herman was tensing up and having spasms that he could not control, which happened to him in scary situations—not uncommon for people with cerebral palsy. His reaction wasn't really any different than what was happening to the other 200+ passengers and crew on the train. His was just amplified significantly.

Finally the speaker in the ceiling of the car started to crackle with a familiar voice. Nick's "in charge" tone of voice helped Herman, and everyone else settle down somewhat.

"Ladies and gentlemen, Nick the conductor speaking. As I said a few moments ago, we are in an emergency. Here is our status as we understand it currently. We received a message from the dispatching center in Omaha, Nebraska, letting us know that a volcano in Yellowstone National Park in Wyoming was blowing up massively. Since receiving that message, we have been unable to contact anyone outside of this tunnel. An eruption of Yellowstone explains the violent rocking of the train. It must have been an earthquake related to the blast. The train stopped because the far west end of the Moffat Tunnel caved in. Our engineers were able to stop the train quickly enough to avoid being crushed. We then backed the train up to where we are now. We are parked on the east side of the apex of the tunnel, the Continental Divide, about a mile from the east portal of the tunnel. The last thing the dispatcher said was that all trains in this half of the country were to seek whatever shelter can be found."

"I am no expert, but from what little I know about Yellowstone and volcanic eruptions, we can expect a massive cloud of dust to reach Colorado shortly, if it hasn't gotten here already. The question is whether we shelter here, inside the tunnel that has already partially caved in, or go outside and take our chances with the possibility of a deadly dust cloud overtaking us. Folks, I'm sorry—I don't know the right answer. What I do know is that when this tunnel was built, the west end was loose and gravelly. It caved in a lot. The east end, where we are now, was solid igneous rock—no cave-ins. Because of that, I think this is the safest place to be right now."

"Here is what I have decided to do as the conductor responsible for the safety of everyone on this train. I am going to shelter the train and all of us in the only structure anywhere strong enough to provide us with real protection—inside this tunnel. The train is going to stay right here. At the same time, we are immediately going to send out teams on foot—one to each portal. They will investigate conditions inside and outside the tunnel and report back to us as fast as possible."

Larry had left the engines and was just reaching the first passenger car behind the locomotives to hear the end of Nick's announcement. He was amazed at how calm and in control Nick's voice sounded.

Christina had stayed on the locomotive. She didn't like being in crowded train cars, especially in a tunnel. Besides, railroad rules required engines to be occupied by a qualified employee at all times when the train had passengers aboard and was on a live main track. Her big fear was not seeing her son again. She had raised him as a single mom since he was five. He was now in college at Flagstaff, Arizona, with his girlfriend. Christina had several pictures of him that she kept in her purse. She took out her favorite one and taped it to the dash of the locomotive. *I'm getting back to you*, she said to herself, as if she were talking directly to him.

Nick's PA announcement continued, "At this time, we need some help. If you are physically fit and can move fast, and if you are willing to run far in near total darkness, come to the parlor car immediately to volunteer on one of the two scout parties. We have to find out what the situation is out there before we risk taking the train into what might be a more dangerous environment than staying put. Thank you for staying calm."

Nick walked, fast pushing his way through the coach aisle, not responding to any of the questions coming at him from all sides. He finally stopped near the end of the car and shouted as loud as he could while standing on the arm rests of two seats to get above the crowd, "I don't have any answers! I just need volunteers to run to the end of the tunnel. Everyone else, just please sit down and stay calm!"

His path opened, and he ran for the parlor car.

The parlor and dining cars were full of people—all talking to him at once. Zach, the big Amish fellow, was at the door. "I can run ten miles," he said.

"You're in! Follow me," Nick ordered. The conductor's hat was still on Nick's head. He decided that the hat would stay on throughout this entire ordeal. It gave him an aura of being in charge, but he knew that wouldn't last long if he didn't lead with strength and clarity. He made his way to the center of the car dimly lit by emergency lighting powered by the car's battery pack.

"I need all the volunteers that are ready to scout out the tunnel portals right here in the middle of the car right now."

A voice came from Nick's left. "I demand that you get this train out of this collapsing tunnel right now!"

"We aren't doing that," Nick replied in a matter-of-fact way, which left no question that the train was staying where it was until the crew knew more about the situation outside.

Nick pointed at three guys to go east. "Take a fully charged cell-phone for light. You will go with me. Who else is volunteering? We need a team to go west."

"Don't bother going west." Larry's voice was resigned. "It's totally caved in and blocked. We were lucky to make it out of there alive."

Nick saw Larry's eyes for the first time since Denver. He felt like hugging the guy. He knew that Christina and Larry had just saved all their lives at the cave-in. Nick trusted the judgment of the old hog-head. Nothing more needed to be said.

"Okay, no west team. East team, let's get to the end of the train and get going. René, we will need your radio to relay messages between the search party and Christina in the locomotive. We can communicate that way."

René gave him her pack-set radio. "You are in charge while I am gone. If anyone wants out, let them go. This isn't train jail, but they are on their own and can't take anything from the train."

"Got it, boss," René replied. Nick was in "take charge" mode. René always said "Got it, boss" in a rather sarcastic way when he got in those moods. The familiar refrain made them both grin for just a moment.

Jim, the parlor car LSA, handed Nick several white N95 COVID masks. "Here, take these, they might come in handy."

Nick hated those masks. He had hated them since they first became a thing in 2020. But he agreed that it would be prudent to have them. He grabbed a handful. He was in a rush to get going. "Thanks, Jim."

"No worries, Nick, we have 2,000 of them." The two friends gave each other a knowing look that simultaneously made fun of and revered the prudent excess of Zephyr Manager Joyce Smyth's train-stocking philosophy.

The search team made their way through the crowded isles of car 510, 511, and half of car 512. Downstairs they found four people waiting.

"We are going with you." Nick didn't know those passengers yet. They were all a little older than him. One lady was clearly the leader. None of them looked like they were in any condition for a one-mile jog at 9,000 feet above sea level.

"You can leave the train if you want, but we are not waiting for you. You will be on your own," Nick told them in a stern voice. *I don't have time for this crap*, Nick thought to himself.

"It's your responsibility to get me to safety!" one of the women demanded.

"What is your name?" Nick asked.

"Karen Allen, and I want you to get me out of here right now!"

Nick looked at her and the others. "Good luck, Karen," was all he said as he and the other people of the team opened the door and left the train.

The tunnel was dark and cold—50 degrees. Water was dripping. The space was surprisingly large without a train taking up most of the hollowed out area inside the solid granite mountain. They began running. The three person team included conductor Nick, Zach the young Amish man, and Knut, the vegan marathon runner from Europe. After about four minutes, they were close to the red signal that protects the portal.

DS051, Nick thought, *about a quarter mile from the opening*. They were able to see other lights.

Large and stable lights were at the ventilation ports right before the big gate that closes off the tunnel when the vent fans are blowing. After every train, fresh air was pulled into the bore to replace the exhaust laden atmosphere. Under normal circumstances, that nearly airtight curtain makes sure the fans suck out tunnel air all the way to the west portal, rather than pulling in fresh air from outside of the east portal in a short loop, thus defeating the purpose of the venting process.

Then the team saw other lights. Nick was surprised and curious at first. Then he realized they were flashlights bouncing along. The team heard heavy breathing and footsteps coming their way. Soon Nick called out, "Who's there?"

"UPR maintenance crew, are you from number 5?"

"Yes," Nick yelled back. Both groups were still jogging toward each other. Finally they met up.

The United Pacific Railways maintenance of way workers were exhausted and out of breath. They took a knee trying to breathe. "What's going on outside?" Nick asked.

"We don't know. *GASP*. We felt the earthquake for a long time. Rock slides were coming down all over the place. We ran to the truck and turned on the radio. *GASP, GASP*. Besides hearing what the dispatcher told you on the train, we heard the emergency broadcast system. *GASP!* Yellowstone has blown." The big man stopped talking and tried to catch his breath.

"Is there a dust cloud?" Zach asked impatiently.

The older UPR man doing the talking looked strong, but a fast long uphill run at 9,000 ft. had whipped him.

"Not yet, but they said hot gas and deadly toxic air was coming fast." He paused to catch more breath.

"Whew!" He wiped his brow as he started to gain his composure. "We didn't want to drive the Highrailer in, because we were afraid you would be backing up into us. We closed the dampers on the fans. Then we started running west to get as far away from whatever is coming as we could."

Nick looked west into the darkness. He saw small lights. Clearly passengers were walking toward them. *Idiots*, Nick thought.

"Do we even know if the cloud can get this far south? I mean, Yellowstone is a long ways away from here, right?" Zach asked.

Nick knew a little bit about volcanic clouds. He tried to remember geology class from Metropolitan State University of Denver, and what Dr. Fletcher taught. He recalled how Mt. Pinatubo blew up in the Philippines in 1991. He'd read about the pyroclastic flows racing down through the valleys, destroying everything in their path, and igniting massive fires. But it seemed impossible that a flow could have enough energy to go 400 miles. But then he thought about the hot springs all over northern Colorado and the bentonite beds along Barbara Gulch and the Big Ten curves. He knew the theory: all that clay was made of ash from ancient eruptions.

"Yep," he said. "It's possible. Ash certainly can make it this far, especially if there were some closer blasts in addition to Yellowstone. And that includes toxic air."

The UPR guys were going west to get away from the cloud. They had sealed the doors to keep the ash out. "Is there a window to see out from the inside of the tunnel at the portal?" Knut asked.

"Yeah," the big guy said. "At the gate, turn right and go to the pressure equalization doors. That will take you to the maintenance office. There is a steel door to the outside with a reinforced window. It ain't locked. You can even leave for all I care, just shut the door behind you."

"Let's go!" Nick said to Knut. "Zach, stay here with René's radio to relay messages to the train."

Zach nodded. Knut and Nick took off, jogging east into the darkness toward the white lights in the distance. Zach, who was clearly not in the kind of shape he thought he was, sat down on the rail. He was happy to stay with the two exhausted railway workers while they continued to catch their breath.

Eventually the group of people from the train who wanted out of the tunnel arrived at the DS051 signal where Zach and the two UPR guys were sitting. The ranks of their small group had swelled to about twenty people. Most had their cellphone lights on. Zach was curious and wanted to look outside too, but his job was to relay radio messages. He reluctantly stayed right where he was as the group passed. Those renegade passengers continued their trek east to the lights at the portal, and what they perceived to be safety.

Zach looked back west, toward the still and silent marker lights of the Silver Sky on the back of the Zephyr more than half a mile away. He looked east to the promising man-made lights at the end of the tunnel. He did not join the others walking by him. He kept his word and just sat there, waiting for a radio transmission from Nick.

Nick was at the end of his endurance when the two runners reached the lights of the east portal of Moffat Tunnel. Knut was barely out of breath. He got to the huge steel curtain first—it was like a massive and impressively heavy garage door. He looked up first, then to his right. *The door!* he thought. He could not figure out how to make it open.

Nick caught up, puffing for air. He grabbed the spring-loaded relief valve in the middle of the door to equalize the pressure in the next room with the air in the tunnel. He opened the first door, and the two men walked through. Nick closed and latched the first door. Then he opened the second door's relief valve that equalizes pressure in the small space they were in with the outside world. Finally they were in the service room of the Moffat Tunnel. They hurried to the window in the door, leading out of the building. They looked through, not daring to open the door.

Everything outside looked perfect.

CHAPTER 10

RUN!

"Cowards judge leaders, leaders save cowards"

—CB

Knut took a look at the door. Unlocked, just like the big UPR guy had said. Knut did not let the door shut, because he was afraid it would lock behind him. He scanned the sky. Everything looked peaceful. Nick stepped through the threshold and silently looked around just as Knut was doing. At first, he could not see much because his eyes were used to the near total darkness of the tunnel. As they adjusted to the daylight, they began to assess their surroundings. Everything looked almost too good to be true.

Nick's deductive mind was racing. *Maybe the cloud didn't make it this far? Maybe this eruption was smaller than the ones that sent ash to Denver and beyond eons ago. Maybe Yellowstone just had a hydro-event where water got trapped underground, expanded as it boiled into steam and then blew.* Nick knew those could be bad, but not nearly as destructive as a magma event would have been. Hope was welling up inside the two men as they considered the possibility that they and over 200 people were safe.

They rocked the door jamb to keep it from locking behind them. Nick used his radio to tell Zach to relay to Christina that there was no ash cloud for now, and that they should get ready to back the train out of the tunnel. Nick looked at Knut with a touch of pride. "Not for nothin', but I predicted this in our crew briefing this morning."

Knut looked back not understanding what Nick meant.

After a few minutes, the crowd of passengers from the train started to show up at the east portal. The first few tried to get through the emergency airlock door, but were having trouble understanding how it worked, just like Knut had. Nick heard them struggling with the door. He went back inside the building and tediously made his way back through the airlock doors into the tunnel.

"Everyone, please step back. I will open the main gate of the tunnel, so we don't have to monkey with the airlocks."

He went to the gate and pressed the gate control switch to open the door. He was relieved to hear the motor engage and see the huge steel barrier begin to rise.

It took a few seconds for the gate to rise high enough for people to get through. As the door opened, everyone shielded their eyes from the sunshine. They all walked out into the open. Soon the relieved passengers raised their hands in celebration.

"We made it!" a young lady yelled as she and her boyfriend danced in circles. More and more people from the train started showing up.

With the gate up and people outside, Nick tried again to reach the dispatcher with his portable radio. No one answered.

After about five minutes, Nick was feeling that odd conflicting emotion of having been wrong about stopping in the tunnel, and being increasingly happy that there was no ash cloud. He thought about his wife and daughter back in Denver, how they would be alive and well when he got home.

Nick overheard Karen Allen talking to others, who had embarrassed looks as they glanced at Nick.

"That dumb conductor thinks he knows what he's doing, but he nearly killed all of us!" she said with a judgmental glare in Nick's direction. "He better get those poor people still on the train out of that tunnel before the rest of it caves in and kills them all," she continued.

Nick had to console himself with his own thoughts. *Well, no one died. We took the safe course.* He refused to let her make him angry.

Karen continued her rant, "The lawsuits are going to flow like water. His job is gone once my lawyer eats into him for putting us in unnecessary danger. I can't wait to post this on social media!" she said as she snapped Nick's picture with her phone.

A few things didn't make sense to Nick. No automobiles were racing to the tunnel with people desperately trying to get shelter. Besides the UPR guys, there were no other people at all. Surely, if this eruption were as big as he had feared, there would at least be some sort of hysteria out here.

He decided the train could come out of the tunnel. *If others were not too concerned, why should I be?* he thought. Once outside, they would wait there until the dispatching center was back online.

Power to operate the curtain was working perfectly. About forty people from the train were outside of Moffat Tunnel. Most were sitting in the shade of the impressive concrete structure, waiting for the train to come out. One person asked Nick about the large brass plaque commemorating the construction of the tunnel.

"It's a time capsule that was opened back in February 2028," he said rather impatiently. This wasn't the time for tourist chatter.

Nick kept trying to reach the dispatcher, but to no avail.

The conductor was just about to call Zach to relay the message that the train should back up out of the tunnel. But something wasn't right.

"See the birds?" Knut asked Nick. "They are flying so fast, and they seem all confused."

"See the plane contrails?" Nick responded. Three white lines of vapor from jets had recently left their mark on the stratosphere. All three had made shape turns to the south and disappeared beyond Rodgers Pass. Something was not right for sure.

A pickup truck suddenly roared to life and sped out of the Rogers Pass Trailhead parking lot, heading east, away from the tunnel, leaving a dust cloud in its wake. Either hikers had gotten back to their vehicle from the woods without Nick seeing them, or they had been sitting there the whole time. Regardless, they were leaving in a powerful hurry.

"Do you hear that? Is that our train?" Knut asked.

Nick thought for a moment. He heard it too. His first thought was that he had not given the order to move the train yet. *Those Prima Donna engineers had better not be taking things into their own hands*, he thought.

He then decided it couldn't be his train, because the growing sound was clearly coming from outside of the tunnel. He knew another train, an empty coal drag, was following them up the hill from Denver that day. But that train should have been about an hour behind them. It had only been a little more than half an hour since the earthquake struck.

A loud and sudden pop on the ground right next his foot caused Nick to look down. Something like a large hailstone, but denser, with a wisp of white smoke rising from the impact, and a few points of something glowing red. A rock falling from the sky! The impact had shattered its hardened shell to expose red-hot innards. Nick looked up. Everybody started running in his direction like people on a beach running from a tsunami.

Small hot rocks started falling all around them.

"Run!" Nick pointed over the crest of Rollins Pass to the north-west. The roar did sound like a train locomotive at first, but as it grew, it was clearly greater than any man-made noise they had ever heard. The gray and white cloud billowed over the last hill between the group of tiny humans and the massive, unleashed fury of the interior of the planet. The cloud was getting closer with the speed of an avalanche. "Faster! Get in! We've gotta close the door!"

Chance Nelson went as quick as he could, but tripped over the rail.

"Get up! Go! Go! Go!" Nick yelled. Chance scurried to his feet and ran for all he was worth through the big entrance of the tunnel and west into its depths. Nick followed, but stopped at the curtain. He was ready to close the door but waited for the others to get inside.

Most of the people who had left the train and gone outside were close to the portal. They quickly raced in through the entrance to escape the cloud. But to his dismay, Nick saw that several people had walked out to the trailhead 200 yards further east. He assumed they had gone to ask for a ride to Denver from hikers. They were running west in a panic between the rails toward the curtain.

"Hurry! Faster!" Nick yelled over the roar of the oncoming wall of death. *BOOM!*

A large rock fell from the sky as the cloud reached the bottom of the valley east of the tunnel. The missile of black and orange rock flattened two cars at the trailhead. Shrapnel from the impact peppered the whole area.

Nick wasn't waiting any longer. He pressed the button to close the curtain. The red strobe light started spinning. Thirty seconds would pass before the curtain started to close. Time stood still as Nick prayed for the people to get in and the door to seal them inside the tunnel.

Three men and a woman reached the tunnel, still ten yards left to go to get to the curtain. The lady was now further behind and at risk of being trapped outside. "Come on! Go!" Nick yelled again, but no one could hear him over the thunderous roar.

The curtain started to move. The closer group of people ducked in as dust started blowing into the concrete structure. They made it under the curtain and kept running for their lives. The lady at the back of the group then fell face first just ten feet from the gate. She tried to get to her feet, but her legs just wouldn't move as fast as her brain was telling them to go. She fell forward again. Laying on the ballast of the railroad tracks just a couple feet east of the rapidly closing curtain, she was about to be swallowed by the darkness of volcanic ash. She looked up at the last moment. Her eyes pierced Nick's subconscious. This woman, who had been dismissive of Nick's authority and insulting of his efforts to save lives, looked at him in a way that said, "Please don't leave me to die out here."

She disappeared in the toxic burning cloud.

It would have been easy for Nick to run for it and get away from the billowing ash cloud. Without regard for his own safety, he thrust himself forward and grabbed her arm. He yanked with all his might. She was moving but he could no longer see or breathe. Using instinct for direction, he powered her under the curtain knowing that if he wasn't fast enough, she would die. He thought he might also get crushed under the weight of the curtain. Suddenly, the lady was moving easy and fast.

They kept going, not being able to see how much farther to go in order to clear the curtain. A mighty rush of wind was pushing them further into the tunnel like a tornado. Nick kept pulling the woman. As the curtain sealed on the floor of the tunnel, the sound of the wind was replaced by wicked rattling of the gate that was protecting them.

"Knut!" Nick yelled. It was the Euro-athlete that had added the extra effort to get the lady and Nick through the threshold. He had come back and risked his life for people he didn't even know.

"The curtain closed!" Knut yelled.

Through the dust, Nick started to make out human figures. "You got her?"

"Yes!" Knut responded with an air of satisfaction. They both heard the lady make a noise that was halfway between a scream and a groan.

"Good, now let's go! Ma'am, get on your feet and move!"

The dust was settling fast, but the rattling gate was still voracious. It was a sound that made a person feel that they would soon be swallowed by a demonic monster.

Nick expected the curtain to give way and a cloud of death to envelope them at any second. He kept yelling, "Run!"

Knut was able to see enough through the dust to help the lady back to her feet.

Nick was up and moving when the lights went out at the portal. *Surely the power lines have been destroyed*, Nick thought. The curtain was rattling with a frightening tempo, but it was holding.

Without the lights of the portal, a whole new kind of darkness overcame them—so dark that it seemed to consume the tiny light of the phone Knut had never turned off. Darkness has a way of amplifying fear. They all felt it instantly reach into their souls to steal away courage and confidence. Then the coughing started, and a powerful smell of sulfur—ten times more pungent than the healing waters of Hot Sulphur Springs. They were choking to death on the stench of rotten eggs in the darkest place they had ever been. *What a lousy place to die*, Knut thought.

Then like a miracle, the lights of the east portal came back on! But it was not a miracle at all. The railroad industry is obsessed with robust redundancy and back-up systems. Instead of supernatural intervention, prudent human preparation came into play.

"The emergency generators kicked on!" Nick yelled.

They all kept moving without speaking. The lady was going as fast as she could. Her breathing was laced with cries of pain, fear, coughs, and exhaustion. Knut and Nick were feeling the burn in the back of their throats as well. Their lungs struggled to clear the intruding toxins with deep coughs emanating from uncontrollable contractions of their diaphragms. They were walking at a quick pace. They probably could have run if they didn't have to practically carry the lady.

As they went deeper into the tunnel, the dust and smell decreased. Breathing became easier. Nick was curious about what was happening outside. The curtain was holding, and the violence of the rattling was clearly beginning to diminish. He chose to stop and have a look back east—to the portal and the curtain. Everything looked stable. Then suddenly the portal lights went out again. "Oh shoot," Nick muttered.

"What?" Knut asked.

"I bet the air intake for the diesel generators got clogged," Nick replied.

In the rush, Nick had forgotten that he had his railroad-issued lantern looped on his arm. He switched it on. Its light felt like a friend.

"You folks go back to the train. I want to have a second look outside," Nick said as he started going back toward the portal.

"You are a crazy American guy."

Nick took the comment from the accented voice of Knut as a compliment. In the light of Nick's lantern, it was clear that the woman Nick and Knut had rescued at the curtain was not Karen Allen, as assumed. It was a different lady named Doris.

"What happened to Karen Allen? The lady you were talking to outside?" Nick asked.

Doris looked angry. "She drove off with two hiker guys that had just run out of the woods to their truck. That woman asked for a ride. There was only one extra seat. So she jumped in and the guys, who looked really scared, drove off. They left the rest of us just standing there."

"My goodness," Nick said with dismay. "She is still out there."

The conductor then refocused himself on the task at hand. "Hello, Zach. OVER," Nick said into the radio.

"This is Zach."

"Zach, tell Christina on the engine that the cloud has hit hard, but the curtain is holding it out. We are going to try and see more. Also tell her that the two UPR guys are walking her way. OVER."

"Okay, I will relay. OVER." Zach responded. He was a fast learner. He was already starting to get the flow of railroad radio procedure.

But no answer came from the train to Zach's transmission. He tried again. There was a moment of silence.

"This is UPR Maintenance-of-Way, we will relay. OVER," came a voice over the radio. It was the big track worker. Zach was too far away from the train for his radio to transmit through the narrow tunnel all the way to the locomotive. The maintenance guys had two portable radios with them. They passed the message from Nick to the train.

"Roger, I will get the message to René. OVER," Christina said on the radio.

"Good, thanks. Out," the UPR the guy replied.

"Ladies and gentlemen, this is René. We just heard from the scout team that went to the east portal. They tell us that a powerful inferno of ash and toxins has hit outside, but the tunnel curtain is holding the storm out. We think that the passengers who had left the train are safe and coming back. Also, two United Pacific Railways Maintenance of Way track workers are coming to the train. They came into the tunnel to escape the cloud. I will share more information when I have it. Thank you."

CHAPTER 11

SAFE INSIDE

"Hope is being able to see that there is light despite all of the darkness."

—Desmond Tutu

Knut escorted Doris through the tunnel to Zach at DS051 then ran back east to rejoin Nick. The two made their way toward the curtain together. Nick was glad to have the company. About 100 yards from the door to the room with the window, they began to smell the dusty sulfur. They put on the N95 masks Jim had given Nick. After another twenty yards they began to feel the heat. They kept going cautiously forward. The curtain was still rattling some, but much less than before. There was a rushing sound coming from the direction of the portal, but it was not like before. It was a continuous dull drone, with crackling and occasional pops. "Fire?" Knut asked.

"Maybe so," Nick said. The heat was getting intense as they approached the gate. They could barely get through the airlocks and into the maintenance office, because everything was getting too hot to touch. They aimed both their lights at the door. It was holding fast. There was no light in the window. It looked like the darkest night, although it was almost midday. Then a flicker. More flickers, then a more constant orange glow.

"I think the forest is burning," Nick said.

"Will the door or curtain melt?" Knut asked.

"I don't know, but I suggest we don't wait here to find out. Let's get back to the train fast."

"I couldn't agree more!" Knut said.

"Nick to Zach—bad sulfur smell, almost unable to breathe close to the portal. Very hot near the curtain, like an oven. Orange glow indicates the forest is on fire. Sparks floating like fire flies. OVER."

"Will relay. OVER," Zach said. He keyed the radio and repeated the news. It was passed on by the UPR guys to Christina.

Finally assistant conductor René told all the people aboard the Zephyr via the PA that the world outside had become a burning inferno.

The sobered band of rebellious passengers who had ventured to the portal were trickling back, past the darkened Silver Sky and into the open door at car 512. Nick and Knut returned as well.

First, they picked up Zach and Doris at DS051, then they finished the walk to the train. No words were spoken. Doris sniveled as they walked. She almost wished she had died. Finally at the train, she spoke. "Thanks for pulling me through the tunnel door," she said meekly.

Nick allowed himself to feel a bit of vindication. "I'm just glad I didn't usher all those poor people to their deaths by taking the train out prematurely," he said with satisfaction. "Seriously, all's well that ends well."

She looked at Nick. "This . . . is ending well?"

The two UPR guys were waiting in the 512 vestibule. "Thanks for the help, guys," Nick said.

"Thanks for being here for us," the bigger man replied.

Nick introduced himself as the conductor.

"I'm Jake, this is Charlie," the man said, tipping his hard hat slightly.

"Well, my friends, welcome to the Zephyr," Nick said, trying to be his usual hospitable self.

Reality began to sink in among the passengers and staff on the Zephyr. Sobbing could be heard in every train car. It was now clear that this was not a common mishap or small disaster. This was epic!

Millions of people were probably dead or dying. People's thoughts ranged between their own plight in a terrifying dark hole thousands of feet underground, and their loved ones on the outside who were exposed to a toxic inferno.

CHAPTER 12

LEADERSHIP

"A genuine leader is not a searcher for consensus but a molder of consensus."

—Martin Luther King, Jr.

We have to manage this, Nick thought, as he walked through the train. He purposely held his own personal grief at bay. His closest people, including his wife of thirty-five years and their daughter were certainly in the sphere of destruction. *I don't have time for grief right now,* he told himself.

He wondered what his goal was. He thought through a few options. He searched for guidance from Scripture. Reading the Bible had always been a source of comfort for him. Preparing for eternity with Jesus might be his top priority, but right now he needed hands-on problem-solving skills to save the lives of his passengers. He thought through a career of experiences on the railroad. Nothing came close to an equivalent situation, not even the derailments or trespasser fatalities he had worked through. Railroad rule books and situational awareness training were key elements to keeping the train and passengers safe in normal emergencies, but this was so much more extreme.

He thought of literature. His mind raced through books he had recently read like *The Midnight Library* and *The Reckoning*. Those stories did not help. He thought of a great book called *The River of Doubt* about President Theodore Roosevelt's voyage on an uncharted river in the Amazon. Great stuff there! Fight to survive, work together, improvise, problem-solve, and never ever give up. But Nick's mind couldn't formulate any of that into a survival plan for his train. Then an idea came to him.

Sir Ernest Shackleton. The great Arctic explorer from the early part of the twentieth century had been in a hopeless situation, with a crew of shipwrecked men a thousand miles from anywhere in the coldest, harshest place on earth. They all survived thanks to Shackleton's leadership. It had been several years since Nick had read *Endurance*, but the story of survival against all odds was still burned into his memory with unusual clarity. Nick tried hard to remember what it was that Shackleton had done that got all those men back to civilization.

It wasn't easy to think. As he and the others walked through the train, people were understandably upset and panicked. "Are we going back to Denver?" he heard from behind him. "Can you get us out of here?" "Is everyone out there dead?"

There was no way to answer such piercing questions. People were in despair, and even denial about the seriousness of their predicament. One passenger even asked if this incident was going to delay the train's arrival in California. Nick had to block them out and concentrate on the problem. Only then could he try to formulate some answers.

"Leadership," Nick said to Knut, who was still by his side.

"Excuse me?" Knut asked.

"Leadership. Our only hope of surviving this is through good leadership, like Ernest Shackleton."

"The British explorer?" Knut responded with a knowing look. It turned out the European reporter was very well read.

Nick looked at him with a touch of surprise. "Yes! I'll explain the details later," Nick said as he began to charge toward the dining car with purpose.

Conductor Nick's thoughts were now focused. *Survive. Everyone on this train must survive—at least until we make it back to whatever civilization is left out there—just like Shackleton got his men back to the civilized world from the Antarctic in the middle of World War I. Okay, that is our goal. Now then, how in the world do we do that?*

Nick finally arrived at the dining car. Sammy, the snack coach LSA, was there with Lorette, the dining car steward, Thomas the chef, and the rest of the crew. Normally during a service disruption, they were a professional and active bunch. Not this time. They were truly scared. They sat silently waiting for more information. Besides the crew, passengers were pressing in from both sides of the train. It was a situation where nobody knew what to do. Everyone was waiting for someone to take charge.

Nick grabbed the PA mic in the diner and began to speak. "Please listen, everyone, this is Conductor Nick. I am going to tell you everything I know, and then tell you how we are going to deal with this truly unprecedented situation. What we know is this: we are about one mile inside the east portal of Moffat Tunnel. The west end of the tunnel has caved in and is assumed blocked. The east end of the tunnel is sealed by a steel door that is protecting us, and the air we are breathing. Outside of the tunnel, the air is completely inundated with what appears to be volcanic ash. Those of us who were at the east portal couldn't breathe the air because of the burning hot dust and toxic sulfur. We believe, from what we saw through a glass window in a door, everything outside is on fire.

"None of us know what we will do next yet. We believe all of this is the result of a massive eruption in Yellowstone National Park, based on what the dispatcher told us earlier. Some people may have used satellite phones outside before we had to run from the ash cloud. They might know more. Since then, we have not been able to reach anyone on the railroad radio. What we have to do now is try to figure out what happened, what will happen, and what we should do."

Nick took a big breath and continued, "I can tell you what our singular goal is. We are going to commit ourselves to getting each and every person on this train back to civilization alive." He paused. "It's as simple as that. We all get out of here alive—together."

"What we need to do first is figure out what to expect. I am calling everyone who has specific training, education, or skills that can help us survive to come to the parlor car now. I'm talking about people who have real knowledge about geology, air quality, human physiology, stuff like that. From there, we will try to decide on a plan of action."

"I know that all of you are just like me—you're scared, and also worried about your loved ones on the outside. We will have time for all of those thoughts. Right now, we are going to focus on our situation and do our best to work through this. I believe that if we work together, we can find a way to manage the situation and get back to those we love."

"So please come to the parlor car or dining car now if you feel you can help us understand what we need to know. Please make room for those folks, so we can talk face to face. Thank you."

Nick replaced the mic in the holder. He took another deep breath and waited to see who would answer the call. Within a few minutes, the parlor car and dining cars were full of chatting people ready to get to work.

Nick was wracking his brain, trying to remember what Shackleton had done to organize and lead his beleaguered men to safety. His first thought was that there was no question through the whole ordeal that Shackleton himself was the undisputed leader. Another thing he remembered was that the toughest people to deal with on the crew were kept close. Nick recalled that everyone on the crew was kept busy; everyone had to contribute to the effort. In the book about the doomed polar expedition, there were amazing photographs. One was of all the supplies, and a guy taking an accounting of all those available resources.

With Sir Ernest Shackleton as a template, Conductor Nick went to work. The first thing he wanted to know was exactly how many people were on board. As the passengers who had something to say gathered, Nick called the train staff together. René was by his side. "Crew, listen up; we have to know exactly how many people are actually on the train, and the physical capability of each person. Dan will count everyone from the middle of the diner back through the coaches." He then asked Jim, the parlor car lead service attendant (bartender), to go from the diner forward into the sleepers. "Pick another person to give you some help. Let's get it done. Thanks, guys," Nick said with a grateful tone of voice.

Passengers and staff still in the diner were looking at Nick. They were waiting to see if he could deal with the challenge before them.

His hat was still on his head, and that made him the leader. He felt the pressure. Nick picked up the mic again. He wanted the whole train to hear everything he said as it was being discussed. "Folks, thanks to all of you who have come to the middle of the train to help us figure out what we should do. The whole train can hear me as we talk through this. First off, who can tell us with some probability what has happened to our world?"

Dr. Michael Sayers pushed through the crowd. He had been the last man in line to get on the train in Denver. He knew what had happened as soon as he understood they were experiencing an earthquake. He had done a full scenario in his head after Nick made the announcement about Yellowstone. That's when he lost all hope of getting to the Granby airport to escape.

He imagined one of his best friends and mentors, old Dr. Fletcher, at his nine-story tall retirement and assisted-living complex in Denver. The two academics had spoken on the phone the night before, after he had his fateful conversation with his boss and Secretary Blackburn. They both felt an eruption was imminent. But the United States Geological Survey (USGS), which Sayers consulted for, could not convince the office of Homeland Security to do more than evacuate Yellowstone National Park itself.

Fletcher had told Sayers that if the eruption starts, at his age, he will not run. Instead he would go to the roof of his building, set up his reclining lawn chair facing northwest, mix a blood and guts martini, sit back, and enjoy the show. Sayers had to smile when he imagined Fletcher laughing at the cloud of death as it approached, pleased as could be with himself for perfectly predicting in terrifying detail to class after class of undergraduates what was finally happening.

Sayers calculated the time. His wife had taken off from Golden, Colorado, driving south at 1:00 a.m. It was after 11:00 now. Ten hours. They should be past Amarillo, Texas. Panicked hordes trying to escape Denver and Colorado Springs, and ensuing traffic jams, would be well behind her. He assumed she and the kids were far enough away to be relatively safe, at least in the short term.

In general, Dr. Sayers was an optimist. He wanted to find a way through the debacle they were in. He knew that the most probable outcome for the people on this train was that everyone would be dead in a few days. But not for sure. He prepared himself to deliver an explanation that would give everyone hope. If he was wrong, the end result would be the same anyway—so why not help them believe they had a fighting chance?

"Hello, Nick, I am Dr. Michael Sayers, professor of geology at the Colorado School of Mines, and scientist with the USGS. I think I can give a decent summation of what is happening with Yellowstone."

Nick was surprised. He remembered the man from the platform in Denver, the disheveled fellow who was last to board. Nick wasn't sure he believed the man, so he asked a couple probing questions. The answers were solid. Relieved to have someone onboard who could explain what was happening out there and being intensely interested to hear what the professor had to say, Nick asked Dr. Sayers if he would be willing to tell the people on the train what he knew over the PA. Sayers agreed.

Nick grabbed the PA mic again. "Ladies and gentlemen, I have with me a professor from the Colorado School of Mines. He believes he can fill us in on what happened. Here is Dr.," Nick let go of the transmit button on the mic for a second. "I'm sorry, what is your name again?"

"Michael Sayers, Dr. Sayers," the professor replied.

Nick went back to the PA. "Dr. Sayers, professor from the School of Mines. Dr. Sayers, please tell us what is going on."

Dr. Sayers was used to speaking to rooms full of mostly graduate students who were highly interested and intelligent. The Colorado School of Mines is one of the best schools in the world for the study of geoscience. The school attracts top students from around the globe. Nick knew right away what a godsend it was to have his wealth of knowledge aboard the train. *Luck,* Nick thought, *was not a strong enough word. Having this guy on board is nothing short of a miracle.*

CHAPTER 13

GEOLOGY AND MATHEMATICS

"Time is not always written in stone."

—CB

Sayers took the mic. "Um, I have spent a lifetime of academic study and research into the cause and effect of geological phenomena. For the past several weeks, I have been in close communication with the United States Geological Survey, and the National Earthquake Information Center. Of main concerns have been the increasing incidences of crustal disturbance related to the Yellowstone Caldera, and other formations along the spine of the Rocky Mountains.

I'm going to give you my best presumption of what is currently happening, from what little information we have at this time. I believe the main magma chamber below Yellowstone has, in all probability, experienced a catastrophic eruption. In addition, several old volcanoes in Colorado that were previously presumed extinct, including areas of the Hot Sulphur Spring Quadrangle, have become very active in the last month. It is possible that they have exploded too—triggered by the convulsions of the Yellowstone caldera. I base my deduction on the observations at the sites over the past week, what we heard from the dispatcher, and the severe seismic event (what most people call an earthquake) that we felt. That earthquake probably had a Richter magnitude of 8, or even 9, to cause the intensity of shaking we felt here in north-central Colorado, which is 400 miles south of the epicenter at Yellowstone. The cause of that shaking, the eruptions, have probably sent a chunk of earth's crust measuring one mile thick and forty miles square, or about 1,600 cubic miles of material, up to fifteen miles high into the atmosphere. That vague guess still does not explain the fact that heat and ash from the blast reached us about forty minutes after the earthquake started. I was one of those who went to the end of the tunnel. The heat we felt there when the ash cloud arrived, and the solid boulder impacts, made it abundantly clear that the amount of material in the air is far too close to have been an expulsion from the Yellowstone Caldera alone. Also, if the forest is already burning, that means the energy emitted was nearby. A nearby volcanic explosion plus the largest eruption the Yellowstone super volcano can produce is my only explanation for what is happening."

"The key questions for us at this time are these: What is falling from the sky? And how long will it keep falling? I cannot say for certain. Typically, a volcano will vent for many hours or even days. My guess is that this will not be the case this time. I believe it will be a short duration eruption. I base that theory on two pieces of information we know for certain. First, there have not been continued earthquakes that can be felt here in the tunnel. Second, the distance the ash has traveled, and the speed with which it reached our location, indicates that most, if not all, of the energy was expelled in one huge series of rapid explosions. Those blasts almost certainly released all their pent-up power at once, like Mt. St. Helens did in 1980. Should my theory prove to be true, it would be very good news for us. This would mean that the ash and toxic gasses, which are for the most part heavier than air, will quickly settle to the ground. My guess is, we will have breathable air outside the tunnel within just a few days, maybe a week."

As soon as Dr. Sayers said the train needed to stay in the tunnel for a week, Bill and Evelyn Pope, two passengers who were science professors from the University of Iowa, started doing the math. "How much oxygen does a person at rest need?" Evelyn asked.

"About 1,000 liters a day for an active healthy person, but I can't remember for sure," Bill answered.

"I need more data," Evelyn said. "How big is the tunnel?" Bill thought he remembered what Nick said in his tunnel announcement.

"Okay, so six miles of good tunnel air. That is 5,280 ft. per mile times six. Then multiply by about fifteen feet wide and cube it at twenty-six feet high." She was thinking out loud while typing into the calculator on her phone, 12,355,200 cubic feet of air.

"Darn it! How many liters in a cubic foot?" She was getting frustrated. "For the love of God, why are we still mixing imperial and metric systems? The rest of the freaking planet is smart enough to go metric. This is so stupid!"

Inside the tunnel, there was no way for outside satellite or cell tower signals to reach the train. It was the first time in decades that Evelyn couldn't instantly access simple information, like metric conversion tables, from the internet. She felt stifled.

"Again, I don't know for sure, but maybe twenty-five liters per cubic foot?" came Bill's answer.

"Okay, multiply twenty-five liters per cubic foot." She was still tapping into her immensely powerful phone computer, which had suddenly been reduced to the capability of a 1970's calculator, without its usual connectivity to the world wide web.

"I need to know how many people are on this train, Bill," she said with urgency. Tim, the car attendant, was near the couple and saw them working frantically. He had already been thinking of asking them to add their expertise to the brain trust in the diner.

"Two hundred and nineteen total," he said to Evelyn.

"Thank you," Evelyn replied without looking up. She kept looking at the numbers, then repeated the entire calculation out loud to Bill.

"Okay, 12,355,200 cubic feet of air, times twenty-five liters per cubic foot, equals 308,880,000 liters of air in the tunnel; 308,880,000 liters, times 21 percent oxygen in good air, equals 64,864,800 liters of oxygen available to people on the train; 64,864,800 divided by 220 people in the tunnel equals 294,800 liters of oxygen per person. 294,800 divided by 1,000 liters of oxygen per day needed. Nearly 300 days of oxygen—awesome!"

"Got it." Evelyn called out. "We've got more than enough oxygen to last us for months."

She was pleased with her results and smiled at Bill, expecting the same reaction from him. What she saw instead was something very disturbing. Her husband was doing his own calculus, and he looked very worried. Bill looked up from his own phone. They both said together, "C02."

Dr. Sayers was still speaking on the PA. "Based on what we think we know about the last Yellowstone eruption of substantial magnitude some 664,000 years ago, I would expect about a meter, three feet, of ash accumulation in the midsection of Colorado over the next several days. Also the atmosphere will be very hot for a couple of days from the super-heated fallout and organic material—forests, houses, grass, et cetera, burning across several states. The fires, like the ones that probably caused the flickering light outside the tunnel, were ignited by balls of magma bursting upon impact, the high temperature of the ash itself, and perhaps even lightning, created by vast static charges generated when ash particles collide in the atmospheric umbrella. It didn't help that this event is happening in the driest season during an already dry year in Colorado. After the fires burn out, the air will rapidly cool because the sun will be mostly blocked from the surface of the planet. I expect we will have a brief window, starting several days from now, when air quality and temperature are conducive to leaving the protection of this tunnel. That window may only last a few days. Then it will become seriously frigid out there. The faster we go south, and lower in altitude, the better. We just have to wait for the air to clear and cool. Timing will be critical."

"That brings us to the next question. Who is left alive outside, and what kind of damage has occurred? Sadly, anyone or anything within the vicinity of Yellowstone will be gone now. In all probability, no life at all survived within a hundred mile radius of the epicenter. Let's call that inner ring the annihilation zone. Beyond that sphere, there is a chance some people could have survived, but only with extreme protective measures, including a very strong and robust shelter, and a source of breathable air for several days—like what we have here in this tunnel. The second zone probably reaches approximately four hundred miles from Yellowstone—about to where we are. We can refer to the second sphere as the dead zone, because everything exposed to the immediate effects of the eruptions will be dead. That zone could be much bigger depending on how many volcanoes in Colorado blew up. Beyond that, survivability rates go up progressively. We can call that next area, between 400 and 600 miles away from the blasts, the Fringe Zone. In that vast space, survivability is possible, but suffering could be intense. Beyond the fringe zone, the immediate effect of the volcano is probably just a thick dusting of ash."

"In summary, Wyoming, Utah, Idaho, Montana, and Colorado will have been hardest hit. Wind at the time of the eruption plays a big role in who lives and who does not. It looked to me this morning like the prevailing winds and jet stream were mildly strong, and due south-east from Yellowstone, directly toward Denver."

The cold, scientific explanation from the geologist was piercing. He had not shared how his own family was somewhere out there, frantically trying to escape due south to get as far away from Yellowstone as they could get. Dr. Sayers had his "professor face" on. He was blocking all his emotions so that he could maintain self-control. His fact-focused lecture was harsh, but what everyone needed to hear—the truth, without any sugar-coating.

Sayers handed the mic back to Nick. The two men looked at each other.

"Thank you, Dr. Sayers," Nick said into the mic. "I am sure there are a million questions people want to ask you. Would you mind making yourself available in the dining car for a few minutes?"

"Sure," Sayers acquiesced.

"Ladies and gentlemen, you heard the professor. We are going to have to live here in this tunnel for several days. Then at just the right moment, we are going to go outside. If no one is there to rescue us, we'll race down the hill to Denver, where I expect to find help."

Bill was busy tapping away on his computer. His conclusion was that if all the air in the tunnel was clean at the time of the eruption, the

CO_2 level would not become dangerous for about thirty to forty days. However, the locomotives had been running for at least fifteen minutes before they were shut off. Bill made a quick guess regarding the production of CO_2 by two massive 16-cylinder engines. He added that sum to the growing volume of the toxic gas created by people exhaling.

"We've only got five to seven days," he said to Evelyn with wide eyes.

Nick was about to say more into the microphone when he heard an emphatic voice. "We don't have a week of air in the tunnel," came a loud voice from the far end of the diner near the premier coach car.

"Let me through, please! Dr. Evelyn Pope here, Mr. Conductor."

Nick turned and looked at the woman forcing her way through the crowd. "Listen, there are about 220 people on this train according to my car attendant."

"Yeah, that is what we have recorded on our EMDs, but there are also twenty-four people from the Silver Sky car. So the total is more like 245," Nick answered.

Evelyn shook her head as if to dismiss the minutiae and get to the point. "Oh, well that is even worse." She quickly did some additional math. "Here is the thing; we did the math. We only have enough air for 220 people to live for 120-160 hours. After that, CO_2 levels will start to weaken our mental capacity. By 170 hours, it is probable that nobody on this train will be able to function. We have to find air with less than 2 percent CO_2 within seven days or we will probably die right here."

CHAPTER 14

SEVEN DAYS

"One of the tests of leadership is the ability to recognize a problem before it becomes an emergency."

—Arnold H. Glasgow

"Damn, we might be screwed after all," Ronald Spruce, the food specialist, uttered.

Nick darted a glance at Ron, then back at the agitated lady. "I'm sorry, who are you?" Nick asked.

"I am Dr. Evelyn Pope, University of Iowa," she said, in an effort to make it clear that she was speaking from an educated deduction of the facts, not just some amateur sensationalist.

"Oh yeah," Nick remembered, "the lady from Iowa with family in Granby." Nick looked at Dr. Sayers and then at Dr. Pope. "Would you two please get together and talk about this? We really only need one piece of information. Exactly when should we leave the tunnel? We will count on you to tell us what our timing needs to be."

"We are going to have to make sure this thing starts up again after a week of sitting here," came the familiar New England voice of engineer Larry.

"Right," Nick said, "we have to save the batteries. Pull the knife switch."

"That's risky too. Those Kraut wagons got all of them computers that have to work or it won't start. You sure we want to hard-cut the power and risk not rebooting properly?" Larry asked.

Nick looked at the most experienced member of the train crew.

"You and Christina do what you think has to be done to make sure those engines restart in five to seven days."

Larry knew Nick was putting the pressure on him to make the right decision. The lives of everyone on-board would depend upon it. It wasn't just the engines that were rapidly burning off stored energy from limited capacity batteries. Each train car had a bank of batteries that kept emergency lights burning. Nick's thoughts about power in the cars were interrupted by a lady with an embarrassed look on her face as she told him that the toilets had stopped flushing.

"Wow," he answered her. "I'm so sorry, we forgot to tell people not to use the toilets when the power from the locomotives (HEP) is off." Nick picked up the mic to tell everyone on the train that the toilets could not be used, when another passenger, an elderly overweight man, said his oxygen concentrator wasn't working because the power strips had no electricity. Nick was starting to realize he could not manage all the problems that were rapidly starting to pile up. *Delegate*, he thought. *No way I can handle all these issues by myself. But if we involve everyone, like Shackleton did, we can do it all.*

Nick picked up the PA again. "Folks, we are facing a huge number of challenges. We are going to need the skills, wisdom, and labor of everyone to help develop and implement ways and means that will give us the best chance of getting out of this mess alive. Dr. Sayers and the scientists from Iowa have laid out our challenge. Now we need to figure out how to meet that challenge—and what other challenges are out there. Please think of ways you can help. Soon we will be ready to involve you. Thanks."

René was right there as Nick was thinking about how to involve everyone in the survival plan. She had a bunch of questions and suggestions. "This is like a military campaign," she told him. "We should act like an army with platoons and squads. Each group will be responsible for one aspect of our dilemma. Teams: One for food, one for dealing with the bathrooms, one for monitoring the air, things like that."

Of course, Nick thought, *lots of little platoons dealing with one problem each.* "Thanks for that idea. Let's do exactly that, René," Nick said.

"We're going to need a leader for each team. We don't want to reinvent the wheel here—we can just use train staff to lead each team. That lead person will report to us."

He remembered how Shackleton maintained the hierarchy of a Naval vessel throughout his entire ordeal, long after *Endurance*, their ship, was at the bottom of the sea. The thought of going forward without a solid recognized structure scared him. The last thing he wanted was people getting tribal, where small groups become combative for diminishing resources. They had already seen some of that when people went outside earlier. *We're not going there,* he thought.

"Organized teams with purpose and a clear chain of command are how we are going to keep order."

René nodded her head in approval. Nick again raised the mic to his mouth. "All staff, please come to the dining car. Thank you, ladies and gentlemen, I am going to meet now with train employees. We are going to work out a plan to break down what resources we have on the train and in the tunnel. Then we will develop a way forward on how we will use those resources to give us the best chance of survival. As soon as we have a plan, we will ask all of you to help us with the tasks at hand by joining one of various teams that will be responsible for working on the problems they are assigned to. Please stand by; it will take us a bit to get this organized. Thank you."

He hung up the mic and looked around. His friends in dark-blue uniformed slacks, white shirts, and lanyards started to show up. Most of them were already in the diner. Plenty of passengers were still in the car, as well. Nick thought about asking them to leave as he briefed the crew, but decided to let those people stay. There was no need for secrets. He was afraid that if the passengers had the feeling staff were holding back information or resources for themselves, things could get confrontational quickly.

"First, let's take an inventory of the people we have," René said, and started to take a roll call of the crew. She wrote down names on the back of her Track Condition Summary (Train Orders, as some still called them).

She read off the names as she wrote them. "Conductor, Nick; assistant conductor, René; coach attendant, Dan; premier coach attendant, Tim. Sleeping cars: 540—Rashid, 532—Jen, 531—Rita. Diner kitchen: chef, Thomas; food specialist, Ron; kitchen assistant, Nathan. Dining room staff: LSA, Lorette; first service attendant, Michelle; second service attendant, Judith. Parlor car LSA, Jim; snack coach LSA, Sammy."

It took Rita and Sammy a bit to get there, but finally the entire staff was assembled. Dan and Jim returned from their count of passengers. "243 people aboard, including passengers, the Silver Sky people, staff, and two UPR guys," Jim said to Nick. "Thanks guys, make it 244—we have one engineer still in the locomotive."

"*Oops*, engineers, Larry and Christina," René said out loud. Christina was still in the cab of the lead locomotive, but Larry was in the diner with the others. "A total of eighteen people on the crew, all accounted for," René reported.

Nick was puzzled. "René, my EMD shows 201 passengers aboard. With the crew, UPR guys, and private car, that should make 245 people?"

Rashid spoke to that. "Karen Allen is no longer with us."

Nick nodded. "Oh right, thanks, Rashid. Our final count is confirmed at 244." He was finally satisfied that everyone was accounted for.

The time had come. The crew would begin the single-most-important crew briefing of their lives.

Nick began, "Thanks for coming so quickly, guys. Let's get right to work. We now have to dedicate ourselves to one hard and fast goal, that every person on this train survives until we are rescued. It is up to us to get all these people and ourselves back to civilization, to safety. So first things first. Based on what we think we know right now, we have to live here in the tunnel for at least four days, maybe longer, up to seven days, but no more. We know we have limited time, because the air in here will eventually become toxic. That means we have to be fully prepared for whatever we might find once we open that gate and plow our way out."

He continued to speak, but in a way that felt different to his crew. He was focused like never before. His voice was not that of the simple railroader with a flair for making people laugh with silly PA announcements. He had become a true leader.

"René and I believe we need to involve everyone on this train with purpose and tasks to keep them engaged and focused on the challenge of surviving. We think everyone should be on a team that will deal with some specific aspect of our situation. So what are our major challenges, and which teams do we need to form to take on those challenges? Next, which team will each one of you lead?"

"You want us to be team leaders?" Sammy asked.

Nick spoke decisively. "Yes, at first. If you decide that a passenger on your team is more qualified to make decisions and lead, you can appoint them to do so. But you will still be the point person that reports to the rest of us on the crew. I think it is important that we retain the official command structure of the train until we can be relieved by someone in the outside world. Otherwise, we risk falling into chaos."

Thomas the chef spoke next. "It's a full-fledged nightmare we've got going on here. I'll tell you what, there's never been anything like it. It's freaking unprecedented." Thomas's deep baritone voice and thick Long Island accent seemed even more pronounced in the stress of the moment. He continued, "I don't know if we can make it, but we're sure going to do our best. I can take inventory of all the food we've got and start a rationing program."

René was taking notes and talking at the same time. "Great! Tommy, you've got the Food Team. Ron and Nathan, can you help him?"

The two younger members of the kitchen staff nodded in a way that made it clear they were unsure of what they agreed to, but they would help as best they could.

"That means finding out what we have in the diner, parlor, and snack cars, and also what personal food people have with them," Nick added.

"That brings up a big point going forward" Nick began. "We are no longer in any kind of normal situation. Things like private supplies, or divisions based on class of service no longer apply. If we are all to survive together, we have to use every resource for the greater good of everyone. We have to assume we will need to survive on this train for a lot longer than just six or seven days, because we still might have to get to Denver after we are out of the tunnel. We might have to live with what we've got for two weeks based on what Dr. Sayers told us. We can't ask folks in coach to live in upright seats that whole time. We will have to rotate everyone on the train in and out of rooms where people can lay down flat and sleep. Everyone also has a need for at least a little privacy over that long period of time. Even our own staff rooms need to be rotated."

The group of employees looked rather shocked. Employees who spend up to six days in the confines of the train tend to regard their dorm room in the crew car as sacred space, their own personal refuge from the daily grind in the public eye. It hadn't even occurred to them that they would have to share their rooms with others. Coach passengers in the dining car were listening in silence, watching to see how the crew, and sleeping car passengers, were responding to that intrusive instruction from their conductor.

For a long pause, Nick scanned the group of staff and passengers for reactions. As he waited, he had a quick recall of a book he had recently read that also had a survival theme like *Endurance*. It was called *The 40 Days of Musa Dagh*, by Franz Werfel, chronicling the amazing true story of 5,000 Armenians who survived the horrific genocide at the hands of the Turks in 1915. Nick remembered that the villagers from different economic levels united all their resources to survive. *If they could do it in even tougher circumstances, we can do it too. At least nobody is trying to kill us—all we have to do is survive*, Nick thought.

Rashid was the first to answer. "We don't have a choice; it is just what we have to do."

Rita spoke up next. "I agree. I don't like it, but I get it. We have to do it."

Nick gave a sigh of relief. His eyes were appreciative as he responded. "Okay, Rita and Rashid, you two are in charge of making a schedule for everyone on the train to get rest and privacy in sleepers."

René added, "It's like hot racking on a Navy ship. The hard part will be getting all the sleeper passengers to agree."

The authoritative voice of Senator Jackson came from the sleeper end of the dining car, "Don't you worry about that." He then pointed at Rita and Rashid. "We will help make sure these two get full cooperation from all of us with sleeping car tickets."

"Thank you, Senator," Nick said.

The man nodded with his wife Janice by his side. Another distinguished passenger, Jay, smiled toward the senator in a way of agreeing. Senator Jackson's parents, who had often been victims of prejudice as children, and later became activists in the Civil Rights Movement, and taught their son to always do what was right for everyone, even if it hurts. Jay had roots as a humble farm boy. He became one of the global leaders in dental surgery innovation. These two self-made millionaires never forgot their roots. Now their shared ethic of *looking out for the little guy* was on full display.

René was impressed. Two of the wealthiest and most influential people on the train, with the very best accommodations available, just gave up their position of privilege for the benefit of others. *How refreshing*, she thought.

If any of the staff were unhappy or angry about the sharing of rooms, they didn't let it show. Perhaps the surprise of the situation had not been fully processed. Maybe they were in denial. Regardless of why, there were no immediate objections.

Dan, the coach attendant, spoke up next. "Hey, we've got a problem that is getting serious fast. We need a team in charge of sanitation. The toilets won't flush until we restart the engines. People have been using them, and it's getting seriously nasty already. I don't even want to think about how things will look or smell in a couple of days."

Everyone on the crew was aware of how quickly that problem can escalate. Often in the past, toilet mechanisms on the trains had failed enroute. The entire staff had lived with the issue since coming to work for the passenger railroad. Thankfully, when Joyce had taken over Zephyr operations, things got much better. She had spent much of her time with maintenance employees in Chicago who were assigned to the Zephyr, working on toilet reliability. She had secured the funds for parts, tools, and training needed to replace or repair components. For her, working toilets were a top mechanical priority on the Zephyr. Sadly, all that work didn't help unless the locomotives were running and providing both electrical HEP power and compressed air to the toilet system. The engines were not going to be running until the train left the tunnel.

"Well, that's a crappy problem to have." Nick tried to inject a bit of potty humor to lighten the mood. It didn't really work—no one laughed.

He cleared his throat. "Clearly, we need to create a way of disposing of our waste. Dan, would you be willing to oversee the sanitation team?"

Dan suddenly regretted bringing up the issue. "Yeah, sure," he said with a frown.

"Awesome," Nick replied. "I suggest quickly figuring out a way for people to go to the toilet. Then let them know on the PA where to *do their business* as soon as you can."

Dan was already thinking it through. "I'll get my shit together as fast as I can." Unlike Nick's joke, Dan's comment was actually funny, and made people laugh.

"People are already asking about water," Sammy—the snack coach LSA—said.

Nick nodded in agreement at her implication that water was of major importance and warranted a team of its own. "Sammy, do you think you can form a water team?"

Sammy was not usually one to take charge. She was good at pointing out what was wrong, but not a real problem-solver. Now she was being asked directly to solve what could prove to be a life-and-death problem for everyone on the train. "I'll need some help," she said, not wanting to be the first to refuse a request. "

We will find the best people we have to help you," Nick said.

Jim, the parlor car LSA, said, "I can help Sammy with that."

Everyone on the staff looked at the two LSAs as they smiled at each other. It was clear there was a thing going on between them.

Nick continued talking. "Besides food and water, we are going to have to manage our clothing and bedding. The static temperature of the rock in the tunnel is only 50 degrees. That means we are going to get uncomfortably chilly pretty soon, even inside the train. It's still late summer, so people probably didn't pack coats. We're going to need every bit of clothing and linen we've got divided up and evenly distributed. Jen, would you mind taking on that task?"

Jen, who had received more customer service awards than anyone else in the company, quietly agreed to do her best.

Rashid mentioned that he had a few people in his car who were not very healthy and needed lots of medications. Nick looked around at which staff members he had left. He knew Tim had a few medical issues of his own, although he had no idea just how serious they were. Regardless, he asked the most senior person on staff to take on the challenge.

Tim looked like he was out of his league. So Nick tried to put the job in perspective. "You will simply be the organizer. Try to find doctors and nurses who will take care of everyone on the train."

"Okay, I'll do my best," the senior coach attendant said.

René suggested that they collect all the oxygen bottles from the emergency refuge locations in the tunnel for use on the train by the medical team.

Nick was starting to feel mental fatigue. He couldn't think of what issues still needed attention. He wished he had gotten better sleep the night before. "Are there any other teams that need to be formed?" he asked the group.

Larry chimed in, "Yeah, we have to prepare this train if we want it to be operational out there in that God-forsaken ash for who knows how long."

Nick looked at Larry with full understanding of just how challenging that was going to be. "Sounds like we need a mechanical team. Maybe two mechanical teams—one for the locomotive and one for the train cars. I can lead the group that will have the cars ready. Obviously, Christina and you are leading the engines team, Larry. Will you need any more help?"

"Sure," the grizzled old engineer answered. "Just don't give me any slackers—we don't have time to pussy-foot around. We'll need real mechanics."

A familiar voice came from the far end of the dining car. "You need a team to monitor air quality."

Nick strained his neck to see over the crowd, just to make sure it was Evelyn Pope he was hearing. She was getting very worried. "All this activity, and all these people doing work would flood the tunnel with CO_2 too fast for the air outside to clear," said the atmospheric scientist from Iowa.

The conductor made eye contact with Dr. Pope. He asked her if she could monitor that. "I can use some methods, but regardless, we must modify behavior to conserve our usable air supply immediately!"

"Okay, I am sorry, but I don't have any more staff members to be on your team. Can you please be in charge of that group?"

"Yes, but right away we need to have people try to relax. That way, they will produce as little CO_2 as possible," she said.

"Okay, I'm on it." Nick picked up the mic again.

"Folks, Nick the conductor again. We are forming teams to preserve our resources while we wait here and prepare the train and ourselves for eventually getting out of this tunnel. Right away I am asking any healthcare professionals to please help us with our medical team. It is important that we assess everyone's physical and mental health. Medications and medical devices we have now are all we are going to get for at least several days. Perhaps we won't have new supplies for up to two weeks. If you have the skills to help, please come to the parlor car."

"This next part is even more important, so please listen closely. We have a huge tunnel with lots of good air. But still, we need to calm our breathing as much as possible to conserve the oxygen we do have. So just sit down, relax, slow your heart rate and rest."

Nick let go of the mic switch and looked at Evelyn. "Will that work for now?" he asked.

She nodded her approval.

Nick heard another voice—rather close behind him. "Sir, I am a military veteran and police officer in Denver."

Nick turned to see who it was. Leonard Gonzales was looking rather concerned. "We are going to see a rapid breakdown of command, cooperation, and control if there is not a police force to keep the peace and enforce the rules. I have seen societies collapse in combat theaters, and it isn't pretty. Let me see if I can get a few people to help me take on the task of maintaining law and order."

Nick looked at the man closely. He wasn't sure if Gonzales had credibility or not, but he agreed with everything the man had said. The Marine Corps tattoo was reassuring. Nick looked at René. "Police force on the train?" he asked her, more with his eyes than his words.

She nodded and Nick turned to Gonzales. "We agree, there should be a group available as enforcers if needed, but nothing heavy handed or violent unless absolutely necessary. Would you please work with conductor René to recruit a team and work out the details of how security should work?"

Both René and Leonard nodded. Soon the two were deep in conversation.

The whole time, Nick had not even thought to speak with the two UPR track workers who had found refuge in the tunnel. Jake and Charlie were there with their yellow reflective vests, hard hats, and radios.

"Guys," Nick said, "we will need to have usable tracks, and tools to fix 'em if they're broken. We're lucky to have you with us to lead the track inspection gang when we leave the tunnel."

The two men looked at each other. "Sure thing," Jake, the foreman, said. "I am the senior man on the crew so I will take the lead."

Charlie nodded.

Another passenger from the crowd spoke up—Dr. Abraham. "With so many people in close quarters for so long without fresh air or reliable sanitation, the odds of a major outbreak of illness are high."

Nick heard her. "What do you suggest?" he asked.

"We have to keep everything as clean as we possibly can, on a personal level and also on the surfaces of the train itself."

"Got it," Nick said. He called Nathan, the dishwasher. "Will you please be in charge of janitorial duties?"

The young man agreed to do it. "Get some help and keep this train clean and sanitized," Nick said.

Nathan looked proud to have a team to lead. "Yes, Sir!" he replied.

Nick said loudly, "I need all the designated team leaders to gather around."

After a bit of shuffling in the crowded train car, the group of leaders was assembled. Nick asked René to read off the teams one at a time.

René began with loud decisive tones that reminded Leonard Gonzales of a capable drill sergeant. "Food, Thomas; water, Sammy; sanitation, Dan; medical, Tim; room rotation, Rashid and Rita; janitorial, Nathan; linen and clothing, Jen; air monitoring, Evelyn; mechanical/locomotives, Larry; mechanical/train, Nick; track inspection, Jake; security, René."

Nick looked at René. "Let's add another team. I want an update every few hours on conditions outside of the tunnel."

"Good idea," she said. Nick turned to Charlie, the younger of the two UPR men. "Can you take on that chore until we get out of the tunnel?"

The young maintenance apprentice looked to be out of his element. "*Um* . . . honestly, I am not great at organizing and such. I can do what I'm told and work like a horse. I can get pretty technical too. But please don't put me in charge."

"I understand," Nick responded as he scanned the train car for a suitable leader for the outside monitoring team.

Knut had been about four rows of people behind Nick for the whole meeting. He felt he could help. He was in good shape and could learn fast about what to look for from people like Dr. Sayers and the professors from Iowa. As a lifelong sports reporter, he was an astute observer. Also his girlfriend Olivia was in great physical condition. They could work together. Nick appointed them co-leaders.

"All of you team leaders, create a plan of action. You need to ask yourselves the following: what are we trying to accomplish?; what resources we need; how many people we need on the team; and what skills those people need. Once you have that information, you should walk the train to gather the team you need. We have a lot of people on this train, and they have a lot to offer. Use them! That's it for now. Good luck."

Nick was relieved that some of the tasks had been delegated. He was starting to gain confidence in the crew's ability to manage their situation.

René spoke up before the group dispersed. "Wait a moment, please."

The room got quiet for her. "We have a list of passengers from Dan and Jim, but we need a lot more information than that. We have to inventory our material resources. We need to know how much stuff we have, and what skills or talents each person on the train has. Stuff like that. How about if I start a spreadsheet and have everyone on the train file by and tell me what their talents are? Then each team leader can pick and choose their teams from the list."

Nick liked that idea. "It's like picking teams on the playground. Anyone disagree with this plan?" he asked the group.

No one spoke up. "Done," Nick said as he lifted the mic once again. Before speaking he turned to René and asked, "Are you ready for them?"

"I will be in two minutes," she answered as she quickly opened a new Excel page on her computer and began creating new headers for the columns. Dan yelled out, "I pick first!" Dan had been an expert at recess team sports in elementary school. "I choose Doug for my team—he's got tools."

"Folks, Nick here. Thanks for bearing with us as we try to flesh out this whole survival plan. In order to get each team populated with the most suitable folks, we need to know what talents and skills each person on the train has. Everyone has something to offer, and we have to marshal every bit of what you've got to give. So I am asking everyone to go single file through the diner. Assistant conductor René will record what you are able to do, and what private resources you might have. From there we will assign you to a team. That team leader will get you involved as needed. I will also be next to René, ready to listen to ideas you might have that can improve our plight, and maybe even our chances of survival."

Linda Madden, a tour director for twelve travelers from England, approached Nick. She had met him on previous trips. She was a kind, witty, organized woman, and charming too. She was also a fierce advocate for her customers. Nick saw her coming and prepared himself for a litany of concerns. To his pleasant surprise, she had quite the opposite message.

"Conductor Nick, I have spoken with the entirety of my tour group contingent. We want to assure you that each and every one of us are at your service, in whatever capacity we are requested and able."

Nick looked at the others in the area. "Friends, that is what I'm talking about!" He then looked back directly at the British woman. "Linda, thank you. Your support is inspirational. But make no mistake, those words are going to be put to the test in ways we don't even know yet."

She smiled at him. As she turned to make way for others, Nick had one last thing to say to her. "Hey, Linda, God save the King!"

She gave him a Churchillian "V for Victory" sign and left the car.

Nick and the others got right to work. Larry was getting ready to return to the engine to talk with Christina about how they would restart the locomotives, and keep them going. He was worried about the prospect of going for days on a single tank of fuel through an ash-covered world. Before he left, he approached Nick about his concerns.

"Slow down, cowboy," Nick said, looking at the man from Boston who had never ridden a horse in his life. "We are on step two. Fuel is, like, step 12."

"Okay, fine. But don't forget that all these lights are running off your emergency batteries. You won't have much light left if we have to stay in here for three or four days."

"Now that is a great point, thanks," Nick said. He sent Jim to race from one car to the next quickly explaining that the lights had to be kept off as much as possible to preserve the batteries.

Nick was looking forward to meeting each passenger face-to-face as they came through the line, which would give him a chance to connect, and hopefully earn their trust. He made sure to keep his hat on and his tie cinched up.

Image matters, he thought.

CHAPTER 15

TEAMWORK

"Alone we can do so little. Together we can do so much."

—Helen Keller

Dr. Abraham, Ingrid's seatmate Susan, who was a nurse, and several others were chosen by Tim for the medical team. Jay, the dentist, and his wife Diana, who had assisted him for years, prepared themselves to deal with any dental problems that arose. The whole medical team chose the lower level of the parlor car as a clinic. Issue number one was to find out who needed regular medications, how much medication they had, and to try to stretch that supply out for fourteen days. Sean from the Silver Sky gang was a physician's assistant with an extensive background in technology. He quickly organized a spreadsheet with paper backup to track and monitor all 244 people on the Zephyr.

Half the first aid kits were brought to the clinic. That stocked the medical team with plenty of basic supplies, and still kept some in the emergency lockers throughout the train. The medical team had all the gauze they needed—so they thought. What amazed the team most was the huge supply of N95 masks. Dr. Abraham said the decision to stock those masks, made by a lady she never met, Joyce Smyth, could end up saving lives in the days to come.

The most immediate weakness in the clinic was a lack of bottled oxygen for two passengers with compromised respiratory systems. Not only was their personal oxygen supply already running low, they were also under extreme stress at 9,230 feet above sea level. Knowing the tunnel had several refuges with emergency oxygen tanks, Sean asked Nick if they could be gathered up. They both agreed it was the only solution to the problem, but hauling those heavy steel canisters for miles through the tunnel would be a chore.

Jake, the UPR maintenance foreman, had forty-five strong people picked out for his track team. He divided them into three "gangs," as maintenance-of-way workers liked to refer to themselves. Once the train was out of the tunnel, his plan was for each gang to work an eight-hour shift and be relieved by the next. He wanted to make the most of the time in the tunnel to prepare his gangs. Jake began a sleep rotation immediately to acclimatize each person to their work hours.

The people assigned to the track team knew almost nothing about train tracks. So during on duty hours of each gang, Jake or Charlie gave classes. The instructions included how train tracks were built, how switches work, what tools they needed, how to use those tools, and how to work safely as a group.

Safety had always been the number-one priority at the UPR. Under Jake's watch, that ethic would not change—especially in these extreme circumstances. He challenged his gangs to execute the next several days without injuries. The entire track team adopted a new theme, "Survive safely."

Thomas took ten people to gather all the food on the train into the diner kitchen. He multiplied 244 people by fourteen days. The food team meticulously divided up the stockpile into 3,416 portions. One ration per person per day. Though not easy to figure out how to do equitably, and it wasn't much food per portion, it was carried out fairly.

Ron was thankful that the kitchen had been overstocked in Chicago. He said to Thomas, "You know, I was dumbfounded by what I thought was a stupid amount of food when we left yesterday. But I can't tell you how thankful I am that our commissary guys did that."

Thomas was a little less complimentary. "We can't serve half the stuff we have until we cook it, and that ain't happening till we get out of the tunnel and turn the engines on for HEP."

He and the others placed all the uncooked perishable items in freezers and refrigerators and planned to keep those doors closed to preserve what they could for as long as possible. They hoped the frozen items would keep everything cold, even without power, until the train could get outside.

Nick assembled eight people to get the train cars ready to face the outside conditions. He assumed the ash would clog air filters right away if the air intakes were not protected. He worried about ash building up on the tread of the wheels and derailing the train. He thought about ash blowing in through end-door diaphragms and other air leaks, choking out passengers in the process.

Duct tape was almost always packed in the grip of railroaders, regardless of craft. Nick's team collected a total of thirteen nearly full rolls. Nick and Larry used it to tape bed sheets over air intake vents. Those sheets were to act as a pre-filter that could be dusted off, or even exchanged, so long as the supply of tape held out. Loose sheets were wrapped around the outside of diaphragms between cars. Of utmost help were all the new rubber gaskets and seals recently installed throughout the train.

Months ago, Joyce Smyth had asked Conrad, the lead Zephyr mechanic in Chicago, to have every car on that train airtight. Nick knew some ash would get into the cars, but thanks to the efforts of the new maintenance department, it wouldn't be much.

Jen, who inventoried the linen, wasn't thrilled to hand over 120 of her bedsheets to the mechanical teams. The Chicago yard crew had loaded the train with enough linen for a full six-day round trip to California. Most was still in the baggage car. Jen counted 840 blankets, 1,520 sheets, 460 towels, and 500 washcloths. About 20 percent of her total supply had already been used since leaving Chicago. Some of those sheets and towels were too messy to reuse. Jen gave Larry and Nick the dirty ones for the mechanical teams. She decided to hand each person on board their share of linen to use as they liked.

Six passengers helped get the stock divided and distributed. Everyone on board got two blankets, four sheets, three towels, and two washcloths. Jen's team kept the remaining supply wrapped up in the baggage car for use as needed.

During normal winter operations, ice and snow did not build up on train wheels because the weight of the train on the tiny contact point with the rail almost always squished frozen water out of the way. Nick feared the denser ash would build up like a snowball until the flange could ride off the rail and derail the train. He and the team preparing the train cars used 4" X 6" pieces of linoleum flooring from the baggage car to clean each wheel. The scrapers were wedged between the outside of the brake shoes and their pressure-producing calipers. Once secure, the fibrous material was bent into shape so that the edge could clean the wheel like an ice scraper on an automobile windshield. To set up the entire train took a couple of days.

Jim turned off breakers to all illumination except the emergency strips on the floor along the aisles. The glow-in-the-dark safety stickers suddenly seemed bright. Nick thought about Joyce Smyth, the Zephyr train manager who had instituted an "overstock policy" months before. *That lady even replaced the old stickers with new ones. She gets a nice card when we get home*, he thought.

But it was more than stickers. Joyce had fresh air filters and spares on board. Lights were going to last much longer because she had insisted on LEDs to replace all the energy-sucking incandescent bulbs. The batteries in each car were new high-capacity lithium ion units that would last as long as anything on the market. *If we get through this, Joyce Smyth will be a big reason why*, he thought.

Dan assembled his people for their sanitation mission. Ten people had agreed to be on his "poop patrol." Perhaps the most useful person on the team was an Englishman, Neville Hampton. He'd spent more time in tunnels than anyone on the train, as a tunnel maintainer for the London Underground for over thirty years. By regularly walking miles of tunnel on the poop patrol, he watched for signs of stress in the tunnel walls and roof.

Collection of the waste was the first challenge. Dan's team gathered ice buckets from the sleeping car rooms and placed them in the toilet rooms of each train car. Lids of the real toilets were taped shut with a note, "OUT OF SERVICE! USE BUCKET PLEASE." Dan and the team emptied the buckets every hour into large plastic kitchen trash bag liners that were doubled up in cardboard trash cans. What to do with the collected waste was a tougher problem.

Neville informed the group that whatever was uphill in a dripping tunnel would eventually come downhill, so he suggested disposing of the material past the apex so that the foulness would flow away from the train. That sounded easy, except for the fact that the apex was nearly two miles west of the train's location.

Dan explained on the PA how the system was going to work less than an hour after he was put in charge of sanitation. His team then began their round-the-clock chore. Whenever someone thanked him for doing that most unpleasant job, he simply responded with a smile, saying, "It's a labor of love."

To make Dan's job easier, Doug (the man with the heavy bags René checked in on the Denver platform) cannibalized four roller suitcases and some interior wall panels from the 512 car to create a cart that could roll on rails. Eight wheels rolled on top of the rail, taking the weight of the whole cart. Four other wheels were secured horizontally against the inside ball of the rail, like the flange on a train car wheel, giving lateral stability.

"That man has skills," Dan said after looking at the contraption. "I'm glad I picked you for my team."

Doug responded, "My secret is that I've got cordless power tools. So long as the batteries hold out, we can do great things."

Neville, who had seen his own brand new suitcase drawn and quartered for the project, praised the invention with typical British re-servedness. He called it "a capable crap cart."

On the first poop patrol run to the other side of the apex, Neville and Doug ventured all the way to the cave-in near the west portal of the tunnel. The rocks Larry and Christina had hit with the locomotives were marked by the violence of the collision. Just beyond those rocks, the two men found an impenetrable chaotic wall of broken concrete lining and shattered granite. Everything was wet. A pool of water was already forming.

Neville shook his head in disapproval. He determined that the roof had not fallen. Rather, the sides of the tunnel had squeezed together. "If only they would have built the tunnel in a complete circle, like the London Tube, rather than with straight vertical walls, the mass of the earth itself would have compressed into a stronger tunnel during the earthquake. Then this structure would not have collapsed."

Doug, who had barely gotten out of high school, but had more common sense than most people, assessed what the educated tunnel expert had said. His response left the witty Englishman speechless. "Yeah, but if it hadn't caved in, the train would have made it out of the tunnel, and we all would have died in the ash cloud."

Doug snapped several photos with his phone before the two men began their return trip to the Zephyr. Along the way, they picked up every tank of oxygen at the refuge points. The crap cart made easy work of the chore. Tim and the medical team were thrilled to receive the vital supplies.

Sammy's job of ensuring a clean water supply was not easy. Without compressed air from the locomotives, the 500-gallon water tanks in each train car were inaccessible at the faucets. Eric, one of the Colorado Buffalo football players, had a degree in mechanical engineering. He offered to help figure out how to get into those tanks.

Nick helped by showing him how to access the water and toilet machine rooms in each train car. They had to go through exterior service doors. It was very tight quarters for the big man. In short order he was able to understand what the various tanks, pipes, and valves were for. He figured out that there was a "tank purge valve" that could be opened to fill buckets as needed.

While Eric was learning the inner workings of train car plumbing, Sammy was busy finding every bottle, cup, jar, and vessel she could. Four others helped her. She and her team went through the trash. They became the best recyclers on the train. Water in the train tanks would be exclusively for drinking.

Sammy's team found a constant drip on the wall of the tunnel outside the diner. The water was clean and tasted good.

Dr. Sayers believed the seepage had filtered through at least 2,000 feet of rock and sand. He surmised it had been in the mountain for several years before finally flowing into the tunnel. The team decided to use that tunnel water primarily for washing.

Sammy used large, fiberglass trash cans in the end lockers of each car to collect the raw water. Each one held about twenty gallons. A can full of water was placed outside each restroom. People were instructed to take a cup of that water to the sinks and use it to wash hands often. According to Dr. Abraham, keeping clean, thus preventing outbreaks of illness, was almost as important as people staying hydrated.

Chance Nelson was feeling a bit left out. He was a new employee of the railroad, but not really a part of the crew. He had just finished his training class for the Information Technologies Department. Still he wanted to contribute to the cause. At fifty years old, he had considerable life experience that could be of use. He had an idea. Chance believed the ordeal they were living through was extraordinary and needed to be documented and recorded. He felt they needed communications with the outside world as soon as possible.

René was close by, so Chance asked her what she thought. She agreed and placed him in charge of the Tech, History and Media Team. Marshall Knight asked to join Chance's team. He was an expert in program development and IT solutions. They could use the machines available to document everything that happened and reach out to the world.

Chance began creating an application on his computer to record the history and report on social media. Marshall walked the train, seeking programmers, photographers, and writers to be on the "history" division. He imagined being an old man reading the book of events that were happening in Moffat Tunnel. He thought about grandchildren being amazed that he and Grandma really lived through all that.

As Marshall asked people to contribute, he encouraged the volunteers to record everything. "We can edit and whittle the content later. Our task now is to gather as much as we possibly can about everything that happened, is going on now, and will befall us in the coming days."

Soon Chance and Marshall had several others on the team. Lisa joined the group because she was an outstanding published writer, reporter, and storyteller. Reagan's mom Claire was added to the team. They would record in meticulous detail everything that was done with names, numbers, dates, locations, and times, and proofread and edit all the material the team produced. Rich Lucky, a renowned videographer of railroad-themed material, was put in charge of video. Altogether, Chance felt he had a world-class group that would be able to effectively tell their story.

When the lights went out, people started using their cellphones for illumination. Nick told dozens of passengers that the 110 volt outlets would not be working for perhaps several days, and that they may want to conserve their battery power for going to the bathroom. He even had to remind some people that there was no cell tower service or Wi-Fi in the tunnel. Even so, some passengers kept trying to call friends or family, presumably out of grief-induced denial and fear.

Eventually, calm began to settle over the Zephyr. Most lights were out. Miraculously, the entire train of passengers and every resource was cataloged, organized, and delegated into functional groups with achievable tasks. It was impossible to tell day from night inside the pitch-black tunnel. Susan, the nurse, suggested that sleep patterns and a sense of routine would be important to maintain. So Nick asked everyone without a specific night job to try to sleep between 10:00 p.m. and 7:00 a.m. Dr. Pope encouraged rest and sleep anyway, as a way to reduce the consumption of oxygen and the production of carbon dioxide.

One particular passenger was a problem. Randal Keaton and his girlfriend Amy were in room B, car 532—a deluxe bedroom. He demanded to talk to the conductor.

Nick came as soon as Jen called him. As he arrived, Randal stood up like a boxer from his corner about to fight a fresh round.

Nick felt the aggression from the man, but introduced himself cordially anyway and asked how he could help.

Randal was clearly upset and shaken, as so many were at that point.

"Listen," the angry man said. "I paid over $2,000 for this room. Now you say I have to share it with others because of something I had nothing to do with? Let me make it clear; this is our room, and we are staying right here until your company gets us safely to Emeryville."

Several others in the deluxe rooms of the car were trying to listen in on the conversation through the thin walls.

Leonard Gonzales showed up in the aisle near Nick. Jen had run to get him, believing that Nick and the passenger might engage in a confrontation. She worried Keaton might get physical, and she knew Nick would not back down. Gonzales was excited about his first police action on the train.

Awesome! Nick thought. *I've got backup.*

Anne Hampton was next door in room C of the same car. Her husband Neville was still out working with Dan's sanitation team. She was disgusted by Randal Keaton's objections. In a very *un-British* demonstration, she noisily gathered belongings and began her trek to the coach class cars. She loudly thanked Jen and Nick for their service, and asked directions to where she should go, making sure Randal and his girlfriend heard and saw what she was doing.

Randal Keaton pretended not to notice Anne. He looked at Nick as if he was a middle school bully staring down a smaller kid.

But Nick was no "smaller kid." He saw Randal's weakness—his girlfriend Amy, who was looking rather sheepish. The obviously embarrassed woman was sitting by the window in the corner of the room. Nick decided to play the "guilt and shame" card.

"Oh, c'mon now, you don't really mean that. You don't want all 242 other people on this train to know that you, and only you, are so intolerably selfish in the face of this life-and-death situation that you would deprive others of sleep for days on end while you lounge in the lap of luxury? And regarding getting to California, we don't have any idea what is even left out there. What I can tell you is this: If we survive, it will be together. Nobody will be able to buy their way to rescue." Nick was looking at Amy while he spoke, as if Randal wasn't even there.

"Hey, you're talking to me, not her. I have . . . "

Nick redirected his overpowering gaze at the short pudgy man and forcefully interrupted. "Sir, you will be a part of the bed rotation. If you refuse, I will instruct our security force to physically compel you to comply. Is that clear?"

The strategy worked. Amy had had enough. "Randal, just do what they ask. It's no big deal." The woman began gathering her things as if she would leave the room.

Randal watched Amy, looked at Nick, and saw Gonzales and René. Their eyes told Keaton that they were ready for anything. He knew he was beat. In his heart he felt fear, but also hate for Nick.

"Okay, off you go." Nick said.

Amy pushed by Randal as if she were ashamed of the man who had bought her way aboard the train. Keaton didn't say another word. He just gathered his stuff and marched off toward the other end of the train.

After Randal Keaton found a double coach seat to himself, an older gentleman approached him. It was United States Senator Antonio Jackson. The senator and his wife had been traveling in an adjacent deluxe sleeper. The two men talked for about half an hour. The content of the conversation was not overheard, and neither man ever shared what was said. One thing everyone saw was a change in Randal Keaton from that point on.

Senator Jackson was a grandfatherly figure. After a long and prosperous career leading a home restoration business in inner-city Baltimore, raising three sons with his wife, and serving on numerous city councils, he chose to make a run for an open US Senate seat in Maryland. He was motivated by the destructive extremism he saw in both major political parties. He wanted to offer a moderate choice to voters. He promised to be a senator who would listen to all sides of a debate and find middle ground without being disrespectful of other opinions. In the end, his movement mushroomed into a whole new political party in America. His victory in Maryland, and leadership of the "Radical Moderates Party" had sent shockwaves through the political establishment.

Now deep inside Moffat Tunnel, his optimism and calming influence were needed more than ever.

CHAPTER 16

DARKNESS

"Perseverance is not a long race. It is many short races one after the other."

—Walter Elliot

Nearly everyone was either trying to relax or already asleep at 11:40 p.m. "Fourteen hours down, who knows how long to go," Nick said to the few people in the parlor car. He had his watch on timer and countdown modes. The eruption happened at about 9:40 a.m. He used that as the start time to get to the 144 hours Dr. Sayers and Dr. Pope thought was the best timing for their exit from the tunnel.

Knut's shift to report on east portal conditions was coming soon. He was already up and in the parlor car ready to go. He'd walk to the portal at midnight to report on the conditions outside. Dan was going to lead his delegation of the sanitation poop patrol at 11:45 p.m. René was relieving Nick of "overall monitoring duties" in twenty minutes.

Nick's adrenaline had kept him going at full alertness since going on duty at 7:20 that morning. He didn't know how he could even begin to fall asleep, but he knew he couldn't keep going without rest. He was glad to see René come to relieve him for a few hours.

Knut and Nick were sitting in the darkened parlor car at a table. Dan and René were chatting at the table across the aisle. "Hey, Nick, before you go to bed, I want to say that you did good today," Knut said to the exhausted conductor.

Nick was still wearing his uniform and hat, now dirty from an extraordinary day of nonstop action.

"How did you know what to do?" Knut asked. The European athlete was amazed how the entire crew, especially Nick, had responded to such insane circumstances with such collected responses. He believed their actions had already saved many lives.

"Well," Nick began, "the official answer is that we have to thank the company and the Federal Railroad Administration." He thought for a moment, and continued, "Actually, there is quite a bit of truth to that statement. You see, all of us employees have had to go to training classes in Chicago every year. We have a thing called PREPARE (Passenger Railroad Emergency Response Education) class. They taught stuff like the hierarchy of command, making a manifest of passengers, delegating responsibilities—things like that. The teacher for several years has been Rosa. She made sure we were ready. She was a conductor, then an engineer, before getting into the training department. She could really talk to us on our level. Of course, in class she was talking about things like a derailment, or a passenger getting really sick, not a major cataclysmic volcano. But the principles are still the same."

"This Rosa must be a really good teacher," Knut said.

"She is," Dan chimed in. "Rosa makes everyone feel like they can get through anything and come out the other end as good as new."

René continued Dan's line of thinking, "Yeah, I don't think any of us ever even thought we were getting ready for the situation we are in now, but Rosa led great discussions in class about survival, even survival in tunnels. We went over what to do if we lost train power, how to deal with darkness for extended periods of time—all that stuff. So her class was actually really close to what we are facing now. When we get out of this and make it back to the real world, we will have a lot of people to thank. Rosa the PREPARE teacher will be at the top of the list!"

Sleep rotations had begun. Rationed food was divided and stored. Water was being collected in every vessel available. The poop patrol was doing what could be done with human waste. The bleak hell-storm outside of the protective mountain was being monitored. Plans were underway that would keep the train moving once they got going again. Notes and pictures were being assembled in a deliberate way to chronicle every detail of the entire adventure. Everyone aboard had a task and a team they belonged to. Things were finally calm. Most people had gone to a coach or sleeper car, if not engaged in one of the many tasks that continued around the clock.

Nick looked at his watch: 10:49 p.m. For the first time since the initial wave of geologic tremors, he allowed himself to think briefly about his own situation. Years of working trains across Nebraska on night shift had taught him to listen to his own body and brain. He knew that once he began showing signs of fatigue, he'd start making mistakes. The only two remedies were rest or total activity. Fully engaging himself only worked for a brief time. It could get a person to the end of a twelve-hour tour of duty, but not much more. Rest was the real relief. He knew the quest for survival that lay before him was not going to be a sprint—it was a marathon. Sleep, not just rest, was invaluable if he was going to be able to give his best effort. Nick looked at the bedsheet Rita made. His turn started at midnight. Room 24, car 540.

Keep watch for another ten minutes, I got this, he thought. He finally allowed himself to think about the most important thing to him—Beatrice and Juliette. His wife and their thirteen-year-old daughter were in Arvada, a suburb of Denver. *Could they have survived? How bad is it in the city?*

His emotions overflowed when he thought about Juliette being afraid during the earthquake and as the ash cloud descended. For the first time since his father passed away, he felt the true pain of heartache. He imagined her in shock and panic as she had to instantly process impossible circumstances, facing imminent death, without her dad there to protect her.

Nick's wife Beatrice was resourceful and resilient. If there was any way for her to get to Juliette and get through this, she would find it.

Hope—don't lose hope, he thought, trying to convince himself not to fall into despair. He grabbed a tissue to blow his nose.

"How long 'till we run out of these?" he said out loud to no one in particular. He was using what humor he could to smooth over his breakdown. The man who had tried so diligently to project an image of strength, leadership, and stability throughout the longest day of his life was reduced to tears. He saw the few people who were still in the diner looking at him. Embarrassed, he tried to turn the crying into a veiled laugh through sniffles and light sobs.

"It's okay, I just needed a moment," he said. Looking closer at the others he saw that his eyes were not the only ones full of tears.

Almost the whole train was in total darkness. Thankfully, a glimmer shone in the floor track lights. Those LED bulbs didn't drain much power. It was the right call to kill the lights and conserve battery power, but it came with a price. Deep in the bowels of the earth, where the temperature was always at a constant 50 degrees, people's minds began to play tricks on them. Darkness had a way of amplifying fear, and many people were beginning to experience a mental state of desperation where it feels like being pulled ever deeper into a bottomless pit with no way out.

Maria and Javier Sandoval, psychologists from San Francisco, had walked the train throughout the afternoon, talking to everyone they could. They had been assigned to the medical team by Tim when he learned of their skill set. He asked them to head up the mental health division. The couple agreed. They promptly formulated a plan and asked for a few more people to help. To some of the nuts-and-bolts-type thinkers, a mental health team sounded like "fluff and stuff" that didn't really make much difference—sort of a filler to give more people something to do. Reality proved it far more vital. Keeping the entire population on the train in a positive state of mind mattered as much to everyone's survival as running locomotives, finding water, or clearing tracks.

The "shrinks," as Thomas the chef called them, got right to work. First they set up an area in the lower level of the 512 coach car that would be a place to go, or be taken, for people experiencing severe or uncontrollable breakdowns. The professionals were certain they'd see plenty of such cases. Next they had a walk through the train to talk to everyone and evaluate the needs of each person. Conversations centered around what to expect. They validated people's feelings and told them to expect panic attacks, fear, deep grief, outbursts of emotion for themselves or others, and much more. They told everyone, "Knowing the overwhelming reality they were living through and not being overwhelmed by doom was possible."

Knowing what was happening in their heads, and understanding that such reactions to their extraordinary situation, was normal and had a deescalating effect.

One obvious fact the Sandovals confirmed was the inadequate supply of antidepressant medication. Nearly 10 percent of the people on the train reported to the pair that they were on such prescriptions. Nick had told everyone to prepare for up to two weeks without outside help. Maria and Javier did the math. People would start running out in just ten days—they'd run out of medication at the time they needed it most.

CHAPTER 17

ALONE TOGETHER

"When darkness, fear, and grief overwhelm, a kind word can restore a battered heart."

–CB

Nick left the parlor car and headed for his room in the 540 car. He would have room 24 to himself from 12:00 a.m. to 8:00 a.m. He felt his way through three dark sleeping cars to get to his temporary refuge. He let his thoughts go to Chicago and all his friends there, like Rosa and all the people he had worked with over his lengthy career. He prayed the ash cloud had not gotten that far, and that they and their families were all right. He also thought about what Knut had asked—how he knew what to do.

I knew the basics of what to do because of railroad training from Rosa and her team for sure, but also because I'm an avid reader, he thought to himself. Books had exposed him to Shackleton's adventure. Books took him down a deadly uncharted river with Roosevelt. True-life survival stories taught him what survivors do to survive. The books he read were part of what made him who he was. Books gave him a wealth of knowledge to draw from in this hour of need. He was deeply grateful for the books he had read. He wanted to recall every important lesson he ever read.

Room 24 was empty and tidy. Clearly, the previous tenant was a neat person who cared about the next occupant. Nick entered. A moment after closing the door, he was surprised to find himself suddenly collapsing once again in a flood of uncontrollable tears. From all he knew about the history of Yellowstone, and everything Dr. Sayers said, Nick was fairly sure there was no way his family, or anyone else, would have survived down in Denver. Fear of losing them overwhelmed him. He sat in the seat, which was still in the upright position, for nearly an hour before turning it into a bed. He prayed for a miracle.

After a long cry, he tried to humor himself out of grief. *I haven't prayed this much since the CU Buffs played Notre Dame for the National Championship in 1991*, he thought.

Eventually he lowered the seat to form a bed in the small room. He lay down in total darkness except for the dimly glowing emergency evacuation stickers on the window. He wrapped his two blankets around himself. His head fell onto the pillow. He submitted to several hours of exhausted sleep.

Hours go by slowly in near total darkness. It can play tricks on the mind. Vertigo and paranoia can creep into a person's thoughts, sucking away confidence and composure. The best way to fight the spiral into despair is to talk. Conversation with others, even in pitch blackness, keeps the mind engaged and entertained. When Nick woke, he decided to make a habit of talking with as many people as he could to help keep his mind off his fears about what might have happened to Beatrice and Juliette.

The next eighteen hours were uneventful. People were adjusting to their plight, though it wasn't easy figuring out how to pass one dark hour after another. Nick was walking the train. He met Herman in the H room of car 531. Herman had paid for a trip to Glenwood for his parents' fiftieth anniversary. He used a powered wheelchair due to quadriplegia, and he was nonverbal due to cerebral palsy. He communicated by leaning his head to his right for "yes" and left for "no."

Herman's caregiver, Rob, taught Nick how to engage with Herman, mostly by asking Yes or No questions. Herman could also use an eye contact-activated computer to write messages.

Rashid and Jen thought it best for Herman and his people to stay in the sleeper for practical reasons. Herman was not happy about that. He could rotate to coaches like everyone else. Nick was inclined to agree with his staff. So he sat down to talk with the man for a bit.

Soon it was clear to Nick that Herman had spent most of his recent life getting excited about his parents' anniversary train trip.

"Your folks need an elegant dinner to celebrate their anniversary properly." The conductor called Lorette in the diner. Together they planned it out. The dining car staff would pull out all the finest equipment and make it as fancy as they could. Rations would be the same as everyone else, but it would be served with style!

Nick went to the bag car and pulled out the emergency ADA Stryker chair. That chair would get Herman through the narrow upper level aisle so he could go to the dining car. Nick warned Herman not to tell too many people about what he was doing, because it was a rule violation to use emergency equipment for parties. Also there was no way, under strict interpretation of the ADA law, to move Herman up the winding stairs to the second level. Everyone agreed that this was a suitable time to make a discrete exception. Nick and Rob carried Herman up the stairwell to the waiting Stryker.

Small electric candles were lit on the white tablecloth. Every piece of china had the Zephyr logo emblazoned across the top. Dim lighting helped hide the fact that there was very little food on the plate. Herman looked at his parents, Aunt Suzy, and his godfather, Rob. He proposed a toast to his parents. It took only a moment, because Herman had prewritten it on his computer, "Happy Anniversary, Mom and Dad—You're the best! I love you."

The happy party of five enjoyed their banquet. Each got a quarter sandwich and ten potato chips. Their wine glasses contained 2 ounces of cabernet. Regardless of the anemic rations, it was a glorious party. One passenger after another came by to congratulate the couple. Herman beamed at each visitor. Nick came by while they ate. He was impressed with what the Dining car staff could present on short notice and with almost no light—even live music. Jimmy, a passenger who was a professional guitarist and singer played soft jazz two tables away.

Nick looked at Herman's parents. "Not bad when every dignitary on the train, including a United States senator, wishes you a happy fiftieth."

Dr. Evelyn Pope walked by. She was having an extremely hard time figuring out how to monitor air quality without instruments. She saw Herman in his chair. After the usual congratulations were given, she asked Herman if his heart rate fluctuated much. Herman's heart rate was almost always at exactly 58 beats per minute, because his physical activity level never changed.

"Do you have an oxygen meter?" she asked. "Yes, a finger gauge and a blood pressure cuff," Herman's mom answered.

Evelyn was a bit sheepish to ask, but she decided to risk being rude due to the circumstances. "Herman, do you mind if I use you as a measuring system for air quality in this train? You see, your vitals seem to be absolutely stable in normal air. If your vitals change, we know we have worsening air quality."

Herman's dad spoke up. "You need a canary in the coal mine?"

Evelyn was afraid she had insulted the whole family. "Well, in a sense, yes."

Marta pointed out that the plan would only work while Herman was calm. "When his emotions are riled up, his vitals could go off the chart."

Herman tilted his head emphatically to the right—his way of saying "YES!"

Herman's parents told him he had to really concentrate on staying composed and keep his emotions at bay. Again Herman said "YES."

Evelyn was thrilled. She had her air quality monitoring system, even if it wasn't perfect, and Herman was delighted to have a tangible way to contribute to the survival effort.

After a delightful dinner, capped with a single piece of lemon cake shared between all five in the party, they all went to get some sleep in the coaches.

When Nick told Evelyn about the need to get a scout party outside the tunnel as soon as possible, she was not happy thinking about the effects of silica ash or sulfur on lungs—even with the N95 masks. Nick figured she would feel that way. He told her about his plan. The Zephyr had a set of breathers—hoods that go over a person's head and connect to portable oxygen tanks. Together they agreed that the first people to venture outside the tunnel would wear them. If the toxins and ash were controllable, others could venture out with only their N95 mask and bandana protection.

Leonard Gonzales and René had organized the security detail. They took all five CU Buffalo football players (who'd been on their way to a reunion)—all big men beyond age fifty who were still in surprisingly good shape. Gonzales deputized them and gave them a crash course on keeping the peace. Their main task was to ensure everyone complied with the food rationing and bed rotation programs.

René's big fear was that some people would figure out a way to scam extra food or sleeper time for themselves. If that happened, the entire system could crumble. She ordered a two-person team from the group to block the entrance to the kitchen around the clock. All food was stored there. Gonzales kept the guard couplets rotating, and started a verification program of supplies; he knew from experience that probable thieves in a stressful environment could be the guards themselves.

Bed rotation was easier. Rita and Rashid would simply call security when people didn't vacate their room when it was time. After the Randal Keaton affair, there were no further problems.

People were always hanging out in the parlor and dining cars, passing the time. A passenger named Johnny, from Pueblo, Colorado, started talking about NFL football. He was a native of Colorado and lifelong, die-hard Denver Broncos fan. He and a couple from Reno were remembering some of the great games of the Raiders-Broncos rivalry. A stout man named Chuck from Louisville, Texas, chimed in, "If y'all are going to talk '70's football, you gotta talk Dallas—how 'bout them Cowboys!"

Jim, the bartender, had already made friends with the man from Texas. He added his two cents' worth. "Excuse me, but what team was without a doubt THE team of the '70's? None other than my own Pittsburgh Steelers!"

The one-upmanship didn't end there. Larry, the locomotive engineer from Boston, wanted in on the banter. "Seventies smededies! Let's talk about real domination. Let's talk Patriots—for the first twenty years of the twenty-first century!" The conversation devolved from there.

Jessica Knight and her kids found the other children on the train—ten were twelve years old or younger. She had been a Sunday school teacher for several years, so she had some experience keeping young people engaged and entertained. Anne Hampton offered to assist Jessica, since she had ample experience with youngsters in England. Together, they invented games that worked in the dim strip lighting on the floor. They made up stories where each child added one paragraph. Jimmy the guitar player had sung songs with them. Before long, the whole gang of kids had every word to "Puff the Magic Dragon" memorized. Mostly though, Jessica and Anne tried to help the kids sleep through the long dark hours.

The Amish passengers aboard had not lived with electronic screens for the most part. They had spent a lifetime entertaining themselves with conversation, jokes, and stories. No other group on the train seemed to adjust to the "black out" better than they. Before long, other people were getting in on the Amish conversations, because they were the ones that were still able to laugh. When the Amish saw that some "English" were listening in, they switched to English from their Pennsylvania Dutch language, so as not to be rude. A number of friendships were created between those vastly different cultures.

Knut, Olivia, and others on the outside monitoring team were bringing back the same news trip after trip to the tunnel portal. The main gate and pressure air lock doors are too hot to touch. Powerful sulfur smell.

Dr. Sayers tried to assure the team, and everyone else, that the ash and heat would subside in time. He just didn't know how long it might be because they didn't have enough data. After just two days, Evelyn was already recording slight changes in Herman's vitals.

The Silver Sky gang was busy rigging a plow for the end of their car. Ash was presumed to be three feet high outside. They used three wheelchair ramps from the sleeping cars to build the protective wall around the end of their car. Noah and his brother Luke removed the beautiful California Zephyr drumhead. They stowed it in a closet under the dome stairs. The ramps were tied on with some ratchet straps Doug had in his tool bag. It made a wonderful-looking wedge plow.

Once the gate was open, they could just push right through the ash like deep snow. Or so they thought.

Randal Keaton was feeling the stress. Time and his talk with Senator Jackson had calmed his anger toward Nick and the others. Still he was in rough shape mentally. His girlfriend Amy argued with him after he had behaved so badly in the sleeping car. He was pretty sure the relationship was over. He felt that everyone on the train was "out to get him." It was a bit overwhelming for him and he decided to change his ways. He sought out Nick to apologize.

On the *Endurance* with Shackleton, a guy named John Vincent had been a troublemaker. Ernest kept that difficult man close to him. Nick saw Keaton slipping into a place where he might really lash out and cause harm. Remembering Vincent from the book, Nick tried to think of how he could arrest Randal's behavior before he had to arrest the man himself.

I have to keep him close, Nick thought. *A historian. He can help Chance the IT guy document all that we do and how we do it. I can have him contribute to that team by observing the crew.*

Nick approached Keaton with the idea. Before Nick could speak, Randal Keaton surprised him. "Conductor, let me just say I am sorry for what I did and how I behaved. I just want to get out of here alive. I still feel I am getting jacked, but I'm ready to do my part to help."

Nick was flabbergasted. He thanked Randal and accepted the apology. He told Randal about the historian job. Nick asked him to "just keep within earshot with pen, paper, and video phone in hand."

Keaton agreed to do his best, and related that he did have some experience in journalism.

The security detail was also preparing for anyone who might get out of hand. They reversed door locks on two restrooms. From then on, those doors locked from the outside, thus turning the small stalls into pseudo jail cells. They also collected cable zip ties, mostly from the two conductors, and other tools that could be helpful in the event of an altercation. Part of Gonzales's security plan was to preemptively broadcast the security measures being taken, and the consequences if anyone tried to violate them.

CHAPTER 18

LOVE

"True love stories never have an ending."

—Richard Bach

Fear, darkness, and loneliness are a wicked triad—the opposite of what people usually want in life—such as security, light, and love. Intense situations sharpen the senses and amplify emotions. People turned to each other for support and comfort on the Zephyr while they were stuck inside Moffat Tunnel. Physical touch, a hand on the shoulder or just the warmth of the person in the next seat, could be therapeutic. In some cases, those bonds grew. During those long dark days of waiting and planning, couples were increasingly leaning on each other for comfort. At first, married folks were the ones noticed to be inseparable. As hours turned to days, other passengers formed strong bonds.

Jim, the parlor car bartender, had always been infatuated with the coach class snack car LSA, Sammy. In her eyes he saw the kind of woman he could fall in love with. Though they never dated because she was a Chicago girl, and he lived in Pennsylvania, in the darkness, they sought each other out. They'd been good friends for the past few years, and their friendship rapidly turned to support and growing fondness. Without even realizing what was happening, Jim had fallen in love with Sammy. He wanted to be with her all the time. But he was afraid to confide to her how he felt. He was afraid she might think his words were just a ploy to get her to let him have temporary comfort in the stress of the situation.

What he didn't know, but kind of felt, was that she had fallen in love with him as well. Light touching on the elbow or shoulder turned into hand holding. Finally she kissed him and thanked him for being the best friend she ever had. Jim was besotted. Their love would last for the rest of their lives—no matter how long or short that would be.

Ingrid, the Austrian girl who had suffered the indignities of Andy "Rad" Richardson, was truly alone. The language barrier was hard for her. All her family and friends were a continent away. People on the train were friendly to her, but that was not a substitute for a close relationship. Her kind seatmate, Susan, had been busy most of the first day, working with the medical team. Zach, her defender, had been gone all day as well. Barely older than a child, Ingrid had spent the first several frightening hours alone in the dark, thousands of miles from home.

Zach didn't know what to do. Ingrid was the most beautiful woman he had ever seen. Her accent made him swoon. He wanted to talk to her, to get to know her. He was, in a word, smitten.

Suddenly, in the dark that first night, he heard her voice. "Thank you, for being strong for me earlier with the bad man."

He tried to see her face, illuminated only by weak floor lights. "Oh, hello," Zach replied. The entire Amish clan tried to look at this girl from Austria.

"*Kannst du mich verstehen?*" she asked.

Zach had understood her—barely. He said so, but he answered her in Pennsylvania Dutch, wondering if she would understand him. She got some of his words, but they continued their conversation in English.

Ingrid said that the obtrusive man earlier that day had really scared her, and that her heart jumped with relief when Zach stood up for her. She asked if she could sit and talk. Soon she was speaking not just with Zach, but with the whole Amish clan. She told her whole story.

Her mother and father had been divorced for many years, and there was nowhere she could really call home. She had always been considered a little bit odd by the people she knew. Her passion was to live a natural life, close to nature. Sometimes that meant she would not eat what was served, or ride in a car when a bus or train was available. She said everyone in Austria was still nice, and her family cared for her as they always had, but she never quite felt like she belonged.

L.T. Miller, the patriarch of the group, imagined how his ancestors from that same part of the world were shunned and persecuted, hundreds of years ago, because of their religious beliefs.

Maybe her walk is not so different from ours, he thought.

Zach and Ingrid talked across the aisle in the diner for hours. The situation was odd in that he was always in the company of others in his group. To Ingrid, Zach was unlike anybody she had met before. He seemed immensely confident in who he was and where he came from, yet there was an innate humility about him. He was such a down-to-earth man who listened and seemed to understand her. They spoke of their worry for people they knew on the outside, and how those people would be worried about them. She was mesmerized by Zach's description of farm life in Kalona, Iowa, with no chemicals or outside electricity. It was almost as if they both had the same attitudes, world view, and thoughts. To say they were falling in love was not exactly accurate. It was more like they were destined for one another, and their lives up to this point had not been complete. Zach started to imagine a life after Yellowstone—a life with Ingrid.

At Tim's request, Dr. Abraham took over leadership of the medical team. She chose Susan to be her main nurse, and Sean as a physician's assistant. Their first injury patient was Chance, the new hire IT guy. He had fallen on the ballast as everyone ran from the ash cloud at the tunnel portal. He gashed his head. Nick sent him to the clinic once everything settled down back on the train. Dr. Abraham asked Susan to patch up Chance.

As Susan worked to clean off the wound, the two talked about where they were from, what they did for a living, why they were on the train—all sorts of small-talk stuff. Her hands felt soothing on his head and neck as she held him steady to apply the Steri-Strips and bandages.

Chance enjoyed the attention of the lovely woman. He noticed her kind eyes and attractive shape. After he left the clinic, he found himself wanting to spend more time with her. He wondered if what he was feeling was a real connection. *Time will tell*, he thought.

Susan was intrigued with Chance's demeanor and wanted to hear his life story. They agreed to talk more when neither was working with their respective teams. *What is going on with me?* Susan asked herself. *I am in a soot-covered, dark tunnel, with no way to properly wash, on the verge of dying a senseless death, and I am feeling an emotional connection? Either this guy is really amazing, or I am going nuts. What an insane reality this is*!

Michelle, one of the two servers in the diner, had only been with the railroad for a couple years. She came to the job, based in Chicago, after a nasty split from her ex. She was a New Orleans girl with a spicy attitude, but didn't want to live in the Big Easy anymore.

She became friends with some of the former CU Buff football players, because they were guarding the food she helped prepare. Before long, she and Cliff were talking a lot. Cliff usually walled himself off from women he didn't know, because most of them seemed to just want his money. He was worth a modest fortune thanks to his investments in lithium battery recycling. Michelle didn't know about any of that. Inside the tunnel, what people had on the outside became somewhat meaningless. Cliff was attracted to her, and she gave him attention without pretense. As the hours became days, they became quite fond of each other.

CHAPTER 19

THE WEDDING

"Marriage is not a noun, it is a verb."

—Barbara De Angelis

On the third day in the tunnel, Jim was feeling like the time had come. He asked Nick if it would be okay with the Silver Sky guys to take Sammy to the dome for a very important moment.

"Sure, they won't mind," Nick said. "What is the *moment*?" he asked curiously, although he had a feeling he knew. For the last few years Nick had felt Jim and Sammy should just admit they were perfect for each other. Jim looked at his friend of fifteen years and simply said, "It's time to do this once and for all."

Nick had one request. "If she says yes, and that is not a given, can we have a makeshift wedding right here, right now—on the train? Everyone could really use a happy distraction."

Jim had not even considered where or when the ceremony would take place. It only took him a moment to think through the fact that they may never get the chance to have a real wedding. After a moment of contemplation, Jim answered with a laugh, "If Sammy says yes, and that is not a given, and she agrees to a ceremony right away, then okay, let's do it."

An hour later, Jim asked Sammy to walk with him to the private car at the rear of the train. Nick had told the people in the Sky what was about to happen. He asked Sean and Alex to turn on a few extra lights for the event. As the couple entered the dome, everyone else went downstairs to the lounge area.

To Jim, Sammy looked more radiant than ever in the "mood" lighting of the glass dome atop the Silver Sky. The words he used were from his heart—too private for others to hear. Whatever the persuasive oration he used, it worked. Sammy said "Yes." They hugged and kissed.

For the first time in a long time, she was crying for joy rather than out of fear or grief. Her cheeks blushed as she noticed they were not totally alone. The sound of cheering came from below.

A few hours later, Lorette, Judith, and the rest of the staff had the dining car all set for the big event. The batteries were still strong in that car, so they turned on the regular lights. Nick had his full uniform tidied up as best he could. He stood at one end of the car. The entire staff became the wedding party—no best man or maid of honor. Jim and Sammy felt they were all equally in this together. As many passengers as possible crammed into the car and overflowed both ends. It felt great to have a moment of full lighting after so many hours of darkness. Nick was asked to officiate.

"Since the first barnacle barge plied the seas, it has been the greatest honor of the captain of the vessel to preside over the joyful and solemn wedding ceremony in emergency situations. Rarely has this privilege been required of railroad conductors. So it is with pride in my craft that I welcome all of you here today for what is—in every way—an emergency. I have known Sammy and Jim for many years. I can testify here and now that they are people of the highest character. It fills my heart with joy to see them choose to unite in holy matrimony publicly for us all to witness, right here, and without delay. Because everyone knows conductors hate delays."

A few chuckled at Nick's weak attempt at humor. He cleared his throat, as he usually did when his jokes fell flat, and continued, "So let me ask you Jim, do you choose to take Sammy as your wife—to love her with all your heart for the rest of your life?"

Jim looked at Sammy sincerely. For him this was no joke; he meant it. "I do."

Nick looked at Sammy. "Sammy, do you take Jim as your husband, and to love him for the rest of your life?"

She quietly said, "I do."

Nick had them exchange rings—donated by random passengers. Nick looked left and right over the assembly of people. "Then by the authority granted to me by the Federal Railroad Administration as a certified passenger railroad conductor, the brotherhood and sisterhood of all railroad unions, and America's passenger railroad, I pronounce you man and wife. Sammy, you may kiss your husband."

Jim looked up in surprise as Sammy laid a huge kiss on his lips. She smiled at Nick in gratitude for getting the secret "kiss plan" perfect.

Jimmy played "Wonderful Tonight" as the bride and groom danced. After that he laid into some Stevie Ray Vaughan blues tunes. Several others started dancing in the narrow aisle of the train car. It was just like any other wedding reception party, other than the cramped venue, chilly temperature, and lack of food, decorations, or festive dress.

Jim apologized to his new bride for not giving her a fancier wedding. She told him that no place or time on earth could have been more perfect.

The happy couple was escorted back to the Silver Sky where the drawing room was immaculately spread out with fresh linens, a quarter bottle of champagne, two crystal glasses, and an entire bowl of Chex Mix.

Jim later said it would have been the most perfect night of his life—if only he had been able to take a real shower at some point.

CHAPTER 20

WE ARE ALIVE!

"This is not the end. It is not even the beginning of the end. But it is, perhaps, the end of the beginning."

—Winston Churchill

After more than five days since the tunnel gate closed on the outside world, Knut's team finally had good news. The gate and air-lock door were cool enough to touch. Toxic odors were far less severe. They donned the rescue breather hoods from the Zephyr and connected them to two half-used oxygen bottles from the medical clinic. They tried to go out the door of the tunnel to the maintenance office. The door started to open.

The world Knut and Chance found was not at all like what they left five days before. They had less than 200 feet of visibility, and gritty haze filled the air. Ash was piled up five feet high in the doorway. With great effort, the men forced themselves through. Once they were away from the building, ash was more consistently about three feet deep, much heavier than walking through deep snow, but it looked similar.

The first object they saw was the UPR maintenance truck. The big vehicle was completely burned out. Tires, windows, paint, plastic trim—everything that could burn, or melt was gone. Knut ventured as far as he dared on his oxygen supply. Overall, the temperatures of the air and ash were hot—maybe 110 degrees Fahrenheit. Even without the heat, trudging through ash to reach any rescue party would be impossible. He and Chance quickly dug down to the tracks. Rails and ties appeared to be in good shape.

Chance had his satellite network phone with him. Only one bar of battery power left after five days of using the light to go back and forth from the train to the east portal. Now out of the tunnel, it beeped, indicating it was receiving a signal! He tried making a call to the Centralized National Operations Center and heard a ringtone. It was working!

"CNOC Operations, Andy speaking, can I help you?"

"Andy, this is Chance Nelson from the new hire IT class last month, can you hear me?"

"I'm sorry, who?"

"Chance Nelson. I am on the Zephyr. Train number five. We have been inside Moffat Tunnel for days. We are all alive!"

"No way! We thought you were all dead! You are the Zephyr that was in Colorado, right?"

Chance took a quick look at his air gauge, and phone battery meter. "Yes, that is our train. Listen, I am almost out of air and power— and it is very hot. I have to go back inside the tunnel. Here is the deal: We are going to push out of the tunnel in the very near future. We need a rescue party to meet us up here as soon as possible."

Andy was frantically trying to get his superiors on the phone with him. "Hold on Chance, give me a minute."

Chance was getting impatient. "Andy, just pass on the word that we are alive—244 of us. We are almost out of all our supplies. I will call back as soon as I can."

"Chance, this is Andrew Sullivan, manager of Eastern Operations. Stay on the line. We are trying to get hold of top management and authorities. We need a lot more information. Can you . . . "

Chance interrupted, "I am sorry—I am going back into the tunnel now. We will call back soon. Have the right people ready to help us. Thank you! Goodbye."

Chance Nelson hustled back into the tunnel as the whistle indicating low air on his oxygen tank started whining. Knut and Chance got back to the train as quickly as they could.

Evelyn needed good news. Herman was breathing much more rapidly. His O_2 meter showed dangerously low readings, and blood pressure was up 25 percent. The inside of the Moffat Tunnel was starting to get toxic. She had already alerted Nick and the rest of the staff about Herman.

Chance, Evelyn, Nick, and a few others met in the parlor car. Chance spoke first. "If we go out now, the heat will make it very uncomfortable—maybe deadly over a long period of time. The sulfur is still really bad too. I won't go out there without a breather."

Evelyn shook her head in disapproval. "You know that we are already seeing serious signs of elevated CO_2?"

Nick tried to break the impasse. "Dr. Pope, do you think we will still be able to function here in the tunnel for twenty-four more hours?"

The scientist knew the air in the tunnel would get much worse rapidly, but she was well aware that she couldn't overreact and send everyone into an ash-covered oven. "Yes, one day only though," she said.

The next twenty-four hours seemed to take forever. People's nerves were frayed. Herman found it bothersome to stay awake. His vitals made it clear that the people on the Zephyr couldn't wait much longer.

Thomas had more than half the food still stored in the kitchen. However, half the remaining sustenance was raw, and needed to be cooked. If the chef couldn't get that meat and other items into the oven soon, it would go bad, because the freezers and refrigerators had lost the last of their chill.

In the early afternoon, a group of passengers came into the diner. They didn't have a spokesperson. It was more like an angry mob. Nick was called to talk with them. About twenty passengers were staring down Gonzales and one of the Buffs, who were guarding the door to the lower level kitchen. "We're starving, and you have plenty of food down there," an angry man said.

"Larger folks need more than your skinny people!" yelled another.

Ron, the food specialist, came upstairs from his work preparing the next round of rations to try and reason with the crowd. "We are doing our best to give all of us the highest possible chance of surviving together."

He tried to continue, but was shouted down.

Nick got there as the conversation was devolving into angry arguments. He quickly recalled how Shackleton had doubled the rations, even though they didn't have enough provisions as it was, to improve morale when spirits got low. That tactic worked a century before in Antarctica. Nick figured it would work in Moffat Tunnel too. He asked for patience, and called the chef.

He asked Thomas and his staff to pass out two days' rations immediately. He then got on the PA to talk to the entire train. "Conductor Nick here, everyone. The ash is still too hot for us to start moving. We believe that by tomorrow, everything will have cooled off enough for us to survive out there. Regardless, we are going to leave the tunnel in the morning. I know that many of you are already feeling the effects of increased CO_2 levels, and we're all hungry. Just hang on one more day. We think it won't be too long before a rescue party can reach us. They now know we are here and that we are all alive. Therefore, I have asked Chef Thomas and the diner crew to pass out double rations right away. Friends, don't let yourselves get discouraged. We got this."

Thomas and his crew passed out the extra provisions. Nick's trick worked. The crowd dispersed and peace was restored. But everyone knew that temporary bit of cooperation wouldn't last long. Nick felt like a man walking across a river covered with thin ice. If he made one wrong move, he could fall through and be swept away by a torrent of chaos.

By 7:00 a.m. the next day, a quick check of the outside ash showed the temperature had dropped to just over 95 degrees. Knut said he almost didn't return to the train because the stench from days of Dan's poop patrol had finally fouled the entire tunnel. Nick thanked Knut for getting them the information they needed, and offered him foam ear plugs for his nose. Knut was not humored, but he gave them a try.

The whole group of team leaders was called to the diner, which only took a few minutes for them to gather.

Nick took the lead. "Guys, it's time. Let's get out of this tunnel!"

A cheer came from everyone in the train car.

"We have been preparing for this moment for several days now. Is there anything we could be doing that we have not done to give ourselves the best chance of surviving?"

No one said a thing.

"Okay, here we go. I believe we are ready. We got this!"

Nick, Christina, Larry, René, and Jake gathered to make a plan based on what they now knew about the ash.

"We can't go far with the Silver Sky on point," Nick stated.

Larry felt that wasn't an issue. "We will just push out and wait for help to arrive. No big deal."

Jake was not so optimistic. "I don't think anybody will come," he interjected. "We need to plan to run this train down the hill to Denver ourselves if it is as bad out there as Chance and Knut say it is."

Chance added that he didn't think anything could drive or fly through what he saw, although he did feel the air might be safe enough to breathe with a really good mask.

Then Knut spoke up, "I don't know about the big gate. It looks really bent and crooked."

Nick remembered the heat he felt that first day in the tunnel. "Okay, Jake and I will go to the east portal and check it out. Charlie, Knut, Yao Ping, Doug, and four other strong guys will go with us. René, please get a crew ready to release the hand brakes. Larry, you and Christina will be on both locomotives to restart the engines once we're outside."

When the guys got to the gate, it was sealed tight. Bearings were wedged into twisted roller tracks. The manual chain did not budge. They worked for an hour with crowbars to dislodge, dismantle, or tear open the gate. All efforts were hopeless.

"Is the train trapped inside?" Knut asked.

"Nope," Jake answered. "We're just going to smash through it, that's all."

Nick looked at Jake. He knew what "smash through it" meant. Jake was suggesting that the Silver Sky be used as a battering ram to punch the gate out of the way.

"Isn't that dangerous?" Knut asked.

"Not as dangerous as staying in here and suffocating," Jake answered.

The gate team returned to the Zephyr. René had Dr. Abraham tell everyone how to prepare themselves to safely ride through the impact with the gate. Yao Ping did some rough engineering math.

"I think 50 mph is needed," he told Nick.

The conductor told Larry and Christina that they needed at least 50 mph at impact to bust through.

"I sure hope we get there with just gravity," Larry answered.

Nick and Randal Keaton would be on the Silver Sky. Nick would give radio commands to the engineers. Randal would man the hand brake in the private car, and record the whole event with his phone camera. René got everyone in the main body of the train ready. Larry and Christina were in the locomotives. Larry flipped the switch to turn on his speedometer screen. It worked. Everyone and everything was ready.

CHAPTER 21

LET 'ER ROLL!

"It is easier to be courageous when no other options exist."

—CB

"We got this!" Nick said on the radio. "Number 5, Nick on the point, good for ten cars, release the brakes. OVER."

Like all good conductors, Nick looked at his watch. He asked Randal to record the time when movement started. Sunday morning, 11:00 a.m. on the dot. Randal took his padded position in the vestibule of the Silver Sky, after he had popped off the brake. Nick peered through the armor of the jerry-rigged wheelchair ramps hung on the outer skin of the stainless steel train car. In the main body of the Zephyr cars, all the brake levers were lifted. Each car made a sound of chains suddenly releasing pressure.

Engineer Larry turned the parking brake lever for the locomotives to "RELEASE." The cold engines were free to roll. For the first time in nearly a week, the mighty Zephyr was starting to move.

"Five mph," Larry called into the radio.

"Here we go!" Nick said with a tone of anticipation. His train had sat still for six days. Finally, some action.

"Ten mph." Larry was keeping everyone with a radio posted on their speed. Reagan, Claire, and twenty other passengers were listening in on the young man's scanner from their protected impact positions.

Nick looked at his radio—still one bar of battery power.

"Twenty mph—remember we got no air brakes," Larry hollered.

They didn't dare try to start the locomotives in the bad air of the tunnel for fear that they would asphyxiate the passengers before getting to the tunnel entrance. Instead, they were letting the train free-roll down the 0.8 percent grade to the gate. Nick was still believing the math Yao Ping came up with. He felt sure the impact through the door would consume most of their momentum, and slow down the train effectively.

"Just let 'er roll! Good for another ten cars. OVER," he called out.

At the hand brakes in the Zephyr, nine people were ready. Slack in the chains was already ratcheted up. René had wanted brake pads to start grabbing the wheel treads and axel disk rotors the moment she gave the signal to tighten the chains. They were told to wait for the word from René on the PA, or relay by hand signs if the batteries powering the loud speakers finally failed. The plan seemed easy enough when the train started to slowly roll, but then it started to go faster and faster.

Larry was getting nervous. "Forty mph!" he shouted as the cab passed the DS051 signal, now dark without power from the outside world. To the experienced crew, it felt like an out-of-control runaway train.

Nick sat into the cushions he'd assembled to lend protection during impact with the gate. "This is it, let it hit hard—Nick. OUT!"

He put on the breather hood and turned on the oxygen. Randal did the same. Nick was bundled behind the couch he used as a protective barrier. At the last moment, he ducked his head. The last two seconds of nearly silent running were eternal.

René had everyone on the train ready. Every person braced for impact. Every head was secured from whiplash as Dr. Abraham prescribed. Larry sank into his seat on the 313. The train was as prepared as they could make it. Everything they could think of had been done. They had passed the point of no return. The train was no longer under their control. The laws of physics would determine their outcome. Gravity pulling steel wheels downhill on steel rails, the Zephyr was ready for an intentional crash.

Larry took a last look at the speedometer: 48 mph.

WHAM, SLAP, RIP, CRUNCH! The Silver Sky lurched upward as all the knuckles and draw bars of the entire train compressed and drove their inertia into it. With the compression came the full force of the nearly 1,500 tons of train bearing down on the steel gate, which gave way with great protest. Parts of the gate whacked the sides of the Silver Sky.

The impact was so violent that two of the custom-made windows blasted inward through their housing and rubber gaskets. An enormous cloud of gray ash inundated the Sky. The car kept moving!

Grumbling and gnawing of metal started to reverberate through the floor. Dull sunlight dimmed by haze and disturbed ash suddenly burst through the windows. The sound of scraping metal and thumping wheels gave Nick a sinking feeling. He imagined the entire train piling up on him and his derailed train car. Gravity and momentum kept the Zephyr moving. Parts of the gate were still wrapped around the end of the Silver Sky.

Nick looked up after the initial impact. Flying ash and dust obscured any view of the outside world. The leading truck was either off the rails or dragging some massive pieces of steel. Speed dropped rapidly.

Larry, in the lead engine, yelled into the radio, "We're out of the tunnel on the head end!"

René rose from her protective position and looked out the window. Even though the sun's energy was heavily diffused by lingering ash and smoke, the blast of light into the pupils of everyone on the Zephyr was blinding. René tried to catch her bearings.

Nick was starting to see beyond the skin of the Sky. "Keep it moving, guys!" he called out. His transmission was a welcome relief for those listening on the radio, because it meant the impact with the gate hadn't derailed the train or killed Nick and Randal.

Larry waited until he could see what he thought was the east signal mast on the main track at the East Portal control point switch. "We made it! Tie the brakes!" Larry barked into the radio.

René screamed into the PA, "Tie 'em now!" Hand brake chains came to instant life.

Within a few seconds, all the hand brakes of the train were tied off tight. The train screeched to a stop. Suddenly there was only silence in the Silver Sky. The two men in the car, bedecked in breather hoods, rose to inspect themselves for injuries. None were found. Nick dusted himself off and walked to the back of the car where Randal had just finished tying the hand brake. They opened the top half of the vestibule door and poked their heads out to survey the scene.

In every car of the train people tried to adjust their eyes to look at the reality of the ravaged landscape. Dust and ash settled slowly. It was a calm day—almost windless. Nick tried to figure out just how far out of the tunnel they were. He could only see two train car lengths—not much, but better than he expected. Inside the train were cheers and high fives. They were out of that wretched tunnel at long last!

No maintenance buildings. No forest. No familiar reference points. Just gray everywhere. For most people on the train, this was the first time they saw the world—their new world—as it had become.

Everyone stuck to the plan. The doors of the train stayed closed except on the Sky. Nick opened the bottom half of the vestibule door and lifted the trap floor that lowered the steps. The bottom rung of the stairs pressed into the ash. He turned so that he would face the equipment as he stepped off. Randal had his phone on video to record the moment, as Nick asked him to do. Still in the full breather hood, the conductor descended the steps and let his boot hit the moonscape below him. As he did, he keyed his radio mic. "That's one small step for a man, one giant leap for . . . Everyone on the Zephyr."

Larry was still tense. There was a lot of work still to do. He got on the radio. "Do you have to joke at a moment like this? I mean really!"

Christina, in the trailing engine, got ready to fire up her locomotive. She smiled a bit at Nick's declaration. She keyed her radio mic and jumped in on the exchange. "A giant leap for passengers and crew of the Zephyr! We got this!"

The joke didn't last long. Nick was first to shut off the oxygen valve and lift his hood. He still had his N95 mask and bandana on. He took some deep breaths. Randal watched intensely to see if the conductor started gagging.

"It stinks of sulfur for sure, but not too bad," Nick said.

"Give it a few minutes like Dr. Pope said, just walk around a bit and see if you have any trouble," Randal replied.

After walking to the rear of the car and back in the deep ash, Nick waded over to talk with Randal. "I think we can breathe out here," he said.

"Hallelujah!" Randal twisted the air valve and pulled his own hood off as well.

"Nick to René, with a decent seal on the N95 masks, the air seems to be good enough to allow a person to work out here, at least for a while."

René answered with the usual one word, "Rog," and relayed the message on the PA. She ordered track teams to prepare to get working as planned.

With their vision unencumbered by the hard-to-see-through hoods, the two sojourners trudged around the end of the Silver Sky to survey the damage caused by bashing through the Moffat Tunnel gate. Much of the steel curtain was still wrapped around the end of the car. As the curtain was pulled apart, the sides ripped out of their steel guides bolted to the concrete walls of the tunnel. Portions of those railings that tore out of their moorings whipped under the car. Sheeting had let loose with such force that when it snapped free, it caused a whiplash effect that whacked both sides of the Silver Sky at once, blasting in windows and flaying the shiny skin of the car. The bottom edge of the curtain balled up and was wedged under the leading axle.

Luckily, the debris stayed intact enough to remain stuck on that bogie. Had it rolled under the whole train, the shredded steel debris would have sliced air hoses, rendering the Zephyr immovable with normal air brakes. Unfortunately, upward pressure on the truck of the Silver Sky from the scrap steel bouncing along the ties of the track had cracked the bulky bolster and center pin that held the entire A-end wheelset together.

Nick stopped thinking about survival for a moment. He started to think about his glorious Silver Sky train car. Her fate was sealed. The damage looked beyond repair. All the work and money to restore it had been for just one fifty-mile jaunt into the Rockies. She was finished. He felt like crying.

Christina started throwing electrical breakers on the back panel of the trailing locomotive. Larry was doing the same on the 313 at the front of the train. Lights came on in both cabs.

At least the batteries have some power left, thought Larry.

Within a couple minutes the engines were ready for a restart attempt. Dim daylight and man-made illumination had already lifted Christina's spirits. "Ready on the 309," she said into the radio.

"Okay," Larry answered.

"You first." Christina pressed the ENGINE START button.

This was the moment of truth. If the engines didn't start, everyone on the Zephyr would have to survive in that lifeless world on foot. If the engines did start, all of them had at least a shot at transporting themselves to some sort of rescue.

Lights in the cab of the 309 dimmed as power drained from the batteries to crank the prime mover. Fuel primer pumps were humming. The electric starter motor engaged and tried to turn the main crankshaft.

Vroom, vroom, vroom tap, tap, tap, then a growling sound of accelerating RPMs. "It's running!" Christina said into the radio with the kind of elation that only those in a life and death situation can fully understand.

René repeated the message on the PA to everyone on board. The cheers heard in the train were reminiscent of a Bronco's victory over the Raiders!

Larry pressed his start button just a few seconds after Christina. "The 313 is running too—we got 'em both going!"

"Train #5 calling anyone who can hear this radio. OVER." Larry and the others were hoping that by some miracle someone was out there. He repeated himself. Seconds passed.

"No answer. OUT," the old engineer said with clear dejection in his voice. No answer meant only one thing—they were alone. No other trains, no dispatchers, and no rescuers were close enough to hear them.

"Nick to Larry, fire up HEP. Let's get some power on this train and see how it deals with all this ash and dust. OVER."

Larry was quick to respond. "Roger that, HEP coming up. OUT."

Volcanic ash is nasty stuff. When it is dry, it floats like mayflies above a fishing hole at sunrise. It gets into everything. It could clog the N95 masks people on the Zephyr used to protect their lungs. When it is wet, it's like glue—sticking to everything and gumming up any moving parts.

When the locomotive started running, they began sucking in huge amounts of air. Sheets taped over air intakes were immediately pulled tight over the steel grids. Ash and dust came racing toward the sheets with the air, but were blocked by the cloth. Dribbles of dry dust fell to earth in micro avalanches of ash. The haphazard pre-filters the mechanical team had taped on were working as intended. When HEP came on, the same thing happened on each car, where sheets protected main filters that cleaned the air people in the train needed to breathe.

Another cheer rang out when the power came on in the train. To feel the breeze of warm conditioned air was exhilarating after a week of stale stench. Toilets flushed for the first time in a week. Thomas and Ron were ready to cook everything they could as fast as possible in the kitchen. Anything that had been raw was fried up fast. Dan, Tim, and other crew members flipped breakers so that lights had full power. Suddenly, the Zephyr started to come alive.

Passengers and crew aboard the Zephyr were no longer isolated from the outside world. Thanks to a massive constellation of low-earth satellites, communication with friends and family was possible with fully functional Wi-Fi. Electrical outlets were working, allowing everyone to recharge their phones. More importantly, the crew now had all kinds of experts to help them make the right decisions that could get everyone on the Zephyr to safety.

Of greatest importance to the crew was learning all they could about their predicament as fast as possible. Railroad officials in the engineering department were ready. UPR people were based in Omaha, Nebraska.

Omaha had been hit hard by ash, but not as badly as Colorado, because the prevailing southeast winds the day of the Yellowstone eruption took the bulk of the material down the spine of the Rockies, rather than east to the Midwest. Power grids were out, but back-up generators allowed the hub of railroad information to function. The dispatching center had turned into something like mission control guiding a spacecraft in distress.

Nick remembered the story of Apollo 13 and Astronaut James Lovell in the book *Lost Moon*. He thought, *We will do what he did— we'll use those people in Omaha for all they're worth.*

The railroad had assembled all the data they could think of to help the stricken train get to safety. A conference call was planned for high noon mountain time. René's laptop computer was set up in the diner. Larry, Nick, René, and Jake were all seated in front of the monitor at 11:59 a.m. The rest of the car was filled with other staff and team leaders. It was less than an hour after Nick's "small step," and the video Randal Keaton had taken of that moment was already trending worldwide, thanks to the social media prowess of Marshall Knight.

The screen flickered. A ringing sound was answered by René tapping the keyboard. Suddenly there were live faces from beyond the deadly grip of Yellowstone. A woman appeared on the screen. She was the CEO of the UPR. With her were several people sporting name tags on lanyards. They were dressed and groomed far less formally than usual, and the men had several days' worth of stubble on their faces.

This is tough on them too, Nick thought.

Still more people appeared on the conference call—mostly from Washington, DC, and the train maintenance shops in Delaware and Indiana. After quick introductions and expressions of elation that the Zephyr and its passengers had miraculously survived the initial blast of Yellowstone, the group got down to business.

"What is the status of the world out there as it relates to us getting rescued?" Larry asked.

The CEO of the UPR, Brenda Bradford, spoke up. "We have with us Dr. Johnston from the United States Geological Survey. He will fill you in."

Johnston got right to it. "The eruption of Yellowstone last Monday was five times more destructive than any geological event ever recorded in human history. In addition, five other magma chambers simultaneously exploded through the surface of the earth in Wyoming and

Colorado. We believe that altogether about 1,500 cubic miles of debris were thrust into the air. Deadly sulfur dioxide levels were far greater than we expected. Apparently, there is a reason they called it *Yellow*stone. The jet stream at the time of the blasts took much of the effects primarily southeast—right toward you and Denver. The combination of the blasts itself, lava missiles, toxic gas, and choking ash created a dead zone shaped like a football that extends over all of Wyoming, most of Colorado, half of Idaho and Montana, some of western Nebraska and Kansas, and a sizable chunk of Utah. Within that dead zone, only a handful of survivors have been able to contact the outside world. Nearly everything that was combustible burned. Your train is by far the largest group of survivors in the dead zone, at least that we know of at this time. We expect the final death toll to be over ten million people. On the fringe of the dead zone, the US government, and everyone else, are trying to help twenty million people survive and get to safer places. That fringe area is double the size of the dead zone and basically the same shape. Beyond that, there is a thick layer of ash and weak sunlight, but nothing immediately life threatening."

"Thank you, Dr. Johnston," Bradford said and continued, "Obviously, since we received the call that you were alive, we have been working nonstop to figure out a way to help you get out of the dead zone as quickly as possible. But there is a lot we do not know yet. All imaging from satellites is blocked by stratospheric haze, so we can't tell you the status of roads, tracks, or anything else. All of our ground-based communications systems and electrical data from the dead zone have failed. Worse yet, the Caldera continues to emit gas and ash. It is not nearly as bad as the initial eruption, but still enormous. We cannot fly supplies to you because the particulates in the air ruin airplane engines and helicopter rotors within minutes. It's like trying to fly through sandpaper. It's not just in the dead zone. All aviation around the globe is currently grounded. Piled up ash on roads that are jammed with burned-out cars hopelessly block every access route. A great number of bridges have collapsed. In other words, at least for a while, we simply have no way of helping you. You are on your own."

Another railroad official spoke next. "We are trying to get through by rail from the east to Denver. Needless to say, coming down from the north, from Cheyenne, is, well, there is no Cheyenne anymore. We have not yet made it west to Holdrege, Nebraska, on the Hastings Subdivision because of wrecked track and disabled trains. The old line from Kansas City to Denver is blocked east of the Colorado border. Further south, no train has gotten beyond Dodge City. Straight south we are working on crossing Raton Pass, but it's a long, slow, dirty slog. The good news is the railroads are doing better than paved roads."

Nick listened with laser focus. What he had just heard, combined with the total destruction of his immediate surroundings, did not give cause for optimism. His first thought was how accurate Dr. Sayer's predictions had been. Nick then asked, "How long do we need to hold on here before rescuers can reach us?"

Bradford sat silent with a grim expression on her face.

Angela Lee answered. She was a deputy with the Federal Emergency Management Agency, FEMA. She introduced herself as an invitee of the UPR. She gave the news everyone was afraid of. "I am deeply sorry to say that we have no projection for rescue. Every resource we have is being taxed beyond its limits as we try to aid the millions of people on the fringe of the dead zone. We are weeks away, at best, from getting to Denver with any substantive government resources."

"My God!" René said.

Nick looked at her and then back at the screen. "Mrs. Lee, we don't *have* weeks. We did good just to survive in the tunnel to this point. We need food, clean water, fuel, and medication."

A long pause ensued.

Larry was ready to deal with the situation as it was. He spoke. "Mrs. Bradford, with all due respect, we are going to need some help here. Just saying you are trying is not good enough."

Another awkward moment of silence.

"If we can't get to you, what do you want us to do?" Bradford asked.

Larry was quick to fire back, "First, we need to have people available to talk us through mechanically, keeping this train running."

An official in Wilmington, Delaware, spoke up and said the passenger railroad had a top team of their best mechanics on locomotives and bi-level cars at the ready 24/7.

"Great, thank you. Next we need to know everything about the status of the tracks before the eruption, and your best guess as to what that status might be now. In other words, do we have any chance of getting this train back to Denver?"

Bradford called on a UPR man, "Jack?"

The man started talking. "Jack Steele here. We had two trains on the Moffat Sub. west of North Yard at 9:40 a.m. on Labor Day, when the earthquake and eruption first began. One was a rail train, you know, a train full of continuously welded rail that was to be installed, a work train. That one was tied down on the Crescent siding. It should still be sitting there. The other train is an empty coal train. We think it stopped just west of the west siding switch at Crescent. In general, all the Class 1 railroads tried to get trains off the main lines and tied down. The Federal Railroad Administration asked us to keep main lines clear as much as possible. Crews on the freight trains knew this before the ash cloud hit them. Sadly, all communication ended shortly after 10:30 a.m. that day. We don't know for sure where trains are now, or their status. What we do know is that there wasn't room in Crescent for the rail train and the coal train. The empty coal train was still in the block west of the Crescent siding when our screens went blank."

"Okay," Larry said, "is there a clear track through North Yard for us to get back to Union Station?"

Nick jumped in, "Larry, we don't even know if Union Station is there anymore. Let's not get ahead of ourselves."

Larry was getting impatient. "I just want to know where we're going, that's all."

Brenda Bradford interrupted the frustrated Zephyr crew with decisive and blunt realities. "We don't know where you should eventually go with your train—yet. We don't know where you will find supplies—yet. We don't know what you will find along the way—yet. What we do know for starters is that you have to make it to Denver. That is the only way you have any chance of getting out of the dead zone alive."

Nick was ready to reassert himself as overall leader, for better or worse. "Good questions, Larry. I think we know our orders: get to Denver with what we've got, whatever it takes. With luck, someone will have help waiting for us before we get down the hill."

Bradford was relieved to hear a bit of confidence and clarity, saying, "That sums it up."

Contemplating what most people would consider nearly hopeless circumstances, the conductor of the Zephyr tried to end the call on a confident note. "Thank you for your time. We will make effective use of the wisdom your people have. We will make it to Denver. We got this!"

Bradford and the others on the call wished the Zephyr crew and passengers good luck and the call ended.

The whole Zephyr staff sat in stunned silence for a moment in the diner. They had a few choice words about being left to fend for themselves. After the mental venting, they got down to crafting a plan to get everyone back to Denver alive.

Nick addressed the entire group in the diner, "Sounds to me like they are a bit overwhelmed. We are just gonna do what we have to do on our own. Step one is to wye the engines, then we set out the Silver Sky. Finally we'll start pushing through the ash down the hill."

After a few private logistical briefings, the staff left to gather their respective teams and get to work.

Ash was thick, dry, hot, and heavy. From rolling over just a few hundred yards of track, they knew that the sticky gray material was too heavy to push with train cars leading the way.

"We have to have the locomotives on point, and they have to have a bigger, tougher plow." Nick told Larry and the mechanical team to work on that. Nick then addressed Jim, Brewster, Jennifer, Noah, James, Sean, Alex, Luke, and the others from the Railroad Museum's Silver Sky. He was blunt and to the point. "The Silver Sky is severely damaged. We need to get it out of the way. We have to set it out and leave it here."

Grim-faced railfans looked at their conductor and friend. They had learned to trust Nick's judgment, but couldn't believe what he just said.

After a long silence, Harry Shaffer, the man who had raised most of the money to restore the car, spoke. "Listen everyone, I know how badly this hurts. But the train car is still just a thing. It is meaningless compared to one single human life. If Nick says it's a problem, it has to go. When we can, we will be back for it again."

None of the heartbroken enthusiasts protested.

Nick addressed the entire train with the PA. He told them about the call with CEO Bradford, and how they were alone—at least as far as Denver, maybe even further. He asked that they all contribute as they can on their teams.

Many people were not listening to Nick's announcement. They were checking texts, emails, and voice mails and making phone calls. Some found joy, but many were in agony and sorrow. Cries of grief-stricken people could be heard in every car.

I can't do this yet, Nick thought to himself as he contemplated trying to learn the fate of his own family.

René, and most of the other staff, did not wait. They made the calls. Rene's husband John was doing some work in Singapore. He was fine and overjoyed to hear that his wife survived the cataclysm. He begged her to do whatever it took to get herself to safety. She knew what he meant by that.

The On-Board-Services employees were from Chicago or further east, so most of their people had survived thus far. Ron met Nick in the corridor of a sleeping car.

Nick asked, "Have you heard from your family?"

"Yes, we just spoke on the phone. Mom, Dad, and my sister are okay."

Nick smiled for his friend and said, "Oh, man, Ron, that is great news!"

Ron then asked, "What about Beatrice?"

Nick looked at his friend stoically. "The odds are not good. I am terrified, to tell you the truth. When the time is right, I will try to reach my family, but right now I have a job to do."

Ron gave his friend some encouraging words before the two went in opposite directions through the narrow passageway.

CHAPTER 22

WYE

"Railroading is simple; trains go from point A to point B. It is the parts in between that can get complicated."

—CB

Christina had moved to the lead unit, the 313, while Larry attended the conference call. Nick called her on the radio. She was excited that the satellite phones reached the dispatching center. But the message she got was grim. "Christina, this is Nick. We have a problem. The bolster on the Silver Sky looks cracked, and debris from the gate is jammed in tight. We have to set the car out."

"Okay, we need to do a runaround and wye anyway. We can set it out on the siding from the east," she replied.

Nick answered, "Agreed. OUT."

Larry was back on the 313 shortly after the call. He took over that engine while Christina went to the 309. "313 to Nick. OVER."

Nick replied, "Go. OVER."

The engineer never willingly broke a railroad rule in his life, and he did not want to start now. "We need permission to use the wye and authority on the main and siding. OVER."

Nick was mildly humored by the formality, considering the situation, but he agreed. Nick called Omaha on the phone. The answer came from Jack Steele. Having been a dispatcher earlier in his career, Jack was well versed in proper procedure.

"Train Number 5, you have authority to work between Milepost

58 and Prospect Junction on all tracks as needed without further permission. Possible trains ahead. OVER."

Jack then made up a new level of track authority to keep the train moving. "And Number 5, you have permission to use whatever means are required to get by all obstacles. OVER."

Nick replied, "Roger that," and repeated the instructions as required by rules. Nick asked if the wye was still safe to use before the eruption. He had not seen an engine use it in years.

Jack asked him to stand by for a few minutes.

In Jack's contacts list, he found the person in charge of track maintenance on the Moffat subdivision, a man he didn't know, named Jake. *He's probably dead, but I'll try*, Jack thought as he dialed the number.

Seconds later, Jake's phone rang. "Hello, Jake speaking," he answered.

Surprised that someone answered, Jack Steele started talking. He wanted to find out what to tell Nick about the wye.

"What? You're asking me? I'm on that train right now. Sure, the wye is serviceable. I will tell Nick and the crew myself."

René and Jake had track teams ready to get off the train and start working on the planned wye and runaround move. The assistant conductor got on the PA. "This is the time, guys . Track teams, open your doors, and go to work." She keyed her railroad radio mic and requested three-point protection from the engineers. HEP power went down on the train.

For everyone on board it was a depressing moment, almost like PTSD. To lose power after only an hour was something they all had to get used to.

Brake pipe and main reservoir angle cocks between the 309 and baggage car were closed. Christina and Larry ran through the locomotive departure tests for each unit. Once assured that both engines were working perfectly, they were ready to roll. Retaining pins were pulled and placed on their respective hooks.

René pulled up on the pin lifter lever of the locomotive. Her jacket caught on a jagged piece of steel sticking out from the end of the baggage car. She used her other hand to release herself. She saw that the whole side of the car was scraped and thought, *It must have hit rocks in the tunnel during the earthquake.*

The lever lifted easily and released the locking mechanism. She told Larry and Christina that she was releasing three-point protection. They acknowledged the release. Then came the time for the power of the Zephyr to finally move under its own tractive effort.

"René to the 313, cuts are made. Pin is lifted. Pull forward easy. OVER."

Drive wheels on the locomotives had not been engaged for a week. Larry fully activated the independent engine brakes and set the reverser to FORWARD. He released the parking brake and pulled the throttle to notch 1. Amps on the meter rose. Ever so carefully, the most experienced locomotive engineer in the system feathered off the independent brake. The lead unit eased forward and yanked on the knuckle of the 309. The 309 bumped westward into its leader. Both engines were powering wheels! The locomotive lash-up moved forward, leaving the train behind. The two mighty diesels rolled past the points of the west East Portal siding switch. Jake led his team forward through nearly waist-deep ash from the vestibule of the 540 car, past the baggage car, and to the switch about 100 yards ahead.

After Larry got the engines past the control point, Track Team #1 began immediately digging and sweeping out the switch as they had been taught. They were all looking at the rail to see how much damage the heat of the fallout and fires had done. "It don't look too bad," Jake said over the radio.

On the other end of the train track, teams #2 and #3 worked on the wye switches. Inside the train, people with phones connected to satellites were passing them around to those who did not have a connection. This was their first connection to the electronic age in nearly a week. For some of the younger people on the train, this had been their first prolonged separation from illuminated screens. At a time when it seemed almost every form of higher technology failed, a simple phone call was a welcome relief. Most phones had been out of battery, but the sixty minutes of HEP before the wye operation began recharged them enough for a few calls.

As instructed, folks who were making the critical calls that would inform them of loved ones, of life and death, sought privacy before pressing the SEND button. Senator and Mrs. Jackson, in a deluxe room, were able to speak with their sons for the first time. The grown man in Maryland was overjoyed to hear his parents' voices, and know for sure that they were still alive. As the Jacksons were on the phone, they heard grief-stricken moans from the next room. The loss and heartache Jay and Diana had tried to prepare themselves for came to pass. Not one member of the happy family they had just seen on the Denver platform had survived.

René was at the west East Portal siding switch lock, which was covered by more than three feet of ash. The track team dug down to the mechanism in no time. Heat and fire had charred all the paint off the shrouds covering the gears of the switch. The padlock itself was blackened. René inserted her key. After a lot of wiggling, she managed to get it to open. She flipped the power lever to HAND, and tried to move the points of the switch with the main lever. She needed help to get it to start moving. Metal warps in hot temperatures, but the railroad uses thick heavy parts that can withstand an inferno. The switch, for the most part, maintained functionality. Zach was right there along with two of the former CU Buffs. Together they got the switch thrown to line it for the siding track.

The mechanical team installed an "ADA ramp plow" to the back of the 309. The bottom of the plow was just millimeters from the top of the rail. Once the work was finished, René got on the radio. "313, okay to go east to the west wye switch. OVER." Christina began plowing fresh ash.

Nick was watching the plow and wheels. "Using wheelchair ramps as plows turns out to be a good idea," he said on the radio, as he walked with the leading edge of the 309. He was almost running as he bounded through the deep ash. He keyed his radio, "Slow down Larry, I can only go at ash speed."

Christina was amused. "Is that a thing? Ash speed?"

"Yes," Nick answered, "It's a brand new thing. OVER."

Larry answered his conductor, "Roger that—ash speed, I like it. OUT."

Track team #2 had the west wye switch dug out and mostly clean, but there was a problem. Wooden ties. Only one year before, the UPR had invested heavily to put in all-concrete ties on the main line and sidings between Denver and Fraser. But that did not include house tracks and other auxiliary tracks, like the Rollins Pass wye. Those 100-year-old wooden ties were burned badly, leaving the underside of tie plates exposed.

Nick had a chat with Jake about the issue.

"I say go for it, slow like. Leave the ash packed around the rails."

"To me, it looks like just surface burning," said Jake.

Nick managed the lock on the manual switch stand and its electric lock, a device that is designed to set off stop signals on the siding when the wye switch is not closed. Both still worked. The fire had warped the rails some. It took real strength with crowbars to bend the switch points to line into the wye. The track team found the metal derail device buried just beyond the switch. Nick unlocked it and flipped it off the rail. They were ready.

"Okay, Larry, go east slowly. We have to see if these burned ties will still hold rail," Nick ordered.

"You want ash speed? OVER." Larry had wanted to use the new term.

"Funny guy, no, slower, one car at a time. OVER." Nick was glad to be back into the normal banter with his engineers.

Engine wheel flanges pressed against the inside of the points on the switch. The rail moved and groaned.

"It's holding up!" Nick yelled up to Christina, who was looking down from the window of the 309.

Track teams #2 and #3 worked fast to clear the north wye switch and other derail device. Nick threw the switches as needed. The locomotives plowed their way to clear the north switch.

Several of the Silver Sky gang were helping on the track teams. Noah looked at Brewster, who had a wistful gleam in his eye. "I was just thinking," he said to the young train fan, "This is the first time since 1928 that the power of a main line passenger train has started up Rollins Pass."

Noah looked at the engines, then at the rail. It was stamped with the year it was forged, 1913. "Well noted for the historical log," Noah said.

The ash was so deep and thick near the end of the tail track of the wye that the engines could barely clear the north switch. Once the points were unobstructed by the locomotives, it was thrown for the east leg of the wye.

Larry in the 313 was back in the lead. He set the reverser to FOR-WARD and eased it slowly into the switch. Nick was a bit concerned because the points had not seated perfectly, but the power tracked through without trouble. The procession went east to the next wye switch connected to East Portal Siding, and then back to the main track, nearly a mile east of the Zephyr passenger cars. The rail was definitely wavy from the intense heat of the eruption, but the clips held them to the ties.

Dr. Sayers explained that ash worked to insulate the rail and put out tie fires, like a blanket being wrapped around a burning person. In spite of that, the rails had still gotten very hot—at least for a while. There was no way to know if the tracks were still in gauge.

Jake made the call to have a walking inspection preceding all movements.

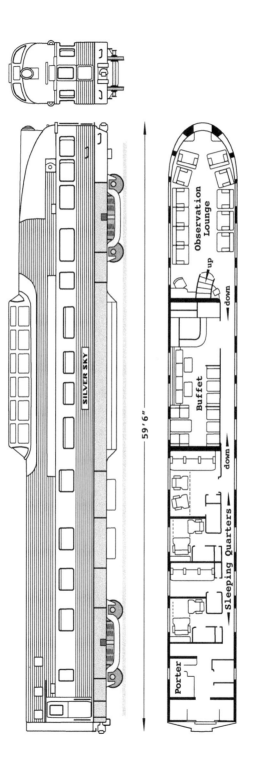

SILVER SKY

59' 6"

Observation
Lounge

Buffet

Sleeping Quarters

Porter

up

down

down

CHAPTER 23

GOODBYE TO THE SKY

"A thing of beauty is a joy for ever: its loveliness increases; it will never pass into nothingness."

—John Keats

The Silver Sky crew was busy getting their beloved car ready to be discarded. They took every resource they could imagine that might prove helpful. The demolished gate of the tunnel was peeled off the rounded end of the car and set aside. The makeshift plow was taken off. Tools, extra air hoses, HEP cables, their FDA-approved 100-foot water hose with "water point" adaptor, two buckets, all the linens, dishes, cushions, chairs, the vacuum cleaner, everything that wasn't bolted down, and some that were, were salvaged. Even the big 12 volt batteries were taken off. All of it was laid in the ash next to the main track. The Zephyr could stop and pick up what was needed as they passed.

Nick's railroad phone rang. Jack Steele from the UPR Operations Department was calling. "Nick, we've been doing the math. You should have enough fuel to make it to Denver no problem, but it might take a long time, and a lot of power to push through the ash. So you have to conserve as much fuel as possible. Don't run HEP if you don't have to. If you find more fuel—anywhere, take it."

Nick wondered how his locomotives, which had just been topped off in Denver, could have fuel issues when they only had to go downhill fifty miles. "Got it, go sparingly on the diesel," he answered.

The knuckle on the tail end of the Silver Sky was opened. Nick and

Christina worked together to bring the power back up the main track and make a joint between the 309 and the Sky. At the other end of the car, René was ready to separate the Sky from the rest of the Zephyr.

After René made all the cuts to the hoses and HEP cables, the 313 pulled the Silver Sky away from the Zephyr for the last time. Clearly the rear truck of the car was not rolling straight. The screeching from the flanges on the ball of the rail was unsettling. With separation from the train, the crew was able to go back and forth enough to free the gate debris from the underside of the car.

The rear truck was badly bent and cracked, but it held together long enough to get through the switch points and into the East Portal siding. To conserve fuel, the crew left the Sky just beyond the fouling point, where a passing train would not sideswipe the car. The hand brake was tied, chocks were placed under each wheel, and a chain was locked around an axle and the rail. Passenger doors were locked (even though two windows were broken in). Nick and Larry pulled the power away to the east.

Both engines passed over the east East Portal switch. Nick threw the switch back to the main line. They headed back west to the train waiting for them on the main track. Nick had Larry stop the engines as they passed the now-abandoned Silver Sky. Alex was with them.

Nick asked Alex how much fuel was on that car. "Fifty gallons of diesel," Alex answered.

"Perfect," Nick said, "let's siphon it out and dump it in our tanks.

"Good thinking," Alex responded.

Knowing what you want to do was often easier than knowing how to do it. The fuel tank on the Sky did not have an easy way for the crew to drain it. The liquid had to be sucked out. The only hose they had was meant for drinking water. Larry called René to send the mechanical team to the engines—a long walk through the ash.

Doug Klaus overheard René discussing the problem of removing the fuel. He gathered a few of his tools into his bucket, exited the train, and started walking. He knew his big Hilti hammer drill and one-inch steel bit were the key implements for the job.

As he left the train for the Sky, René stopped him. "How much does that weigh?" she asked.

"Oh, about forty pounds," Doug answered.

She looked at him, frowning. "Then your tool bucket weighed way more than fifty pounds, like you told me on the platform in Denver." René hated nothing more than to be lied to.

Doug was unfazed. "No, Ma'am. It was fifty pounds on the button. I put my clothes with the drill to lighten the tool bucket. I put the other tools in my backpack and suitcase. Each one was fifty pounds." He smirked at René.

With a motherly look of pleased disapproval, she said, "Fine. Just get going."

Nick told the mechanical team not to use the water hose. He didn't want it contaminated with petroleum, ruining it for drinking water. They might need it later. He suggested they use the backup hose Dave put in the 512 car storage locker after making the joint with the Silver Sky back in Denver. The team tried Nick's idea, but the two-inch air hose was too fat to fit through the inlet of the Silver Sky tank. They were trying to decide what to do when Doug showed up.

"Guys, let me use my drill to punch a hole in the bottom of the tank. We can fill buckets to transfer the fuel to the engines."

Everyone agreed that Doug's out-of-the-box thinking was perfectly brilliant. The battery-powered drill was awesome; the hole was bored through in seconds. Fuel gushed out into a waiting bucket. When that bucket was full, Sean's gloved hand plugged the hole in the tank. The contents of the bucket were dumped into the fill pipe on the 313. The process took twelve trips from the car on the siding track to the engines on the mainline. The fuel gauge on the 313 barely moved, even though they added forty-eight extra gallons. All activity on the private car was finished. The 313 and the 309 proceeded west to pick up the Zephyr.

Ben Batton, curator of the Colorado Railroad Museum and primary leader of the Silver Sky restoration project, was the last to descend the vestibule steps and leave the beloved train car. Suddenly the Silver Sky was left still, silent, and alone. Its fate was unknown. There it sat at 9,000 feet above sea level, axel deep in a sea of gray ash. Her marker lights were dark, interior stripped, skin battered, and glass shattered—an inglorious end to the most glamorous train car of the golden age of passenger railroading.

"We have our hatchet," Nick said to Doug on the short ride back to the Zephyr.

"Huh?" Doug replied.

Nick explained, "I read a book with my son when he was in middle school. *Hatchet* was about a kid who crash landed a small airplane in the Canadian wilderness. He was alone. His only tool was a hatchet. That one tool gave him what he needed to survive until a rescuer arrived. Your bucket of tools is our hatchet."

"Dope!" replied Doug with a modest smile.

Minutes later, the engines were hooked up to the Zephyr. Nick and René plugged in the HEP cables and buckled the air hoses.

Nick ordered, "Light up the HEP 313. OVER."

Christina hit the button in 309. RPMs jumped, and the amber HEP cab light came on. Inside the train, cheers rang out again.

Power to the wall outlets was restored. Phones, computers, and other devices started recharging. The kitchen grill and microwaves were cooking. Surprisingly, the climate control systems in the cars turned on the heaters. No one had noticed that the outside temperature was dropping below normal for early September.

Nick and René walked both sides of the train during an activation of the brakes and walked back to witness a brake release while Larry held engine brakes tight with the independent lever. Each brake was working. The mechanical team double-checked all the wheel cleaners they installed.

Before leaving east portal, Charlie, the junior UPR track maintenance guy, wanted to dig through the ruins of the sheds for useful tools. His team found rock bars, spike pullers, rail cutting wheels, several chains, picks, shovels, re-railer plates, and many other items. All the wooden or fiberglass handles had burned away, but a few tools had intact steel shafts.

Some of the people on track team #1 were trying to cut off poles from a chain-link fence for shovel handles. Doug had a Sawzall that cut off ten shafts before the last of his blades were rendered useless. One thing they did not find was a single functioning engine or motor of any type. Every gas tank was either blown up or melted. All wiring and cowlings were burnt to uselessness. Aluminum engine blocks were hopelessly warped. Only the thick, hard hand tools were still valuable.

Every tool they found was put on the 512 coach car. Fence poles were bolted to tool heads with Doug's drill and scavenged screws from the interior of the Zephyr train cars. Floor carpet was cut and taped around the poles for a better grip.

A snow plow designed for a pickup truck was found under the ash. It was sitting by what had been a railroad shed. Twenty people from the mechanical team heaved that perfectly shaped piece of steel and fixed it to the front of the 313 with fence wire and chains.

L.T. Miller and other men in the Amish clan showed the team how to use chains wrapped under the plow, and around the shoulders of the people on both sides, to easily manage the burden. The plow was twice as big as the regular plow on the locomotive. With luck, that salvaged piece of steel would clear their path to Denver.

CHAPTER 24

THE SCREAM

"Vitriolic ignorance often results in eternal silence."

—CB

The train was finally ready to begin the descent to Denver. The track teams sent two people ahead of the train on foot. Jake cut a piece of interior aluminum trim from the 512 car exactly four feet, eight-and-a-half inches long. The plan was for two track scouts to use that template to measure the gauge of the rails. The teams would use their feet to feel the rail through the ash. If anything started to feel wrong, they'd dig it out to test the width between rails. The first stop was to pick up salvaged supplies from the Silver Sky. All those items were placed in the baggage car.

It was fifty rail miles to Prospect Junction in Downtown Denver from East Portal siding and the Moffat Tunnel. The train began moving east as they rounded the first turn. Moffat Tunnel, that incredible refuge that saved everyone aboard the Zephyr, was fading from view.

Brewster stood in the vestibule of the 540 car. Out loud, he said, "Good-bye, Mr. Moffat, we all thank you."

After picking up the Silver Sky supplies, it took over an hour to go two miles, performing Jake's foot rail inspection as they went. Some drifts of ash were too deep to get a good sense of width between the rails with just kicking. Holes were dug every ten feet. Though slow and tedious, no serious anomalies were found.

Visibility through the hazy ash was still only about 200 feet. The train was nearing the first bridge. That span went over Rollins Pass Road. The powerfully built and recently updated bridge held up well. It was passable, but an ominous sight came into view as the engines crossed over the bridge. Cars, trucks, and jeeps were lined east of the bridge bumper to bumper as far as the eye could see through the haze.

Some members of the track team scurried down the slope to see what had happened. Two charred and crumpled vehicles, now covered in ash, were wedged into the narrow passage under the tracks. It looked like they had collided, thus blocking the path to Moffat Tunnel. Motorists trying to find refuge from the firestorm bearing down on them from the north had been trapped east of the tunnel. With the road blocked, those desperate people had been baked alive while trying to breathe toxic sulfur dioxide.

All the vehicles were completely destroyed. No machine was going to ever run again that wasn't protected by a bomb-proof bunker when the volcanic cloud hit. Everyone on the train knew right then that the Zephyr was their only hope of getting out of the mountains. Some passengers only realized at that moment what a protective cocoon Moffat Tunnel had been.

Track team investigators who went to the road saw that only one vehicle was on the west side of the crash—a pickup truck. They looked inside at a shocking sight. Although the ash made shapes hard to distinguish, there was no mistaking three human skulls in the cab. The sight was grizzly, like a scene from an apocalyptic horror film.

Several others came down to get a look.

"That sure looks like it could have been the truck Karen Allen took off in," Paul Brown commented.

"Then that must be her in the back seat," Knut said. They all looked at the sobering sight of her skull kinked back with her jaw wide open, as if frozen in a terrifying death scream.

After a long look, they all trudged back up the hill to the bridge and the Zephyr. As they went, Knut spoke to Nick. "All the people in those other cars—they would all be alive with us now if there had not been a crash right under the bridge."

Nick thought for a moment then answered, "Probably, but if they all made it into the tunnel, they would have over-taxed the air supply and made us run out of food too quickly. It might just be that the car wreck, and the reckless abandon that caused it, is why we'll make it back to civilization."

For both men, and everyone else on the Zephyr, it was impossible to know what might have been. Regardless, it didn't change the way things were, or their mission. They had to move on, on to where they would be rescued.

CHAPTER 25

VOICEMAIL AND TEXTS

"Grief and resilience live together."

—Michelle Obama

Darkness was falling. They had worked an entire day and only progressed four miles from the tunnel. This was going to be an awfully long trip. To save fuel, Christina shut down HEP. The lights on the Zephyr were back to half off. Not as bad as the way it was during those long, dark days spent inside Moffat Tunnel, but depressing nonetheless. At least everyone knew the batteries were recharged, and power would come on again at regular intervals.

People were receiving calls and messages from loved ones and friends in droves. Christina made a rare appearance in the parlor car. She wanted to report that she had heard from Mary and Margaret, the station agents that left for Hawaii the morning of the eruption. They had talked on the phone just minutes before. She said the two couples made it to the airport, and were on their airplane when the earthquake hit.

Once the news about Yellowstone exploding circulated through Denver International Airport, people rushed for any plane they could get on. Planes took off as fast and close together as possible. Landing gear blasted over big cracks in runways and taxiways, which had been opened up by the earthquake.

Near Concourse A, the wingtips of two planes collided, and both machines burst into flames. Air traffic control and ground control towers had collapsed, so there was no guidance—just a mad dash for the sky. The plane Mary, Margaret, and their husbands were on was loaded down with twenty more people than it had seats. A push-back tractor driver shoved the plane away from the gate, got his vehicle out of the way, and was hoisted into the plane through an open door.

The bumpy, weaving race to a runway was harrowing. The aircraft was overloaded, but it got into the air. The plane headed straight southwest. Passengers could see the cloud of ash swallow the airport, and then the city behind them. The pilot tried to get around the west edge of the cloud, but it was too wide and fast. In a last ditch effort to save their lives, she turned abruptly south and made a full throttle race for Phoenix.

At 600 mph, the 737 was just able to stay ahead of the deadly wall billowing after them from the north. As miles passed, the intensity of the cloud diminished. They had to descend to Sky Harbor Airport because their fuel was running dangerously low. The airport was jammed with jets, but they found an open runway. The pilot drove the plane right into an open field next to the runway to free up space for more planes. The cloud got there, but it was weak. The airplane had outrun certain death. Everyone aboard, including Christina's friends, had survived.

Nick felt some joy that their friends cheated death—a welcome bit of good news in the face of so many tragedies being realized by other passengers and staff on the Zephyr. Finally the time had come. He went to his room at midnight to do what he had dreaded for a week.

He picked up his private phone, which had to be turned off per FRA regulations while he was working, and turned it on. His hand was shaking. The screen read, "12 new text messages. Voice mail received."

Nick hit the speed dial button for the voicemail account set up just for his wife and daughter, mostly to coordinate rides to school and other logistical stuff. The familiar automated voice spoke, "Seven new messages, and one saved message."

First message: "Hey, Dad, this is Juliette. There was just a really big earthquake or something. We are waiting in the storm shelter at school. Mr. Nelson and Ms. Andrea are still with us. The other kids from the carpool are still here too. Nobody's parents can get to us. Everybody is really scared. I tried to call Mom. I hope you are okay. Call me as soon as you can. Love you."

Next message: "Nick, I am on my way to try and get Juliette, but the roads are jammed. NPR says Yellowstone blew up, and an ash cloud is going to cover us soon. I don't know what to do, Nick. Damn it! I'm just gonna try and drive through the prairie. I love you!"

Next message: *Click*

Next message: "Mr. Jay, this is Juliette's orchestra teacher, Mr. Nelson calling. Listen, things are not good here. You have to get your daughter, and the others if you can. Ms. Andrea and I will stay with all the students till the last one is picked up, but please hurry! Thanks."

Next message: "Okay, Dad, Juliette again. So now there is, like, this huge cloud and everything is starting to burn. I'm really scared. Come get me please! Hurry!"

Next message: "Nick, the car is covered in dust, and I can't see a thing. There is no way I can make it to the school. This might be it. It is getting really hot. *BOOM! AHHH!* The car next to me just blew up. I love you forever, Nick . . . I've loved every single day with you!" *Click*.

Next message: "Dad, am I going to die? *Sniff.* I'm afraid! Mom won't answer her phone (background sound of Ms. Andrea's panicked voice, saying, 'Just huddle together with me and Mr. Nelson in the corner, kids—c'mon'). The smoke is too thick. Help me, Daddy, please help me." *Click*.

"You have no more messages." *Click*

Though Nick knew he'd hear something like what he just listened to, he had no way to prepare his heart for the reality of it. His phone fell to the floor and he slumped to his knees. He heard himself make the same indescribable grief moans he heard coming from sleeping car rooms earlier that day. His mind was in a fog; he had not even remembered to close the door. Thirty minutes had passed when Reagan walked by his door with his mother. Claire took her son on walks the length of the train when he got fidgety. The boy saw Nick dissolved in grief and gently took Nick's hand. He opened one of Nick's fingers. Then another, and so on. At the same time, he counted. "One, two, three, four, five."

Reagan told Nick, "Do that over and over and over. It helps me. It helps me. Just count. Just count."

Nick wrapped his other arm around the boy and sobbed.

After Reagan and Claire left to continue their walk, Nick called his grown sons. They both lived in Europe, so he was pretty sure they were fine. They all cried together. His sons had lost their mother and sister. They knew their father was in mortal danger, and there was nothing they could do, no flights back to the States, no ship they could catch. Even if they could get to the East Coast of North America, there was no way to get into the Dead Zone of Yellowstone. They were left to pray and try to motivate people to mount a rescue for the Zephyr.

Nick collapsed in tears again after hanging up.

Herman sensed the despair many were experiencing on the train. He told his parents, and his godfather and caregiver Rob, that he wanted to encourage everyone to carry on and survive. Herman had his dad, Mitch, write, "BE STRONG," on a headband. His mom Marta put it on Herman's head, and Rob rolled Herman through the entire train on the Stryker chair.

Another hour passed before Nick found enough composure to pick up his phone again. He had a few text messages waiting, most from his sons as they had frantically tried to find out his situation. The last text, from his oldest son, included a news clip that was only three hours old. The report was about the revelation to the world that the Zephyr had survived Yellowstone and was now trying to get out of the Dead Zone. Spontaneous prayers came from around the world for the survivors on the train in Colorado. People had gathered in churches, mosques, synagogues, temples, and other places of worship to beseech God's favor on behalf of the imperiled passengers and crew.

One congregation no longer praying was Nick's own home fellowship, Quaking Aspens Christian Church in Coal Creek Canyon. Nick was sure, from what he saw and heard so far, that everyone in his neighborhood was either dead or out of town. He saw a group text from his pastor, Neal Rosen, to all the church members, dated last Monday, Labor Day, at 10:20 a.m. Nick imagined the terror Neal must have felt at that moment.

Nick felt some comfort believing that, only moments after Neal pressed the SEND button, his soul was in Heaven. Nick knew Neal was fully aware that the end for him and his wife was upon them. Still the pastor had taken some of his last moments to reach out to others. It was a humbling experience for Nick to read Neal's note. Every poignant word touched him deeply.

Dear Brothers and Sisters of Quaking Aspens Church,

Our time is short. There is too much to say. You are loved. You are dear to the Lord, and to me. Know that no matter what befalls you, because of His great love we are not consumed (Lam. 3:22). I beg your forgiveness for the times I have failed to love you as Christ has loved you. I am grateful for each one of you, and I know that this ordeal is merely a momentary light affliction, and we'll soon experience together a glory beyond all comparison (2 Cor. 4:17–18). I'll see you soon, in His presence!

Pastor Neal and Shelly

CHAPTER 26

ON THE MOVE

"Few things are as alleviating as a moving train after a lengthy delay."

—CB

All the while, the train kept pushing east. After a few more miles of walking rail inspections, Jake decided the whole process was overkill. On straight stretches without bridges, the rail was almost certainly secured to the powerful concrete ties that United Pacific Railways paid so dearly for over the last year. Jake wanted to just push through the ash in those areas rather than slowly slog through by foot to inspect every inch of track. He suggested his idea to the Dispatching Center in Omaha.

The civil engineers calculated the thermal dynamic math. They agreed with Jake. Now Larry and Christina could plow forward without waiting for rail inspectors over much of the line. After a couple of minutes, Omaha called back and made a request, "Do not exceed four miles per hour. You still might have solid debris under the ash."

Larry felt like he was free! "Oh boy, four mph! Here we go!" he said sarcastically.

All the mechanical preparations were paying off. The plow and wheel tread scrapers were stopping ash from building up. Air intakes were staying relatively clean as long as the team beat the dust off the taped sheets at regular intervals. Bed rotations and food rations continued as they had in the tunnel. Three days' worth of food was left on the train. After that, everyone would go hungry.

Headlight beams made a very horizontal reflection through the ash. Track team #3 and Larry were straining to see if the Highway 119 bridge at Rollinsville had fallen on the tracks. Ash seemed thicker. News reports said that Yellowstone had another minor eruption—minor for Yellowstone. This latest explosion sent more ash into the air than all the Icelandic volcanoes for the last half-century combined. Visibility was down to only 100 feet after sunset. Omaha reported that they believed the sulfur dioxide levels were much lower than during the earlier eruption. So crews could still work outside, but they needed all the dust masks they could get to protect their lungs.

Larry knew they were getting close to the bridge when it was suddenly right in front of him, just a few feet away. "Larry to Nick, 119 is still standing, we're going through! OVER."

It was Nick's rest time in room 24. "Roger that, Larry, maybe this run won't be so tough after all. OUT."

Each time the train came to a cut or cliff, they encountered small rock slides, presumably caused by the initial earthquake. Between Moffat Tunnel and Rollinsville were only a few small slides. The plow easily busted through those. Other slides encountered east of the Highway 119 bridge required backbreaking hand work with sledgehammers and rock bars to clear.

Pushing forward only got tougher. Narrow Sphinx Canyon had ash six feet deep with avalanches of debris actively falling from the cliffs above. Nick set all the track teams to work at once to try to push through as fast as they could before the accumulating material was beyond their power to clear. Fortunately the canyon was short, and the muddy current of South Boulder Creek was still strong enough to carry away much of the ash. The Zephyr entered the short tunnel at the end of the canyon as wet, mucky ash and debris finally dammed up the flow of the river and began filling the chasm behind them.

Track teams rotated shifts as planned. Everyone was eager to get out of the mountains. Motivation among the workers was not an issue. Even so, it took hours to go a mile. As the pale light of Monday morning began to glow, the Zephyr was passing Lincoln Hills. That glorious historic resort was unrecognizable. Every building was reduced to nothing more than debris-filled foundations.

The ash was so heavy that the locomotive engineers had to add power up to notch three just to push through on track where normally the train would race downhill out of control within seconds without brakes. Each time the track teams had to dig through that heavy debris, friction was applied between their hands and the tools they were using.

Dr. Abraham in the medical clinic called for Nick. "We are getting loads of guys with severe blisters on their hands. You have got to find more gloves. Also most of the people outside are coughing their lungs out from the ash. The N95 masks alone are not good enough."

Conductor Nick, still in shock after his personal phone calls, made a PA announcement right away. "Folks, we need more gloves and masks. We are already using all the ones we had. So I am asking Jen and the linen team to sew up new work gloves and face coverings from whatever materials we've got. Thanks."

Within minutes, team leader Jen, Herman's Aunt Suzy, and his mother Marta were in the diner, ready to start stitching together safety gear. Several others, including Jay and Diana, and all the Amish women, showed up as well. They cut up the window curtains and turned them into the tough outer mittens. Dining car tablecloths were used for inner linings. Extra stitching was added to the palms to add strength and protection.

They worked fast, knowing how desperately the diggers needed them. Between all the sewing kits brought onboard by passengers, they had more than enough needles and thread to make hundreds of pairs of gloves. Ingrid, with her Austrian textile skills, joined the group. Bedsheets were turned into large face coverings. Most of the sewing team were glad to have a way to help further their cause.

Workers from the track teams came to the sewing team in the diner for fitting. The tables in the car resembled a nineteenth century sweatshop factory.

Zach came in to get his hands fitted. He had worked almost non-stop since the train departed the tunnel, but he did not have blisters yet because of the callouses built up over years of hard farm work in Iowa. Regardless, he went to Ingrid to have her trace around each curve of both hands. The two smiled as they chatted.

Lorette, the dining car LSA, saw it all. "Oh, I know that look," she said to Judith. The two coworkers giggled a bit.

CHAPTER 27

THE SURVIVALIST

"A hero does what has to be done to stop evil deeds before the evil act is done."

—CB

The tedious push through the ash went on. Nine hours had passed since Nick listened to his voice mails. Four people from track team #1 were in the 313 cab as they approached a bridge over South Boulder Creek. The locomotive was plowing ash to both sides of the track. They were at milepost 38.7. The four-person team climbed down and walked forward to begin probing the rail over the sixty-foot span. René led the group on the bridge. Shortly after they started working, a Silver Sky passenger named Hugh noticed something new. He took another look, removing his safety glasses to see better. "Tracks!" he yelled to the others.

They all looked up from their brooms and shovels incredulously.

"*Um*, Hugh, there are supposed to be tracks here; it's a railroad." René responded sarcastically. The others on the team laughed a bit.

"No, I mean human tracks. Look!" He pointed demonstrably. It was true. Two trails of what looked like human footprints showed through the deep ash coming from the hillside to the north. They were fresh.

"Someone survived!" Hugh said.

He looked closer to try and figure out where the tracks came from and where they were going. Whoever it was, they seemed to have come down to the railroad tracks and then went back up the hill to what would have been the forest, but now was just debris, ash, and charred tree stumps.

René keyed her mic. "Nick, you better come have a look at this. OVER."

Nick had to compartmentalize his anguish to get back on the job. He took a deep breath and got ready to answer. He thought about how relieved he was to have a fully charged radio again.

"This is Nick, on my way, René. OVER."

He walked through the train from the 540 car, now near the rear of the train, to the last coach, which was the new front behind the locomotives. He bound his mask around his face and raised his bandana over his nose. With glasses and gloves donned, he opened the door of the 512 car, stepped off, and began trudging through the ash alongside the train. He marched on past the engines. He inspected the sheets covering the air-intake grids as he went. Everything was working as planned.

So far, so good, he thought.

He got to the front of the engines and took the path the work party made just a few minutes earlier. The walk through the ash reminded him of a time just a few years prior when he was the conductor of the Ski Train. Deep snow had rendered a power-switch inoperable near the same location at the West Cliff control point. On that frosty morning, he walked through three feet of snow with his shovel in hand. It was a calm, cobalt-blue winter day in the Rockies with brisk air hovering 5 degrees below zero. He remembered his breath crystallizing in front of him. Today it was a struggle just to get a deep breath of air at all through the filtration on his face. The temperature was about 45 degrees, but the ash made everything feel hotter.

Nick got to the bridge to find René's team idle and leaning on the long handles of their tools. *This is bad if they can't keep working*, he thought.

Nick assumed the bridge had severe damage. He got to the group, but before he could ask what was wrong, René began to speak, "Look at that," pointing at the mysterious man-made tracks though the ash.

Nick's first reaction was to wonder who left the group to go on a nature hike. But all four people in the work party were where they were supposed to be. He quickly realized what was so exciting to the work group; they were not alone! Others had survived the earthquake, ash, and fires.

"Anybody out there?" Nick yelled in the direction of the disappearing tracks. No answer.

Hugh chimed in louder, "HELLO! ANYBODY THERE?"

Two dark figures started moving in the gray landscape. People! Survivors! The figures continued walking closer.

"Boy, are we glad to see you!" René yelled to the survivors, walking cautiously toward them. The walkers didn't say a word. They were about thirty yards away when the work party began to have defensive feelings regarding the silent moving figures. Judging from the way they walked, it was almost certainly two men. As the pair approached, it was clear that both were carrying assault rifles in a ready position.

"It's okay; we are from the train. We were in the Moffat Tunnel. You can come with us," Nick yelled out as the men were now only twenty feet away.

The armed men were ready to shoot. Both had one hand on the barrel and the other at the trigger, with the stock already up against the shoulder. Still not a word.

Nick and René felt a piercing dread when they recognized one of the men—Rad!

"Well, isn't this just perfect?" Rad said with unhidden glee.

"I'm glad you survived, Andy, you and your friend here are welcome back on the train. We are going to try to make it back to civilization," Nick said immediately in an effort to preempt any misunderstandings.

"There is no civilization! There hasn't been for a long time," the other man barked out. "The world became too evil. Now it's gone, and only those that were prepared are left. We survived because we are the chosen ones. Now here you are trying to do the work of the devil and poison the future with your filth from the past. I am not going to let that happen!"

This guy is nuts, thought Nick, trying to think of a strategy to deal with this man who could easily kill all of them in a moment. Then there was Rad, who probably wanted to kill them all regardless of the situation.

Rad began to speak, "You ain't so arrogant now, are you, Mr. Conductor? See after you kicked me off the train, the cop said I was on my own. I had to hitchhike outta here—not even cellphone service to call a cab. Bob here saw you kick me off the train from his Humvee. So he picked me up," Rad said as he nodded to the other man. "Turns out we are of the same mind on a lotta things. He invites me to his place. When the earthquake hits, we go to his bunker. We rode out the ash cloud with his gas masks. So then . . . "

"Shut up. They don't need to know our business," the other man said, turning to Nick. "Let me tell you what you're going to do. First, you have everyone throw all the food you've got off the train in plastic bags. Next, you'll leave here with that train and go down them tracks, and don't even think of coming back. We could kill all of you right here, but you'll be dead soon enough regardless. Besides, we need to save our ammunition."

"Don't forget the women!" Rad pleaded.

"Oh yeah, you'll also leave the two women that Rad knows with us."

The ex-con from Joliet Prison laughed and said, "That's right, suckers, we gonna' make a new world, and them chicks that complained about me and got me kicked off the train—they gonna be ours!"

Rad is sly, Nick thought. *He met this crazy survivalist, and in just a couple of days he became exactly who that guy wanted a partner to be. Very impressive.*

Nick surveyed the survivalist for any glimmer of distraction he could use to deescalate the situation: military shirt, full military-looking outfit, sergeant chevrons, "Miles" above the left chest pocket, mean-looking rifle, clips of ammo, many other pieces of gear on the belt.

Sergeant Robert M. Miles, US Army. Had Nick and the others from the work party known who they were dealing with, they would have understood just how dangerous Miles really was. He had served six tours of duty in combat theaters, four in Afghanistan and two in Iraq. He was decorated numerous times for bravery. Miles had over fifty verified kills or captures. He had witnessed the very worst of human nature many times over. He saw women stoned to death publicly. He watched many brave American soldiers die needlessly. Finally he watched as political powers chose to abandon all that he and his brothers in arms had fought for. He cracked mentally, shunned all help, and cut himself off from civilization.

He had seen enough to lose all hope in humanity. His way of dealing with the world was to shut himself off from it and protect himself. The VA, his family, and those he had fought with tried time and again to reach out and help the tortured soldier, but Miles ignored them all. His thinking had gone deeper and deeper into the survivalist netherworld. Just a few years after beginning to set up his compound and bunker near Pinecliffe, he was getting close to complete insanity. He found it hard to get things done. It was increasingly uncomfortable for him to venture into town for supplies. He wanted some help though— he wanted a slave like he saw occasionally in combat zones from enemy fighters. He was hunting for someone to do his heavy lifting and run his errands. Then like a gift, the train and sheriff handed Andy "Rad" Richardson into his clutches.

"Don't just stand there—get it done!" Sergeant Miles shouted.

Nick replied calmly, "You can partake of everything we have, but not all of it, and no one stays here with you."

Robert Miles was impressed with the calm bravery of this civilian conductor. Nick reminded him of some of the Afghans he fought with. *But those guys were probably all dead by now*, he thought.

"This isn't a negotiation," he warned, "I want your food and the girls right now, or we start shooting!"

The impatient reply from the insane-soldier-turned-mountain-man left no question that Nick would either comply with his demands or die in the next few seconds.

"Just let me shoot this wannabe tough guy conductor in the head right now. Then they will get the picture," Rad said to Miles.

The former special ops Army sergeant had seen the power of fear in the population after a leader was eliminated. He knew the people on that train would do whatever was demanded once they knew that he would kill, and that their leader was already dead. Robert Miles smiled with his eyes and began to respond, "Maybe that's not such a ba . . . ."

POP! Robert Miles' head suddenly flopped to the side. Flakes of flesh flew from his neck. Before his body could even begin to crumple to the ground, Rad spun backward as his left shoulder took a severe impact.

Nick didn't think; he just jumped at Rad to grab his rifle; there was still some fight in Rad. The two struggled and, in no time, Nick had help from Hugh. Rad was overwhelmed; he gave up. He wasn't going to fight much longer anyway, the wound on his shoulder was spewing blood.

Nick looked to make sure Miles wasn't going to fight anymore. He saw the nearly decapitated body of the man, who thought he could take whatever he liked from the train, lying dead in the gray ash.

Nick looked up to try to figure out what just happened.

René stood motionless. Legs spread slightly wider than shoulder width. Both hands on her Glock 9mm Shield EZ pistol pointed straight up from her elbows that were locked at 90-degree angles. Her face was covered with the bandana and N95 mask, but she'd removed the scratched safety glasses for a better view of her targets. Her eyes were laser focused like an Old West gunslinger.

No way! René? Nick thought. He turned back to Rad.

The criminal was gasping for breath, but not like choking on ash or running too far and being out of breath. This was the sucking sound of lungs filling with fluid, probably his own blood. "I'm a goner," Rad said between half coughs and gasps. He tried to use his right arm to pull his mask down.

Hugh grabbed the hand before it could do anything, thinking the man on his back might be going for another weapon.

"It's alright, Hugh, let him get a breath," Nick said.

"Am I really gonna die?" Rad asked with watery eyes.

"Yeah, I think so," Nick said.

"Oh damn," he gasped again in terror. "I don't wanna die."

The tattoo-covered face of the dying man froze with eyes open. Gurgling sounds came from somewhere inside him.

"He's dead," Hugh said after a pause. His tone wasn't sad really, but there was no joy in his voice.

René walked the few steps from where she fired the deadly shots, to where the foul-mouthed Andy "Rad" Richardson uttered his last words.

Nick looked up at her, still in disbelief at what she just did.

She looked down at the kneeling conductor and at the dead man with the tattooed face. In a moment of pure emotion, she kicked the still warm body as hard as she could with her right foot and let out an angry grunt of power as she did it.

"That'll do, René," Nick said. "It's okay. Are you alright?"

She looked at her conductor with a purposeful stare and said, "Let's get this bridge inspected and get out of here before any other lunatics show up."

Zach asked if they should take the weapons from the bodies.

"Yes!" Nick said, realizing there could be more crazy people along their path to the civilized world. A little firepower couldn't hurt their chances for survival.

Several others from the train rushed to the aid of the work party after hearing the gunshots. One was Leonard Gonzales, of the security team. René looked at Gonzales. Leonard had a look that somehow combined surprise with pride.

Leonard and two others from his team searched the two dead men. No one else in the group understood the weaponry they were looking at. Leonard's first words were, "Whoa, this guy was geared up for a serious battle!"

He looked at René with astonishment. "Ma'am, do you realize you just took out a seasoned warrior? This soldier, insane or not, was extremely well outfitted. He was no ordinary survivalist; this guy had enough firepower to take out a battalion. I bet he was special forces at some point. You got him with one shot. Damn, girl!"

René didn't care. "He threatened us. I hate bullies, and I hated him. I'm glad he's dead." She said it with steely conviction, then walked off to the engine.

Rad only had an AR15, a gas mask, and the clothes he wore when

Nick kicked him off the train the week before. Hugh checked out Rad's rifle—"No bullets!" Hugh and Nick looked at each other.

Robert Miles didn't trust Rad enough to let him have bullets. All he wanted Rad for was a bigger show of force. They now knew Rad had been subservient to Miles at best, perhaps even a prisoner of the insane soldier. They all suddenly felt some small amount of pity for the foul-mouthed ex-con.

Zach, Hugh, Leonard, and Nick grabbed the tools and weapons before hurrying back to the railroad bridge. René climbed into the lead engine with Christina and Larry.

"Good job, René, you saved all those guys' lives," Larry said in all sincerity.

René looked at him and at Christina, who rose from her seat to hug René. The two professional railroaders hugged in an embrace of support.

René started sobbing uncontrollably.

"The bridge is good, Larry, push it forward. OVER," came the order from Nick.

"Roger, forward." Larry sat down in the seat Christina had been sitting in. He manipulated the controls, and the train began to ease forward.

As the engines slowly passed by Nick, he looked back at the two dead bodies of Robert Miles and Andy Richardson. Their skin had taken on the gray hue of the volcanic ash all around them. Blood was bright crimson and provided the only real contrast to the subdued scene, like an image from a bad zombie movie; but this was real, and those were the bodies of human beings. Nick was glad the evil men were dead, but sad that it had come to that.

"That will do, number 5. OVER." Nick tried to stick to railroad operating rules regarding radio procedure in an effort to cling to some form of civility in the face of the barbarism he just lived through.

The train stopped. Nick climbed on the dorm car 540 with the others that had gathered around. He called out on the radio, "Highball ash speed. OVER."

Larry replied, "Ash speed. OUT."

While the train was stopped, René walked back to the 512 coach car from the engines. Nick met her in the diner. They needed to talk.

Nick started, "First, thank you for saving my life. I seriously thought I was finished." René smiled as he continued, "Okay, now go ahead and explain the gun."

They both knew what Nick was referring to. Railroad rules and policy are crystal clear that there be no weapons on the property at any time other than those properly checked and locked in the baggage car. Guns are certainly never to be in the possession of employees. Suddenly an assistant conductor who was considered one of the most caring, compliant, and kind people on the payroll pulled out a gun and used it with lethal accuracy.

"I didn't want to tell you before, because you would be in trouble too if I ever got caught. I have been packing this thing at work for about four years. You remember that time I got assaulted and my stuff stolen, on track 4 at Union Station?"

"Of course I do," Nick replied.

René continued, "I almost started carrying my gun then. I had a concealed carry permit at the time. But I thought I better not, because it was against the rules. Well I never told anyone, because I don't want to be looked at as a perpetual victim. But I got mugged another time too. It happened while I was walking to my car at the RTD Park-n-Ride. The Zephyr was late. It was about midnight, and pitch dark. They stuck a gun in my face and made me do what they said. Luckily, they were just after stuff and didn't hurt me physically. But they took my keys, phone, purse, money, IDs, all of it, and made me take them to my car so they could steal it. Then they were gone, and I was left just standing there in the dark parking lot with nothing. After about ten minutes, I found another person who helped me call the police and my husband John. Within an hour, the cops caught the guys, and I got all my stuff back. The car wasn't even damaged."

"As you can imagine, after being thankful that I was fine, John was enraged. He said I was going to be armed from then on, or not go to work at all. I felt so conflicted, but in the end I had to agree. I had been shooting my whole life. So we went to the store, and I got a little Glock 9mm EZ Shield that would fit neatly in the bottom of my purse. When I am alone in a vulnerable place, I put my hand into my purse, and I am ready. We built a little gun range on our property. I practiced all the time. Since the earthquake, I have had it under my blazer in a side holster," she finished and looked at Nick, expecting some form of judgment.

"I don't know what to say," Nick said. He was still in a bit of shock. "Wow, I don't know what to think. What I do know is that because you chose to be a secret rule breaker, I get to keep on living," he said in an almost providential tone.

René had one last thing to say. "I used to feel bad for people who appeared evil. I even felt empathy for Rad until he pointed his gun. Now I have killed two people because they were bad enough to kill. I don't feel bad for them anymore. I don't think there was any good in them. They made me kill them. I hate them for that." She sobbed again briefly.

Nick handed her a tissue and thought for a moment.

"René, I've known you for a lot of years. You are not a killer. You're a giver and protector. As far as I am concerned, you didn't kill them. You protected us. You just did what comes natural to you. It was the right thing to do. Now it's over. Typically, we could have a few days off after an event like this, to process the whole thing. But we don't have time for that out here. So like it or not, we have to put this episode behind us for now and press on to Denver."

He smiled at her and added, "We still got this, because you did that."

René looked at Nick and said, "Roger that."

Leonard Gonzales was entrusted with the weapons and gear from Miles. He was told to store them in the baggage car gun locker.

Nick's thought was that if they needed weapons, they would come get them. A bigger danger, in Nick's mind, was that a person on the train could go nuts and try to take a weapon if starvation or other stressors pushed them over the edge. He asked René to lock her gun in the locker as well.

She never said if she would comply or not.

CHAPTER 28

ZEPHYRING

"Do what you can, with what you have, where you are."

—Theodore Roosevelt

The second eruption of Yellowstone was cruel to the Zephyr. Wind accompanied the fallout. Ash deepened. The added ash further slowed the progress of the beleaguered train. During Christina's shift at the controls of the 313, she found that more and more throttle was needed to keep pushing through the thickening mass of debris that fell like snow, but plowed like sand. At last she found that the power and weight of the Zephyr alone was not enough to push the deepening drifts out of the way.

Between tunnels, Nick's phone rang, Jack Steele, in Omaha calling. "Nick, you'll have to start using momentum as a plowing technique."

Not sure what that meant, Nick asked, "Momentum?"

"Yes, hit the ash drifts at about three miles per hour, and keep going until wheel slip begins, then back up a bit and hit it again. Use momentum to break up the drifts and blast them out of the right-of-way."

Nick liked the aggressive plan of attack. "Oh yeah, we got this!"

Christina was more than happy with the new plan. "We will just kick those drifts to dust!" she said with a degree of grit Nick had not heard from her before.

Larry was awakened by the back-and-forth jolting of the train. He got up earlier than required and made his way to the front of the train, now the 512 car. Nick was there with track team #2, about to go on duty.

"What's happening now?" Larry asked.

Nick explained the new tactic of busting through the ash. "It worked great, except for the few rock slides that blocked easy progress," the conductor told his engineer. René was on the tail of the train (the back of the baggage car), giving clearance for the backup moves.

"So we are just beating the ash down?" Larry asked.

Nick thought for a second and answered, "Not really, I mean, it's a totally new method of railroading. It deserves its own name."

Larry thought back to his days working freight yards in Boston. "It's kind of like working in a hump yard."

Nick hated it when Larry tried to "old head" him; he tried to one-up the old engineer, saying, "Well, Larry, I did plenty of humping at Balmer yard north of Seattle in my day, and this is nothing like it. This is more like trying to pack as many cars as you can into a stub track with a really strong bumper."

Feeling a bit disrespected, Larry quipped, "Okay, wise guy, why don't *you* try and make up a name for what we're doing."

Nick thought for minute. This was a historic event in railroad lore—a solemn moment when a new word was added to the eternal lexicon of railroad lingo, joining such great terms as "highball," "kick it," and "dog catch!" Not a decision to be taken lightly, the new term had to be worthy of the greatness of the moment.

Larry knew Nick had a knack for noteworthy nomenclature. He eagerly anticipated the brilliance to come.

"Zephyring," said Nick finally. "We are zephyring through the ash heap of hell on our way to salvation." Nick looked at Larry for approval.

"Zephyring? That's all you got—zephyring?" Larry asked incredulously.

Nick looked at Larry with wide eyes and nodded, as if to say, *Yep, how do you like it?*

Larry paused a second and said, "Well, I can't think of anything better. But you're starting to slip a bit on your game here. I expect better from a man of your talents."

Nick was pleased. That was a better endorsement than usual from the crusty old hoghead.

"Nick to Christina. OVER."

"Christina on the 313 answering. Go ahead. OVER."

"We are going to call our current technique of back-and-forth through the ash 'zephyring.' OVER."

"*Ha ha*, sounds great! Engine 313, zephyring at ash speed!" she said in a tone of jocularity.

CHAPTER 29

THEY DID THEIR JOB TO THE END

"Heroism doesn't always happen in a burst of glory. Sometimes small triumphs and large hearts change the course of history."

—Mary Rosch

Zephyring through the ash was made easier by numerous tunnels east of Pinecliffe. The makeshift plow was aimed to push debris north, off the edge of the cliff and down into the South Boulder Creek Canyon. Progress seemed a little faster. In just eight hours, the Zephyr was nearing Crescent siding. Approaching tunnel 22, it looked like the west portal was blocked. Charlie, the junior UPR track man, was leading a scout crew for track team #3. It was just starting to dawn. Light was dim, but he could tell there was a problem. He and two others quickened their pace through the ash to see what was up there—something big, shrouded in gray ash and about twenty feet inside the tunnel. "It's another train!" Noah shouted.

The UPR 6413 was facing them, as predicted by the engineering team in Omaha. "That's the train we hoped was in the siding," said Charlie.

He called to report to the Zephyr. "Charlie to Nick. OVER."

"Nick answering, go ahead. OVER."

"Yeah, bad news, Nick. We found the empty coal train. It's on the mainline, head end inside tunnel 22. OVER."

Nick and the others had been afraid of this. He immediately started getting his gear on to go out in the ash to assess the situation and plan how to deal with the issue.

"Nick to track team #3, inspect, but do not touch the train. We will be there in a few minutes to make a plan to move it out of our way. OUT."

Nick never once thought the freight train meant the end of the line for the Zephyr. Others were not so sure.

Christina was at the helm of the 313. She came to a stop 250 feet from the knuckle of the freight engine facing her. Her heart sank.

How do we get past that beast? she wondered.

Charlie, Nick, and several others started going over to the empty UPR coal train. Under the veneer of ash, the investigators found charred remains from the violent inferno, even inside the relative protection of the open-ended tunnel. No way any of the locomotives would ever run again; their fuel tanks appeared ruptured and empty, perhaps from boiling or burning off. The aluminum skin of the coal cars was twisted and contorted by the heat of the ash cloud, but the all-important running gear (the iron wheels, bogies, draw bars, center beams, and knuckles) all looked in good shape. Parking brakes on the engines and hand brakes on the first twenty cars were all tied tight. The investigators took over an hour to get to the end of the coal train due to the drifting ash and the five short tunnels the train was in.

No one on the inspection team had gone into the cab of the 6413, the lead locomotive of the coal train. Eventually Jake, the UPR maintenance foreman, walked back to look for himself. He was friends with the two men who had been running the train when the eruption hit. Both of those railroaders often operated work trains that Jake managed. He tried to prepare himself for what he would find. He climbed the rear side ladder of the 6413 and peered inside to where the engineer would have sat. He saw no floor, seat, or human bodies . . . at first. He pushed his way in, careful not to fall into the charred remains of the complicated equipment below the burned-off floorboards.

Fire is brutal, with no respect for persons or things. Jake looked closer, taking a moment to focus on the ash-dusted shape—no mistaking what he saw. A human skull is not easily reduced to ash in a fire. Soon more personal stuff came into view: a Leatherman tool, belt buckle, and steel-toe boots. Jake knew it was the body and belongings of Bruce Springfield, a twelve-year veteran of the rails. Jake figured Bruce died in the engineer's seat. He had done the best he could when he received word about Yellowstone from the dispatcher; he got into the longest tunnel they could reach.

Where is Zane? Jake wondered.

Charlie and the scout team were told via radio that the engineer's body was found in the 6413. René heard it too, as she inspected the twenty hand brakes that had been tied down. She yelled to the team, "Guys, you better look closely around that twentieth hand brake and the car behind it. The freight conductor is probably laying out there somewhere."

"We found him," said Charlie.

Like Jake, he had worked with the same crew often in the past. After the initial shock of seeing the body of a friend, Charlie smiled in appreciation at his dead colleague. All the professional railroaders knew what the freight conductor, Zane, had done.

Nick thought it through as he looked at Jim, the LSA. He imagined what must have happened. "Those guys knew things were nearly hopeless. They did what they could to save themselves, but they also saved all of us."

Jim looked confused, responding, "They left a train blocking our path to Denver?"

"I know," Nick replied. "But can you imagine our predicament if they had not tied those hand brakes? They would have died just the same. In time, air in the brake cylinders would have bled off, releasing the brake shoes on the wheels. What's left of that train would have begun a runaway descent on a 2 percent downhill grade. The coal train would have built up speed until it jumped the tracks and piled up. That train wreck would have torn the tracks to ribbons. Had that happened, we really would be stuck. They knew they would die, but they still did their jobs to the bitter end."

The two men stood in silence, contemplating the heroic efforts of Zane and Bruce. Charlie and the others were almost to the end of the train. Another engine was there on the rear of the coal train—what the railroad industry calls "distributed power" or DP units. DP units supply power to move the train, and air to set brakes. Sophisticated radio signals allowed the engineer in the leading cab to control all engines at once, including the DP units, with the same controls.

The rear unit was in really bad shape, not in a tunnel, and therefore took the full force of the superheated ash cloud. It looked like it had melted in the middle, probably because of its diesel tank either burning or exploding. The mighty locomotive was sagging in the middle, between the trucks. The contorted fuel tank was touching the ball of the rail. Somehow, the rail itself still looked serviceable.

"Nick to Christina, this is going to take a bit. We need to consult the help desk in Omaha. You better fire up HEP for an hour to get the phones charged. We need the best minds we've got working on this one. We have to move this whole train out of our way. We might only have one shot at it, so we'll have to do it right the first try. No screwups allowed."

In spite of the words being said, Nick's tone was so confident that it caused everyone to believe they could simply move a 3,000-ton train out of the way and keep moving.

René and Marshall Knight got the call organized with the mechanical and civil engineers in Omaha. The Omaha guys needed thirty minutes to figure something out. Finally the whole gang was ready for the conference call to plan their attempt to move the ruined coal train.

Back on the Zephyr, pictures and descriptions from Nick and the others were streaming to René and Marshall. They were all on the conference call with the Omaha team, who also had access to the data feeds. The experts at the dispatching center asked for a few more minutes to review the situation.

While the brightest minds in railroading were working on the problem of the 6413, a gang of Silver Sky passengers and Amish men were digging two graves. They dug down below the ash and into real rock and soil. Carefully, and with utmost respect, they laid the remains of Zane and Bruce to rest. The graves were marked by chiseling an X on the rock cliffs beside the last resting places of the two courageous railroaders. A proper marker could be placed later.

A junior dispatcher, John Crisantian, had returned to the Omaha Dispatching Center to help as he could. His personal hobby for the previous year was to help build a modular N-scale layout of the Moffat Road for the Colorado Model Railroad Museum. Being a new employee with the UPR, he didn't have enough seniority to get the holiday weekend off. Otherwise, he would have been in Denver for the first unveiling of the massive modeling project at Train Days. He would have died there with Michelle and the others from the museum.

Because of that modeling project, John knew every contour of the landscape the Zephyr was trying to get through like the back of his hand, having formed it to scale with his hands. He interrupted his supervisor as the team of engineers tried to brainstorm a way to get the Zephyr past the dead coal train, "If you can just get that train moving, and aim the tracks off the cliff from the Crescent siding a bit east of the first switch, the whole train should roll off and into the deep canyon there. Then it would be out of the way."

John showed surprising confidence in his deductions as he continued, "Then the Zephyr can reline the siding switch for the main and continue down the hill."

The supervisor looked at John and thought for a moment. Then with a determined look, pushed toward the front of the room, and shouted over the conversations others were having to get the attention of the man in charge. "Steele! I think we have an idea."

CHAPTER 30

END OF THE WORLD

"Never tell people how to do things. Tell them what to do, and they will surprise you with their ingenuity."

—George S. Patton

The conference call computer rang. The Omaha meeting began without introductions. "Nick, from what we can see, the freight train should be able to move downhill," the first voice said; it was Jack Steele, the UPR dispatching supervisor. "Your people will have to find a way to simultaneously release all the brakes on the coal train to see if gravity can push the sagging DP engine, the one at the rear, without derailing."

René was almost humored. "Release all the hand brakes at the same time on a long train without any airbrakes. Sure, no problem. What's next?" she asked sarcastically.

A different voice came on from the UPR, a civil engineer. "Before you do that, you have to line the west switch at Crescent for the siding. And you will have to cut the rails 140 yards east of the switch points. Then shove the siding track to the left twelve feet—without exceeding a 14 degree radius."

Steele came back on. "What you are trying to do is run the whole freight train off the cliff and into South Boulder Creek Canyon."

"Oh, c'mon, I thought you guys could help us do something that we could actually accomplish. How are we gonna cut rail, bend steel, and realign tracks?" Larry asked.

But Nick had been thinking along the same lines as the UPR men, even before the call. "We got this, Larry. I think I know how to make a rail cutter, and a track alignment tool."

The UPR team snapped to attention. The truth was, they didn't have a clue how it could be done. "You do?" Jack Steele asked Nick.

"Yep, we take a rail saw abrasive cutting wheel, the one we took from the maintenance shed at Moffat Tunnel, and fasten it to the rear wheel hub of one of the bicycles hanging in the bag car. We plop the bike down on the rail and tell the rider to peddle like crazy. It should cut the steel. Regarding lining the rail, we can use rail tongs, or something like that, to hold a twelve-foot piece of 120-pound-per-foot rail. Then we swing the rail into the side of the tracks to scoot it over, one blow at a time, until we have it to where we want it."

Only stunned silence came from the UPR people on the conference call.

"What do you think?" Nick finally asked.

Steele pondered this for a short while more, before he said that it might just work.

Larry jumped back in. "I am just going to play devil's advocate here—what about getting the brakes off the coal train all at once?"

Nick was ready for that too. "We don't. We buckle on with our train to hold the coal train in place. Then we put rock chocks under the wheels. With the train secure, we kick off the hand brakes one at a time. With the brakes off and rocks holding the coal train in place, we'll unbuckle our train. Finally, all at once, people at each wheel, using sledgehammers, will knock out the rock chocks and let the train roll. If it doesn't roll on its own, we can shove the whole mess off the cliff and into the canyon with a butt joint on the 313." A butt joint was like two friends doing a fist bump rather than a handshake.

René wanted to side with Larry. She thought the plan was really risky. But she couldn't think of a better way to get the coal train out of their way.

Neither could Larry, although he seemed to enjoy the role of the skeptic. In the end though, he was usually the one who tried the hardest to make sure things worked. "Okay, fine. We are doomed if we don't try something. Let's go!" he said.

Steele spoke up again. "We have one more good idea for you. Couple into the UPR 6413 that was in the tunnel and keep it with you. You will use that as a battering ram if needed down the road. Cut away from the freight train between its lead unit and the second engine.

After a moment of silence, René spoke, "Okay, thanks for the plan. Can you talk us through the details?"

For about thirty minutes, the gang discussed each part of the procedure. René would use the mechanical team to make the joint with the 6413 and figure out how to get the makeshift plow shifted from the nose of the 313 to what would become the new leader of the Zephyr, the back end of the UPR 6413.

René started organizing a team to set rock chocks and kick off the brakes of the freight train. Jake and Charlie got all three track teams together to go whack the Crescent siding to a new and ominous alignment.

René, Christina, and the mechanical team got the plow off the front drawbar of the 313 and prepared for a joint on the lead unit of the coal train. Knut, Doug, Yao Ping, and others went to the bag car. Knut made sure he had his emergency bike tools. biking shoes, and water bottle. Out of sheer habit, he wore his bike helmet. Dan brought the cutting wheel. Doug had his tool bucket.

It took some thought to come up with a way to connect an industrial 30" cutter wheel designed for a large gas-powered machine to replace the rear wheel of a bicycle. Yao said the key was to fabricate an adaptor to go between the rear bike axle hub and the cutter wheel.

Everyone in the group was dumbfounded, except Doug. He thought he could make an adapter using wall board from the bulkhead of the 540 car. It took him a couple of minutes to explain how he'd do it, but it sounded like his idea just might work. The others in the group looked at Doug with amazement. Yao spoke up, "You are a smart guy, let's try it." It took over an hour to assemble, but the contraption seemed to be strong enough to work.

It hurt Knut's feelings to see his $8,000 mountain bike ruined. "If this doesn't work, I will lose my bike for nothing," he said.

"What good would your fancy bike do you if we all die up here?" Doug quipped. "Tell you what, if we get out of this alive, Yao will buy you a new GIANT bike."

Everyone looked at Yao, who stood there without expression. The whole group took the bike, with the newly installed rear rail cutting wheel, out the bag car door, and headed for the Crescent siding.

The team began referring to themselves as the biker gang. After arriving at the west Crescent siding switch, they marched off another 140 yards further east, to find the right location to cut the rail. They adjusted the spot slightly so that they would cut the inside rail six inches closer to the switch than a bolted joint on the outer rail. They did that because they only wanted to cut one rail, not two. The other rail could be unbolted, and joint bars removed. Also, as the tracks were shoved north toward the drop-off point, they would need a little extra clearance for the inner rail to pass the outer rail.

The biker gang was ready to give their invention a test run. Knut was in the saddle. Four members of the team held the bike in place, using a shovel handle as a crossbar, with the front wheel on the ground, and the cutter wheel above the rail.

Yao Ping told Knut to start pedaling. The cutter disk on the rear hub began to spin. Knut shifted gears and got the disk going faster. The team carefully lowered the spinning cutter wheel to the rail. When the big black disk hit the rail, the bike and Knut shot forward, and everyone fell over.

"We're sure glad you wore your helmet, dude!" Doug said as he helped Knut back on his feet.

"I think the front wheel is of no use and may be causing us problems," the European athlete replied as he got up out of the dusty ground, trying not to cry. He looked for blood. "Please, just take off the front wheel, and let me balance on the front fork alone."

"Wait, guys," Paul Brown said as he ran toward the team, waving his hands. "What you are trying to do is build a chop saw. I have analyzed hundreds of chop saws for a woodworker magazine, so I know what I am doing. First, we need a solid base. Second, the angle of attack should be lower than the fulcrum. Third, the saw should be locked at 90 degrees." Knut looked at Paul as if to say, *Could you have thought of this a little sooner?!*

Everyone agreed with Paul's points and started trying to figure out how to make the suggested modifications. To stabilize the bike at the right height, they kept the front wheel on. That wheel was sandwiched between the two rail joint bars from the outside rail, which were re-bolted together. The team found two more joint bars and some wire from what had been a fence next to the tracks. The fence wire was used to tie those plates perpendicular to the joint plates connected to the front wheel. The setup made a heavy-duty bike stand. Finally, Doug's drill was used to poke a hole through the frame and front fork post of the bike. A salvaged bolt from the train was stuck through the hole to pin the bike at a secure 90-degree angle.

The biker gang was ready for a second go at cutting the rail. Everyone looked at Knut expectantly as he tightened the straps on his helmet. He got the cutter spinning. The disk was lowered to the rail by two men holding the shovel handle on either side of the bike. Sparks flew. The rear of the bike went a bit left, then right. The guys on the team worked to stabilize the apparatus by tightening the fork bolt.

Sparks turned to an orange glow, like a real rail saw. Slowly, the steel rail was succumbing to the power of Knut's pedaling and the ingenuity of the biker gang. After fifteen minutes of stationary spinning at top speed, the steel ribbon of rail was divided. Knut was completely spent after breathing hard through his N95 mask. He emptied his water bottle in big gulps while everyone cheered. No race victory could have been more satisfying.

While the biker gang was building the rail cutter, Jake's track team had been busy making a tool to realign the track. His gang started with Nick's idea of whacking the track with a heavy piece of rail. In short order, they figured out a way to turn three ten-foot chunks of rail, found near the Gross Dam Road crossing, into a battering ram—like a weapon from medieval siege warfare.

Marshall Knight and his son Kevin took the idea from a battle scene in the *Lord of the Rings* trilogy by Tolkien. Some chains were wrapped around a twelve-foot-long piece of rail to provide the necessary swinging motion. Doug used his drill to bore a hole through two rails, and join them into a large A frame with a rail joint bolt. The A frame supported the bulk of the weight of the swinging rail. That allowed the workers to simply guide the force. They assembled the contraption just west of where the biker gang cut the rail. They called their new tool "The Rail Wrecker."

It took several tries to get good at aiming the force of the blows, but in time the system began whacking the tracks connected to the switch bit by bit to the north. The team moved the A frame several times to inch the whole track in the right direction. Some track team members dug out ballast from the butt-end of the ties on the north side to reduce resistance to the force of the impacts from the Rail Wrecker. After two hours, the south inside rail of the part being moved passed the outside rail of the siding track that was still where it had been. The tracks were lined in a slow arching curve that ended in oblivion. They had created a new end of the tracks, what railroaders call "The End of the World."

With the siding track realigned, Nick opened the west siding switch itself. He walked back to the DP unit a quarter mile west as the moment of action drew close.

"Jake to Nick, the tracks are now lined, ready to send that worthless hunk of metal to its doom. OVER." Jake was starting to get into the melodramatic language the conductor and passenger crew enjoyed using.

"Oh yeah, baby, you're ready!" Nick answered with bravado.

While the biker gang and track teams had done their work, René worked on the freight train brakes. First, she had coupled the 313 with the Zephyr behind it, into the UPR freight engine, to hold the whole thing from running away out of control. Then they started kicking off hand breaks one at a time. After only three brakes, the freight train tightened the joint on the Zephyr's knuckle.

René had the mechanical team place moderately sized rocks under twenty-four axels on the north side of the coal train. She had Christina relax the Zephyr brakes to allow the whole train to snuggle into the "rock chocks." The rocks held the train in place. Then more hand brakes were kicked off. After all cars on the coal train had the hand brakes released, the freight locomotive parking brake wheels were slowly unwound. The train still didn't move.

Next, the Zephyr, with the UPR 6413 attached, was uncoupled from the freight train and backed up slightly. The coal train stayed put. René closed and locked the knuckles of the 6413, and the 7906, the second unit in the coal train lash-up. She called Nick and Jake on the radio. "We are about ready to cut the freight train loose. Are your people in the clear? OVER."

"This is Jake, we are lined, clear and ready. Let 'er roll! OVER."

"Nick to René, we are ready at the east end of the train. OVER."

"Roger," she said, "here it comes. OUT."

René gave the sign. Simultaneously, twenty-four people swung their sledgehammers into rocks that had kept the coal train wheels from turning. The rocks either popped out of the way, or were crushed. The coal train started moving. Then after about twenty feet, it stopped.

"Nick to René, the sagging DP unit at the rear of the coal train is dragging on the rail. It's enough to stop the train. OVER."

"Roger that, shall we push it? OVER."

"We have to, it's our only option. Push into the 7906 with a butt joint to give the train a bit of motivation. OVER."

Christina and René were prepared for that. "Roger, the 313 is pushing forward. OUT."

Added pressure from the Zephyr got the freight train moving again. All wheels were turning—the journal bearings had not completely seized in the heat of the fires. The DP unit was starting to throw sparks as the burned out fuel tank scraped over the rails.

"Faster 313! OVER," Nick called out. "We have to have more speed to throw this thing into the ditch!"

Christina went to notch 5. She looked at the speedometer: 12 mph. *We need at least 25 mph*, she thought. Notch 6. If she gave too much power, it could cause the dragging DP unit to derail, throwing everything into chaos. Speed increased to 16 mph.

The track gang sitting on the slope above the drop off point heard the DP unit round the curve just west of the switch.

"A hundred yards to the switch 313, lay into it! OVER," Jake yelled as he gained sight of the leading edge of the train. A few seconds later he continued, "Fifty yards to the switch." Jake's voice was calm and confident.

Christina went all out: Notch 8. Still only 22 mph.

Nick was not as placid as Jake; he yelled into the radio, "Kick it!"

Christina yelled back with a Scottish accent, as only engineer Trekkies can, "I'm givin' it all she's got, Capt'n!"

The DP unit swayed as it went through the switch points at west Crescent, and aimed into the siding. Sparks flew as the stricken engine scraped steel over steel. Jake strained to see if the locomotive would tear up the switch points, or ride safely over them. The crowd of workers on the slope above the switch rose to their feet cheering, like fans doing the wave at Mile High Stadium.

Christina backed off the throttle the second the speedometer hit 25 mph. Then she applied blended brakes to stop the Zephyr. The last thing she wanted was to follow the coal train off the end of the track: the "end of the world."

The sight of a huge SD70MAC locomotive flying in midair was beyond description. The sound of it landing on granite rocks was deafening. To witness multiple coal cars following that engine into the chasm of South Boulder Creek was like nothing anyone there had ever experienced before. Once the DP unit, with its dragging fuel tank, was off the rails and flying into the depths of the canyon, the coal train accelerated rapidly. Train car after train car was flung into the abyss. It was an awesome explosive spectacle that just kept going on and on.

The track team and Jake saw it all. Thanks to Marshall Knight, so did nearly ten million viewers via his Virtual Railfan livestream feed to the whole world.

Christina applied more braking effort to slow the 313. She was just a quarter mile west of the west Crescent switch. The coal train quickly ran away from the Zephyr. If the freighter went too fast, the front of the train, now the rear end of the movement, could flip or derail on the sharp curves of the switch. But at that point, no one could do anything about it. Christina and the Zephyr stopped with a hundred yards to spare.

As the 7906 hit the west Crescent siding switch, it swayed dramatically. Some members of the track team thought the north wheels may have come off the rail as it entered the switch, followed by the south side wheels rising on the straightening part of the siding just east of the frog. Everyone feared the worst. But it stayed upright! The 7906 held the rail, until there was no more rail to hold. It rode, and then flew, its course to a brief but impactful end.

Nick ran to the end of track on the siding to survey the pileup below. "We did it!" He yelled at Jake and the track teams.

The whole group was already looking over the cliff.

Jake and Nick, the two old railroaders, contemplated what had just happened. "You know," said Jake, "I've spent a career making sure the railroad is a safe place . . . I have always taken pride in my work. No train has ever crashed on my watch. Now suddenly I am overjoyed that an entire coal train, a hundred million dollars-worth of hardware, flew off the end of the world, and piled up in the canyon. What a strange legacy to have."

Nick looked at Jake, who continued trying to see through the disturbed ash to the destroyed train below. "You did good, Jake. You've done really good."

CHAPTER 31

ROCKSLIDE

"It is not the mountain that we conquer, but ourselves."

—Edmund Hillary

Nick got the west Crescent siding switch restored to the main track position. Christina, René, and part of the mechanical team backed the Zephyr up to retrieve the plow, then eased their way down to the site of all the commotion. Everyone on the train tried to see the wrecked coal train below them. Ash had settled somewhat. The tangle of train cars and engines was an amazing sight. John, the junior Omaha dispatcher, had been correct; there was just enough space down in the canyon for the whole coal train. All the workers on the track teams got back on the cars of the Zephyr, except track team #2, which would lead the way further east, toward Denver.

Nick had to ride point on the B end of the 6413. After only a few hundred feet, he realized it was miserable, perhaps even dangerous. Ash was kicked up all around him as he stood on the back platform of the dead freight engine. He got on the radio. "Once we get out of the Tunnel District, the point person is riding on the roof!"

The rest of the track team didn't have it much better on the walkways of the same engine. Nick asked the engineers to keep it at about 2 mph to reduce the blowing dust.

Larry had relieved Christina at the controls of the 313. She made her way to the 540 car to get some well-deserved rest. René met her as she walked through the parlor car. "Great job, Christina! We did it. By the way, you sounded just like Scotty back there."

Christina chuckled a bit as she often did before speaking. "I take that as a compliment. Just don't give me a red miniskirt; those things were sexist, and also, it was always the red-shirt guys that got killed."

René, who had also grown up with Spock and Kirk on TV, had always enjoyed sharing occasional *Enterprise* moments with her colleague and fellow *Star Trek* fan.

Before going to bed, the two railroaders saw Herman rolling through the hallway on the Stryker chair with Rob pushing. His new headband read "PRESS ON." He had decided to have a new slogan each day. Herman smiled at the two women. They smiled back. They both felt a strange motivation from his subtle statement.

The track team loaded as many tools off the abandoned work train on the Crescent siding as they could. It was still tough going. They would need all the resources they could get. Ash was as thick and heavy as ever. The wind had increased the night before and drifted some of the gray, dusty, sand-like mass almost five feet high.

Several hours after leaving Crescent siding, track team #2 came upon a new rock slide. Unfortunately, this one was huge! Just west of tunnel #8, a wall of fractured sandstone boulders completely blocked the right-of-way. Nick called Jake to come check it out. It was twenty feet high. The rocks were of all sizes—some as big as an SUV. The pileup had fallen right at the west portal of the tunnel.

Nick thought about it for a minute and looked at Jake. "We can't punch through this with the engines, or the rocks will get wedged in the curving tunnel." Jake knew this would have been a challenging job for his guys using all their cranes, back hoes, and front loaders—and now he had to get it moved by hand!

Nick tried to be clever and funny in the face of the back-breaking labor that awaited them all. "It is going to take a bunch of bold brethren to bash these boulders into bits."

Jake, and the few others who were there all looked at Nick without laughing. Dan, the coach car attendant, said what everyone was thinking, "Please don't ever say that again."

The group all smiled under their masks and started for the train to gather tools and recruit more workers. Every sledge hammer, crow bar, track tool and shovel were employed on the slide. Bit by agonizing bit, big rocks were whacked into smaller rocks and pushed aside.

More than 150 of the Zephyr's 244 people were digging. Within eight hours, only a few of the largest boulders remained. But getting that far had been costly. Several times it happened that a worker moving a rock triggered a mini avalanche of stones and ash. Many diggers incurred minor flesh wounds. There was even a broken arm recorded in the log. Dr. Abraham, Sean, and Susan were going through first aid supplies fast.

Jake and Charlie had a team bring out the A frame Rail Wrecker to the site. It took twenty strong people to move the device. They tried using that simple machine to break the big boulders into manageable stones that could be moved with muscle power.

Victor Homko, from Ukraine, had spent a career breaking rocks right where he wanted them to split. He was an expert stone mason. He could read the fractured lines of a rock better than a PhD geologist. He guided the Rail Wrecker team with unparalleled expertise. Ever so slowly, the rocks succumbed to the relentless pounding. Finally, the 6413 under the power of the 313, pushed the last of the debris off the rail.

To protect the engines, reinforce the plow, and move rocks off the right-of-way, the mechanical crew chained four slices of rail found near the tracks to the leading end of the dead UPR engine. When finished, the back end of the UPR 6413 looked like it had a giant cow catcher, like those used on old steam engines. The burned-out hulk still had the vague outline of the American flag visible on its side. Against the post-apocalyptic scene of gray cliffs and burnt stumps, the UPR 6413 looked like a vehicle from a *Mad Max* movie.

West of tunnel #8, boulders falling on the rail had caused some damage. The rocks apparently bounded off the tracks and over the cliff. At one point the gauge was nearly five feet, rather than the standard gauge 4'8 ½". Some of the tie slots that held the rail clips in place were broken as well. For a normal day on a passenger train, this would have ended the trip, or meant at least a several-hour delay. But not for this group on the Zephyr. People on the track teams had become well-seasoned units of efficiency. Using the Rail Wrecker, they forced the track back into place in less than a half-hour.

Larry was given the signal to pull forward at ash speed. When he released the brakes, he was hoping that the realignment would be the last of their trials getting down to Denver. But he knew better; there was no way their luck would improve that dramatically. He was impressed, however, by the ability of that motley gang of people to get through as much adversity as they had.

CHAPTER 32

THE FIREMAN

"Firefighters never die, they just burn forever in the hearts of the people whose lives they saved."

—Susan Murphree

Surprisingly, the Zephyr was able to go ash speed through the rest of the tunnel district. The train made it past Plainview without any major interruptions. At about 2:00 a.m., members of track team #3 noticed their breath was steaming and hands were getting numb. Cold was creeping up on them just as Dr. Sayers said it would.

Rounding the horseshoe curve at Coal Creek Canyon, the tracks cross over Highway 72 on a steel bridge. Between the main steel girders of the bridge, and the train tracks, was a thick old wooden deck that held ballast and ties. This one, like the Union Station bridge, was among the last of the old unrenovated bridges on the Zephyr line. As the train approached, people on the track team could tell that the rail and concrete ties were sagging deeply. At first, they worried that the whole bridge was gone. They could not see well at night. The locomotive headlight was still aimed too far to their right, and it was blocked by the 6413. Upon further inspection, they found the girders were good; only the wooden deck was burned off. The ballast had fallen onto the roadway and the ruined cars below. The team decided to rest inside the train for the couple of hours remaining before daylight. Illumination would help them overcome this latest challenge.

As the pale light of day started to glow, a sobering site came into view. Cars were stacked up in a massive traffic jam along the highway. All of them were in the same state as what had been seen at East Portal, Rollinsville, and Pinecliffe—no windows or tires. Just ash-covered hulks. But this was different, bigger. Hundreds of cars and trucks had stopped in their tracks. Some were crashed into other vehicles. Cars were all pointing east in both lanes and on the shoulders. Some were in the fields on either side of the road. Looking at the remains of that panic-stricken morning, a person could almost hear the echoes of honking horns, screaming people, and the roar of the deadly ash cloud bearing down on them. Now all was silent. People on the Zephyr saw no sign of life.

Unlike the bridge near East Portal, nobody on the Zephyr wanted to look closer inside the cars along the highway. They had seen enough dead bodies. There was another ominous aspect about the traffic jam of death they were looking at—ash had drifted up to the roofs of the cars on the south side, like the scene of a closed road during a massive winter blizzard.

"The wind must have really been blowing here," Charlie said to Jake.

The older boss looked at the young man grim faced, knowing what that meant down in Barbara Gulch. *Worry about that when the time comes*, Jake thought. *First we have to cross this bridge.*

Trains can deal with a decent amount of misaligned track sideways or up and down. Vertical and horizontal stability of the roadbed below the rail is important, but there is some leeway—perhaps an inch or two. The loss of decking on the highway 72 bridge left rails, with concrete ties still attached, sagging almost two feet across a span just forty feet wide!

Jake checked out the girders below the dangling tracks. They looked and felt strong. The concrete abutments on both sides appeared solid enough to hold the weight of a locomotive. He climbed off the remains of the bridge to tell his track team what he thought.

Nick, Christina, and a few others were waiting for Jake at the west end of the bridge. As the "fresh" group of track workers started to show up at 8:00 a.m., Jake gave his assessment, "We can cross this bridge— but we have to shore up the tracks between the girders and the ties."

Nick thought that sounded easy enough. "Okay," he said. "How do we do that?"

Jake looked back at the bridge with a degree of reservation. "We have to lift the track up to grade level, then find something to support the weight of the train to stick between the bridge girders and those tracks. Whatever we find has to be stable, so the whole thing doesn't get out of balance and fall apart while the train rolls over it."

Rails and ties weigh thousands of pounds. Lifting that mass is not a job mere muscles can do. Mechanical assistance was needed. They needed rail jacks, of which they had none. That was just step one. Next they needed about twenty inches of supporting material. Wooden railroad ties would work, but those had been replaced over a year before with concrete ties.

Brewster, from the Silver Sky group, had lived in Coal Creek Canyon for decades. He knew most people up there had rugged jeeps and SUVs with off-road repair gear on their vehicles all the time. "I bet we could find a few big jacks on some of the jeeps down there." Nick nodded.

Charlie remembered how "steel gangs" he had worked on before the eruption would connect just one out of three ties when they had to get a passenger train over a work zone. He looked at Jake. "What if we unclip two out of three ties and stack 'em under the others for height?"

Jake thought about it for a moment and said, "That's a good idea."

The two track men told Nick about their plan.

Nick smiled at the quick thinking and "never say die" attitude the group of survivors were manifesting. They were starting to believe in themselves. They were not getting discouraged anymore by the hardships before them; they were just looking for a plan to overcome the obstacles and move on.

One group from the team went to work on the ties, and another left to find car jacks. After setting the plan in motion, Nick shouted out to everyone, as they were leaving the briefing, "We got this!"

No one had any doubt about it.

Brewster and a few others scurried down the steep embankment from the tracks to the road below. Everyone was amazed at Brewster's agility in spite of his seventy-eight years of age. They started walking the line of burned-out automobiles. A smoky, musty stench was heavy in the air, enough to overpower the ever-present sulfur stink. Eventually they found two high lift 5,000 pound capacity jacks on the back of a single jeep.

Breaking the jacks free of the locks and cables that secured them to their vehicle was a challenge. Noah wisely suggested they should see if the keys to the locks were on the keyring hanging from the ignition. Fire had warped the thin bits of metal, but eventually they got the key to work. The jacks were freed. The team cheered when the lock opened. But Brewster was looking sad. "What is it?" Noah asked him.

"Oh, it's just that this is Jason's Jeep. He was a fireman in Boulder, and a neighbor. He lived about a mile from my place. I bet he was trying to get to his station house after the earthquake, you know, trying to do his job. That's him there," Brewster said, pointing to the charred human remains on the wire and metal frame of the seat.

The group went silent for a brief moment then hauled the jacks up the slope to the crippled bridge.

Dropping an 800-pound railroad tie and putting it in the right place to balance on a bridge thirty feet above the ground was a scary proposition. To make the operation safer, Jake had the team use a piece of rail from the Rail Wrecker laid over the bridge rails to act as a pulley. Chains were strung over steel, and around one tie at a time. A worker knocked out the clips holding the tie to the mainline rails, then the gang eased the chains to lower the tie to the girders below. The whole job could be done with most of the gang safely standing on solid ground.

With each tie that was dropped to the girders, the burden the jacks had to lift decreased. The first ten ties were on the girders before the jacks were employed. The devices from the fireman's Jeep managed to lift the rail with ease. The second row of ties were dropped into place.

It only took two hours to stack the ties under the tracks. The alignment still sagged a bit, but it felt secure. "Let's give this a try," Jake ordered.

Nick called Larry on the radio. "Number 5, ease it forward—balancing bridge speed. OVER."

Larry looked at Christina, who had come into the cab for the move. "Why does he always have to try to be so funny?" he asked.

Christina smiled at Larry, picked up the mic and responded, "Roger that, balancing bridge speed. OUT." She hung up the receiver and smiled again at Larry.

He looked back at her with a grimace, released the train brakes, and feathered the independent engine brakes to slowly coast over the span above Highway 72.

It worked perfectly! A few bits of ash fell as the pressure of the train crossed over the makeshift supports, but nothing scary happened. Lisa and Randal Keaton were taking photos and video, as they had since the Moffat Tunnel, to record this latest event. This was just another in a string of hurdles the Zephyr was clearing.

Claire and Suzy were writing down names, times, locations, and descriptions for the official log. They all knew about the intense interest their drive to survive was garnering around the world. They knew what they were chronicling would be seen or read by millions of people. All of them had visions of what that fame would be like once it was all over—if they could just survive.

CHAPTER 33

HIGHWAY 93

"No barrier is strong enough to stop those determined to pass it together."

—CB

Hours of tedious drudgery through deep ash continued. But things were changing. The total depth of ash seemed to be on the decline. Unfortunately, in places it had been drifted by the wind. On the Big Ten Curves, the first major drift was encountered at the wind-break hopper cars. It was short—only thirty feet long, but it was twelve feet tall!

Nick and Larry agreed to hit it at 20 mph to knock the piled up silica and other elements off the rail. The curve, they thought, should make it an easy push. They hit it hard.

"We are not doing that again!" Nick said into the radio, after the battering ram 6413 was nearly tipped over by the weight of the drifted ash when the Zephyr smashed into it.

Larry sat in the cab fuming; he knew better than to do that. But like everyone else, his nerves were getting a little frayed, and he wanted to keep moving. The good news was the ash drift did succumb to the power of the train—barley. Luckily, they learned that lesson up there where the drift was small. Had they been able to see through the gray haze, they would have seen the mega drifts that awaited them.

Nick's phone rang, a Washington, DC, number calling. "Hello, this is Conductor Nick."

203

"Nick, this is CEO Qwana Rice. I want you to know we are all impressed with what you all have done so far, and that we are praying for your safe return."

Nick had not met his new CEO yet. "Thank you, it's an honor to speak with you, Ma'am."

Rice got to the point of her call. "Nick, please listen, we have people here to help you make good decisions. Use them. That stunt on the drift of debris was foolish and dangerous. We expect better. Just take your time. Ask for our help, and let's get you out of there alive."

Nick felt a bit sick in his stomach. "Understood. It won't happen again. We will use all our resources from now on."

Rice was known for being a great negotiator who could get people to see things her way.

"Thank you, Nick. And remember, your leadership is vital. Be strong."

An earthquake can do a great amount of damage to human infrastructure, especially bridges. Up to milepost 17, only one bridge went above the railroad, highway 119 at Rollinsville. That bridge had tipped and sagged a bit, but not enough to interrupt the slow progress of the Zephyr. Now they were entering highly developed areas where every kind of overhead peril could have fallen onto the rail.

Colorado Highway 93 marked the line between the mountains and the city below. It was notoriously dangerous for motorists. Steep grades, tight curves and blind entries caused untold accidents and heartache. As the train got close to the bridge that takes the road over the railroad right-of-way, the Zephyr crew realized that the west side of the span had collapsed. It looked like a solid wall.

"Highway 93 strikes again," Alex said to Noah, as they pushed through the ash for a better look.

Within minutes, everyone on the Zephyr was looking at the fallen bridge. Officials in Omaha and Wilmington were pouring over the photos streamed to them. What they found was that one huge beam of solid concrete, and the paved deck above, had crashed into the cut, through which the train needed to pass. Apparently, the shaking of the earth had wiggled the beam downhill to the point that its north edge slipped off the lip of the abutment. As the beam fell, it cracked, turned on its side, and broke in several places. It had landed on the tracks like a bent elbow held together with strings of rebar. The other beams of the bridge were still sitting precariously on the sill of the abutment.

"If we smash into it too hard, the other beams might fall," Charlie said to Jake. Christina, Larry, Nick, and René were looking at the screen, hoping the brain trust from the outside world had some brilliant ideas.

Finally, a person spoke up, Hank Doney, a civil engineer from the UPR bridge department. "Are Jake and Nick there?" he asked.

"Nick here, Jake is still out looking at the bridge."

The man on the screen didn't want to wait. "Here is our best guess on getting that debris out of your way. Basically, you will use your power, your locomotives, to pull the big chunks west, away from the bridge. With luck, the disturbance won't drop the other beams. We think the gas pipeline between the first and second beam kept the rest of the bridge from bouncing off the abutment, so you don't want to break that. If the broken beam blocking your tracks moves, but it doesn't leave the right-of-way, which we don't think it will, you will have to smash into it to either shove it out of the way or bust it into more manageable pieces. You will have to use the 6413 to do that."

Nick had a million questions for Hank. But they could wait. He asked the man to remain available to help talk them through the procedure. Marshall Knight was to keep the lines of communication open. Nick asked the staff for another briefing to go over the plan. He waited for Jake to join them. The plan met with skepticism from almost everyone.

"I'm sorry, how do we pull huge chunks of broken concrete with railroad locomotives?" Jim asked.

"We have some chains; we can do this. It just might take a while," Jake said. He was already pretty sure they could pound away enough material around the rebar to wrap a chain through those weak parts of the broken span. Then it was a matter of power, weight on drivers. In other words, how much tractive power could they cajole out of the 313 and 309.

Nick got on the PA and shared the news about the bridge with all the passengers. They had sat inside Moffat Tunnel almost a week, and then worked their butts off three days straight so far, only making it 33 miles from where they had started. Being told that a collapsed roadway was now blocking their path was just too much for some of them. Many started to cry. Some cursed openly, and some were overcome with desperation.

Nick knew they were wearing down mentally as well as physically. He felt he had to address that.

"Folks, I know how tough this is on all of us. I am sorry it has not been easier, but we don't get to choose our fate. We do get to choose how we respond to our situation. Make no mistake about it; we choose to make it out of the dead zone alive! That is what we are doing. That is why we are going to punch through this bridge. That is why we are going to get through the next challenge too, and every challenge after that. We are just going to keep going no matter what. We don't have any other option!"

He hung up the mic, grabbed a sledge hammer, and headed to the bridge. All the people on track team #2 who were going on duty at that time followed.

All the tools were pulled off the train for the work crews. René and Larry backed the Zephyr up about half a mile, tied down all the brakes on the cars, and cut off the engines. They pulled up to the work site with just the locomotives, or "light power" as railroaders call it.

By the time they got to the bridge, it was already a hive of activity. Chains from the tunnel shed were being snaked around giant blocks of reinforced concrete. The knuckle of the 6413 was brought right up to the edge of the first piece to be moved. Chains were wrapped as tightly as possible around the 6413.

Jake and Charlie were talking as they used track bolts to secure the chains. "It will hold. These things are designed for pulling massive loads," Charlie said. Jake agreed regarding the chains, but he didn't think passenger engines could pull apart the whole beam.

Back in Omaha, Hank was looking at pictures, listening to Jake and Nick, and clicking on his computer. "Don't try it, you'll snap the chain," he said. "You have to get the concrete to about half that size to have any chance of the chain holding."

The work crew got word of what the trained civil engineer was saying. Discouragement was getting real. "No way we can bust this beam in two with the tools we have," Charlie blurted out.

Nick agreed.

Hank heard their thoughts and started brainstorming for a better idea. He felt there was enough tractive effort on the locomotives to pull the 5,000 ton beam. They just needed stronger chains. "Guys, can you add about five more chains?" Hank asked.

Nick wished they had taken the time to look for more chains back at Moffat Tunnel. "That's all we've got," he answered.

As Nick spoke, Hank saw a big burned-out Ford F-350 in the corner of his screen, with a winch! "What about getting chains and cables from vehicles on the road?"

Everyone looked up at the endless lines of dead cars and trucks.

After a few hours of salvaging, there were enough cables and chains for eight lines around the concrete beam. The track team had used the time it took to gather the added chains and cables to clear as much of the smaller debris as possible away from the tracks. Bigger pieces of the beam would have an unobstructed path when the locomotives pulled them.

Some of the cables were wrapped around the entire UPR locomotive to improve the weight distribution. Hank had never seen such a thing. He did the math on his computer. Two younger engineers were looking over his shoulder. They all felt the beam should move. They also knew it might tear up the tracks as it did, but that was a problem for later on.

"It's Go time. OVER!" Nick said on the radio.

René came on next, "313, René on the point, you are clear for twenty cars, bring 'em back." Larry put the engines in reverse, and added throttle to notch 1. Then he feathered the independent brake lever. Chains and cables tightened. Everyone stood a good distance back for fear of breaking chains and winch lines. UPR CEO Bradford was watching. Everyone inside the train, and around the world, had a real time livestream view. Fingers were crossed. Some folks held their breath.

"Notch two. Notch three!" Larry called out as he added power to the wheels. Sand was gritting the rail as the mighty engines labored under the strain. *POP!*

"That will do Larry! STOP!" Nick was as urgent as he could be. Larry threw the throttle to idle.

"A chain broke. It's okay, no one got hurt." Nick said.

The engineers in Omaha looked again at their calculations. "Oops, sorry, guys, the beam must have more resistance than we thought. You have to get more chains."

Nick looked at his phone a few moments later. He read a text: "Rice here—keep at it. You got this." Nick appreciated the confidence his boss showed in him, and the personal touch.

Brewster, who had first thought of looking for jacks on cars at the previous bridge, made his way to Nick. "You know, Nick, if you need chains, the dump is just over that hill." He was pointing south. "Bulldozers and garbage trucks are loaded with chains."

Nick looked at the old railfan with indignation. "You had to wait till now to remind me about the dump?" Nick directed a crew toward the landfill. Three hours later, thirty people from the Zephyr emerged from the haze, dragging chains through the surreal gray landscape. Nick thought they resembled the ghosts from Dickens' *A Christmas Carol*, hauling their burden through eternity. Brewster had been right again.

The second try at pulling the beam looked ridiculous. Twenty loops of chain connected to the 6413. Larry added power. The huge concrete casting groaned. Then to the surprise of some, it started to move. Once freed from its settled spot, it slid more easily. After pulling 100 feet, Nick directed Larry to stop pulling. The beam was away from the immediate bridge area. Unfortunately, it was still on the tracks. The beams still holding up the rest of the bridge had not fallen when the broken beam was removed. So far so good.

The entire effort was taking on a life of its own. Outside media reps, who were monitoring every move the Zephyr made, dubbed it, "Operation Beam Buster." For the people on the Zephyr, it was not a slogan; it was life or death. Either they got by that bridge, or they would most likely die.

Larry gave some slack on the chains. The 6413 was untethered from the beam laying across the tracks. The mechanical team buttressed up their cow catcher on the battered UPR engine for ramming. Larry pushed into the isolated beam. It moved to the side a little. He backed up. Then he slammed into the massive dead weight again with a bit more umph.

Larry smashed the 6413 into the concrete five more times. He hit it a little harder with each impact. Finally the obstruction was out of the way, and the entire locomotive could pass by the huge chunk of concrete and rebar.

Dragging and ramming the beam had destroyed some of the main line tracks. Jake and Charlie, along with track team #2, used the Rail Wrecker to try straightening things up enough to allow the locomotives to go forward, but it was no use. The ties were smashed to bits. Twice, the crew had to use the rerailing plate to get the leading axle of the 6413 back on the rails.

Nick racked his brain for a way to repair the track. *Ambrose!* he thought. *Nothing Like It in the World* by Stephen E. Ambrose, the story of the building of the Transcontinental Railroad. Nick's plan was simple. Don't waste time trying to fix what can't be repaired. Instead, build a new track in place of the broken track. Nick gathered his key track guys— Jake, Charlie, Christina, Larry, René, Alex, and a few others. "Guys, more than 150 years ago, the Union Pacific Railroad was built by hand across a vast wilderness. All we have to do is fix a little 100 foot section of rail on broken ties. If they could do what they did, we can surely do this."

Two teams got to work. One started working to tear out the hopelessly broken track. The other went to get materials for rebuilding the line. Knut and his biker gang started cutting out the worthless twisted rail.

The second team went back west 400 yards with Larry and the locomotives. They were looking for some short pieces of rail from the house track back on the Rocky siding. Rails on the house track were spiked into wooden ties. Those ties were scorched on top, but not burned through. The crew unbolted joint plates, pried out spikes, and lifted off the rail piece by piece. They dug out thirty of the best wood ties they could find under the ash. The materials were lashed onto the walkways along the sides of the 6413. Larry then ran the power back toward the bridge, delivering all the materials to the work site.

Some jobs are tough physically. Nobody on the work crews had ever had to work as hard as they did that day. The bike cutter was still working well, but it wore out peddlers every fifteen minutes. Lifting ties and rail into place and then driving in spikes to keep tracks steady is backbreaking. Hands were worn raw through the improvised work gloves. Lungs strained to suck in air through dust masks. After a few hours, it was almost impossible to move on. And yet they all kept moving. Slowly, progress was being made.

The problem with Highway 93 was not over when the tracks were fixed. Some dangling slabs of roadway still hung down over the track where the beam had been. About ten pieces of rebar were still connecting the fallen concrete and asphalt with the upright part of the bridge. All day long Knut, Olivia, Yao Ping, and other peddlers had used the bike and rail cutting wheel to slice through broken tracks. Now they had to drag the bike up onto the bridge deck and tackle the tangle of blue-green rebar steel.

In the midst of the drudgery, Knut remarked to Olivia, "If we get out of this alive, I'm never riding a stationary bike again!"

The bike was perched up on the unstable bridge at an odd angle to reach the rebar. It was scary work. The biker gang used safety harnesses around the rider, the two guys supporting the bike, and the bike itself. It didn't take long to slice the first several strands of rebar. They were down to the last two places they needed to cut. Halfway through one of the last inch-thick steel reinforcers, the whole section of dangling roadway broke loose. It snapped the remaining rebar and fell to the ground.

The harnesses worked. The workers and the bike were pulled to relative safety. Below, workers building the new track heard the scream and ran. They all bolted as fast as they could. Everyone got away. About twenty tons of road deck had fallen thirty feet.

The only injury was Chance's leg. He was peddling at the time of the mishap. His leg was caught between the safety strap on the bike and the part of the road that fell. He had a serious gash. Yao and the others did quick first aid to stop the bleeding. Two of them helped the man back to the clinic on the lower level of the parlor car.

Nick saw Chance being hobbled off to Dr. Abraham and nurse Susan. Once he knew that the injury was not life-threatening, he looked at Chance. "You did that on purpose, didn't ya?"

Chance looked at Nick with confusion.

"Look, if you wanted to hang out with Susan, all you had to do was ask." Everyone grinned.

Chance looked at the conductor. "Guilty," was all he said.

After more than thirty hours of constant toil, the collapsed portion of Highway 93 bridge over the tracks was sufficiently removed to allow passage of the Zephyr. Once east of the blockade, Nick ordered a three-hour break to rest, eat rations, and hydrate. Everyone collapsed into coach seats or beds. The health clinic was jammed with minor cuts, blisters, and cases of dehydration. There was pride in what they had accomplished, but everyone knew that Highway 93 was only the first of many bridges as they headed into the Denver metro area. They all wondered how many more broken bridges lay ahead.

Tim, the premier coach attendant, had waited patiently for a chance to see Dr. Abraham. The two were on a first-name basis by this point. The old railroader required a cornucopia of medications to give him the ability to function in spite of his inoperable cancer. After nearly two weeks away from home, he only had two days' supply of medication left.

The doctor had him reduce doses by one third, to stretch out his supply one more day. "After that, there is really nothing more you can do," she told him.

"Okay," Tim said. "I'm just really hoping to live long enough to see my dog one more time."

Susan was listening. "What is your dog's name?" she asked.

Tim looked at her and smiled. "David Moffat," he said.

CHAPTER 34

BARBARA GULCH

"Nothing reflects so much honor on a workman as a trial of his work and its endurance of it."

—Charles Spurgeon

When progress resumed, track team #1 was back on duty. Almost immediately, the train had to come to a full stop again. Ash was too deep to push through. The north side of Barbara Gulch had nearly 20 feet of ash drifting over the rails. It would be a tough dig. The drift was nearly half a mile long. Without much talk, most of the people on the Zephyr took whatever tools they had and dragged themselves outside to start digging.

Conductor Nick started walking through the drifted ash up the hill to the north. He was waist deep. Nobody knew why he was leaving. He seemed to be in a trance. Randal Keaton pointed him out to a small group of workers resting in the 512 car.

Rashid said he heard Nick say, "Her school is right over that hill."

It didn't take long for them to figure out what was happening.

Rashid slipped on his mask and started after their conductor. The big man from Chicago had to work hard to catch up with Nick. When he did, he found him completely dissolved in grief. They were right on the crest of the slope. What they saw was devastating.

North of the gulch, on a plain called Rocky Flats, the first large community of the Denver metro area lay before them. Technically, it was part of the city of Arvada, but everyone called it by the development name, Candelas. Hundreds of relatively new and expensive homes neatly lined on tree-adorned streets with a large school, an attractive shopping center, recreation parks, and more. It was the quintessential American bedroom community.

When Rashid and Nick got their first glimpse of Candelas, it looked like a nuclear bomb had gone off. Not one house was left. Only a few walls and chimneys made of stone remained standing. Every vehicle was a destroyed hulk. Fire had consumed everything, and now all of it was covered in wind-whipped ash.

Nick saw Rashid and started talking, "She's right there. I just had to see where she was . . . is . . . had been when . . . "

Rashid put his arm around Nick as the conductor started to cry. He tried to reason with Nick. "I know, but you said we don't have time to feel sorry for ourselves; we have to survive first. Then we can have our break downs."

Nick looked at his friend. "You're right. I'm not really going to go all the way to where she must have died, but I wish I had been there." He shook his head. "I wish I were dead," he said in a moment of complete despair. He placed his bandana back over his dirty N95 mask when the sting at the back of his throat reminded him of where he was.

Rashid was just listening, just being present, and trying to catch his breath through his rapidly clogging mask. After a long silence, with only the sound of Nick sobbing, Rashid spoke. "Come on, buddy, let's get back to the train. They need us there. There's nothing we can do up here."

Nick wasn't done yet. "It's not just Juliette; it's Beatrice too. She's out there in our car somewhere."

Rashid knew Nick's family because they rode the train on occasion. He saw how they all loved each other. He had seen the close emotional bond that connected Nick with his wife and daughter. "It's okay," he said. "They are both in a much better place than this. Now c'mon, let's get back to where we can do some real good. Somebody out there loves the people we are saving. We are going to save them, so their people don't have to feel the way you feel now." He led his conductor back down the embankment.

The walk, the cry, and the support from his friend were good therapy for the burdened conductor who was leading this bedraggled band in a banged-up train. The sight of Candelas completely destroyed seemed to sap hope from Nick's heart. He was tempted to quit, just walk away. *The others can save themselves if they want*, he thought, *but I don't feel like going on.*

This was a pivotal moment for Nick. He had to decide what he was going to do with himself, what kind of man he was going to be. He thought of his two sons living in Europe with families of their own. He was afraid they would be ashamed of him if he gave up. Another thought pulled him back: his job wasn't finished. His father had taught him that winners in life finish what they start. Quitters might suffer less, but they never win. Nick, and everyone else on the train, had committed themselves to survive together. They weren't done yet.

Finish what you started, he told himself. He raised his head, took as deep a breath as he could, and pushed powerfully through the final steps to the vestibule door of the 540 car. At the threshold, he thanked Rashid for joining him on the slope. The two were warmly welcomed back on the train.

The Sandovals were busy in the bottom of the crowded 510 car, operating the mental health clinic. One person after another came to them to talk about feelings of giving up, grief, fear, and despair. Some had depression so deep that suicide felt like a real option. Rashid suggested Nick go chat with them.

The seasoned conductor had never been to a "shrink" before in his life. But he could feel his grip on sanity slipping. He paid them a visit. Maria, Javier, and Nick talked for twenty minutes. When Nick left, he was ready to lead again. His grief was not quenched by any means, but he found a way to compartmentalize it. His loss would not dominate his thoughts, at least not yet. He would allow the full impact of the most emotional event of his life to hit him, but on his terms and in his timing.

Nick took Reagan out to dig. They worked for two hours in the filthy dust. At the work site, they saw Jay, a man well over eighty years old, giving all the effort his body allowed. Noah, Alex, and Luke were still working hard without any complaints in spite of their youth.

Brewster, Harry, and James, the three oldest train fans from the Silver Sky, were dragging piles of ash down the slope away from the tracks. Musician Jimmy had pulled the hinges off his guitar case and was using the big half as an ash scoop. Nick saw Senator and Mrs. Jackson, covered in volcanic debris, toiling away at the endless burden before them. Literally everyone was involved in the massive effort. Neville, tour director Linda, and the whole British group were making use of the "crap cart" to haul ash out of a drifted cut.

What a beautiful sight, Nick thought, *to see the young and old, rich and poor, strong and weak all working for a common purpose.*

Patty and Sharon, friends from Hastings who had originally taken the train to visit Yellowstone, had been digging for hours. They were exhausted. Patty, in an effort to lighten the mood, said to Sharon, "I'm so thirsty I would even drink a glass of warm Kool-Aid."

She knew Sharon was on the town council that promoted the Kool-Aid Museum. The humorous dig did not sit too well.

"Patty, right now I just don't want to hear it. I'm tired, I am hurting all over, I'm hungry, I'm thirsty, I'm scared, it's cold, and I want to go home." She started to cry.

Patty felt terrible. She hugged her friend.

Rob and Herman rolled through the Zephyr. Discouraged and worn-out people lay exhausted in the seats and rooms of the passenger train. They all looked to see what Herman had to say on his headband this time, hoping for some kind of inspiration.

Herman didn't smile as usual. He was more determined now. His message was blunt: We don't quit!

After six hours of hand digging and "zephyring," the train crew was finally able to punch through the drifts of Barbara Gulch. It felt like heaven to be rolling on a relatively open track as they approached Leyden siding. Every one of the diggers were spent. Water was given freely, even though tanks in two cars were already dry.

CHAPTER 35

COLD WAR HORSE

"If there must be trouble, let it be in my day, that my child may have peace."

—Thomas Paine

"How ironic," engineer Christina thought as she gazed upon the desolation from the cab of the 313. She had almost bought a home in Candelas ten years earlier, but chose not to because she was afraid of radioactive contamination. The ground just north of where the Candales community was built had been a weapons factory during the Cold War. Rocky Flats built enriched plutonium triggers for America's nuclear arsenal. After a billion-dollar clean-up, homes and stores were allowed to be built on the fringes of the site.

The government claimed it was safe, but Christina would have had to sign a "release of liability" form to buy the house she wanted. Any possible future links to health problems related to the radioactivity of the land under the home would have been at her own risk.

At the time, Christina had felt rather vulnerable. She had recently been divorced and was raising her son as a single mother. All her decisions were made to give herself and her son the strongest possible chance for a comfortable and secure life. She knew there wasn't enough money to take unnecessary risks. She didn't say much about it. She simply moved to Highlands Ranch thirty miles to the south. That choice was typical of the kind of person she was: quiet, prudent, and deliberate.

Christina often wondered if she was overreacting back then. *Only time would tell*, she thought. As it turned out, there wasn't enough time to find out. The town, built next to the birthplace of so many weapons of mass destruction, looked like it had lost a nuclear war. Utterly lifeless, shattered, burnt, and silent. The Red Horse statue referred to as the Cold War Horse, dedicated to the memory of those who worked at Rocky Flats, was melted into the ground.

Energy and endurance were running out on every level on the Zephyr. The amount of effort it took to get by the Highway 93 bridge, through the drifts, plowing the rock slides, shunting the dead freight train, and more, had taken their toll.

On a physical level, workers were hungry and thirsty. They were doing herculean labor on starvation rations. Muscle mass, stamina, and coordination were on the decline for everyone. Small and annoying physical irritants like old injuries and hurting backs were becoming harder to ignore. Compared to the thin air up at Moffat tunnel, breathing was easy down in Denver. But it was still hard to get enough oxygen through the rapidly degrading masks. Ash and sweat had a way of caking up in a person's hair, but there was no more water for washing. Life was miserable, and getting worse.

Fuel, food, water, and battery power were all running low. Comforts and protective equipment like gloves and regular clothes were worn thin. Hope itself was starting to wane. Where were the survivors in Arvada? Surely someone would come out of the ruins to greet them, or at least beg for supplies and a ride. No one was there.

René looked at the internet to see what people outside the Dead Zone were saying about the Zephyr. She went to the Friends of the Zephyr page. There was Derek's shot of the gleaming train reflecting a brilliant sunrise through crystal clear skies at Barr Lake more than ten days prior. She peered out the window. The train was on a curve. She could just see to the end of it. The skin of the train cars was filthy and horribly scratched in places. Light from the sun was hazy and obscured. There was nothing beautiful about the train anymore. She wept. She was homesick for beauty and vibrant color.

In the health clinic, a young woman, Alison, came seeking help. She had nausea, headaches, and was not feeling herself. It had been going on for three days. Dr. Abraham was busy, so nurse Susan made the initial diagnosis. *There is something familiar about this lady*, Susan thought.

She asked where the woman was from, and where she had been traveling to. She and her husband Brian were returning to their home in Provo, Utah. She had just auditioned at the Juilliard School of Music. Her dream was to make it into the Mormon Tabernacle Choir. His parents had bought them a sleeping car room. It was like a honeymoon—at least until Yellowstone.

As soon as the lady said, "Sleeping Car," Susan knew who this person was. As Susan had waited on the platform back in Omaha, the train rolled by with two very engaged and surprised lovers frantically trying to close the curtain of their lower-level bedroom window. The crowd on the platform cheered and clapped as the car rolled past to the far end of the station.

The nurse held on to her professional demeanor. "From the symptoms you are describing, my guess is you are experiencing morning sickness."

"You think I am pregnant?" Allison asked, sounding a bit surprised.

"Is that possible?" Susan wanted to know.

"Yes, we have been trying for a few months now. But this is a terrible time to be pregnant."

Susan agreed, but did not let her opinion show. "Let's not jump the gun. We are going to use one of our four instant tests donated by other passengers."

The test was positive. Susan had a look at the paper strip. "Well, congratulations! Now don't you worry about a thing. We will help you through these early stages. Then we will be rescued. You and your baby will be just fine."

Allison was shell shocked. She thanked Susan. "I can't wait to tell my husband. He is out digging ash now, but his shift ends soon."

That's when Allison finally asked if Susan had seen something "interesting" on the platform in Omaha. Susan didn't answer right away, not knowing what to say. Susan was embarrassed. "Oh, my goodness, are you one of the people who saw us?"

"Um, I . . . "

"It's okay, I just don't think I have ever been more embarrassed in my entire life," the blushing young woman said.

Susan was kind. "You have nothing to be embarrassed about. It is our secret." The two women smiled.

CHAPTER 36

NOBODY?

"When left to stand alone, the brave stand together."

—CB

Getting past the first parts of the Denver metro area was relatively easy. Bridges over the tracks all held up. Over-engineering and investment by the railroad and the Colorado Department of Transportation were paying off for the Zephyr. Other than some automobiles that were stuck in traffic jams as they had tried to cross the tracks, no major obstacles challenged the Zephyr. Christina plowed through the abandoned cars and trucks with the 6413, like Eric Bieniemy used to run through the Nebraska defensive line. It was easy, but the noise was explosive. Nick thought it ironic that those crossings were designated "quiet zones."

The promise of resupply upon entering the city quickly faded. Fires had burned everything. Still-smoldering piles that had once been houses lined both sides of the tracks. Not a usable drop of gas, not a functional vehicle, not a living thing—anywhere. Just deadness wherever anyone looked. Nick had seen something similar before. On December 30, 2021, the Marshall Fire engulfed over 1,000 homes just twelve miles north of where he had lived. The scene he was seeing was the same, only multiplied a hundred fold. *At least back then there were some surviving homes and trees*, he thought.

FEMA coordinators were not giving the Zephyr any good news. No other survivors from the entire Denver area had communicated with the outside world in days. The few that did manage to live through the first harrowing days, had either died since, or found a way to get south, out of the dead zone. Most simply stopped communicating.

The Zephyr pushed on. With only a few hundred yards of visibility through the haze, no one could see the towers of Downtown. When the train finally got close to North Yard, the tall grain silos came into view like a beacon.

"You think there is anything in those that we can eat?" Thomas asked Ron in the kitchen of the diner. In order to keep the work crews going, Thomas had given out rations faster than planned. The shelves and cupboards of the diner were now frighteningly bare.

"Maybe we need to tell Nick to let us have a look in the silos," Ron said.

"I'm on it." The chef headed upstairs to get a hold of Nick on the PA.

The train was stopped at CPDS 003—Utah Junction. Track team #2 was busy cleaning out switches. Larry, Christina, René, Nick, Jake, and Charlie had already spoken to railroad leaders. They all felt the main track to Prospect Junction would be free of parked freight trains. They assumed the Zephyr should be able to cross the Balloon Bridge and head south on the Pikes Peak subdivision, the old joint line to Pueblo and beyond.

Another conference call began at North Yard. "What is the status of rescue from the east?" Nick asked.

"Nick, there is no nice way to say this: Nobody is coming to help you. It isn't that we don't want to help. We just can't get through. I'm sorry," said Qwana Rice, CEO of the passenger railroad company. "But we are not giving up. We will do all we can for you from here. I am working with Bradford at the UPR to get a train loaded with military troop carriers from Texas to run as far north as we can. Right now, all those vehicles are being used in Kansas and Oklahoma to evacuate civilians from the fringe zone. I think soon they can load up a flat-car train and maybe get to Colorado Springs. You guys had to do so much to get to where you are now. But we have to ask even more—you need to go south on the Pikes Peak sub. Get close to Cheyenne Mountain."

Nick knew what she was saying. "So the military is willing to go get the Brass out of the bunker at NORAD, but not us. We can hitch a ride if we find a way to get there?"

Rice put it differently, "The railroad is coming for everyone we can rescue. Because we need the military's help, we are allowing their personnel and civilians to hitch a ride with us."

Nick replied, with a hint of sarcasm, "Oh, well then, on behalf of the crew and passengers of the Zephyr, when you put it like that, we feel much better."

CHAPTER 37

RESOURCES

"When all effort proves insufficient, a little bit of good luck can go a long ways."

—CB

Yao Ping was with the search party sent to check out the grain silos. The imposing concrete structures still retained warmth from the eruption ten days before. Steel doors in the walls of the silos were discolored from fire. Using rock bars, the team was able to pry open an unloading shoot. In normal times, grain would have spilled onto the loading dock. Nothing came out. Inside they saw blackened charcoal that appeared to have been corn at one time. The chef and his food specialist were ready to go back to the train in defeat.

"Wait, do not go," the Chinese man begged. "We must dig deep—to the core. We may find good seeds." Yao Ping knew that fire needs three things: fuel, spark, and oxygen. He thought there was not enough oxygen in the silo to create fire. So even though the grain near the burning hot concrete walls would have cooked and turned to charcoal in the eruption, the further into the middle they could get, the better the seeds should be.

Using the longest implements the team had, they dug a two foot diameter hole eight feet deep into the contents of the silo. It was still a blackened mass, but some streaks of color in some kernels gave hope that deeper in, there might still be some life-sustaining grain. No one on the team wanted to crawl into the hole to dig further for fear of a cave-in.

"Maybe we will find food in a grocery store further south . . . "

Before Ron could finish his excuse for giving up on the silo full of corn, the small, highly educated man from China scurried into the black hole with a shovel and started whacking his way deeper. If the unstable roof of the charcoal hole gave way, the young man would be crushed and die in an instant. Black debris shot back at the men still outside the silo. They rapidly scooped out what Yao Ping sent them. Then they heard rumbling from deep within the bowels of the massive structure.

First there were dirty tennis shoes. Then two legs blasted out of the hole. A moving mass of yellow corn surrounded the rest of Yao Ping as he burst out of the silo. The slight man jumped back to his feet, gasping for breath as tons of yellow kernels flowed to the ground like water.

"You did it!" Thomas yelled at Yao.

The diminutive man smiled broadly. The whole team started filling the containers they brought along. They returned triumphantly to the Zephyr as the train was ready to proceed on the main track through North Yard.

"Food! We've got tons of food!" Ron hollered to the people at the open door of the diner. They ran out to help. Nick got to the diner shortly thereafter.

"Corn?" Nick asked as he looked at the bounty of yellow sustenance.

"Yes, isn't it beautiful!" Ron said with excitement.

"Um, yes—great. I love corn." He didn't let anyone know about his allergies that had forced his family to leave Iowa more than fifty years before. *I still hate corn. I have another ten pounds or so to shed before things start getting serious for me. I can keep going without eating corn,* he thought to himself.

Nick asked one of the locomotive engineers to come to the kitchen. Christina showed up. Thomas and Ron were looking at bushels of beautiful corn just waiting to be turned into something edible.

"I can't give you cooking power—HEP—because we are getting very low on fuel," Christina explained to Ron, who replied, "But I have to make bread, or something with this stuff. We can't eat it hard and raw like this."

Just then Jake, who had walked south to the yard office, keyed his radio and shouted out to all those who could hear him, "I found fuel!"

Jake was at the UPR tower and engine servicing facility.

"What?" Larry asked.

"The fuel tank of a SD70ACe-T4—the UPR 3010! It looks like it is intact and sounds full when I knock on the tank walls. We can siphon fuel from this engine and keep going."

Paint, decals, hoses, battery box, wires, and glass were burned off the 3010. But the fuel cap was on the fill spout and the tank itself had not blown up or warped, as the other older engine tanks had. Jake twisted the fuel cap off, taking care in case there was built-up pressure inside. With the cap off, he could tell that the inside of the tank was not damaged.

Nick and Larry got the mechanical team stirred up to help Jake.

There was no fuel gauge left on the 3010, so the team had no way to tell for sure how much fuel was in the tank. If the engine had been serviced and fueled before the eruption, it would have 4,800 gallons of fuel to siphon off and put in the Zephyr's two locomotives. If it had just been delivered from a long run and not fueled, the tank would be nearly empty.

"It has to be full," Alex said. "The fuel itself was cold when the hot ash hit the area. The tank of the new EPA-compliant engines insulated that fuel. It must have been enough to keep the temperature of the fuel low enough not to blow. It was enough insulation to give time for the outside temperature to drop."

"I think you're right, Alex." Jake said. "We've got fuel! Now all we have to do is transfer it to our engines and cruise south."

René and Nick tied down the train and cut off the two good locomotives and the 6413. The train crew left the Zephyr cars so the teams could gather and load more corn. The power lash-up went to the engine servicing track switch. They backed up on an empty yard track adjacent to the 3010. Their power just made it under a half-collapsed bridge. It was West 48th Avenue.

Doug got his drill and buckets in short order. Unlike the small fuel intake on the Silver Sky, the big orifice for the freight unit tank allowed the two-inch caliper backup hose to fit. No need to drill holes, Doug shoved the hose as far into the tank as it would go. He got as low to the ground as he could get and prepared to suck on the end to create the needed siphon.

"Stop!" yelled Neville Hampton from England. "We have a Hoover—don't risk your lungs."

Everyone looked at the aging Englishman. "What's a Hoover?" Doug asked.

Jake answered, "That's British for a vacuum cleaner."

Neville nodded his head, realizing he had used a term that was just too foreign for the people he was with.

"Duh, thanks," Doug said.

"That thing sucks," Luke said, in an attempt at some humor. Within minutes the vacuum cleaner from the Silver Sky was fetched from the train, and hooked up by electric extension cord to the 110-volt outlet in the cab of the 313. The hose end of the vacuum was shoved up the valved end of the backup hose. The machine was turned on. The valve was opened. Fuel was sucked into the hose. "Siphon accomplished!" Luke proclaimed.

"That's dope!" Doug said.

Like magic, the pinkish-brown liquid was filling white plastic containers. In between buckets, the valve on the end of the hose was closed to hold the siphon pressure. An inverted safety cone from the Sky worked as a filling funnel on the 313 and 309. Transferring thousands of gallons of fuel with just three five-gallon buckets took a while, but it worked.

The path between the two engines was made easier once ash was packed. Enough people were employed to make a "bucket line" that rapidly moved the diesel. Dr. Sayers was in the line. He told the person next to him how ironic it was that the fuel that was possibly going to save them from the effects of Yellowstone had probably been created because of huge peat bogs buried by Yellowstone, more than 600,000 years before.

While the head end of the Zephyr was getting some much-needed fuel, the Silver Sky guys were on the back of the train at Utah Junction. Jennifer, an avid steam engine fan, had helped prepare the North Yard water tower for the BIG BOY. From where they sat, she could just see that structure through the haze. "Guys," she said, "I know we had the water crane full the day of the eruption. Look, it's still standing."

Jennifer, Alex, Noah, and Jim made their way to the tower.

The tank was full of water and standing strong! "How come it didn't burn and warp like everything else?" Alex asked.

Jennifer, a science teacher, and an expert in thermodynamics, explained that the single-walled old steel tank was kept cool by the water inside due to its high specific heat. By the time the water got hot enough to boil, the heat blast was already past. Since the tank did not take a direct hit from a lava bomb, it weathered the storm. The ground around the tower had minimal grass and no close trees or buildings. As she spoke, Jim found a valve. He twisted it. It squeaked as it turned, and like a fountain in the desert, fresh clean water without any contamination spewed forth.

Noah ran back to the train. "We've got water!" he yelled when he got inside the train. "Thousands of gallons of beautiful clean water!"

The message was relayed to the mechanical team siphoning fuel. Nick said that after every drop of diesel was transferred into the 313 and 309 from the UPR 3010, they would come back to the train, hook everything up, and then nuzzle up to the water crane.

Three hours later, the 313 fuel gauge read 1,850 gallons and the 309 showed 1,722 gallons. The engines were back on the train.

"Light up the HEP for Ron and Thomas," Nick ordered.

Usually, a passenger train never carries a water hose on the road. Private cars, on the contrary, often pack a conduit for filling their potable water tanks. The Silver Sky had such a hose. Her crew had been wise enough to grab it before abandoning their car near Moffat Tunnel. They took the hose and wedged it onto the drain pipe of the water tower. The other end, with its FDA approved water fill nozzle, was plugged into the 540 car. The valve opened. Water flowed.

"The tank on the car is filling up!" Nick reported on the radio. René relayed it on the PA. The whole train cheered again.

In a matter of four hours, the Zephyr had replenished its supplies of food, water, and energy. Nick and Larry backed up the train one car at a time to fill every water tank. With water plentiful, Rita organized a rotation for everyone to take a badly needed shower. Newlyweds Jim and Sammy were allowed to have the first symbolic showers.

The train sat there until the next morning. Sleeping cars were filled with water four times before everyone had a chance to wash. Lena, from Ukraine, taught everyone how to wash their clothes in the sinks. Sadly, it was a skill she learned after the Russians destroyed the water and electrical systems in her village and took every washing machine during the 2022/23 war.

It seemed as if everything was better. The train had fuel, water, food, and electricity. Herman typed out on his computer "VIDEO GAME." His dad didn't understand. "You want to play a video game?"

"no"

"You have something to say about a video game?"

"Yes"

Herman started typing again. Slowly, he got it out. "WE ARE IN A VIDEO GAME."

"We are? Why do you say that?"

Herman had spent a lifetime playing video games. He knew how they worked. "EACH LEVEL HARDER. IF WE WIN, WE GET STUFF."

"Oh, of course. It's like we are living through a real-life video game. We must have won because we found food, fuel, and water. Right?"

"NOT OVER. NOW IT GETS HARDER." Herman smiled. He liked the game. He was excited to see how it would end.

CHAPTER 38

TIME PRESSURE

"Don't watch the clock; do what it does. Keep going."

—Sam Levenson

Senator Jackson and his wife were in an economy bedroom on their regular rotation. He got a call from his chief of staff who had run his campaign. He and Janice listened to what the man was saying. It was hard to believe. The staffer said he had gotten insider information that a coalition of political opponents from the extreme left and far right had secretly conspired against him. Their diabolical plan was to prevent help from getting to the Zephyr, in hopes that Senator Jackson would die out there. Without Senator Jackson, they believed, the independent moderation movement would end.

After the call, the Jacksons had a serious conversation. The senator did not want to let his enemies win. Mrs. Jackson spoke sternly, "Now you listen here, Tony; this isn't about politics anymore. This is about the lives of the 242 other people on this train. We cannot put them in any more danger than they are already in. We have to do whatever it takes to make sure we don't cause extra harm to any of them."

Antonio agreed with her, as he usually did. "So, what can we do? Do we just walk away into the ash?"

Janice didn't know. "Why don't you give Qwana Rice a call? We know her. She's trustworthy," his wife suggested.

Aunt Suzy heard what Herman had said to his dad about their whole adventure being just like a video game. She asked if Nick would come talk to Herman. The conductor, freshly washed and shaven with clean, although still-damp uniform, came to the coach car where Herman was sitting.

"Hi Herman, what can I do for you?"

To save Herman from the exhausting effort of typing, his dad told Nick about the video game analogy.

Nick responded, "Herman, that is very astute of you. But this isn't a game, and I don't believe things will get tougher before we are rescued. I think we have done pretty darn good to get here, and it will be smooth sailing from now on."

Herman was working on a statement when Nick's phone rang.

"Conductor Nick here."

"Nick, Jack Steele at Omaha. Listen, I don't know if you have been following the weather, but we're getting concerned."

Nick looked at Herman with a momentary glance. "Oh? Go on."

Jack laid it out straight, "We have two massive storms brewing. One is a hurricane in the Atlantic, and another is a full-fledged typhoon in the Pacific. They are acting oddly, perhaps because of the disturbance to the upper atmosphere caused by Yellowstone. Anyway, it looks like the hurricane will hit hard in Texas, then stall over western Kansas and south eastern Colorado. The typhoon remnants are predicted to linger just east of the Continental Divide west of Canon City, Colorado. Both are expected to dump unprecedented amounts of rain. Perhaps causing catastrophic flooding right on your path out of the Dead Zone."

Nick was perplexed. "Okay, so we better just sit right here and wait for you with a rescue train, or the army, or something." Jack's tone was somber.

"That won't happen Nick. All our efforts are being redirected from pushing to Denver. Authorities are trying to save folks in cities that are still full of living people, like Lincoln, Wichita, and Sioux City. They are giving up on you."

Nick felt acid in his mouth. He was angry, scared, and feeling betrayed all at the same time. He did his best to think it through. He knew they were leaving him and everyone on the train to die. But if he demanded help, it would be at the expense of many others who would die instead of them if rescue efforts were redirected to the Zephyr.

We have to save ourselves, he thought.

After a long pause, Nick answered. "When does the rain start falling in Colorado?" Jack was not too clear, but said the best guess was forty-eight hours. Colorado Springs to Trinidad would be hit the hardest.

Nick did some fast calculations. He was 300 miles from the edge of the Dead Zone going east, but only 200 miles from the southern border. The closer they got in the train, the fewer steps on foot. He decided they had to either go south, as CEO Rice had instructed, or stay there for who knows how long.

Dr. Abraham called for Nick to come to the health clinic. He got there expecting a report about a serious injury. It was worse. "Nick, there are thirty-five people on this train that need medication critical to their survival. Mostly heart, diabetes, and blood pressure meds. Sean and I have stretched what we have as far as we can, but now most supplies are out, and people are starting to fade. Here is the deal: Either we get a fresh supply of five different medications in the next few days, or people start dying."

Nick had already spoken with Reagan's mom Claire about his behavior issues and her dwindling supply of meds. He kept listening to the doctor as the realization set in that lack of medication was a far bigger problem than just a few tantrums.

Abraham continued, "Also I am starting to see some beginning effects of malnutrition. Corn and water can help us hang on, but not indefinitely. As bodies weaken, susceptibility to illness grows. You have to expect waves of people getting sick, really sick, like a pandemic on steroids, and soon. Nick, HIPAA laws would nail me for saying this, but one of them is your friend Tim."

Nick looked at the doctor who had selflessly served the people on the Zephyr for days on end as he contemplated their grim situation.

Nick dialed up Omaha. Jack Steele answered the phone. "Listen up, Jack, we are going to go south as fast as we can. And when we can't go any further, we are going to walk on—no matter what the weather does. Can we just go into Cheyenne Mountain? When we get there, we could wait out the storm with the military guys? They should have enough food, medicine, and water."

Jack had been briefed on that question ahead of time by FEMA. The agency had been instructed by the US Joint Chiefs of Staff. "Nick, this comes from the very top. You and the people on the train will not be allowed into the secure military facility of NORAD. They do not have the means to sustain all of you for any extended period."

Nick had no words for Jack. He had to think for another moment. He wanted his message to be heard by those who had decided who should live and who should die. "Jack, let everyone know that the Zephyr and all its people are not going to quit. We are not going to die because of a rainstorm. We are heading toward Texas by rail. We are going to go on and on and on! And when we make it back to civilization, I want to meet with the director of FEMA. Because I'm going to shove a fist full of volcanic ash right down that moron's throat!"

Nick thought about Herman's prediction. The conductor went to see him and explain their situation. Herman smiled as if he was saying, *I told you so—now you have to get through the advanced levels of the game.*

Nick called Jack Steele again. "Yeah, Nick, I'm here."

Nick tried to compose himself. "Sorry about that ash-in-the-throat thing, I'm a little emotional right now. So tell me, this superstorm we are about to get hammered by, does it have a name yet?"

"It's two storms, Wanda in the Atlantic and Xina in the Pacific."

"Okay, can you please call the combined storms over Colorado Superstorm Herman?"

Steele replied, "I can ask—I think NOAA decides names. Why Herman?"

Nick answered while looking at Herman, "Because he is the man who correctly predicted that things would be getting much worse."

"Okay, Nick, as far as I'm concerned, Superstorm Herman it is."

Nick briefed everyone on the train regarding their status. He said they would fill up as much as possible with supplies, and go as fast as they could southbound to beat Superstorm Herman. He figured if they could get to Trinidad, Colorado, they would have a shot. It was 220 miles. They had two days. He ended the blunt statement, "We leave in twenty minutes. Be ready to roll. And don't worry, we have already done so much to get this far. We are just going to press on. We got this! Let's go."

Senator Antonio Jackson came to Nick with a disturbed look in his eyes. "Conductor, may I have a word with you in private?"

Nick was angry and feeling betrayed. *Why didn't the government bend over backward to save a senator?* he wondered. Before Jackson could begin talking, Nick's phone rang, Qwana Rice again.

Jackson told Nick to take the call and put it on speaker phone mode.

"Nick, I know the senator is with you. Now please listen closely and keep this 100 percent confidential. We have reason to believe that there are forces in the United States Government that do not want you or any of your passengers to survive. Their reason is simple—they want the political movement Senator Jackson is leading to die with you out there on that train."

Nick was stunned by what he was hearing. He looked at the tall older man, dumbfounded.

Jackson spoke, "It is true, Nick. My people and sources confirmed it."

"That's why we are not getting rescued, and they won't even let us into NORAD?" Nick asked.

Rice answered, "We believe so. Rescuers couldn't get to Denver regardless, but they are not going to send any real help any time soon."

Jackson nodded, and began speaking, "Nick, I am so sorry my presence is imperiling everyone on this train. Janice and I would gladly just walk away if that meant you all will . . ."

"Hold on a minute!" Nick demanded. He was truly angry.

"Nobody is walking anywhere. This is crap! We are not going to allow some kind of petty political bickering to stop us. We are ALL going to survive this together. ALL OF US!"

Nick was not finished. "Qwana, you muster all the support you can. Pull any string you've got. Get someone to come help us. While you do that, we will rescue ourselves. We'll make our own way to Colorado Springs. Then Pueblo. Then Trinidad. Then Texas if we have to!

We are going to get this man back to civilization. He is going back to the US Senate. And whoever is orchestrating this treachery had better watch out, because the Zephyr is coming back! And Senator Jackson is going to be alive and well and stronger than they ever imagined!"

After a brief pause, Rice spoke again. "Wow, that is some serious resolve. It sounds like you really mean it, Nick. If you are sure about that, I will get with Brenda Bradford at the UPR. Together, somehow, we will find a way to get you the help you need. Senator Jackson, Nick, God bless you all. Goodbye."

Jackson turned to Nick after the call. "Are you sure you want to fight this battle? You will be a marked man, just like me. Just like all of us who are trying to end extremism in our country."

Nick did not hesitate. "Senator Jackson, I have never been more sure of anything in my life. Let's get this done!

CHAPTER 39

SOUTHBOUND

"Victory at all costs, victory in spite of all terror, victory, however long and hard the road may be; for without victory, there is no survival."

—Winston Churchill

Water was frantically poured into every tank, bottle, and bucket on the Zephyr cars. At 11:10 p.m., Nick called on Larry to proceed. He used the familiar "ash speed" command. But he added "only faster now," at the end. They needed to average about 5 mph—more than twice as fast as they had been traveling, to beat Superstorm Herman.

Omaha had cleared the Zephyr to run south on the Pikes Peak Subdivision. Jake was the only one on the train who knew the track. He would not rest again while the Zephyr was underway. Omaha believed it would be possible for the train to weave past the few parked freight trains on the route. Most of the line was double tracked, referred to as "the joint line," because one track used to belong to the Rio Grande, and the other had been owned by the Santa Fe Railroad. From what the dispatchers in Omaha could tell, it looked like the crews manning the trains on the line at the time of the eruption had heroically tried to free up the main tracks before they were overcome by the ash cloud, just like Zane and Bruce had done near Crescent siding.

The first thing the Zephyr crew had to do was veer west in North Yard and take the far right track to the Balloon Bridge.

They didn't get far. The half-collapsed 48th Avenue bridge, which the engines were just barely able to squeeze under for their fuel run, looked to be too low for bi-level passenger cars. Larry thought the train could fit, but it would be very close. Jake, Nick, and Christina watched from the ground as Larry eased under the broken bridge. The 6413 and Zephyr power got through with a few inches to spare. But the 512 car, and all the bi-levels behind it, were too tall. They were about four inches higher than the bridge span would allow.

"Dig out from under the rail," Jake suggested. "We can clear out a couple inches to drop the train under this thing."

Nick looked at him with consternation. They were chewing up time they didn't have. He thought they should just go for it and rip off a tiny bit of the roofs. They called Omaha for a suggestion. While the experts worked on the problem, Charlie summoned the track teams and any others who still had any strength left to get ready to dig again.

It was not easy for the people in Omaha to make engineering decisions because, as usual, there was not enough data. No one enjoyed guessing, but that is what they had to do. The big worry was that the broken bridge was not stable enough to withstand the pressure of the train hitting it. If the bridge fell on the train, any hope of the Zephyr getting further south would vanish. If digging took too long, the storm would flood the tracks before the train got far enough south. It took a certain amount of bravado to make the call. "Dig," Jack Steele said on the phone.

The people from the Zephyr dug furiously. It is amazing what a hot meal of tasteless corn porridge, plenty of water, and a shower can do for a work force. Nick, René, and several other crew members were picking away at the fist size ballast rocks. Ingrid was using a crowbar to loosen material under the ties. Sammy liked the technique, and started doing the same on an adjacent tie. She asked Ingrid if all Austrians were as tough as her.

"Oh yes. Every one of us. Without exceptions," Ingrid remarked with a smirk.

Tracks were undercut four inches deep along a 200-foot section below the bridge. Luckily, the track had been freshly regraded and tamped by maintenance crews just a few weeks before the eruption, so the rocks were not too tightly compacted. They dug out rather easily. Ash was thin compared to what the train had encountered up on the Moffat line. The entire chore took less than forty-five minutes.

"Nick on point, forward 313—ash speed. OVER."

Larry gave some throttle and cut loose the brakes. Engines sank into the depression created by the work crew. The first bi-level car came to the cracked span above. Its corner cleared by an inch! As the middle of the car reached the concrete, a terrible sound of scraping metal was heard. It only lasted a couple of seconds, then the sound was gone. The second car cleared on the ends, but scraped in the middle.

"It's okay, Larry, keep pulling," ordered René, who was on the ground.

Each passenger car roof crumpled a bit as they went under the bridge. Several rips appeared in the stainless steel sheeting. René watched the beam wobble under the upward pressure.

Tim, the premier coach attendant, heard the awful noise from inside the 510 car. He coined the phrase "low centering."

Nick kept the train moving. The beam didn't fall. Cars were damaged but still functional. Tim reported to Nick that the torn roofs should not be too much of a problem, as long as it did not rain. The two men looked at each other with blank stares, knowing their train was about to face more rain than ever before.

Finally the whole train was past the 48th Avenue bridge. They proceeded under I-70 and I-25 without issues. The train was skirting alongside the South Platte River when Nick, who was riding point on the 6413, looked north as they passed beside the 23rd Street bridge. The Zephyr had crossed that bridge just after departing Union Station before Yellowstone ruined everything. It was a sobering sight. The wooden deck was completely burned off. All that was left were twisted rails and main girders.

They approached the balloon bridge, the one they were to cross.

"It looks good to me. OVER," Nick said on the radio. "Keep going, ash speed." The recently rebuilt concrete bridge was as good as new. Crossing the river was no problem. Nick looked down at the waters of the South Platte River.

What a difference a few days and a major disaster can make, he thought. The channel was a braided tangle of flowing mud. The crystal clear water the train had passed as it left Union Station was but a distant memory.

Nick stopped the train at the first control point after the bridge and inspected the switch. It was lined against them. After he and track team #3 dug away the ash, he set the switch lever to manual operation. He threw the bar to move the switch points. Steel moved and seated nicely for the Zephyr's movement. René came to relieve Nick on the point of the train. They were finally making real progress on their way south.

Hugh, Noah, Jennifer, Jim, and others from the Silver Sky group came to Nick in the diner, as he sat down to see if he could choke down some of Ron's corn porridge. The train was just starting to pass by Union Station, two blocks away. They asked if it was possible to stop and inspect the status of the depot and the BIG BOY.

Nick looked at his friends with bemusement. "Really? You want me to stop this train, which is now under serious time pressure, so you can go do some foaming? Guys, I realize that being a train fan is a deep and incurable disease, but c'mon."

The group of enthusiasts looked at each other. Brewster finally spoke up. "Right, well then, we will just show ourselves to the door, and back to our seats. Thank you for your time."

He and Nick had always enjoyed being self-deprecating toward one another. As they were leaving, Hugh went up to Nick. "You know you wanted to go see the big steamer too."

Nick looked at his friend of thirty-five years. "Yep, just please don't tell anyone." The two had a good chuckle.

Track team #3 spent over two hours getting from the Balloon Bridge to Cherry Creek, the next bridge the Zephyr would have to cross. Piles of building debris were everywhere. Dawn was finally breaking, shedding diffused light over Denver. For the first time, people on the Zephyr saw the devastation wrought upon the inner city. Every structure was a burned out shell. Nearly all the windows were shattered. Most skyscrapers were still standing, but some had fallen into massive heaps that looked like the Twin Towers of New York after 9/11. Some of the debris was on the railway.

Cherry Creek bridge was intact and ready to pass, but several power lines and other debris impeded the path. The biker gang was employed to cut through the large power cables tangled on the track. The 6413 was to be used to smash its way through fallen steel poles, wrecked cars, and a collapsed wall. It was going to take a bit to get through the mess.

All the while, there was a stench in the city, the smell of death. Victor and Lena knew the smell from the Russian-Ukrainian war. They told people not to look, just keep their eyes forward and keep on working.

While the track teams worked, Nick asked Noah and others from the Silver Sky group to see if perhaps something, especially insulin and other pharmaceuticals, might have survived at one of the stores nearby. He asked Noah to form the search party. Then he whispered, "Maybe get a picture or two of the BIG BOY while you're out there."

"YES!" Noah responded and took off to gather his group.

"You've got one hour—then we come looking for you. Don't make me do that," Nick told him.

Sean, the physician's assistant, joined the group. He and Dr. Abraham had put together a wish list: Insulin, clonidine, atenolol, Depakote, and Keppra. He would also search for a few things the Sandovals requested: Prozac, Zoloft, and Celexa.

Forty minutes later, a dejected group of railfans returned to the Zephyr. Everything had collapsed and burned up, nothing in the stores. In fact, there were no more stores—just piles of charred rubble.

Noah did have some good news. His assessment was that the BIG BOY, although badly damaged, could be restored. Nick smiled. He loved optimism.

"One more thing," Noah said. "Miraculously, the *Travel by Train* sign atop Union Station is a bit wavy now, but still standing strong."

Shortly thereafter, the track was clear. The Zephyr could continue south. Although there were several small obstacles, all the major bridges were passable. By 10:00 a.m. the train was crossing over Colorado

Highway W 470. That interchange had the largest bridges the Zephyr would face on its route to Colorado Springs. If those spans failed, everything would be lost. The structures were too big and long to fix with anything people on the train would possibly be able to invent. Visibility was starting to get better, nearly 300 yards in the morning light.

"The bridges didn't fall!" René yelled into the radio. The train pushed forward across steel and concrete structures. After clearing the highway bridges, the relieved Zephyr crew stopped the train. Nick took over for René on the point of the 6413. Christina rotated with Larry at the controls of the 313.

Stops were numerous, but not long. Usually they just had to clear small obstacles. During one such stop, Rita used her training and replaced the air filter in her car, car 531. Dan, Tim, Rashid, and the other crew members did the same. It was a tricky process because the duct-taped sheets were still attached over the air intakes. But it was worth it. The old filters were clogged with ash. Breathing inside the train got much better immediately. Christina turned on the HEP for two minutes every half-hour to run the blowers and clear the air through the filters.

Rita brought a used car filter to Dr. Evelyn Pope, who had said she wanted to inspect one. The atmospheric scientist was impressed at how well the device worked. She took it to show Dr. Abraham in the medical clinic. Abraham was thrilled. HEPA filters! No wonder we have not been hit too hard by outbreaks of illness. Hearing the report from Rita made Nick appreciate the excessiveness of Joyce Smyth yet again.

Omaha kept the train on a clear path. Nick and track team #1 rolled on Main Track 1 the entire shift. Every switch had to be dug out and inspected. Progress was slow, but the train was still moving. By noon, they had gone forty miles—almost 20 percent of their quest for Trinidad. But they had chewed up 25 percent of the time they had left before Superstorm Herman might wash away their hopes of survival. They were racing the storm, and the clock.

Railroad CEOs Bradford and Rice were hard at work getting a clandestine rescue effort organized. They were able to find an Army unit not tapped by FEMA, stationed in Texas, to make a run for Trinidad,

Colorado. The commanding general of the base was a friend of Qwana Rice. He was willing to risk his career to help her. His troops volunteered for the mission. They had thirty Bradley armored personnel carriers, and four fuel trucks to make the attempt. Sergeant Major Justus Anton eagerly volunteered to command the operation.

Bradford had a train put together to haul the vehicles as far as they could get by rail. She had the route cleared and train operating crews made ready. This would be the hottest hotshot ever to Trinidad. By the time the Zephyr was leaving Denver, Anton had his vehicles prepped, loaded on Bradford's train, and ready to roll. His troops were put in a separate passenger train Qwana Rice had commandeered from one of her routes in Texas. Before Anton departed on his mission, the general handed him two large grocery bags. "It's the medication the people on that train need. My wife had to steal it from the BX."

The two trains raced northwest on green signals.

Darkness had fallen. The train was inching its way over the apex of the route at Palmer Lake. Nick was on point. The cow catcher on the 6413 was looking pretty ratty after numerous impacts with rocks, building debris and other obstacles. He didn't know if the frame of the dead engine could take much more abuse before it buckled or threw a wheel. He felt much better after they crossed the summit. Ash was not as deep. Drifts were smaller. There were even some places that hadn't completely burned.

Nick had been told a new crew of officials were finally able to reach the dispatching center in Omaha. The new group would come on duty shortly. The people helping the Zephyr had been in the building without relief for days. Nick called to thank them for all they had done.

Jack Steele responded for the entire UPR team. "It was our privilege," he said. "You and everyone else on that train have been an inspiration to the world."

Steele was interrupted, then he spoke again, "Hold on, Nick, I have CEO Bradford here."

The most powerful person in American railroading began to speak. "Nick, Godspeed to all of you. Make our efforts worth it—survive this ordeal. We know you can do it. We are going to keep working on every level to get you the help you need. I am leaving for a few hours, but I will be back."

Nick appreciated the support. "Thank you. Thanks again for the help from you and your people. Together, we will survive. We got this!"

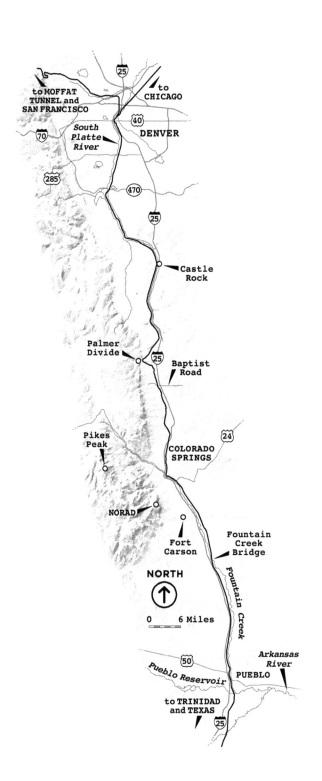

CHAPTER 40

VICTOR'S VICTORY

"Necessity is the mother of taking chances."

—Mark Twain

By sunup the train was at Baptist Road. "Stop the train. OVER," Nick called to Larry on the radio. "Nick to René, we have a partially collapsed road ahead. We need all the track teams up and at 'em. OVER."

René was bummed. Everything was going so well. "Damn. Got it, boss, work crews coming your way. OUT."

Earthquakes are funny things. One building will stand while another falls. Same with bridges. The Zephyr had passed dozens of bridges that were all strong and standing. Then they came upon this one, which had collapsed on its south side. Dr. Sayers, the geologist, was perplexed, not knowing why the anomaly had occurred.

Nick and the others surveyed the situation with Omaha. There was a large crack in the middle of three beams. Those beams had fallen and blocked the tracks. Everyone was depressed. Two days ago, one single fallen highway beam had taken hours of brutal labor to get by. Now more than twice as much bridge had fallen in front of them. To make matters worse, they had no spare time because of Superstorm Herman.

Nick addressed the work crew next to the bridge. "It does not matter that we don't have time for this. We have to deal with it as fast as we can and move on. Omaha says to punch it, then pull it back with chains. The idea is to try and fatigue the structure and weaken it to the point that we can remove one piece at a time. They believe the part of the bridge that has not fallen is secure enough for us to be rather aggressive. So stay back, keep safe. We are going to use the 6413 to beat this bad boy to dust!"

Four hours later, only a few pieces of the bridge had been moved off the tracks. It was like trying to dig a hard rock tunnel with hand tools. Then Nick noticed the thing he had been afraid of. It wasn't a big raindrop. Just enough to see it on his sleeve. But it was real, and it was early. He called Omaha. "I thought we had another day before the storm?"

Jack Steele was back on the line. It turned out he never left the Dispatching Center. He had slept in a corner. Steele felt totally invested in getting the Zephyr over his tracks. Now he was back on the job. "Nick, I really don't know what to tell you. The National Weather Service did their best. It isn't a storm yet. Just keep hacking away at that damn bridge."

Nick stood there, looking at his battered train and exhausted workers.

Everyone was looking to him for some kind of reassurance. For the first time since his breakdown in Barbara Gulch, Nick contemplated what it would be like to simply give up.

"Hey, Nick, you need bigger, faster bomb." It was Victor Homko from Ukraine. He continued speaking with his Slavic accent, "In war we hit Kherson Bridge many times with HIMAR rocket, but bridge stayed. It was damaged, but it stayed. We did not have big enough rocket. Here at Baptist Road, we needed big, fast bomb in just the right spot."

Nick listened. There was no one he had more respect for than the brave Ukrainians who had fought the Russians. But war stories were not going to save them today. "Thanks, Victor, but we don't have a bomb."

Victor disagreed, "You have 150-ton bomb. And you can make it go to right spot. Simply go fast, maybe 100 miles per hour."

Nick finally understood—back up and disconnect the Zephyr. Then kick the 6413 engine by itself into the bridge at insane velocity.

"What if it doesn't work? Then we will have to dig out a smashed engine as well." Victor had learned while fighting the Russians that sometimes it is best to take chances when there are no good options. "I think like so—what if it *does* work? Don't think; what if failure. If we not try, we will not know. Do you have better idea?"

There was now a steady drizzle of muddy precipitation. Each drop was picking up micro ash particles as it fell through the haze. Nick knew that soon it would be a deluge, then flooding. They would be stuck in rain-soaked, sticky ash . . . they would never get out. He called Omaha about the "Victor plan."

Omaha said the odds were small.

Nick asked if they had anything better to suggest. They did not.

"Well then," Nick began, "I guess we are finally going to see what happens when an unstoppable force slams into an unmovable object."

Nick had about fifty workers stay near the bridge, but at a safe distance. The train crew then backed the whole Zephyr up about two miles. All remaining chains were wrapped around the cow catcher rails on the 6413. René tied the hand brake on the dead engine while the Zephyr was prepared. The plan was to use the 313 and the 309 to get the 6413 moving.

Nick had Larry ease the Zephyr away from the UPR locomotive, which was being repurposed into a rail bomb. Jim and the other On Board Service employees tied down the Zephyr cars with hand brakes. Zephyr power pulled away from its train. Knuckles were closed in a butt joint between the 313 and the 6413. Larry moved the Zephyr power forward to the freight unit. He disengaged all the speed restriction seals and valves. There were no limits.

"Nick to Larry, are you ready for this? OVER."

"Yeah, Let's get it done. OVER."

Rene kicked off the hand brake and descended off the 6413. It started rolling slowly downhill. Larry bunched the knuckles together, then went to notch 8. "Godspeed, Larry!" Nick yelled through the open cab window to his engineer friend.

Larry waved a thumbs up. He was thinking that this would never work, but neither would anything else. Knuckles bumped several times as speed increased. Going downhill over the track already cleared of ash allowed for rapid acceleration. Larry had the UPR unit and both passenger engines going 50 mph in no time. He started to get scared as the speedometer went past 80 mph. He had not exceeded that speed on a locomotive since he was an engineer on the 150 mph Northeast Corridor back in the nineties. He stayed in notch 8.

He got on the radio. "Ninety mph. 100 mph. 105 mph. I'm backing off."

Larry hit the brakes hard; the 6413 took off into the haze.

God help us now, he said to himself.

People near the bridge heard the rail make noise. Then they heard whining axle journals that were being pushed too fast. The big engine leaned around the broad curves north of the bridge but held the rail. There was a brief flash of rusted color as the 6413 flew past the crowd. A split second later, an absolutely deafening blast and shockwave was accompanied by the blinding light of raw energy release. The sound of settling debris reverberated for about ten seconds; then there was an eerie silence.

Several people ran to the bridge immediately after the impact. Dust made the already murky haze nearly impossible to see through. Drizzling rain started to clear the air. Cautiously they walked beside the tracks. Larry got on the radio. "313 to everyone, I am stopped. OVER."

The work party went into the area that had been the Baptist Road Bridge. "Am I seeing what I think I see?" Charlie asked.

"You have got to be kidding me!"

"No way!" Accolades poured forth from everyone. It worked! Grown men were dancing in circles. To Jake, the grizzled old track worker, it was the most beautiful thing he had ever seen.

"God loves us! God is Great!" Rashid yelled. He sank to his knees, palms skyward, eyes closed in thanksgiving. The Amish guys and several others hit their knees and covered their faces, overcome by emotion.

Victor surveyed the scene like the veteran warrior he was. His face stayed deadpan as one person after another thanked and congratulated him on his bold plan that had reopened the path for the Zephyr.

The 6413 had hit the bridge debris so hard that the spans completely shattered and blasted away from the track as the engine smashed through. Cow catcher rails lifted the heavy beams off the track and cut the rebar holding them together. When the downward pressure of the bridge was off the locomotive, it literally popped into the air and came down on its side to the west of the rail. Miraculously, tracks were easily repairable into passable condition with a few hits from the Rail Wrecker. The path was just wide enough for the train to slip by unencumbered.

Larry backed up to gather the Zephyr cars. The rest of the crew and passengers got to see what some considered divine intervention. Larry could not believe it. Nick hugged Victor, who did not like being hugged. Lena stood next to Victor beaming with pride.

Everyone in Omaha stood and cheered as the dust settled and the screen revealed the passable track. After picking up all the work teams, the train passed the United Pacific Railways 6413 for the last time. Her main motor was dislodged from the frame. The cab was sheared off at hood level. Wheels had flown off, landing in ballast several yards away. The unit that had blasted a hole for the Zephyr to sneak through was finished.

One person was not looking jovial while the others celebrated what became known as "Victor's Victory." Dr. Sayers approached Nick. "Conductor, something is wrong."

Nick gave the geologist a questioning look. "The impact that wrecked the bridge, I don't think that was a lava bomb, or the earth-quake. It's the only downed bridge we've seen in fifty miles. The impact area was only dusted with ash, while everything around it was two-feet deep in the stuff."

It dawned on Nick where Sayers was going. He asked the obvious question anyway, "What are you saying, doc?"

Sayers looked very serious. "I found two pieces of shrapnel while I was digging in the bridge debris." They looked at the metal shards. They were about ten inches long. "Nick, I think the bridge collapse was a result of man-made sabotage. A bomb of some sort."

Nick thought for a moment. The evidence was hard to argue with. Motivation by Senator Jackson's opponents was known to be real. It could be that someone was usurping America's own military weapons against the Zephyr to try and stop Jackson's political movement. Suddenly the prospect of being left alone by the government had become frighteningly real. It now looked like someone was actively trying to block the Zephyr's path to rescue. Perhaps they would even be directly shot at.

Nick looked at Sayers. His feelings reminded him of the way he reacted to the terror attacks on September 11, 2001. He remembered feeling as if it was really bad luck when a plane hit the first building, although it didn't make sense. Then when the second plane hit the other tower, everyone knew it was deliberate. That same sinking angry feeling was back. At first he thought the Baptist Road bridge was just bad luck. He never thought it was the result of treachery. Suddenly, he was forced to face the truth. The final piece of evidence convincing him that the tracks were being attacked was that the broken Baptist Road spans appeared to have been knocked out from the south—not the north. Not from Yellowstone, but from the opposite direction . . . *Damn!* Nick thought.

"Please keep this quiet. We don't want panic to rise among the others on board. As you know, we have a controversial political figure, Senator Jackson, with us. We have been informed that there may be forces within the US government that do not want him to survive and return to Washington. It could be that those people shot at our tracks. Even if that is the case, will it change our course of action? No. There is only one thing we can do: drive this train south to survive. Every other option ends in near-certain death."

Sayers went pale. "This whole thing is even worse than I imagined. I will keep my mouth shut."

Nick thanked the professor for sharing his expertise, and for his silence at this crucial moment.

Leonard Gonzoles and René were briefed by Nick about possible sabotage by unknown forces. Nick asked Gonzoles to personally take on the task of protecting Senator Jackson.

Evening fell. Inside the train, 244 people pushed on. The annoying drizzle was over. It had become a full-fledged rainstorm. Nick told the engineer to push a little faster. Larry and Christina were both in the cab of the 313. They were glad to no longer have the big hulk of the 6413 impeding their view. But neither were experienced on that section of track. That made running a train scary, even in normal times. Jake was with them, but his knowledge of the tracks was only from a maintenance point of view. Christina felt it was nearly insane to race forward in the dark during a deluge.

It was cold, dark, muddy, and getting wetter. They were out of time. Trinidad seemed like a million miles away. Nick's thoughts were even harsher. *On top of everything else, we were now getting shot at by some rogue force with access to military missiles. Now we really do know what the Armenians felt like on that mountain in 1915—many family members dead, low on every resource, impossible terrain, severe weather, no allies close enough to help, and an enemy from within their own country shooting at them.*

Then his phone rang.

"Conductor Nick here."

"Yes, Sir, Conductor Nick, it is an honor to speak with you, Sir. This is Sergeant Major Justus Anton, U.S. Army. I want to inform you that I am in command of a platoon of rescue vehicles currently heading north to your location from Trinidad, Colorado."

"WHAT! I thought the government wasn't going to help us, that we were on our own?!" Nick shouted with shock in his voice.

Anton continued, "Sir, we could not skip out on this mission. My commanding officer may be in the brig when we get back to base, but we intend to return with all of you alive. Our unit was delivered to Trinidad by rail one hour ago. We are now driving north. We are currently thirty miles from Pueblo on what is left of I-25."

Nick replied haltingly, "Sergeant, I don't know what to say—thank you."

The veteran soldier let down his military veneer for a moment and let his true nature show, saying, "Sir, I've got to tell you, I feel like I have trained my whole career for this moment in time. We are honored to be part of this rescue operation. We LOVE the action!" His tone was almost giddy.

Nick was still reeling from the realization that elements of the military were actively trying to stop the Zephyr. "Sergeant Anton, you will have to forgive me, but we think our tracks have already been shot at. How do we know you are on our side?"

The commander, risking his career and possibly his life on that mission, was quick with his response. "Sir, I was briefed that you might have trust issues. I was instructed by two railroad executives, Qwana Rice and Brenda Bradford. They said to use the code phrase that will ease your mind."

Nick had not been told about any code. "What code phrase?" he asked.

"Sir, we got this!"

Nick smiled quietly to himself. "Sergeant Major Anton, thank you for all you are doing for us. Here we come!"

Anton had one more message: "Please let a young man named Reagan know that his father, Terry, has been allowed to temporarily reenlist so that he can contribute to this mission. He is now our chief mechanic."

CHAPTER 41

PINS AND KNUCKLES

Two hours after the first call from Sergeant Anton, another call came. It was Anton again. "Bad news, Sir, flooding has been severe in Pueblo. We cannot find a passable bridge. You will have to make it to us. We cannot get to you."

Nick was impressed that they had made it that far so quickly in the storm. "You guys keep yourselves safe. We will be there in a few hours if all goes well."

Anton liked the moxie of that train crew. "Roger that, Sir. We will be ready for you in Pueblo."

The rain was relentless. Puddles became ponds and ponds became lakes. Christina pulled the Zephyr through the heart of Colorado Springs without being able to see the ball of the rail most of the time. She was going 15 mph—it felt like they were flying. To say the scene in the cab was tense would be an understatement. Charlie, Larry, Christina, and Jake were all standing—straining to see through the filthy windshield. Omaha had instructed the train to take the old Rio Grande track, the east line, south from Colorado Springs. The track had been lined right through to Pueblo, and no freight trains were on the track when the eruption hit.

In the body of the train, things had gotten more miserable. Muddy rainwater was pouring into every car through the gashes torn when the train "low centered" under the 48th Avenue bridge back in Denver. Passengers did their best to huddle together under bags and blankets. Spirits were low.

Somehow the tracks were clear enough to pass without stopping all the way through "The Springs," as people called the second largest city in the state. Without saying it out loud, Nick was amazed that whoever bombed Baptist Road didn't aim at any of the numerous bridges in the city. All he said to the people in the car was that he was relieved the tracks were clear.

Victor responded to Nick quietly, "Rockets too small for such big bridges."

Nick looked at the Ukrainian curiously. Victor looked back at Nick with knowing eyes. "They must not have heavy artillery. I know how it feels. I lived this life before, in Ukraine."

Nick thought he was starting to understand a little bit of what war felt like. He knew Victor's experience had hardened him. He had a knowing, yet somehow empty look in his eyes. Nick spoke to the former fighter with more reverence than before. "You survived once, you will again."

South of the city, the train passed the switch that leads to Cheyenne Mountain, and the NORAD underground complex. The refuge that America's government would not allow the people on the Zephyr to enter. No one on the train said a word as they went by. They simply kept slogging through the muck. Things went surprisingly well for the next thirty minutes. Nick was starting to feel like they were almost there. They had nearly reached Sergeant Anton. He allowed himself to believe that they were really going to pass the greatest test of their lives, and survive.

"Stop, Christina!" Charlie yelled. She instantly killed the throttle and laid into the brakes. The other three tried to see what Charlie was seeing.

"Fountain Creek!" he said. "I ain't never seen it like that." The others could now see what he was looking at as the train stopped.

Usually, Fountain Creek in September is a small trickle of a stream flowing under the steel overhead girder bridge. Now it had become a cascading torrent of roaring fury. The one railroad bridge that crosses the terrifying channel was bowing in the middle, but it was still intact.

"That bridge doesn't look too stable to me," Larry said.

"Look, either we get across this river, or we will be stuck right here for who knows how long," Christina declared. The rush of gray, thick muck lapping at the bottom of the bridge looked overpowering. All four stared from the cab of the 313. Jake felt the weight of the train and the flow of the water together would doom the bridge and kill everyone on-board, but he didn't want to say it because they would most likely die anyway if they didn't get across. To him, it was a lose-lose proposition.

Larry made a quick call to Omaha. They had to defer to the crew onboard the train.

"Jake?" Christina asked, looking at the track man. "Go for it, but hit it moderately fast and keep going—no matter what."

Jake hadn't lied. He didn't say he thought they could make it. He just said, "Do it."

Nick and René got in on the job briefing by radio. "Okay, we don't have any time to waste. Christina and Larry will be in the cab. René and I will be in the bag car at the tail. We will back up a quarter mile or so. Then you guys get 'er going about 30 mph. Once we get safely over the bridge, I will let you know. Then we can slow down. Does that plan work for everyone?"

Everyone agreed. "Okay, let's do this."

Hunger and exhaustion were definitely affecting Nick. Unlike the others, he was not eating the corn porridge or soup. He was men-tally frayed, and physically he was starting to get a bit clumsy. Nobody knows if he knew it himself, but he was not on his game 100 percent.

After leading the shove a short ways, Nick closed the rear door of the bag car. Muddy rain got on his safety glasses. "Okay guys, highball!"

Nick felt the tug forward. The mighty engines tacked up RPMs. Wheels began turning faster. It felt like warp speed after crawling and feeling their way for more than 150 miles. The leading wheels of the train crossed the edge of the bridge at 30 mph. Christina closed her eyes as they thundered over the weakened structure with a bow in the middle. Both engineers felt a sway to their left.

"OH," Larry moaned as the far bank came closer. Chaotic water littered with ashy debris was violently sloshing below.

"We made it!" Christina yelled as the engines felt a distinct rise to crest the abutment of the south end of the bridge. Every person on the train felt the swaying and uneasy movement as car after car of the Zephyr flew over the chaotic chasm.

"I'm getting stuck!" Christina yelled into the radio.

Nick was in the bag car, feeling it drift to the side and then drop like a gut punch on the rear. He heard the binding of the knuckles and drawbars. *Damn!* he thought. The train stopped so abruptly that he and René were thrown forward through the bag car.

Christina immediately went to idle on the throttle and made a full service set on the brakes. The undercarriage of the bag car was scraping steel on steel and trying to pull the train backward into the river. All movement came to a halt.

Nick knew the "H" knuckles and drawbars were interlocked. If the bag car rolled over into the river, the whole train would be laid down on its side, just like the derailment of the Southwest passenger train in Missouri back in 2022. He ripped open the end door next to the 540 car to escape. René was right on his heels. They both raced as fast as they could up the stairs, to the middle of the dorm car and down to the vestibule. Nick ran out of the dorm car and dropped down into the soaked muck to survey the situation from the ground.

The bridge was still there, but was bending terribly in the middle. The west rail in the middle was already under the flow of Fountain Creek. The middle of the baggage car was touching the rail. The front truck was right on the abutment at the south end of the bridge, but the rear of the car had dropped so far that it was high-centered and twisting with the bridge. Sounds of straining steel were reverberating over the roaring rush of water.

"We've got to cut it off now!" Nick yelled at René through the vestibule. "You've got that side; I'll do this one."

The conductors ran through the slop along the steep slope to get to the joint between the 540 car and the bag car. It took courage to climb under that tangle of hoses, pipes, power cables, and blunt chunks of metal, all of which were contorting unnaturally. Dan suddenly had his tactical flashlight shining down on the imperiled joint where the conductors were working. René dove under the end of the 540 and closed the brake pipe and main reservoir angle cocks.

"Forget the HEP cables, just lift the pin!" Nick yelled as he struggled to get the cotter key and pins out of the tell tell holes of the lifter mechanism. Usually, the pins were carefully placed on their hook for the next use. That time Nick dropped them as soon as he had them off—there was no time for neatness. Nick and René finished their tasks and began yanking on the pin lifters. Nothing moved.

"They're jammed!" René yelled.

"Christina, I need a hard pin now, then pull for all you're worth!"

Without a response on the radio, the train plowed back into the rear car. The bag car lurched. Release of pressure from the train allowed the flood to finish off the bridge. Rails broke, girders snapped, and the whole ensemble began to roll over. At that very second, René and Nick both yanked with all their might on the pin lifter levers.

"It's free!" René called out. The drawbars had lined up for a microsecond. Miraculously, one of the two conductors had put just the right amount of upward pressure on the lever at just the right instant to open the knuckle and free the bag car from the rest of the Zephyr.

The moment the drawbars let loose of each other, the bag car slid back and sank on the rear. That forced the front, where the two conductors had struggled, to thrust violently upward. René wasn't sure exactly what she saw, but the flash of Nick's reflective vest and railroad lantern caught her eye. To her, it looked like he had jumped toward her. A split second later she saw him fly higher—too high. She reached out for him. Everything seemed to go in slow motion.

"Nick!" she heard herself yell after the conductor, but it was like listening to someone else. The bag car rolled all the way over and turned to join the flow of the river, throwing wheels and axles out of their bogies and into the water like toys.

René was clinging to the grab iron with her right hand on the end of the 540 car. She was being dragged forward by the power of Christina throttling up after the reverse pin move. Without realizing it, she was still reaching out hopelessly to help Nick. She yelled again, "Nick! NO!"

The moment the knuckles released, the power of the uncontrolled movement had somehow knocked or caught Nick. His body was flicked into the sky, which was still filled with pelting raindrops. He flew like a rag doll being tossed. From what René could later remember, he landed on the corner of the bag car, began to reach his hand for anything, thrashed his legs in a vain effort to find foundation, and made a final lunge to escape the rolling train car. She saw him get wedged and smashed between the roof of the car as it rolled over, and the girders of the broken bridge.

Her last sight of Nick was his contorted vest, left arm and head being pulled under the current. He disappeared in the churning mass of metal, muck, and the macerated remains of a smashed world. Within seconds, the bag car, the remains of the bridge, and the conductor of the Zephyr were gone—trapped in an undeniably deadly torrent.

"STOP!" René screamed into the radio with a degree of terror that no one had heard from her before. The elation Christina and Larry were feeling because of the unrestricted forward movement of the train was suddenly tarnished by the tone of her screeching plea. Christina immediately idled the throttle and set air for the brakes.

René felt the train stopping. She let go of the grab iron and started running toward the river—toward Nick. Dan caught her before she could get close enough to fall into the river. He had seen it all from the rear door of the 540 car—now the end door of the train since the bag car was gone. He saw Nick's last harrowing moments. He was in shock, as René was, but still thinking clearly enough to chase after René so that she wouldn't become the second casualty of the night.

He had to tackle her to make her stop. "We have to find him! We got to save him!" René pleaded as she looked at Dan, who was holding her back from the slippery edge of the river. Her eyes told the whole helpless story.

"He's gone. We can't help him now." Dan said to her to get her to stop acting crazy. "Nick is gone, René. All we can do now is save ourselves. We've got to get back on the train and get out of here!"

She didn't want to hear it, but somehow her mind heard what her heart couldn't. In a daze, she nodded and let Dan hold her arm and lead her back to the train.

Soon more people were out in the soaked muck rushing to help. Sammy and Jim helped René, relieving Dan of the uncomfortable duty. They all were jogging back to the train. Dan turned to look again. There was no bag car to be seen. Twisted rail ended where the bridge had been. He saw a flash on the ground just a few feet from the destroyed end of track. It was the reflection of light glinting off the shiny conductor badge on Nick's hat. Dan ran back to retrieve it.

Noah and Alex arrived too late to help. Realizing they had lost Nick was paralyzing. After a few seconds, Alex said, "We have to get back to work. There's still a long way to go to the Army convoy."

The two men took a quick look at the end of the 540 car to make sure it was still on the rail. Everything was in order. However, Noah saw the knuckle. It was open. It was René's side of the joint that had freed the train from the deadly connection to the doomed bag car. Nick's efforts were heroic, but in fact he didn't lift the critical pin. The pivotal action had come from René. Noah left the knuckle open for all to see. He climbed onto the train.

"What's happening back there?" Larry asked with heightened concern. Rita and Rashid were at the vestibule door to help Dan, Jim, Sammy, and the others get back in the car. They pulled both of René's arms to get her back onto the Zephyr.

"Where's Nick?" Rita asked almost as if she already knew the answer from the look and body language of René and Dan. She held her hand over her mouth in frightened anticipation of what she would find out.

Dan just shook his head to simply say "no." He shut the door. Rashid was horrified and in disbelief. "Don't shut the door, please, Nick is still out there," he pleaded in desperate hope that what he was seeing was not really true, and they were just being forgetful.

René was sobbing uncontrollably. Dan was not an affectionate man. He was glad that others were there to hold and comfort her. He knew his clumsy and insecure attempts at empathy would be feeble at best.

Christina pushed the radio button in the locomotive. "Is everything alright back there? We are not stuck anymore," she said.

The answer only came after a long pause. It was not the usual voice of Nick or René. "Stand by please," the voice said. Dan held the radio mic that René handed to him, feeling she could not speak at that moment.

Dan was glad to have something else to do with his hands. By then, several people were in the small space between the vestibule doors.

Lorette and Judith came bounding down the stairs to the 540 vestibule. "Is Nick gone?" Judith asked in a panic. A passenger had told her they saw the bag car snap off the train and what looked like a man in a safety vest was swept away.

Dan looked right at the two women. He nodded to confirm that Nick was gone. Judith felt her whole body get weak and out of control.

"No! Not Nick!" Lorette sobbed.

René gestured to Dan to give her back the radio mic. "Is everyone back on board?" she asked. She got the words out as well as she could.

Jim looked out both vestibule windows. He looked back at her. "Yes, everyone is back on the train."

Dan handed the radio to her as she gathered her composure. In half starts and rhythmic gasps for air, she pressed the mic button and told the head-end crew the news. "René to number 5, the bag car is gone."

René took a couple deep breaths. She tried to say it twice before the words finally came out. "Nick got caught as the car rolled into the river." More breaths. "He is presumed dead." She finally got it out. "Okay to proceed. OVER."

René was determined to keep going. To reach the Army convoy—to survive. Her husband John expected nothing less. Her conductor would have ordered it. Now she had to assume the leadership role and get it done. By railroad rules of hierarchy, René was the new conductor of the Zephyr.

Larry realized he had just lost one of his best friends. Christina sat silently, tears running down her cheeks. There was a long pause.

"Let's get a search party and go find him," Larry said as he looked out into the darkness shrouded in a gale, dimmed by muddy pounding rain.

"Negative," said René, sobered by Larry challenging what she said. "There is no way ... we can't, the risk is too high, and we saw him get ... " She began to lose it again. "We saw him get killed. Pull—ash speed." When she used Nick's term, she lost it again and began to sob.

Larry couldn't speak.

Christina, who was still sitting in the seat, spoke softly with a halting voice, "Roger that, conductor René. Ash speed. OUT."

She manipulated the levers. The train was moving—pushing muddy ash out of the way. They were leaving Nick, or at least Nick's body, behind in the dark muddy muck. Jake stood between the two engineers, scouting the track that only he was familiar with. They rode on in silence but for the occasional sniffle.

Word of Nick's demise spread throughout the train within minutes. Learning that their conductor had died was a gut punch. Everyone felt they had lost a friend—more than a friend. He had been their leader, and they trusted him without reserve. They all knew a big part of why they were still alive was Nick's commitment to bring back his whole crew and all his passengers. Many were terrified of going on without him in the lead. Doris blurted out the question many were wondering: "How can we do this if we don't have a conductor?"

"We have an excellent conductor," Senator Jackson said. "Rene has been at Nick's side this whole time. She's proven herself time and time again. She will get us through."

There was hardly a dry eye on board when Dan got on the PA: "Ladies and Gentlemen, just to confirm what I am sure most of you already know. Conductor Nicholas Jay, Conductor Nick, in his efforts to save our lives, lost his own. He freed us from a damaged baggage car that was stuck on a bridge so that our train would be able to carry on. In doing so, he was caught up in the current of the river and carried away. I saw it all happen myself."

Dan took a few long breaths to settle his emotions. "We are back on the move. We are getting close to the Army. Just a few dozen miles is all that is left now. Nick wanted each of us to survive, and that is what we are going to do—survive."

Knut, Olivia, Susan, Chance, Jay and Diana, Senator Jackson and his wife, Ingrid, Zach, most of the Amish group, and a host of others gathered in the diner. Nobody said anything. They didn't know why they had even gathered. They didn't know what to do. Rob wheeled Herman into the diner on the Stryker chair to join the others.

Many found it hard to believe that Nick was really gone, especially the younger folks. It took time to realize Nick was not coming back; that he would not pull off another clever miracle and jump back on the train. The man who had made them believe they could cheat death was dead.

Herman said through his computer, and with the help of his god-father, that he wanted to honor Nick. He took a few moments to get it out. People from every faith on the train, and many nonbelievers, were there. Senator Antonio Jackson suggested a moment of silence. No more words were spoken. After a few minutes, they all went slowly back to their seats and rooms. Their journey was not over yet.

CHAPTER 42

SERGEANT MAJOR
JUSTUS ANTON

"Superhuman effort isn't worth a damn unless it achieves results."

—Ernest Shackleton

The makeshift plow was working better in the soupy slurry than before the heavier rain. Ash seemed to flow out of the way and off the rail. Ash was also thinner—perhaps only six inches above the ball of the rail. Christina opened up the speed to 10 mph. Three hours passed uneventfully. The rain tapered off as the train approached Pueblo. Ash appeared to start falling again. But it wasn't ash; it was snow. The Arkansas River loomed ahead. The last train through before the eruption was a coal drag that was two signal blocks south of Pueblo at last recording. That meant the tracks were lined straight through town. To say there was trepidation about another river crossing would be an understatement. Flat out fear was the case for most everyone on the train. A gray dim light began to glow in the sky; another day was dawning.

Larry was at the controls, trying to conserve what little fuel still sloshed around in the tanks. The 309 was shut down. The train was getting drive power from the 313 alone. HEP would not be turned on again. Larry and Jake strained to see through the haze as they believed the bridge was close.

Leonard Gonzales felt naked. He was getting close to an armed group of soldiers who still could turn out to be hostile. His weapons were lost with the baggage car. If the platoon of soldiers were in fact there to kill Senator Jackson, there was almost nothing he could do to defend the politician. Gonzales would shadow the senator throughout the entire rescue.

"Look there!" Jake said. The bridge was gone, but on the far bank was the first vehicle they had seen since Yellowstone that was not burnt. This was a glorious moment! Atop the first Bradley fighting vehicle that came into view were the bright colors of a United States flag. They had made it! The last major danger before the Arkansas River was behind them.

Cheers rang out in every car. "We got this!" Larry yelled.

René called Justus Anton on the phone. "Hello, Sergeant Major, this is conductor René on the Zephyr. We can see you on the south bank of the river here in Pueblo."

Sergeant Anton could see them as well. "Good job, Conductor René. Waters here on the Arkansas River are already receding. However, all bridges over the river are destroyed. It looks like ash and debris clogged the river upstream for several days. When the debris dam finally broke, a wall of water about thirty feet high washed out all the abutments and bridges. That flash flood is gone, and the damage has been done, but don't worry, we fashioned a raft ferry and secured a line to transport everyone to our side."

"Where is Conductor Nick?" Anton asked.

René's husband John was a military man, so she understood the need to save grief until after the mission was complete. To her, it was a battle—a battle for survival. She said it quickly, matter of fact, and without emotion, "Conductor Nick drowned. He is dead. I am now the conductor of the train."

Justus Anton had plenty of experience with the loss of fellow soldiers. He instantly reverted to his training in dealing with death in combat. "Understood. My condolences."

A squad of soldiers covered in gray filth were pressing forward from the river bank to the tracks and the stricken Zephyr. Larry blew the whistle. It didn't work. *Probably filled with ash,*" he thought.

He brought the train to a stop 100 feet from the broken end of track. Jim, the bartender, and proud husband of Sammy, opened a door on the parlor car to get a better look at the rescuers.

"Tie the brakes," Larry yelled into the radio. René was in the parlor car. She had organized the Buff men and others to be at the ready, knowing the brakes would have to be tied once stopped. She gave the hand signal to the guys on the brake levers. Within seconds, the rattle of brake chains was ringing throughout the train—for the last time.

The Zephyr was at full stop, out of fuel, reeking of unwashed humanity, filthy with the muck of the greatest cataclysm in human history, missing its glorious private historic dome car, stripped of its baggage car that had been carried away with so many vital supplies, and—in the end—deprived of one of its conductors.

Christina grabbed the photo of her son, still taped to the dash of the 313, and climbed out of the locomotive. Larry centered the reverser switch. He set the parking brake. He flipped off the breakers on the back panel. After one last look around, he opened the door and went down the ladder of the last locomotive he would ever operate.

"Sergeant Major Justus Anton at your service," the commander of the convoy said to the locomotive engineers.

"Larry Cohen, engineer. Thank you for coming to this place, at this time, to save us."

"We've been dreaming of this moment for two weeks!" Christina added.

"My pleasure. And if I may, I just got to tell you . . . ," Sergeant Anton looked around at his men helping others, then back at Larry with an excited gleam in his eye, "we love the action!"

Passengers and crew were pouring out of the train. They had gathered up what few things they wanted to keep, and stepped off the Zephyr. There were still 200 hundred yards to go to get to the rafts and rope to ferry them across the Arkansas River. One of the soldiers with Sergeant Anton was Reagan's dad Terry. He finally was able to hug his son and his wife Claire—a beautiful and powerfully emotional moment. So many others on the Zephyr would not get to enjoy such bliss.

After nearly two weeks of trying to survive with dwindling resources, seeing the abundant assets of the United States Army was a vision of beauty. The boat ride was no joke. Water still swelled beyond the natural banks of the river. Debris, including parts of burned tree trunks and man-made junk, flowed by with harrowing speed. Anton and his troops attacked the task of getting the civilians from the train to the river and then across the water like a wartime campaign. Those soldiers seemed to relish the challenge of defeating the angry current and accomplishing their mission.

Within a couple of hours, only René, Larry, Christina, and Jake were left by the train with Sergeant Anton. "Well, we got through it after all," Larry said, looking at the battered front end of the 313.

"Nothing else from Denver made it this far," René added.

Jake spoke up, "We freight guys always thought of passenger trains and the people that worked on them as weak and sissy, but it ain't true. This was one tough battlewagon that got us here. And you folks have nerves of steel." He lifted his hard hat that seemed molded to his head. "Hats off to the Zephyr and her crew!"

They all smiled at the grizzled old UPR track man.

René addressed Jake, "The resilience of the railroad industry got us through. Hats off to the UPR!"

Sergeant Anton had some words too. "You can all be proud of what you did. Millions died. Nearly everyone in Colorado is gone. You saved 244 souls who were sure to die without you doing what you did."

The four railroaders looked at each other. Then Larry looked at the soldier, holding back tears. "We are only 243 now, Sir."

On the other side of the river, people were shunted into the troop transports. Herman's Stryker chair was used instead of his own powered chair. He still had on a headband. His last message had been written before Fountain Creek—before Nick had died—when it finally looked like they were going to make it. The inscription seemed to sum up the entire adventure: "We Got This!"

Once in the military vehicle, Herman complained, via his still operational computer, about the comfort of the military seats—that he could not sit in. "A BRADLEY? I PREFER STRYKER."

Everyone smiled at his joke, as they began devouring MREs and guzzling bottled water.

As the convoy departed southbound, they rounded in a circle with hatches open to let everyone have one last look at the train, which had been their home for so many days. Although all the people rescued were thrilled to finally be free of the train and the terror that seemed to wait for them at every turn while they were aboard, they also felt a certain sadness in leaving it behind.

"She sure was a tough old train," Larry said to René.

"She sure had tough engineers," the conductor said.

Christina looked at René with pride and reverence. "And she sure had a tough conductor—both of them."

René took charge. "Enough sentimentalism, let's go," she said.

Larry looked at her and replied with a smirk, "Got it, boss."

As they departed from that last resting place of the once mighty train, they could not help but be thankful for the protection and deliverance their silver steed had provided. Many people waved. Some cried.

They had done more than just survive. They proved what people in grim circumstances can do when they unite around the cause of saving each other. They would be revered forever. They were among the lucky and resourceful few who had survived the Dead Zone of Yellowstone. They rode into history and were eventually intertwined into the fabric and lore of the American West. One of them, conductor Nicholas "Nick" Jay, rode all the way into Glory itself. They had all ridden to victory together—aboard the last Zephyr.

EPILOGUE

The Yellowstone eruption turned out to be the greatest disaster in recorded human history. The initial blast and toxic ash cloud killed nearly ten million people. In the following years, famine caused by particulates in the upper atmosphere, blocking sunlight, killed almost a billion more people. A dozen small wars, and two large ones, were fought as nations struggled for access to dwindling energy and food supplies.

The United States of America, which had suffered the greatest initial hardship from the eruption on its own soil, fared better than most. After ten long harsh years, planet Earth was starting to feel "normal" again. The skies were clear. Rain and snow were no longer clogged with micro glass shards and silica. The enormous Dead Zone in western America had turned green, and experienced some initial repopulation.

It was more than four months after the rescue before people would be back in Pueblo. The last Zephyr sat on the rails tied down on the banks of the Arkansas River for more than two years.

Nick's body was never found, but the baggage car was. At the end of the car next to the pin lifter, searchers found a tangle of cloth, including parts of what was a white shirt and some of his yellow safety vest. The clothing was snagged tightly on a small piece of protruding steel that had been ripped from the side of the car. René surmised that it was similar to what she had been snagged on at East Portal the day the train slammed its way out of Moffat Tunnel. Although the opposite end of the car from where she had gotten caught, it was apparently the same long gash caused by the car being dragged across rocks after the initial earthquake.

Long-distance passenger trains would not return to the western United States for five years. Only excursions would ever roll on

American rails in the west again; the nation, massively depleted of resources by Yellowstone, had to focus on national survival rather than passenger travel. Leadership chose to devote itself to modern technologies that were more resilient and efficient than surface roads, or airplanes, or even railroads. Sub-surface hyperloop, thanks to amazing advances in tunneling technology, would eventually become the backbone of American transport.

Senator Antonio Jackson and his wife Janice returned to Maryland after being rescued. He remained a senator until his death seven years later. He preceded his wife into eternity by just three months. Those in political power who had sabotaged rescue efforts of the Zephyr were identified. They came from both extremes of the political spectrum. Their alibi was that they were simply trying to ensure that limited resources available were to be used to save the greatest number of people possible without regard to wealth or position. That argument ultimately held up. No one was ever charged with a crime.

The metal fragments Dr. Sayers found were indeed from a medium range tactical missile. The destruction of the Baptist Road bridge was determined to have been caused by such weapons. The missiles had been fired approximately eleven days after Yellowstone first erupted. They were launched from a HIMARS vehicle that was protected in a secured bunker at Fort Carson, Colorado. Persons unknown had apparently survived the eruption and obtained the weapons on the abandoned compound. Investigations continued for years, but no definitive conspirators were ever found.

Although sympathy following the Zephyr odyssey gave moderates a political boost, Senator Antonio Jackson never lived to see his movement reach the zenith of political power in America. However, moderation and compromise continued to gather strength year after year—from school boards to Capitol Hill.

Those who were on the Zephyr that Labor Day in Moffat Tunnel had their lives irreversibly altered. Some, like locomotive engineer Christina, chose to leave everything behind and try to forget the trauma of those harrowing days. Others were obsessed by all that happened.

Some relationships blossomed into lifelong bonds. Regardless, all had become, in some way, eternally connected.

Zach stayed committed to his Amish family and faith. The most glorious day of his life was when he married Ingrid in a decorated barn on his parents' farm. They would remain happily together in Kalona, Iowa.

Olivia and Knut went back home to Vienna, Austria, nine months after the rescue. Olivia started *Maisl*, an upscale vegan bistro in Vienna's first district. The main ingredient in each entree of the carefully curated menu was corn. Knut wrote a global best seller called *The Endurance of Survival* and sold ten million copies.

Yao Ping returned to China after finishing his PhD at Stanford. He became an officer in the ministry of agriculture. The video of him shooting out of the corn silo went viral worldwide. He was revered in his home country as a national hero.

Sammy and Jim never had a wedding ceremony besides the quick little gathering on the Zephyr deep in Moffat Tunnel. Three years after being rescued, their happy life together was accented by the honor of tossing the Super Bowl coin together to start the game—the first major American sporting event held after Yellowstone. The Pittsburgh Steelers played against the Chicago Bears. The game went into overtime.

Victor and Lena Homko returned to their home in Ukraine, where they lived out a quiet and peaceful life of retirement not far from a Black Sea beach near Yalta.

Michelle and Cliff's romance did not last too long. Cliff found that although he loved her dearly, and they remained the best of friends, they were simply not right for each other. He returned to Nevada where his business thrived, and she eventually went home to New Orleans. She never had to worry about money again.

Susan and Chance became close friends and kept in contact. They married five years after being rescued. They made their home in Wilmington, Delaware. He continued to work for the railroad in information technologies, while she worked as a nurse at local hospitals and taught classes at the university in Newark. He often injured himself on his bicycle. She was always happy to nurse his wounds.

Marshall and Jessica Knight's kids finished school and went to college. Kevin, the oldest, studied agricultural sciences. He called his friend Doug (who never went to college) often for practical help designing greenhouse machines. The younger Knight girls both studied psychology. The family lived in Texas for eight years before moving back to Colorado. They all go to the circus together whenever they can.

Joyce Smyth, who was as vital to the survival of the people on the Zephyr as anyone, even though she wasn't on the train, retired in the wake of western trains being discontinued after Yellowstone. She lived out a happy life, leading one project after another at a retirement community in South Chicago.

Dr. Sayers reunited with his wife and kids in Brownsville, Texas, one week after Sergeant Major Anton rescued the Zephyr. She had just made it through Albuquerque when the eruption struck. The family moved to Hilo, Hawaii, where Sayers continued to study and teach about volcanoes.

Nine months after being rescued, Neville and Anne Hampton, Linda Madden, and the rest of the British tour group were finally able to safely fly home to England. Upon arriving at Heathrow airport, they were met by a large gathering of friends, family, and well-wishers, including the King and Queen. The royal couple presented the Hamptons with a new matching set of luggage, constructed with heavy-duty custom rollers—replacement bags for the ones Neville had sacrificed for the "crap cart" in Moffat Tunnel. Each piece was emblazoned with the inscription, "Keep Calm and Carry On."

Farming in America was tough after Yellowstone. Patty's crops near Hastings, Nebraska, were completely destroyed that first year. She plowed, tilled, and fertilized the land as best she could, but the half foot of ash she had to mix into the soil was lifeless. The year before the Yellowstone eruption she had raked in over 220 bushels. Thankfully, the Federal government kept her from financial ruin. After a decade of toil, her land yielded 160 bushels of corn per acre.

Tim, the premier coach car attendant, made it back home to his dog David Moffat, but passed away shortly thereafter. Some others, like

Jay and Diana, Larry the engineer, Brewster, Harry, and Randal Keaton passed away in the first years following their struggle on the Zephyr.

Ten years after the eruption of Yellowstone, there was a reunion of everyone still living from the Last Zephyr. All passengers and crew were invited as well as the soldiers who rescued the survivors, the mechanics who had prepared the train, the whole team from Omaha, Joyce Smyth, family and friends, rail fans, and hundreds of others.

They gathered at the East Portal of Moffat Tunnel. They had to come by car and bus. The Moffat Tunnel Subdivision was never put back into service as a railroad after Yellowstone.

Herman lived to be older than any other person in human history born with quadriplegic cerebral palsy. He was there with his Aunt Suzy and Godfather Rob to remember his parents.

Two days before that Labor Day ceremony, Sean and a few others hiked into the area near tunnel #22. They found the "X's" that had been chipped into the cliff by the tracks. They placed a cross where Zane had been buried, and a Star of David at Bruce's last resting place. They went to look at the coal train those two railroaders had secured, thus giving the Zephyr survivors a fighting chance. It was still piled up at the bottom of South Boulder Creek Canyon. Seeing the wreckage, they could almost hear the crashing sounds again.

For the ceremony at Moffat Tunnel, speeches were made by dignitaries—including former CEOs Qwana Rice and Brenda Bradford. Memorials and prayers were offered; testimonials were recited.

Retired conductor René was the Master of Ceremonies. She had been the principal organizer of the event. The Rocky Mountain Railroad Club and ColoRail, although depleted of members by Yellowstone, together had done all the legwork and fronted the money to make the event happen. A plaque was embedded into the concrete portal façade of Moffat Tunnel next to the 1928 time capsule, placed to immortalize the courage, resilience, and ingenuity of the passengers and crew of the Zephyr. The names of every survivor, as well as Conductor Nick, were inscribed.

Reagan, Claire, and Terry, plus twenty family members were there.

Reagan rubbed his fingers over the inscription of his own name repeatedly. He told his mother how he wished his grandpa could be up there too. He said it several times. On his belt was the old scanner his grandpa had given him.

Not far from the gathering sat the Silver Sky, still exactly where it was left ten years earlier. Vandalism and weather had taken their toll. Surprisingly, the drumhead Noah had removed and locked under the dome steps was found where it had been left.

On a cloth-draped table, near the podium, that California Zephyr drumhead was displayed, along with conductor Nick's hat, the locomotive number plates off the 313 and 309, and several photos taken throughout the ordeal. Those artifacts, plus many others, would be archived by History Colorado.

A standing ovation was given for the mechanical crew from Chicago, who had prepared the Zephyr so well. A similar ovation was given to the UPR for maintaining such a resilient railroad, and helping guide the train to rescue.

Rashid closed the proceeding with a prayer of thanks and remembrance. The ceremony ended with the raising of a large American flag on a brand-new flag pole. Members of the military rescue team hoisted it. Commanding the soldiers once again was General Justus Anton. Allison, Brian, and members of the Mormon Tabernacle Choir led the singing of "God Bless America." The couple's nine year old daughter, Zephyr, sang along.

Conductor Nick's two sons attended. The occasion was the first time they met most of the people their father spent his extraordinary last few days with. People could see Nick's eyes in those of the two middle-aged men. One couple came to greet the brothers after most others had gone. They were trying to keep control of a young son who was full of energy. The poor kid was tired and restless after sitting through endless speeches.

The mother called to the boy, "*Nikko, sei bitte eine Minute lang geduldig!*"

The boy settled down for a moment and stood by his mom and dad.

The father said his name was Zachary Miller. He introduced his wife Ingrid. "We want you to meet our eight-year-old son," he said, obviously holding back tears.

My mother, in her adorable Austrian accent, finished the introduction, "This is our little Nikko. His given name is Nicholas Jay Miller."

"Nikko, these gentlemen are the Jay brothers. Their father was the conductor we told you about."

I was that boy. I immediately stopped fidgeting when I realized who the two men were. Those men and I, along with many others there that day, built strong friendships that have lasted a lifetime.

—Nicholas Jay Miller, 2059

GLOSSARY OF TERMS

24/7. Twenty-four hours a day, seven days a week.

737. Passenger jet aircraft.

A.C. Assistant conductor.

ADA. Americans with Disabilities Act.

ADA ramp plow. Makeshift plow made from wheelchair ramps.

Air brakes. Compressed air to signal and actuate friction brake applications.

Angle cock. Valve to open or close an air hose.

Automatic brake valve. Lever on a locomotive control stand that controls brakes to the entire train.

Axel springs. Thick springs between axles and bogies in a railroad bolster.

B End. The end of a piece of railroad equipment that has the hand brake.

Back-order. List of supplies needed at the next commissary.

Back-up hose. Connected to the brake pipe to allow the conductor to stop the train with an emergency application of the brakes; equipped with a warning whistle.

Bed Sheet. List of railroad crew members who will check into a hotel between shifts.

Bid. Railroad employees "bid" for job assignments; seniority determines outcomes.

BIG BOY. Largest steam locomotive type ever built.

Bite. Powered wheels adhering to rail, causing movement of a locomotive.

Blended Brake. Use of dynamic and air brakes at the same time with the automatic brake handle.

Blood & Guts Martini. Two shots of Bombay gin, one shot of vermouth, four drops of tabasco, a pinch of freshly ground black pepper. Shake with ice. Serve with a sword (must be a sword) skewered through two cherry tomatoes.

Bogies. Metal encasements to hold railway wheels and axles in place and connect to the car body.

Boiler. Portion of a steam locomotive above the fire box where water boils to steam.

Bolster. Housing connecting axles and center pins to railroad equipment.

Brig. Military jail.

Butt Joint. Two pieces of railroad equipment with knuckles closed before coming together so that they do not couple together.

BX. Store on an Army Base.

Car attendant. Employee responsible for cleanliness and hospitality in a passenger train car.

Carman. Railroad mechanic who works on train cars, not locomotives.

Chocks. Blocks that prevent train wheels from rolling.

Chop Saw. Hinged stationary circular saw.

Class 1. Highest level of FRA designation for railroad track.

Coach Cleaner. Employee that performs janitorial duties on trains at terminals.

Colorado Railroad Museum. Golden Colorado.

ColoRail. Rail Advocacy organization in Colorado.

Commissary. Department responsible for stocking supplies on trains at end stations.

Conductor. Person in charge of train operations.

Consist. Line-up of railroad equipment that makes up a train.

COVID-19. Viral global pandemic that began in 2019.

CPDS. Control Point Denver and Salt Lake. Designation for dispatcher-controlled switches and other controlled interlockings on the Moffat Line, followed by milepost number.

Craft. Railroad occupation, i.e., locomotive engineer, conductor, or OBS.

Crew brief. Meeting to plan a course of action among crew members.

CU. University of Colorado.

Delayed in the Block. Railroad rule allowing a stopped train to proceed to the next signal.

Derail. Metal device to prevent equipment from entering a track by derailing it.

Derailment. When wheels of railroad equipment are no longer on rails.

Diamond Track. Where two tracks intersect at right angles.

Diaphragms. Flexible connecting apparatus that allows passengers to pass safely from one train car to the next.

DP. Distributed power, locomotives not connected to the head end, operated by radio.

Drawbar. Primary hinged coupler component on railway cars and locomotives.

Drumhead. An advertisement or logo hung on the back of a passenger train.

Duct Tape. Gray industrial tape.

Dumbwaiter. Elevator system between upper level dining area and lower level kitchen of a railway passenger dining car.

DUS. Denver Union Station.

Dynamic brakes. Reverse polarity in traction motors to retard momentum of a train.

Electricians. Railroad employees that work on all electrical systems.

EMD. Electronic mobile device.

End of the World. Where railroad tracks end.

Engine Service Employees. Locomotive engineers.

Engineer side. Right side of a forward-moving train, side of the locomotive with a control stand.

EPA. Federal Environmental Protection Agency.

F5 tornado. Most severe rating for tornados.

FCC. Federal Communications Commission.

Fireman's side. Left side of a forward-moving train, side of the locomotive without a control stand.

Foamer. Derogatory term for a train fan (as if fans froth at the mouth when a train goes by).

Foaming. Derogatory term referring to the act of enjoying trains and railroading (See Foamer).

Fouling Point. Closest point to a switch where railroad equipment can be without being sideswiped by a passing train.

Friction brakes. Retarding momentum of a train by applying pressure on wheels with brake shoes, or axle disks with brake pads.

Frog. Separation point on the inside rails of a switch.

Glad hands. Metal ends of hoses that allow quick connections and release when pulled apart.

Graduated release. Easing pressure in brake cylinders incrementally.

Grip. Railroader's bag for personal items and required railroad equipment.

Hand brake. Ratchet method of manually applying brakes to railroad equipment.

HEP. Head end power to provide electrical power to train cars.

High Ball. Depart at maximum allowed track speed.

Highrailer. Road vehicle with railroad capable wheels that can be deployed.

HIMAR. Highly Mobile Rocket Artillery System.

History Colorado. Official Colorado historical organization.

Hoghead. RR slang for "locomotive engineer."

In the seat. The locomotive engineer operating the controls of a train.

Independent brake. Black handled lever that controls just locomotive brake applications.

Journal bearings. Sealed railroad axle bearings.

Kick it. Order to push a piece of railroad equipment and let it roll on its own with built up momentum.

Kirk. *Star Trek* captain.

Knuckle. Portion of a coupler that locks two cars together, opens by raising the pin lifter lever.

LSA. Lead service attendant.

Lash up. Two or more locomotives coupled together.

Lifter pin. Portion of a coupler that locks the knuckle in closed position when lifted allows the knuckle to open.

Light power. Locomotives without cars.

Making a joint. Coupling two pieces of railroad rolling stock together.

Manifest. List of passengers and other details.

Marker lights. Red lights signifying the end of a passenger train.

Mechanical. Term for all coach cleaners, pipefitters, carmen, machinists, and others in the mechanical department.

Mic. Microphone.

MOW. Maintenance of way.

N95 mask. Face covering that blocks dust, germs, and other particulates.

NEC. High-speed rail route known as the North East Corridor.

New hire. A person working for the railroad less than two years.

Notch. Position(s) on a locomotive throttle lever. Idle provides no power. Power increases 1 to 8 in ascending order to either add tractive effort, or increase dynamic braking.

NRHS. National Railroad Historical Society.

Number 5. Westbound Zephyr.

Number 6. Eastbound Zephyr.

OBS. On board services employees who work on passenger trains providing hospitality services.

OTP. On time performance.

PA. Public address system used to communicate to an entire interior of a passenger train.

PREPARE. Passenger Railroad Emergency Response Education.

Pack-set. Portable railroad radio used by trainmen.

Pin. RR command to have the engineer release pressure on knuckles.

Pin Lifter. Lever on the end of a piece of RR equipment that unlocks a closed knuckle.

Pipe fitter. Railroad plumber.

Prime mover. Internal combustion engine of a railroad locomotive.

PSI. Pounds per square Inch (used to measure air pressure).

PTC. Positive train control, used to automatically stop a train before it can violate a basic railroad rule.

QR Code. Quick response code used on digital devices.

Rail Yard. A collection of RR tracks used to assemble trains.

Railroad Tie. Wood or concrete foundation piece to hold rail in place and at the correct gauge.

Rank-and-file. Employees that pay union dues.

Red Cap. Station employee that assists with baggage and mobility.

Rerailer plate. Metal plate shaped to roll a RR wheel back onto the ball of the rail.

Reverser. Locomotive gear shifter for forward, reverse, of centered (neutral) position.

Rolling Stock. Passenger and freight railway cars.

RPMs. Revolutions per minute.

RR. Railroad.

RTD. Regional Transportation District; The mass transit bus and rail company for the Denver metro area.

RTD A Line. Commuter rail line between Denver Union Station and Denver International Airport.

Running gear. Components of a railroad car or locomotive that are part of the movement structure (wheels, bogies, couplers, air brakes, etc.)

Scotty. Engineer of the Starship Enterprise (fictional character) on *Star Trek*.

Seated switch points. How points of a switch fit into the adjoining rail.

Set-back. When a train crew is told to report for work later than their scheduled sign-up time due to their train being delayed.

Short Timer. A RR employee due to retire soon.

Signal bridge. Large span to hold RR signals above designated tracks.

Signaled blocks. Length of railroad track between signals, typically 2–6 miles long

Silver Sky. Bullet end sleeper dome observation car built in 1949 for the original California Zephyr.

Skates. Metal chocks that keep train wheels from turning.

Spock. *Star Trek* science officer.

Step box. Used to give passengers a step between a low platform and train car entrance.

Stryker chair. Emergency wheelchair thin enough to maneuver in a train car aisle.

Stub track. Railway track that ends usually with a bumper post.

Suites. Derogatory RR term for management employees not affiliated with a union.

Swag. Novelties, promotional items.

T&E. Train and engine service.

Tail track. Length of track needed for RR equipment to clear a switch.

Tell tell hole. Hole that opens under a drawbar when the knuckle is locked in the closed position.

The Tunnel District. Section of the Moffat Subdivision between milepost 22 and 41 that features twenty-eight tunnels.

Three point protection. Used to keep trainmen safe working on, under, or between train cars.

Tie. A cross beam holding rails at the proper width, providing foundation ("sleeper" in British English)

Tie clip. Small metal device that connects railroad ties to the rail.

Tied down. Hand brakes applied to prevent a train from moving.

Tier IV locomotive. Highest rating of railway power per EPA certification.

Track Condition Summary. Daily train orders for T & E crews.

Train Days. Fictitious rail fan event held on Labor Day at Denver Union Station.

Train service employee. Conductors and assistant conductors

Tunnel district. Part of Moffat subdivision between mileposts 24 and 40.

Turnover. Briefing between inbound and outbound train crews.

UPR. United Pacific Railways, fictitious future company that owns and operates several railways in the Western US.

USGS. United States Geological Survey.

Vestibule. Doorway on or off a passenger train car.

Water crane. Water tower with hardware to water steam locomotives.

Wheel slip. When power applied to drives wheels exceeds adhesion and wheels spin without moving the locomotive.

WYE. A triangle-shaped assembly of tracks and switches that allow rail equipment to reverse directions.

Wi-Fi. Wireless internet signal with an emergency application of the brakes when needed, and provides warning whistle.

Zephyr. Long-distance overnight train operating daily between Chicago, IL; and Emeryville, CA.

Zoppe'. Italian family circus that performs in the USA.

ACKNOWLEDGMENTS

The Last Zephyr exists because of the support, direct assistance, and inspiration I have received from others. My heartfelt gratitude goes to all the following people, and many more who are too numerous to mention. Thank you to Barbara, who had to endure one idea for this story after another, and wisely weeded out the bad ones; and my thanks go to the people who helped by beta reading, giving ideas, and adding inspiration. Among them are my mother Diana, my sister Laura, and a great number of other friends and work colleagues. I appreciate the support, skill, and talent of Mayfly Design, and the editing mastery that Marly Cornell brought to the book.

I am grateful for many institutions, including the Colorado Railroad Museum in Golden, ColoRail, The Rocky Mountain Railroad Club, the Colorado Model Railroad Museum in Greeley, History Colorado, the Colorado School of Mines, Metropolitan State University of Denver Hospitality Department, and others.

As a person who has had the privilege of earning my living on the rails, I am proud to be a part of one of America's safest, most resilient, most stable, and most powerful industries. Those well-deserved accolades are a direct result of the thousands of people, past and present, who have dedicated themselves to making the railroad an enduring part of this wonderful country.

ABOUT THE AUTHOR

CB (Conductor Brad) is a real conductor on passenger trains in Colorado. He has spent a career delighting people as they travel on fantastic journeys by rail through some of the most exciting parts of America. *The Last Zephyr* is a continuation of that passion.

Early in his passenger railroading career, he worked in Washington State. On September 11, 2001, CB was a conductor on the only train that left the United States after a terrorist attack knocked down the twin towers in New York City, killing thousands. The Federal government asked Amtrak to run from Seattle to Vancouver, British Columbia, Canada, to pick up diplomats and others whose planes had been diverted from US airspace. CB was in the line-up to work that train.

On the trip back to the American Mainland that evening, with a train full of weary and bewildered passengers, CB felt trapped. The world he had known until that morning was gone. What lay ahead was unknown and frightening. Bradley fighting vehicles and soldiers were stationed at grade crossings. Military jets screamed by overhead. A cold west wind drove dark waves into the shore along Chuckanut Drive. Everyone on the train felt trepidation, but also resolve. Resolve to weather the storm and press on together, regardless of what the future might hold. *The Last Zephyr* is a story designed to capture some of the energy and emotion of that fateful day and its aftermath.

CB wanted this story to also highlight some of the wonderful places and experiences found aboard, and along the route of his trains. For CB, geology in the west is a big portion of the fun. The ability to visit, touch, and experience the daunting power of our earth is what draws passengers to places like Rocky Mountain National Park, Glenwood Springs, and other remarkable destinations.

Often, CB goes fly fishing in the icy waters of the Colorado River, and later jumps into a geothermally heated pool of 105-degree steaming water at Hot Sulphur Springs. He loves to try fathoming the unbelievable energy it takes to heat millions of gallons of nearly frozen water to the boiling point every day all across the Rockies—and this has been happening for thousands of years on end! No place on Earth displays this power more dramatically than the super volcano at Yellowstone National Park.

The Last Zephyr releases that energy in an imagined and grandiose cataclysm of destruction. CB's research found that the best modern scientific analyses say such events are inevitable, although not necessarily imminent. However, every highly educated assessment ends with the ominous warning that such calming predictions are merely theoretical. Though CB's story is "not probable" in our time does not mean it's "impossible."

Now at the twilight of his time as a professional railroader, CB shares stories, real and imagined, in conversation on trains and on the written page, to share his own experience of color and excitement on the rails.

Printed in the USA
CPSIA information can be obtained
at www.ICGtesting.com
LVHW011339240224
772668LV00001BA/121

9 780972 595513